THE WOMAN WHO SWAM
IN THE NUDE

GARY BENASSI

Visit our website at www.StillwaterPress.com for more information.

First Stillwater River Publications Edition

ISBN-13: 978-1-946-30069-0
ISBN-10: 1-946300-69-1

1 2 3 4 5 6 7 8 9 10

Written by Gary Benassi
Cover design by Kody Lavature
Published by Stillwater River Publications, Pawtucket, RI, USA.

DEDICATION

To my English teachers past,
who provided me with the vision and skill to write.
And to my wife, Frances.

PROLOGUE

osetta Rossi stood at the stern of the ramshackle steamer, DiMarlo, as it slowly coursed its way along the coast of the Italian Riviera. The morning sun shone brightly down on the craft. The forecast called for a warm, dry day. The sea was relatively calm, and was due to remain so for the balance of the day.

Rossi was checking her dive equipment alongside her companions Barbara Danilo and Ann Carter. Her daughter, Ariana, who'd not dive with them stood by, intently watching the women. All three of the women wore neoprene composed dive suits, courtesy of an auction of discarded U.S. Navy UDT (Underwater Demolition Team) equipment. Their ensembles were replete with dive hoods, masks, regulators, weight belts, fins, and oxygen tanks.

Rosetta Rossi checked and rechecked her equipment, paying particular note to the oxygen tanks and regulators, which would literally be her lifeblood during the mission. Everything seemed set, they were ready to go. She looked over at her lifelong companion and friend Barbara, and thought back as to how this project, this endeavor had started. Barbara glanced back at Rosetta, winking at her while simultaneously giving a thumbs-up. Rosetta had always been able to count on her friend over the many years from when they had first met. Barbara Danilo had always been the rock, always unflappable, no matter the situation. She had always been able to keep Rosetta on an even keel whenever a crisis had been encountered. Rosetta would rely heavily on Barbara during this dive.

The third woman was relatively new to the two Italians. Her name was Ann Carter, a former diplomatic administrator at the British Legation to the Vatican in Rome. Ann had been posted there from 1943 to 1946 and had worked closely with Rosetta and Barbara, relating to the underground mission of hiding escaped British and American prisoners of war from the Nazis. Carter, largely with the influence and efforts of her colleagues, had developed a powerful body which set upon her 5' 8" frame. Her dive suit concealed her rock-ribbed mid-section, her heavily muscled upper arms, and her powerfully developed thighs. Carter was now capable of hoisting great weights on deadlifts, bench presses, and arm curls. She would come to rely upon this power shortly.

"Well girls, I think we are ready," Rosetta exhaled to Barbara, Ann, and to Ariana. "I want to thank all of you for joining with me on this mission."

"You don't have to be so formal with us, Rosetta," Barbara said as she feigned boredom at her long-time friend.

"Well, you know, none of you had to come on this... on this... this expedition," continued Rosetta, who seemed to be struggling to convey what she meant.

"It's nothing, Rosetta," said Barbara. "We didn't have anything else in particular to do. Did we, Ann?"

The British woman had stood silent as the Italian women had bantered back and forth. Indeed, she wouldn't have missed this opportunity for the world. Probably, Ann Carter would have joined any endeavor that Rosetta Rossi and Barbara Danilo would have put forth before her. How far she had come in the time she had been in the company of these two remarkable women.

Ann now felt herself empowered to do just about anything she put her mind to. She now possessed a magnificent body, which partially helped to offset the fact that she was not a raving beauty. Attractive yes, but it was her body which now attracted men as she had never been able to do before. Her sex life with her new boyfriend had been spectacular.

"Don't you agree, Ann?" interjected Barbara, seemingly perturbed at Carter's inattention.

"Yes, yes. Absolutely," stammered a flustered Ann Carter. She now stood up abruptly, almost coming to attention.

"At ease, Private Carter. At ease," said Rosetta in a joking manner. All of the women laughed, helping to ease some of the building tension. The girls virtually considered themselves professional divers. They were all expert and accomplished swimmers. Ann Carter had not been at the time of her introduction to Rosetta and Barbara. Ariana, too, had turned into a top swimmer and diver in just the past two years.

Rosetta's husband, Bob, looked over at his wife, stepdaughter, and their companions and silently marveled at them. A US Army officer veteran, Bob Rossi was now the unofficial salvage director of the group's operation. He never could have imagined just a short time ago he would now be where he was and involved in something as daring and fraught with potential danger.

"Well, what do you think?" he asked his wife.

"I think that we're ready. Everything is set," Rosetta replied in a firm and confident voice that she did not quite feel.

"I think you and the girls have done everything that you could," Bob resumed. "Although, I do believe that at some point in the future we'll have to bring in a professional salvage crew."

"I know, I know, but I think that for now, we should keep things low-key. At least, until we're sure," said Rosetta. At this point, she turned to him and looked in his eyes. The two embraced one another and exchanged a soft kiss. Rosetta felt a tingle run through her body.

"It's time, Bob. I'm going to join Barbara, Ann, and Ariana and put on our equipment.

"Good luck, dear. Take care," he replied with intense feeling. Rosetta made her way to the stern of the DiMarlo, where she began her preparation with Barbara and Ann. The three women strapped on their oxygen tanks and checked their regulators. They slipped on their neoprene gloves. All checked again their weight belts, their dive meters and their dive watches.

Barbara, Ann, and Ariana then joined hands as Rosetta recited the "Lord's" prayer. With that, they were ready to go forth. Rosetta, as the team leader, would dive in first. At the very edge of the boat she paused and placed he mask over her face. She then inserted her mouthpiece, checking that there was the proper air pressure. Rosetta looked at her companions, her friends, and nodded.

She stepped over the low rail with her right leg and without hesitation, dropped into the waiting ocean water.

CHAPTER ONE-
RENEWAL

Rosetta Rossi stood over the barbell on the floor in front of her. She was about to attempt a dead-lift the equivalent of 500 lbs. She tightened the weight belt that encircled her waist. Rosetta's hands were coated with a mix of rosin and chalk dust to better enable her to grip and hold the great weight attached to the bar.

Rosetta closed her eyes momentarily as she contemplated what she was about to do. She envisioned herself bending and gripping the bar and then summoning all her strength, she hoisted it above the floor and held it for the requisite five seconds.

Activity in the gym had slowed as those gathered stood by to witness the dead-lift attempt of their leader. Rosetta Rossi was ready. She now bent down and took hold of the bar. Her fingers felt the etched markings that ran around it, to better allow for the weightlifter to obtain a firm grip. Closing her eyes, Rosetta heaved the weight off the floor. She slowly straightened her muscle-ripped back. Her powerfully developed upper arm muscles and her bulbous thigh muscles tightened. Rosetta grimaced, her teeth gritted, her hazel colored eyes flashed, but she held the 500 pounds for the full five seconds. Her close and long-time friend, Barbara Danilo, sat before Rosetta and had silently counted out the time… *uno, due, tre, quattro, cinque.*

Rosetta then proceeded to drop the weighted bar to the floor, where it clattered and bounced on the mat. Rosetta leaped into the air and pumped her right fist. She had just achieved a personal best in the dead lift.

"Bravo, Rosetta! *Bravissimo!*" cried out Barbara as she bounded out of her chair and rushed over to congratulate her friend. She slapped Rosetta on the shoulder. Those gathered round duly raised a thunderous applause.

"Grazie, grazie, Barbara. It was nothing," replied a modest Rosetta as she flexed her arms before her. Indeed, she had made the lift look easy as she did in nearly all the things she ever tried in the gym and in the swimming pool. Rosetta Rossi stood 5' 8", unusually tall for an Italian woman. She now weighed what would equate to 142 pounds. Her physical dimensions were 44-28-40.

As aforementioned, she was ripped from head to toe. This was also unusual for an Italian woman, who were usually considered as fit only for the home and domestic activities. But not for the likes of Rosetta, or Barbara, and the other women who routinely worked out at the gymnasium the two women had founded the previous year.

Rosetta now proceeded to lie down on a bench which held another bar with 250 pounds attached. She reached up and grasped the bar. Barbara and another woman, Ann Carter, would be her spotters, in case she should falter, which did not seem likely. Rosetta took hold of the bar and lifted it up off the clips that had held it. She brought the weight down to a point just above her chest. With unseemly ease, she powered her way through a repetition of five lifts.

"I knew we wouldn't be needed," said Barbara. Ann Carter merely nodded. She had never had any doubt Rosetta would be able to lift the weight.

After she had rested for a few minutes, Rosetta walked over to another apparatus, upon which hung nearly 600 pounds of weights. They were held by a set of clips on two parallel poles. Rosetta placed her shoulders under the bar in a squatting position. She heaved the weight upward until she was standing straight up. Rosetta then lowered herself back down to her original squatting position. She then performed four more reps.

Everyone in the gym silently marveled at this woman's immense strength. Rosetta Rossi had always maintained her figure, going back to before the war. And luckily, she had always been able to maintain her good health. The end of the war brought immense relief to all Italians, Slowly, gradually, food became more plentiful and with that everyone, it seemed, began to achieve much better health in their own right. Everyone's outlook began to change as well. There was optimism and hope for a better future. Rosetta, like most Italians, could not remember the last time when one could feel cheerful about anything.

* * *

The Second World War had changed virtually everyone's lives in Italy. Large parts of the country had been devastated and brutalized, particularly in Sicily and the battlefields south of Rome. Places like Messina, Naples, Anzio, and Monte Cassino had since become immortalized in literature and film in the United States, Great Britain, and Italy. The war had caused untold suffering and deep personal anguish for nearly every family in the country. Hardly one had not been traumatized by the loss of a loved one: father, mother, sister, brother, or a close, personal friend. Along with this, those who had survived had had to undergo hunger, cold, and a sense of longing. Many thought they would never be able to recover, either physically or emotionally.

Rosetta Rossi lost her husband Paolo in the fall of 1942. He had been killed in action in some God-forsaken place in the Libyan desert. He had been a proud member of an elite Bersaglieri regiment. These troops were considered the very best men that Italy had ever brought forth to any battlefield. Rosetta had once thought that she would never get over the loss of Paolo. What would she do? After all, her two children, Ariana had been fifteen at the time, and Marco, their son, had been only thirteen. Their father's death had been devastating to them.

Rosetta had been able to partially assuage her loss by immersing herself in the clandestine work of a monsignor in the Vatican. The Irish priest ran an escape ring hiding escaped British and American prisoners of war from

7

the Nazis, right in the heart of Rome. Through family connections and personal wealth she had been able to provide for herself and her children. But they never lived too comfortably. Many a day and night had been spent shivering in the cold of their apartment on Via Frattina. The street was located quite near the legendary Spanish Steps. The cold had also been punctuated by pangs of hunger, as food, any kind of sustenance, became increasingly harder to find as the war wound on during the trying years of 1942 to 1945.

Rosetta Rossi overcame almost all the devastation, the cold and hunger, and the death of her husband, because she always possessed and maintained the necessary intestinal fortitude. She never lost sight that there could be, would be, a tomorrow. A morrow filled with hope and sunlight, laughter, and love. Rosetta had been determined to overcome all the odds for herself, Ariana, and Marco… and for her close friends, as well as anyone who was in need.

Rosetta's vision included the creation of a center for women, especially those who might have suffered the loss of a loved one or a friend. This center would not be just a meeting place for having an espresso or about chatting over idle things. It would provide a sense of renewal and rejuvenation for these women. The center would offer them the sense of participating in athletic activities that would empower them to hone and develop their bodies, as well as their fractured minds.

* * *

In the immediate aftermath of the end of the war, Rosetta had sat down with her old friend, Barbara Danilo, to put the framework in place to open the gymnasium for women. The two women had to obtain a suitable location, and they had to acquire some of the necessary equipment: barbells, benches, floor mats, ropes, etc. All of this had to be coordinated with their own personal day to day lives. Rosetta was working for the US Military Mission in its efforts to aid and assist the citizens of Rome adjust back to their normal, peace-time lives. She was frequently engaged in performing translation services for those who could only speak Italian. Barbara Danilo was employed as a regional sales representative for the Maserati automobile firm.

Rosetta was able to take out a lease on an abandoned building that sat on Via Vittoria. Its location was perfect for her as it was only six blocks away from her own residence. It was also quite suitable for Barbara, as her own home was on Via Brunetti, less than a half mile away. The building had once housed a metals work assembly factory. Its machines had long since been dismantled and shipped off to Germany. Broken glass hung from cob-webbed window frames. Ample water damage was also in evidence on the decaying walls and dilapidated floors, courtesy of a damaged and leaking roof.

Rosetta had turned to her husband, Bob, for assistance and, more critically, for securing financing for the extensive rehabbing of the building's shell. Robert Rossi was, in 1945, still an active duty officer of the US Army. He had met Rosetta during the war when he had been in hiding from the Germans there in Rome. Upon their first meeting, a spark had been struck between them. A kismet had been born. The rest soon became history. The couple were married in December of 1945, and there had been no time for a proper honeymoon. Both decided to postpone a true one until a suitable time in the following year.

Rosetta had set her eye on an excursion to the Italian Riviera, as Punto had long been considered an exotic and intriguing spot, particularly for newlyweds. It was in a rather secluded area and it also contained a beach for nude bathing.

* * *

The gymnasium required a lot of work, more than Rosetta and Barbara had originally bargained for. But slowly, it began to come together and by early 1946, it was at last ready for its grand opening. At first glance, it was a rather modest affair, rather utilitarian. It did serve its purpose for the two women and for the other girls who had joined in membership. There was Ann Carter, the young Englishwoman, and Paula Baccari, a thirty-five-year old woman. Also, there was Monica Lamonica and Barbara Diala, both Romans, and both in their thirties.

All had suffered deep and personal losses because of the war. All needed no, desperately needed to get back some sense of renewal, something for them to grasp hold of, to help close the emotional voids in their lives.

* * *

"Rosetta, don't forget your appointment with Mauro Guzzo tomorrow," Barbara Danilo said as she poked her head into the office.

"*Grazie*, Barbara. I have not forgotten about Signore Guzzo," replied Rosetta as she contemplated her upcoming interview with the *Corriere della Sera* journalist.

"Rosetta, I have no right to advise you on what you should say to Guzzo, but I do believe that you should be careful. Not circumspect, but careful. Personally, I think his newspaper is just a conduit for the church and some of the other stuck-in-the-mud characters in the city," Barbara sniffed.

"Do not worry," Rosetta said as she looked up at her friend. The atmosphere in the room had taken on a slight chill for Rosetta. She had always felt that she was quite close to Barbara, almost considering her a sister. Nevertheless, Rosetta could never help but feel that there was something else going on when it came to Barbara.

Rosetta Rossi had known Barbara Danilo for seemingly forever. Before the war, the two had frequently gathered for afternoon tea in each other's homes. Neither of the two had then had to work. Rossi's husband was the inheritor of his family's estate which consisted of substantial land holdings within Rome and out into the surrounding countryside. Barbara Danilo's husband had once been the director of a vast olive oil processing firm.

Barbara Danilo had always possessed a wild streak. She had always been considered a rebel. In Italy, at that time, it didn't take much. Even while she had been married to Vincenzo, there had always been persistent rumors of affairs with various leading men of the city. The woman had a magnetism about her, a sense of dynamism, to all who came within her orbit. There had been no children in the marriage. Barbara had always outwardly maintained a correct, virtuous façade in public in regard to her husband, but inwardly she smoldered. There was a raging volcano within her body.

10

Barbara Danilo stood 5' 8", again, unusual for an Italian woman. Some conjured the idea that she could not possibly be Italian, what with her height and her frizzled blonde hairstyle; that together with her piercing blue eyes and fully developed figure. Barbara had always been able to maintain her superb body from even before the war and then on through the trying years of 1940 to 1945, when nutritional requirements were hard to meet. She had run the streets of Rome, lifted weights, swum in the Metropole pool. Barbara Danilo had never cared about any criticism cast her way, any sniping remarks from the upper crust of Roman society, or the Catholic Church.

Her long and lean and well-sculpted body had always helped her attract members of the opposite sex. Often, her liaisons had been with younger men. But Barbara was never better than when she was in bed with any man. She had always favored mounting her partner as she looked down and took in the pleasure each man invariably showed. Barbara liked the power she felt from being able to dominate the relationship.

Rosetta knew of Barbara's reputation and yet, had never felt uncomfortable with it. What the woman did in her private life was of no concern to her. But now, she felt that her friend might have been trying to assert a sense of dominance in the relationship between the two of them. It seemed to her that Barbara was being over competitive in the gym, that there now existed a personal duel as to whom could lift the greater weights… who could swim more laps in the pool.

It always seemed as if Barbara was trying to outdo Rosetta. Maybe just to impress the other women, Monica and the other Barbara's. Or perhaps, it was to satisfy some internal, primal urge of Barbara's own mindset. There was that unspoken edge to all things physical between them.

After a day of fulfilling her duties at the US Military Mission, Rosetta arrived at the health club. She had just settled into her chair in her not so plush office. The wall clock read 4:30 PM. Barbara Danilo walked in soon after.

"Is there anything that you wish for me to do, Rosetta?" Barbara asked. "Would you like for me to join you for the interview?"

"No, I believe I'm ready to receive Signore Guzzo and I think I will do the interview alone. I hope you do not mind," Rosetta answered guardedly. She thought Barbara might well attempt to take charge of the session.

"No, of course not. I don't mind," Barbara said with a degree of indignation. Who did Rosetta think she was? Who had been the one that had had to prop up this teetering organization with her own money? She had been a co-founder along with the great Rosetta. Barbara took all this as Rosetta asserting her own dominance over the situation. She would remain silent for the moment, but the time was fast approaching when the two women would have to settle things between them.

"I would like for you to check in with me about fifteen to twenty minutes after Guzzo sits down with me. I will signal you by nodding my head for you to come over and join us. Find some pretext to interrupt. Perhaps you could say a telegram just arrived and it requires my attention. Something like that."

"All right. As you wish," Barbara said with a piquish accent to her voice. *There you go again, Rosetta. As if you are the queen*, Barbara thought to herself. She tried mightily to maintain her composure but it was becoming increasingly harder for her to do so.

"Is everything all right, Barbara?" asked Rosetta as she looked over at Danilo.

"Si, si, everything is fine. Yes, everything."

At promptly 5:00 PM, Mauro Guzzo arrived at the gymnasium. He was shown into Rosetta's office by Barbara.

"Signora Rossi, I would like to personally thank you for allowing me the opportunity to interview you," Guzzo said in a gushing manner.

Rosetta rose to shake the journalist's hand and took in some measure of the man. He was a rather handsome man who appeared to be in his early forties. Brown, well cut hairstyle and brown, lucent eyes. He had a way of looking at his subject in a disarming way. A person who put you at ease. Rosetta knew the man was unmarried, his wife having been killed Mussolini's Fascists several years before. Guzzo stood around 5' 10" and looked to be in good physical condition. He was no muscle-bound hunk, but definitely possessed a solid foundation.

12

The more Rosetta gazed at Guzzo she could see that, despite a rather plain face, it was punctuated by a narrow, aquiline shaped nose. Interesting. As she looked further, she could see that he was dressed rather nattily in a navy-blue suit, in good condition. It was not threadbare by any means. A bright red tie sat upon a crisply pressed white dress shirt. There was a slight oddity to Guzzo's presentation though. His dress shoes were definitely not new: scuff marks and scratches were noticeable.

Rosetta offered her guest a firm handshake. "It's my pleasure to be interviewed by such a distinguished journalist of Corriere della Sera. But, please, I would like for you to call me Rosetta." She playfully batted her eyelids.

Guzzo answered, "Of course, Rosetta it is. And you can refer to me as Mauro." He felt a charge of electricity from the woman. She was every bit as formidable in person as from her growing reputation concerning her athletic exploits.

"May I offer you some coffee or tea? Or perhaps mineral water?"

"No, signor... er... Rosetta. I am fine."

"*Bene*. Then, we can begin. What would you like to know about me; about our organization?" Rosetta asked, looking straight into Guzzo's probing eyes. She would try to steer the interview in her direction as much as she could. Rosetta sensed that she was tilting Guzzo her way. She was well aware of the man's reputation as a formidable, but honest and straightforward journalist. He had already suffered greatly for this honesty and professionalism by having served several years in one of Benito Mussolini's most notorious prisons, Regina Coeli. "Well, first off, what inspired you to create this...this athletic organization? Why did you want to do it?" Guzzo sat back in his chair. He did so hesitantly, as he swore he could distinctly feel a tenderness from the creaking sound he heard.

Rosetta allowed herself a small smile. It would not do for this man to suddenly find himself on the flat of his back. He may have then immediately rendered an unfavorable opinion of not only her, but of the club as well. Just another group not to be taken seriously.

"During the war I, myself, suffered the loss of my husband, Paolo. It was devastating, not only for me, but for my entire family. Many women and young girls also lost loved ones or close friends. Together with my close friend, Barbara, we conceived of the idea of doing something. Something…to empower these women to regain some sense of their dignity, their well-being. Something to help them regain their sense of balance. A self-confidence, if you will." Rosetta settled back into her own chair, all the while maintaining a light gaze on Mauro Guzzo.

Guzzo took down some cryptic notes, occasionally looking up into the mesmerizing eyes of Rossi. Increasingly, minute by minute, he began to see and feel how this woman could well entice and lead these other women, these victims, as she had so eloquently put it, to come within her orbit of thinking. "And, Barbara," continued Guzzo as he pointed across the room at Danilo, "was, I am assuming, instrumental. Is that correct?"

"That is correct, sir. Barbara, please, why don't you come over and join us," Rosetta said graciously. "Mauro, you've already met Barbara." Rosetta had decided to forego the secret signal.

Danilo walked over and took Guzzo's offered hand into hers. "Indeed we have. You, see, Mauro, it was just something we had to do. To have just sat back and done nothing. Well, that is not who we are," Danilo said as she pointed back and forth between herself and Rosetta.

"I see," mused Guzzo. This Danilo woman was revealing herself to be an intriguing specimen in her own right. What was it with these two? There was a charge in the air. Impressive. "Are there any of the other women here now?"

"I do believe that one or two are working out now on some of the apparatuses, as you can see." Rosetta led Guzzo to a window that looked down on the gym floor. "I will definitely invite you back when the gym is at full bore for you to get a better look. This will enable you to get a better feel, an idea, as to what we are trying to do."

"I would like that very much, Rosetta. Tell me, without giving away too many secrets. Can you describe some of the women who work out here?" Guzzo had framed his question carefully. "I understand that an Englishwoman, an…" he consulted his notes, "Ann Carter works out here?"

"I would be most happy to, but, discreetly, of course," Rosetta said, nodding, "As to Miss Carter. She first came to us as a result of her work at the British Legation at the Vatican. Ann worked very closely with our escape organization. She lost several very close friends as a result of the war. Ann has been a most valuable asset to us, wouldn't you agree, Barbara?" The other woman nodded solemnly. "Some of the other women include Paula Baccari, Monica Lamonica, and Barbara Dworetz. There are others. Paula Baccari endured the loss of her husband at the Battle of El Alamein in North Africa. Some of her family members were also killed during the war.

"You just mentioned a Barbara Dworetz," Guzzo said. "Could you tell me a little about her?"

"*Si*, I can. You see, Barbara lost her entire family in the holocaust. Everyone. She has been able to restore some semblance of humanity and… dignity to her life," Rosetta said delicately. "She has a tremendous work ethic. One day I will introduce you to her. I think you will be most impressed."

"I shall look forward to it," Guzzo said earnestly. "Now, perhaps, we can discuss some of your war-time activities. That is, if you do not mind?"

"No, I would be happy to," Rosetta said. She then began to relate about her work in the Vatican escape network. Before she realized it, Rosetta began telling Guzzo some things which would have been better left unsaid. He looked over at Barbara, who was silently shaking her head, as if to say, "do not go there."

Meanwhile, as Guzzo went on dutifully taking down his notes he could not help but notice Barbara and her impressive body. The woman was dressed in a black leotard top which accentuated her large bustline. Her upper arms were highly developed and when Danilo crossed her long-muscled legs, he unconsciously arched one of his eyebrows.

Barbara took note of Guzzo's interest in her physique and did little to discourage any further attention. In fact, at one point, she crossed her arms just underneath her breasts, enhancing their presentation to the journalist.

Rosetta knew what her friend was up to; she had seen it all before many times. She pretended not to notice anything untoward, but she well knew Barbara was prepping Guzzo for an interesting evening.

"If you do not mind, Rosetta, I would like to ask your friend some questions?" asked Guzzo coyly.

"No, of course not. I don't mind."

15

"Rosetta briefly described some of what you do here at the club. While trying to remain objective as a journalist, I must say that I have been most impressed. What do you feel gives you the most pleasure?" Guzzo reclined back into his still creaking chair.

By this time, Rosetta had begun to feel like a third wheel. She could clearly see how the dynamic was playing out. She did not think Mauro Guzzo would have many follow-up questions for her. Her friend had done it again. And she had hardly had to extend herself in doing it.

"You mean beyond being under the sheets with a well-hung man?" Barbara responded evenly.

Rosetta rolled her eyes. "Now, please, do not quote me on that." Barbara did not display a smidgeon of embarrassment. Guzzo was openly taken aback. Rosetta's face continued to redden.

"*Si*... er... beyond that," a recovered Guzzo stammered forth.

"Yes, of course. No, seriously, what we are doing here is simply something that had to be done. These women's self-preservation was at stake. I do not want to go on with cliché expressions. I do want to say, that it has been primarily Rosetta's vision and determination that has been vital in the success of our endeavor."

"And, it must continue. Signore Guzzo, I also want to say that her drive and energy has been unsurpassed." And with that, Barbara sat back with her arms crossed over her now heaving bosom.

"*Grazie*, Barbara," said an appreciative and moved Rosetta. Barbara's declaration may have seemed outwardly imperious and a little over the top, but Rosetta felt that her friend had really meant what she had said to Mauro Guzzo.

"*Grazie*, Barbara," noted Guzzo.

Mauro Guzzo continued with his interview for another twenty minutes, when he decided to end the session. "Well, I believe that just about covers everything. I will now take my leave of you two fine ladies. You have both been most generous with your time and with your thoughts. I do hope I did not probe too deeply, especially those things involving the war. *Grazie*."

"*Prego*, signore, it has been our pleasure. I do hope that we have given you a little more insight into our organization, Rosetta said as she took Guzzo's proffered right hand. "I will have Barbara show you out."

All three stood and exchanged handshakes and air kisses. On the way out, Barbara slipped a note to Guzzo. Rosetta observed this but did not say anything. She knew what the words on the note would say.

Outside on the sidewalk, Mauro Guzzo paused and opened the note:

Signore Guzzo.

I hope that I do not appear to be forward, but I would love for you to join me at my home at 23 Via Brunetti at 9:00 for cocktails. I think it will be worth your while.

Ciao, Barbara.

Rosetta was busy with her paperwork when Barbara sauntered back in. "I hope you did not mind, I mean, having changed the playbook."

"No, no, of course not. I was a little surprised."

"How do you think it went?" Rosetta asked.

"Well, I think it went well. I am sure Signore Guzzo obtained a rather favorable impression of us."

Rosetta did not immediately reply to her friend, but thought she was intimating about how things had gone between her and Guzzo.

"I would be careful."

"I always am. You know I just like to have a little fun, especially if it is with an attractive man."

* * *

At precisely 9:00 PM Mauro Guzzo found himself standing in front of the home of Barbara Danilo. Although it was April, on this night was just the hint of a chill in the air. Guzzo had to admit that the building before him was impressive looking, with its granite-stoned exterior walls and its

17

exquisitely framed windows. He walked up to the front door and knocked on it with the lion-headed escutcheon.

Barbara let her guest wait for a minute or so before she answered the door. She was dressed in tight-fitting black slacks and an open-necked white blouse which revealed a remarkable view of her spectacular breasts. Completing her ensemble, Barbara has also chosen to wear a one carat diamond attached to a gold chain. The diamond nestled seductively in her cleavage.

Barbara rose from her chair, straightened her hair, and looked quickly around her living room. Strangely, she felt a tinge of nervousness. Why so, this was after all her home turf. She had been around the block, so to speak, many times with a succession of lovers. Barbara went to her front door, paused a moment and then opened it. "Ah-h, Mauro, how nice to see you. I was not sure that you would come. Please, do come in."

Mauro Guzzo stood momentarily speechless at the woman he saw before him. She had clearly made a formidable impression on him. He quickly took in the full measure of the woman. Her bright and smiling eyes, her spectacular breasts, and her tight-fitting pants. Most unusual for 1946 Italy.

"*Grazie*, Barbara. I said I would be here or, at least, I thought I had indicated my acceptance to your invitation."

Barbara glanced down at her guest's crotch and swore she detected a stiffening behind the layer of gabardine fabric. "Well, do come in. I am so glad you could make it. I really had wondered what I was going to do with myself." Barbara noted to herself that Guzzo, being so punctual as to his arrival, indicated, in an unspoken way, that he indeed wanted to bed her that very night, and it might well be done quickly. There was protocol and certain niceties to be observed before the couple could commit themselves to coitus. "Let me show you around."

Barbara swept her hand around the room and Guzzo noted some impressive artwork and tapestries.

"Oh, please, forgive me, Barbara. I did bring a you a gift." He removed a small bottle of Chanel perfume from his jacket pocket. "I realize it is French, but—"

"No, no, Mauro, that is perfectly all right. But you didn't have to. I'm thankful for your thoughtfulness," exclaimed a not so surprised Barbara.

18

"Please, let me continue." She led Guzzo through the kitchen and, of course, her bedroom.

Mauro Guzzo couldn't help but notice Barbara's fulsome buttocks as he walked behind her and how well they filled out her tight-fitting pants. He could feel himself hardening again. "Very nice, Barbara. Do you do much cooking?"

"Well, I have started to lately. I kind of lost my touch during the war. As you well know, pickings were rather hard to come by. But I've begun to make a comeback. And over there, are the bedrooms." Barbara had every intention of introducing her guest to her queen-sized bed in short order. "Ah, how remiss of me. What would you like to drink, Mauro? I have wine, beer, scotch, cognac?"

"I think I would like a cognac," Guzzo replied.

"A very good choice, I might add. Ah-h-h, I also have a cheese plate prepared, if you would like?"

"No, I think I will just stick with the cordial for now. Thank you for offering," Mauro replied smoothly. "I also would like to say I will not try to interview you this evening."

"Oh, that is all right. I don't mind."

"No, this will be just an evening of pleasure—I mean, of relaxation," Guzzo stammered embarrassingly. Sweat began to break out on his face. "That was a rather stupid thing to say," he said to himself.

"I would most like it to be a night of pleasure, er... *Si*, I mean one of relaxation as well. Perhaps both. You wouldn't be trying to seduce me, Signore Guzzo, would you?"

"I am not sure who may be seducing whom," he responded evenly.

Barbara took hold of the cognac decanter and removed its cap. She poured a generous three fingers into each of the cut glass tumblers. She then handed over a glass to Guzzo and together they clinked their glasses, murmuring, "Good health," to one another. Mauro Guzzo could not help but stare in to the wondrous mammary glands of Barbara Danilo. He felt himself stiffening again.

"*Bene*. Let me show you something, Mauro. Please, sit." Barbara went over to a dark, walnut-stained roll-top desk. She removed a photo album from it and brought it over to the Natuzzi leather sofa where Guzzo had remained reclining. Barbara sat down next to him, not too closely, but close enough. Amour would come soon enough. It was inevitable, and both knew it.

"These are some picture from the war years." Pictures poured forth of her, and of Rosetta, some were of family members. In almost all of them, the subjects seemed to be displaying a haunting, sometimes gaunt look, as if everyone could not bear the war and its effects any longer. Barbara occasionally described who some of the people were.

Guzzo found himself staring at the flipped pages almost absentmindedly. He could not help himself as he continued to feel the increasing pull of the woman who sat next to him. He was absolutely enthralled when Barbara would lean forward and her breasts plunged, at times they nearly fell outside of her blouse. His penis was filling; it was taking on a life of its own. He wasn't sure when or how it happened, but at some point, he leaned toward Barbara and his mouth found hers. His left hand went to her breast. Guzzo could feel the tautness of the woman's nipple as it filled and hardened. Their tongues attacked one another fiercely, almost savagely.

Barbara placed her right hand on Guzzo's crotch and began stroking his hardening penis. "I think we should go to the bedroom. It will be more comfortable," she said as they broke from their embrace.

Guzzo did not reply, but simply nodded his head. He followed Barbara while she held his hand. He couldn't help it. He was powerless to resist it. This emotion … this feeling. He wanted this woman more than anything in the world. And he wanted her now.

Once in the boudoir, Barbara quickly removed her blouse. She had not worn a bra. She then took off her pants and panties. They lay scattered about the floor.

Mauro Guzzo stared in awe at what he saw before him as he gazed at Barbara Danilo. Her body was even more magnificent than he had ever imagined. Her breasts were absolutely huge and full. They were mounted firmly on her now heaving chest. Her arms and thighs were powerfully developed, real musculature, and her mid-section was more than breathtaking. It was not only very flat, but she possessed a rock-ribbed six pack.

"Mauro, you can get started," Barbara said gently to Guzzo. She was clearly enjoying the fact that her lover for the evening was in awe of what he was seeing. Barbara wanted him to reach places to which he had never been, and he hadn't even touched her body.

Regaining his senses, Mauro Guzzo hurriedly, frenziedly removed his suit jacket, tie, shirt, and pants. By the time he had dropped his underwear he was fully elongated.

Barbara smiled at what she took in. She was going to love the feeling it would give her as it penetrated her. She would set forth on leading her lover through a whirligig of sexual techniques. She opened herself to Mauro's tongue as he began probing her vulva. She loved the exquisite feeling of her impaling herself upon Guzzo's throbbing penis. She stayed atop him the longest time. Then, Barbara went onto her back as he penetrated her once again.

Barbara Danilo brought her muscled thighs up and around to grip Mauro Guzzo's torso as he drove himself with a fury. Minute followed upon minute as she gripped him fiercely. Her feet floated above his rapidly thrusting buttocks. Barbara couldn't recall the last time a man had been inside of her, remaining hard, and then, at the moment of her sexual arousal, Barbara climaxed as Guzzo ejaculated into her.

Afterward, Barbara and Mauro reclined in her bed.

"Would you mind if I had cigarette, Barbara?"

"No, I would not mind."

"Would you like one?" he asked.

"No, Mauro. Perhaps, I may take a drag or two from yours. Smoking takes away from my lung capacity. This works against my swimming and free diving."

Guzzo got up from the bed and went to his suit jacket pocket and removed a pack of Marlboros. He lit one with a silver Ronson lighter. He then turned and got back into the bed. Barbara thoughtfully placed an ashtray on his stomach. She always had one available for when she entertained.

21

"At least it's not one of those God-awful Italian brands," Barbara sniffed as she took hold of the offered cigarette from Guzzo. She inhaled and blew out a couple of puffs.

"The Americans know how to make a good cigarette. I have to hand it to them," Guzzo agreed.

"Mauro, would you mind if I asked you something?"

"No, I do not think so. What would you like to ask me?"

"I know that your wife died during the war. Please stop me if you do not want me to go on."

"It is all right. *Si*, my wife was killed by Mussolini's Fascist goons. I suspect it was a way to get to her or to get back at me. You see, before and even during the war, I was not always the most complimentary in my commentary about il Duce, or on the conduct of the war."

"I see, it must have been hard for you," Barbara offered tenderly. She snuggled herself closer to Guzzo's body. He brought his right hand around her neck and started to fondle her breast. Barbara liked it.

"*Si*, it was very hard. But you see, I had already had some experience."

Barbara seemed confused. "What do you mean, you had experience? I don't understand."

"In 1941, my wife and I had had to endure the loss of our only son, Marcello. He was killed in action during the Italian invasion of Greece. There was nothing left of him to send back to us. His commanding officer wrote us saying that his body had been completely obliterated." Mauro Guzzo anguished again as he recounted the grim story. Tears had welled up and started to run down his cheeks.

Barbara was stunned at what she had just heard. She gripped Mauro's hand with both of hers. "I am so sorry, Mauro. I do not know what to say. Only, that I am here for you."

Guzzo did not reply. Barbara had planned to resume more sexual intercourse with her man, but not now. She just could not bring herself to do it. It was not the time. And it was slowly dawning on her that there might be something more important than merely indulging in a sexual escapade. Barbara was glad that she had given herself to this suffering man. Perhaps, her offering of her body to Mauro had helped him to assuage some of his personal pain and torment.

Barbara pressed herself closer to Mauro until they both fell into a deep sleep. There would be other occasions when the two of them could indulge themselves in libidinal matters.

CHAPTER TWO -

HOLIDAY JUNE-1946

T he weather had just begun to turn warmer, almost overnight in the Rome area. Rosetta had been working herself very hard of late. It had seemed like this for more than a year, what with her job with the US Military mission and her duties with the athletic club, in addition to her own physical workouts. Not to mention trying to also be a wife and a mother. The only break she had planned for, had been her postponed honeymoon with her husband in late April. They had chosen to holiday at the quaint seaside resort town of Savona, just to the southwest of the famed port city of Genoa.

The couple had engaged themselves in an almost non-stop sexual romp for more than a week. Rosetta truly enjoyed having sex with Bob. He was an experienced and thoughtful lover who more than fulfilled her craven sexual needs. How she loved mounting him, her heavy and firm breasts swaying above him. His endurance and stamina matched her own fevered libido. Rosetta was always able to achieve multiple orgasms during their sexual trysts.

Yes, it would be a good time to escape the capital city.

She asked Barbara, who quickly accepted to join her when they journeyed to the little-known town of Vento, located scant miles from Savona. What few people knew about Vento was the almost totally obscure nude beach, accessed by a very narrow pathway. Those in the know did not refer to such spots as nude beaches, or themselves as nudists, but preferred the more elegant and proper term of naturists. Neither Barbara or Rosetta considered themselves naturists. They did enjoy sunning themselves and swimming in the warm and soothing Ligurian waters, sans articles of clothing.

For a woman, going topless was practically considered standard or *de riguer*, on virtually all European beaches. To go completely naked was, at the time, considered risqué. This had never deterred formidable women like Rosetta and Barbara, especially a titan like Barbara. The two women seemed to revel in rebelliousness.

Journeying to Vento would be by train from Rome to Genoa and, then, they would rent a car to get to their hotel in Savona. The state-run railway was still in the process of recovering from the devastation of the war. Mussolini may have made the trains run on time during his reign as the all-knowing, all-conquering Duce. In 1946, nearly all the trains were tardy in their departures and arrivals. All in all, it was still considered the best way to get to their destination.

Rosetta enjoyed sitting back and taking in the rolling Italian countryside, mile after mile. From her vantage point she would see the open spaces, occasionally field workers would appear. Many of these people were the poor and downtrodden of Italy. During the war to be working in the fields often provided more sustenance than was experienced by the more upper-crust citizens who resided in the cities.

* * *

The women left Rome on a warm and sultry Monday morning, although the sky was overcast with a hint of rain in the forecast. It just had to improve, it would not do to holiday with any kind of inclement weather in the air. Rosetta almost immediately fell into a light sleep as, in the background, could be heard the click-clacking of the rail cars as they glided upon the rails. She periodically broke out of her daydreams and thought about a number of things. But it was the memory of her first husband, Paolo, that kept coming to mind.

Paolo Consento had been among the most handsome of men. And he was dashing as well. Rosetta had first met Paolo in the early fall of 1924. She was just twenty. Paolo was barely older. He hailed from a fairly well-to-do family, with distant strands, it was said, of royalty with the House of Savoy. The two fell for one another quickly, despite the fact that Rosetta's family thought her young suitor was just a bit too dashing, too sure of himself. It did not matter to Rosetta, as it was she, not them who wanted and loved this man.

The children came along, but not right away, contrary to the unwritten Italian custom that wives should bear as many children as possible, soon and often. Ariana was always vivacious and keen-witted. She had the look, one could tell even from a young age. Marco, their son, had always been a more withdrawn child, much less outgoing than his precocious older sister. Some attributed this to a lack of intellect. But Rosetta had always felt that her son was just shy. To her, it was just natural, but Paolo felt, and at times to Rosetta's frustration, expressed the need for the young man to toughen up. One day he would have to be masculine, he might as well be availed of this as soon as possible.

Benito Mussolini and his Black Shirts seized control of the Italian government with their legendary march on Rome in 1920. They soon set about strengthening their grip on the country, seemingly being everywhere at once. At first, it had seemed new and exciting for many Italians, especially those from the younger age groups. But as the twenties gave way to the thirties it had become tiresome, monotonous, and, for some, quite dangerous.

In 1936, Paolo Consento arrived home one bright and sunny day and proceeded to inform Rosetta that he was going to join the army. He said that he had thought long and hard and was now determined that he wanted to serve his country. And not only would he serve, but he would seek entry into the most elite of Italian commands. Paolo Consento would become a member of the Bersaglieri brigade. These men were the best of the best, and with their distinctive dress and black feathered bedecked headgear, they stood over and above all others in the Italian military.

As Rosetta heard her husband going on and on, she thought he might have lost his mind. She tried vainly, and ultimately futilely, to talk her husband out of this mad-capped fantasy. But he refused to listen to her arguments concerning his present occupation in the family business, or his community obligations. And most important of all, his obligation to his very own family. To her, it was beyond belief that her husband would want to tramp all over the place with other men, running and crawling through mud and barbed wire. He also stood a very good chance of getting himself killed or, at the least, dismembered or disfigured. In due course, Paolo matriculated his way into the Bersaglieri Corps. He even seemed to develop more joie-de-vivre than he had already possessed. Consento knew things were moving at an increasing pace internationally and his services would be needed in the not too distant future. Italy had already attacked and subjugated the poor and destitute kingdom of Ethiopia in East Africa in a brutal campaign. Ethiopian troops and civilians had been subjected to poison gas, in direct contravention of the Geneva Accords. Now, Italy had joined herself at the hip of Adolf Hitler's Nazi Germany.

Paolo Consento's military career flourished as he quickly ascended the ranks and by 1940 had achieved the rank of major in the aforementioned Bersaglieri. In late 1941, Consento was posted to the Libyan campaign in North Africa. And what he observed first-hand came as a profound shock. Italian troops were often ill-equipped, underfed, and, most of all, badly led by a martinique and uncaring officer corps, who seemed more concerned with the cut of their dress and which wine should be selected for their next meal. All of this he conveyed in his letters to Rosetta with the proviso that she withhold it from their children. There was no need to unduly alarm them, no good could come from it, aside from the fact that they badly missed their father. He, of course, desperately missed them. How he longed to be with them again. And he missed Rosetta and her exquisite body.

The blow fell in the late fall of 1942, when Paolo Consento's Bersaglieri regiment had been attached to the Trento Division. The British, led by General Bernard Montgomery, opened their attack on the Axis forces with a devastating artillery barrage. A Captain Augusto, Paolo's executive officer, wrote to Rosetta some time later. In his letter, Augusto had expressed his deepest condolences to her and to the children. Paolo had been a fine and caring officer, who had always been more concerned with the welfare of his men than he was with his own well-being. The strange thing, Augusto had noted, was that Paolo had died without mark on him. As if he had been merely asleep and at peace with the world. Later, a small incision had been found on his chest, near his heart. A small sliver of shrapnel had pierced it.

"Rosetta? Rosetta?" Barbara was trying to get Rosetta's attention, shaking her arm.

"Mmm?" Rosetta mumbled as she came to a full consciousness. "What was it you were saying?"

"I was just trying to ask you when you thought we might be arriving in Genoa. You seem as if you were in a trance. Hypnotized."

"Indeed, I was. Don't you know, I have picked up some of the rudiments of hypnotism. I was thinking of setting up a practice to conduct seances."

"Always joking," Barbara teased back, lightly brushing her friend's arm.

"No, I was just thinking back to earlier times. Happier times. You know, before the war. Paolo. The children," Rosetta mused. A tear, then a trickle began to roll down one of her cheeks. "I still miss Paolo. I suppose I always will. I think it has been the hardest on Ariana. Almost as if she blames me for his death. I do not even seem to know her anymore."

A middle-aged woman who was in their compartment looked over at Rosetta and shook her head, a look of contempt on her face. "You think you have suffered? You lost your husband. I lost my husband and my three children. All of them. Do you understand? All of them!" Her voice had taken on a tone of hysteria.

Rosetta stared back at the woman. "I am so sorry for your loss, signora. I really am."

"Never mind, Rosetta!" cut in an angry Barbara Danilo. "Do not pay attention to this… this shrew."

"Shrew, you say? Why I ought to really give the both of you a real piece of my mind in the form of my right fist!" The woman's eyes blazed with hate and fury.

28

Barbara started to rise up from her seat, shaking off Rosetta's attempt to calm her down. Barbara removed her light jacket, exposing her pile-driven upper arms to the woman.

The woman looked down. Clearly, she wanted no physical part with Barbara. "I am sorry. It is just that we have all suffered because of the war. Some more than others."

"You do not have to apologize, signora. You are quite right," soothed Rosetta.

"Rosetta, why don't we step outside for a moment. Perhaps, we can have a smoke," said Barbara. With that, she got up, brushing past the legs of her adversary.

"*Si, si,* that is a good idea," replied Rosetta. She thought she might like the calming effect of a cigarette, despite the fact that she wanted to give up all smoking. It was not good for her workouts, nor for her swimming and diving activities.

Barbara led the way out of the compartment and walked halfway down the corridor. She stopped and paused, then proceeded to lower one of the facing windows so as to allow for some ventilation. Of course, this also let in some of the exhaust smoke from the suffering and wheezing locomotive steam engine. Its soft chuff-chuffing sound in the background.

Rosetta accepted the proffered unfiltered Lucky Strike cigarette from Barbara. Her companion brought up a silver-plated Zippo lighter. Rosetta sucked in a couple of quick breaths until the cigarette was fully lit. She dragged a puff deeply into her lungs, exhaling a cloud toward the window. "Barbara, there is more going on than you may realize." And with that, Rosetta opened the way to what she most desperately wanted, needed, to say at this moment in the company of her good friend.

"What is it that troubles you, my friend? I know that you may sometimes think of me as a rival of yours. No!" Barbara held up her right hand. "It's true. We have known each other for far too long. But, rest assured, I am here for you."

"*Grazie,*" said Rosetta, who in that moment. looked to her friend, as someone who was so forlorn and downcast. "I may as well just come right out with it. You see, I have been troubled for some time now by Ariana.

More specifically, by her coterie of friends. Friends..." Rosetta had bitten off the words as is she had encountered a sour taste. "More like street toughs and thugs. I don't think I've spoken with her more than two or three times in the past month. She disappears for days at a time. Thank God for Marco. I can always rely on him. But, anyway, as to Ariana, I have this deep and abiding fear that she is going to show up one day and announce that she's pregnant."

Barbara stood and watched her friend, as she listened to her torment. "Rosetta, Ariana is at a difficult age. I will not try and lecture you. That is not what you need at this time. What about Bob? What does he say?"

"Bob, well, he loves them both, as if they were his own natural-born children. But he feels powerless, especially with Ariana. It seems as if she blames me for Paolo's death. And, how dare I should have taken up with another man. She cannot fathom that I've had to move on. Besides, Paolo would never have wanted for me to don black clothing and to sit and mourn for him for the rest of my life." Rosetta finished the rest of her Lucky Strike. The countryside, in all its pleasantry and tranquility, rolled by for mile after mile.

"Do you think she resents the things we do in the gym?"

"Perhaps, she does. I haven't really thought about it from that angle. I've attempted to get her to come by and work out, but she's shown no interest. I don't know... I just don't know where to go from here. Well, there, I've gotten my burden off my chest."

"Your well-endowed chest, no less," Barbara reposted. After a moment, both women looked at one another and began to laugh uncontrollably. They then returned to their compartment, whereupon they found that their disagreeable companion had departed. Just as well. Now Rosetta and Barbara could talk to one another without having to be circumspect.

"Next stop Firenze!" called out the conductor. Rosetta and Barbara simultaneously checked their wristwatches. Rosetta's, a Benrus diamond studded timepiece that Bob had just recently given her for her birthday.

"We have made good time, considering the state of the current Italian railroad system. "Oh, if only we still had *il Duce* at the controls. At least, he had made them run on time," scoffed a not so serious Barbara Danilo.

Rosetta merely shook her head with a rueful smile. "I'm glad the Duce no longer occupies high office."

Barbara feigned indifference as she resumed her gaze out the window of the car. "You know, Rosetta, I do think things will work out. They usually do."

"I hope you're right. Well, we're changing trains at Firenze, are we not?"

"*Si*, we are. I don't think, at least, I hope we won't have to wait too long for the next train. By my reckoning, we should be in Genoa in about three hours. Late afternoon, I hope that we will still be able to pick up our rental car. Would you like to drive, Rosetta?"

"No, I don't think so. I will defer to you. I only ask that you don't drive like a bat out of hell. I'd like to get to our destination in one piece, or at least in some semblance of one piece," Rosetta responded with a feigned smile to her friend.

Arrival in Genoa was just before 4:00 PM. Low-scudding clouds danced their way across the sky above. The air in the station was still on the sultry side as the two women gathered up their bags and handed them to a waiting porter. Rosetta and Barbara exited the crowded platform as quickly as possible from the clinging crowd. Once out on the street, they hailed a taxi which took them to the car rental agency less than a half mile away. They made it just before closing.

Offered a choice of vehicles, Barbara hinted that she preferred a Maserati open-topped roadster. After all, if she was going to drive, she may as well do it in style.

The women roared off just after 5:00 PM, daylight was still in its full effect. The wind ruffled and threw back Barbara's frizzled hair, as she put her foot to the floor. She wore a pair of aviator styled sunglasses, somewhat masculine appearing, but she did not care. Rosetta sat back in the passenger seat and managed to resist the urge to clasp a white-knuckled grip on the door handle. Barbara had mentioned arriving at their hotel in Verazze within the hour. At their current breakneck pace, at times topping 80 mph, they might well arrive within the next ten minutes. Providing, that is, they survived some of the hairpin turns Barbara was deftly maneuvering along the scenic coast road.

The Maserati roared up to the front entrance of the Hotel Brentano at precisely 6:00 PM. Rosetta could feel some of the grime on her face, picked up during their drive. It would be good to get settled in and, perhaps, get a libation or two. A warm, soaking bath would do as well

Rosetta and Barbara approached the front desk, only to be greeted by an obsequious, oily, man. Rosetta thought he strongly resembled the Italian-American character actor, Vito Scotti, sans the charm and good naturedness. She took an instant disliking to the man, even though not a word had been spoken.

"*Si, signora*, how may we be of service to you?" the man asked in an unctuous manner.

"We have a reservation for the next several days under the name of Rossi. Rosetta Rossi." The clerk looked at Rosetta and Barbara. Both were dressed in low-necked blouses. The man made sure to fully take in their presentations and, Rosetta later swore, practically leered at them.

Barbara could hardly constrain herself from delivering a right-handed haymaker to the man's, (his name tag identified him only as Vito,) kisser.

"Ah, let me see," he said as he made a big pretense of looking for Rosetta's name. "Ah, yes... here it is. One of our best rooms, overlooking the water I might add, has been duly reserved for *Signora* Rossi and guest." Vito looked to Barbara, who merely stood in front of him, stone-faced. She was really going to have to control herself from hauling off and whacking this odious man before the week was out.

Rosetta signed her name to a registration form and both she and Barbara handed their passports to Vito. These would be forwarded to the local police prefect, which was standard European procedure. The clerk was about to summon a bellhop to take the women's bags up to their room when Rosetta held up her hand.

"That won't be necessary," Rosetta instructed. "I think we can manage on our own, thank you." She and Barbara easily hefted their bags. Vito could not help but notice and admire the musculature of the women's upper arms. He also thought they might just be cheap, denying the bellhop his tip. And, perhaps, this pair might not be as straight-forward as they wanted to appear.

It was somewhat frowned upon in Italy, but two unrelated women rooming together might cause some tongues to wag.

Once in their room, both women threw themselves down onto their beds. "It is too bad for you Bob isn't here right now," Barbara said.

"*Si*, it is, but he is trying to arrange things so he can get here by Wednesday or Thursday at the latest."

"That would be good. Do you want to do anything tonight?" asked Barbara with a slight lilt in her voice.

"No, I would just like to relax, take a bath, have a drink. Maybe some dinner." Rosetta paused a moment before enumerating, "No, definitely something to eat."

"Now that I think of it, I am famished. I agree. Maybe, there might be an eligible handsome man available. I most certainly hope so." Barbara grinned with a look Rosetta knew all too well.

The next morning dawned bright and sunny, the air less humid and sultry to Rosetta as she awakened. She looked over at the next bed to see Barbara still asleep. Her friend had remained in their room the night before. Even she had apparently been a little too tired for any search of eligible men. There were several more nights ahead when Barbara could fulfill her libido.

Rosetta and Barbara grabbed a quick breakfast in the hotel restaurant that consisted of oatmeal, fruit, and coffee. They were served by their genial host, Vito. They just could not get themselves away from this cretin. Rosetta had not changed her opinion of the man from when they had first met. Barbara couldn't help but notice the way he continued to leer at them. She might very well have to hit him before she left; she just knew it.

Barbara took the wheel of the powerful Maserati as they headed off to Vento Beach, a scant ten miles down the Gulf of Genoa coast. There was not a cloud in the blue azure colored sky by this time as Rosetta gazed upward. Once again, her right hand was in a white-knuckled grip on the door handle as Barbara careened along at breakneck speeds. She, in a way, admired Barbara's sure-handed driving skills and yet, she herself would never attempt her hand at the wheel of this automobile at such speeds.

Shortly after 9:00 AM, the girls arrived at Vento Beach. Barbara parked the vehicle in an abandoned field that resembled a parking lot next to the road. She and Rosetta gathered up the things they would need for the day, which wasn't much, and headed toward a nearby narrow trail. This would take them to their secluded destination. As Rosetta walked along the trail, she was gazing out at the partial view of the water offered to her, not paying any particular attention, when she took a wrong step and twisted her right ankle. "Oh, damn!" she cried out. Barbara did not seem to hear her as she continued walking ahead on the narrow path.

At last, they came to the beach. Surprisingly, there did not appear to be anyone in sight. Maybe it wasn't so surprising. After all, how many in Italy could spend idle time, let alone spend the money to holiday mid-week. Rosetta dropped her bag and reached down and took out an old Italian olive-drab army blanket. She took hold of one end, Barbara the other, as they spread it out on the sand. Some smoothing out was required to remove some of the pebbles and small stones. That done, the two women quickly and unceremoniously removed their articles of clothing. Rosetta took out a bottle of the American brand "Coppertone" sunscreen and began to lather herself with it. She would never consent to using any of the Italian brands available. They always left her feeling like a basted chicken. Rosetta handed the lotion over to Barbara. Each of them spread the sunscreen on the other's back, then lay down on the blanket side by side to take in some of the sun's warming rays. Both of the women were already fairly well tanned.

Rosetta and Barbara had not planned any regimen to follow. They were there to relax. They would get in several hours of swimming; this would, in part, help them to maintain their superb physiques and also because they both enjoyed the sheer exhilaration of the salt water. During the war, this sort of activity had to be curtailed.

After less than half an hour, Rosetta looked up and noticed that no one else was on the beach. Barbara appeared to be engrossed in a paper- back novel, some steamy romance type. As if she of all people needed any pointers. "I think I am going in."

"*Si*, that sounds like a good idea," Barbara agreed as she dropped her book without having bothered to mark her place.

Rosetta took out a pair of goggles from her bag and handed a pair to Barbara. They both stood and started down to the water. If anyone had been watching, they would have observed two magnificent physical specimens, one in her early forties, and the other in her early fifties. Neither looked remotely like their age and certainly carried themselves as being much younger.

* * *

"*Scusi, Cardinale Maggione,* you asked for me?" asked a tremulous Pasco Gonevento as he stood before the imperious and menacing Ernesto Maggione. The cardinal did not immediately look up, but continued writing.

"*Si*, I did Pasco. You have something for me, I take it."

Gonevento thought the cardinal to be rude and disrespectful, not only to him, but to all others that he routinely dealt with. After all, this was a supposed man of God, one of the upper echelon of the Catholic Church. "*Si*, I just received word through a source in Verazze in regard to Signora Rossi." Gonevento offered nothing further.

"And? What did this source have to say?" queried Maggione, now having deemed it necessary to face his novitiate.

"Well, it seems as if Signora Rossi and her friend Barbara Danilo checked into the Hotel Brentano. It was noted that the women are staying in the same room."

"Mmm, I see," Maggione said as he steepled his fingers in front of his face. "And? Is that all this source has been able to come up with?"

"I am afraid so, *Cardinale*. At least, for the time being." Gonevento felt sweat breaking out. The imposing grandfather clock ticking in the background. Gonevento had always thought of it as an instrument of foreboding... of doom.

"Pasco, as you may well know, the Church and I are in full agreement as to some of these activities of Signora Rossi and her friend..."

"Barbara Danilo," Gonevento offered.

"Ah, *si, si*. This Danilo woman. As I was saying, the Church, and I also mean the Holy Father, frown upon this *group* of women. What with their grunting and sweating in that so-called gymnasium of theirs. It is very undignified and unladylike, if you will. What is more, some of the leading noblemen of the city feel essentially the same way," Maggione monotoned. He was now sitting back in his red-leather upholstered armchair. The one he had immediately appropriated from his deceased brethren, Cardinale Pacheco. "Anyway, I think we are going to need more information. That is, something of more substance. Do you catch my meaning, Pasco?"

"I think so, your eminence. You would like our source to come up with some…" Gonevento hesitated and then just blurted out, "dirt on these women?"

Maggione shook his doleful head slowly and tut-tutted. "Pasco, not dirt, but something that if it were brought out to the public's attention, as it should be, would cause for a reappraisal of Signora Rossi's operation. As it is, all we now have is a report that two athletic looking women have checked into a hotel and are staying in the same room. I realize that many people may find this as unseemly and may construe some unsavory thoughts as to what these women may be engaged in. Well, in any event, this source, who is being paid good money, must bring us more. That will be all, Pasco." And with that, Cardinal Maggione dismissed Gonevento as he went back to his correspondence.

Pasco Gonevento bowed to his superior and quietly left his office. His head whirled in a maelstrom of conflicting thoughts. Why was Maggione and, by extension, the Church, so interested in the personal habits and lifestyle of one particular woman? He thought he knew the answer. The Church, be it in the form of the Pope or the Cardinals, and those others, Maggione had called them noblemen, all saw Rosetta Rossi and Barbara Danilo as a threat. A threat that was too real and too immediate to them, and to their world.

Women, from whatever walk of life, were supposed to know their place, and it could not be condoned for them to deviate. Gonevento was aware that Maggione and others in the Church would stop at nothing to silence these women, even if it meant smearing their reputations. He shuddered with an inward disgust. He did not know how much longer he could continue to participate in this sordid activity.

* * *

36

Rosetta and Barbara, goggles fixed, dove into the gentle swells off Vento Beach. They swam, in powerful Australian overhand strokes out to a point about two hundred yards away. There they paused for a moment as they treaded water. Rosetta moved out a few yards and then took in a big gulp of air and dove under. Barbara did the same, almost simultaneously. The two women swam powerful breast strokes under the water as they drove themselves onward. Rosetta estimated that they had gone 300 yards when she surfaced. Barbara was not to be found, she must still be under. Again, Rosetta thought to herself, the competition. Barbara was determined to show, despite being ten years older, that she was a dominant force.

Rosetta continued treading water when she saw her friend another 100 yards away. Barbara waved and then she dove under again. Rosetta took in a large breath of air and went under. This time she dove to the bottom. She would linger her way along the seabed. She would also see how long she could remain underwater before she would have to surface for precious air.

As Rosetta swam along the bottom, she noticed that the water felt somewhat cool, but not uncomfortable. It was just about right for that time of year. Occasionally, her breasts brushed against the sea floor. She liked the titillation she felt.

Rosetta was truly free and completely at home within the depths of the sea. It had always seemed so for her; she always had had an aquatic bent, and her superb training regimen allowed for her to spend hours in the water at a time. During her dive, Rosetta had not noticed anything of note. There was the usual detritus one would expect to find: tin cans, pieces of wood, the usual. After she had been down for what she guessed to be about four to five minutes she surfaced.

Not ten yards away waited Barbara. "Well, my friend, you were down for quite a while. I can see that your lung capacity has not been impaired in any way."

"I was just trying to see how long I could stay under," Rosetta said as she pushed up her goggles. Saltwater splashed up against her face, momentarily stinging her eyes. I think that I'm going to resume some more diving. Please, join me, its lonely down there."

"*Si, si,* that is a good idea," agreed Barbara. "We should try and stay within sight of the beach, just to be safe." Barbara checked that her goggles were firmly in place and then swam off a little way before she dove under. It was a textbook perfect swan dive as she flipped her torso over, her legs straightened out and knifing through the water with barely a ripple.

Rosetta took in another huge rush of air and went under. She spotted Barbara about thirty feet away from her, headed for the floor. Rosetta thrust herself downward through the use of her powerfully developed arms and legs. Within a minute, she was nearly even with Barbara who acknowledged her presence by giving an okay sign with her right thumb and fore-finger. She then cupped her breasts and mouthed the words, "Hubba, hubba," to Rosetta.

Rosetta actually felt herself blush, as if that were possible thirty feet underwater. Quickly regaining herself she swam after Barbara. The women lingered along the seabed, again with nothing securing their attention. Once again, Rosetta found herself luxuriating in her comfort in the water. She was proud of the fact that she could swim and dive so well. It was another aspect of her on-going and growing sense of empowerment.

The two women remained in the water for what they thought must have been close to two hours. This was little effort for these two accomplished aquanauts. Before the war, they often spent up to four hours at a time before they sought rest. The girls swam a variety of strokes: overhand crawl, backstroke, breast-stroke, and the demanding and punishing butterfly. Rosetta had been able to perfect being able to stay under for three breast-strokes before surfacing for air on the fourth. Barbara settled for the more conventional two-stroke method. It was a sight to see their glistening, muscled bodies rise up out of the water as they took breaths. During the butterfly, both Rosetta and Barbara would rise up out of the water for a breath.

On one underwater foray, Rosetta felt the hands of Barbara grip her hips and felt her breasts along her back. Rosetta just maintained her strokes, as Barbara supplied supplementary kicking power. The pair swam like this for about a hundred yards.

Upon surfacing, Barbara only said, "I just thought I would hitch a ride from you."

"Think nothing of it, dear," replied a non-plussed Rosetta. She had paid no mind to Barbara's overture. After all, she did not consider herself a lesbian, and she did not think Barbara was one as well. "I will return the favor. You will have to provide transport for me as well."

"I look forward to it," said Barbara as she winked back. She then resettled her goggles, took a deep breath, and then jackknifed under the water. Rosetta immediately followed and soon found herself just behind and atop Barbara's position. She dove downward and brought her hands to Barbara's waist. Barbara kept on swimming as she brought her hands back to briefly touch Rosetta's. She resumed swimming and began to drive herself through the water.

The girls emerged from the surf and Rosetta could not help but notice as they walked in some coils of rusted barbed wire off to the left side. *Strange,* she thought, as scrap metal scavengers had pretty much devoured up almost any type of metal for redemption on the metals market. *It won't be there much longer,* she continued her thought. She also now saw a few people without clothes on the beach. Some were young women and there was one man. All seemed to remain amongst themselves.

Rosetta and Barbara slathered more sunscreen on their bodies and took to their blanket. This time they rested upon their stomachs. After a few minutes, Barbara turned her head to Rosetta. "I've been thinking. I am a little concerned about our friend at the hotel, *Signore* Vito."

"Concerned? Why, whatever for?" questioned Rosetta as she looked back. "I mean I do think that he's an asshole, but harmless."

"No, no, he may well be a spy. You know, Rosetta, you have some enemies, especially among some of the higher clergy and upper crust Roman men. There's something that isn't quite right. I mean, beyond the obvious in that the man is a full-class jerk. There's something… *oily* about him. The way he practically leers at us."

"I know. He makes my skin crawl, too. But, what can we do?"

"Leave it to me. I am going to contact Mauro, and I do know a good private detective. He is most discreet. I can't help but have the feeling that something untoward is about," Barbara said thoughtfully. "I won't make any calls from our hotel. That snake would probably have that covered. In any event, what are we going to do about this evening?"

"I thought, and you do not have to agree, that we could have a quiet dinner at that restaurant next door to our hotel," offered Rosetta.

"That would be fine. Yes, I think that is a good idea," agreed Barbara. Her mind soon drifted back to her evening with Mauro Guzzo. It started to make her feel warm all over her body, aside from the obvious heat of the sun's rays beating down. It had been most pleasurable for her from the sexual standpoint. But is had also provided her with something else. Guzzo's gut-wrenching story of his son's tragic death had been heartbreaking. It had made her consider, even if briefly, there might be more to life than merely fulfilling one's carnal desires. Still, she felt that here and now, she needed the company of a suitable younger man's body. Perhaps, this evening while at dinner, someone might appear.

Later that afternoon, after the girls had returned from Vento Beach Barbara Danilo left on her own and drove over to the nearby town of Scarano. She stopped at what appeared to be a tavern, but she wasn't sure. It certainly wasn't much to look at, but it did possess a working telephone as a sign indicated. After a delay and a degree of frustration, Barbara was able to place a call through to Mauro Guzzo. Luckily for her he was in his office. "Mauro, is that you? Ciao, how are you? This is Barbara," she enthused into the phone.

"Eh, Barbara, how are you? Where are you?"

"I'm on holiday with Rosetta up on the Ligurian coast. We're well, but there's something I would like you to do for me." And with that, Barbara proceeded to inform Guzzo about *Signore* Vito Cardoso. Could he find out anything about this man. Barbara would contact Guzzo again on Thursday.

Unbeknownst to Barbara Danilo, a lone man was waiting and watching the tavern from his white Lancia sedan. The man had been instructed to follow Rosetta Rossi and Barbara Danilo. He had been unable to follow them when they had left for Vento Beach, so he had waited for them at the Hotel Brentano. Now, he would wait for this attractive and obviously well-built, middle-aged woman to emerge from the tavern. He would then go in and subtly question anyone who may have overheard what she had said. She must have chosen this ramshackle place to use its telephone. Why else would she have selected it?

Moments after hanging up from Mauro Guzzo, Barbara fished more coins from her purse and dialed her old friend, Stefano Lucca. The man was one of the pre-eminent private detectives in all of Rome. And, he had once been one of Barbara's most ardent lovers. After dispensing with the usual pleasantries, Danilo got straight to the point. "You see, Stefano, I think that I'm being followed. And, it's not only me, but also involves my good friend, Rosetta."

"I'm not surprised, Barbara. That club of yours has got the clergy and other circles in an uproar. Do you suspect something sinister?" asked Lucca.

Barbara proceeded to tell him of their encounter with the greasy Vito Cardoso. What could he find out about this cretin?

"Give me a couple of days. I'm right now in the middle of a nasty divorce case. It seems as if the male party, my client, is being two-timed by his outwardly appearing pious wife. To hear him tell it, the woman presents herself as some kind of religious apparition. She's devoted herself to God, but not to him. At least, not in the bedroom. Seems she's been humping the brains out of this doctor on Via Navona. Well, I must be boring you, Barbara, I will do what I can," Lucca finally concluded.

"No, you are not boring me. You know I always like a story with a twist, particularly one with a sexual connotation. I would most appreciate anything you can find out. Ciao, Stefano, all my best."

* * *

The old, gray-haired man led Rosetta and Barbara to their table. He informed them that he, Gaetano, would be their waiter for the evening. The women were seated and handed plain, non-descript paper menus listing the various specialties of Rossini's. Rosetta looked over her menu absentmindedly. She was thinking about what Barbara had broached to her earlier that day. Maybe they were being spied upon. But why? Yes. Barbara was probably right, it all centered around their gymnasium. One would think that members of the Church, particularly high-ranking ones, would have more important things on their plates. Italy was still a devastated country, and it would take years for it to finally get back on its feet.

Barbara settled on a main course of veal saltimbocca, accompanied by asparagus, and roasted potatoes. In addition, she selected an appetizer of clams casino. Rosetta agreed to the same dish, despite Barbara's brief insistence that she try another main course. Barbara then filled her in on her calls to Mauro Guzzo and Stefano Lucca.

Across from the women sat two men, both appeared to be in their late twenties. Carlo Tresca and Mario Casso had noticed Barbara and Rosetta when they had walked into the establishment. The two debated as to whether they should approach the women. Clearly, they were older than they were themselves, but it might be amusing to try and pick them up.

When Mario Casso noticed that the girls were about to finish their meals he got up and walked over to them. "*Scusi, signorine*, my name is Mario and over there," he pointed to Carlo Tresca, "is my friend. May we join you for a cordial? I do hope that I am not imposing."

Rosetta was about to dismiss this young whippersnapper when Barbara said, "Ah, how kind of you, young man. That is lovely idea, don't you think, Rosetta?" She received a slight kick to her shin. Rosetta could have killed her friend; it was a good thing a pistol was not at hand for her to do so. "Well-l-l…" she stammered. She knew what Barbara was up to and she was powerless to stop it.

Casso signaled to Tresca to join them, which he did, but haltingly. He was not as sure as his friend that this was a good idea.

For the next hour, Barbara and Casso conducted virtually on their own private conversation. Rosetta knew her friend would lead Mario Casso to bed later in the evening. She could see that Tresca was miserable and wanted no further part in the proceedings. Rosetta actually felt a little bad for him. He was not rude to her, he simply appeared to be tongue-tied. She did notice that her low-cut lilac shaded blouse had gotten his attention.

Finally, to Rosetta's immense relief, Barbara said that she and Casso would be departing for a stroll along the waterfront. Tresca, too, looked

42

positively relieved and promptly paid his respects to Rosetta and then nearly ran out of the restaurant.

* * *

Earlier that day, the strange man emerged slowly from his worn and beaten down Lancia, just as Barbara Danilo had driven off in a cloud of dust. He looked to both sides of the road and slowly approached the tavern. Once inside, he strolled over to the bar and addressed the man he presumed to be its proprietor.

"*Scusi, signore*. I am an inspector with the Carabinieri and involved with a most important criminal investigation. Might I have a word with you?" The man, dressed in a rather worn, belted trench coat, flashed open what appeared to be an authentic police badge.

The man who looked at the stranger was Alberto Conti, a small diminutive person whose head was topped by a graying mop of hair. Conti, who had no love of the police of any kind, knew he would have to tread carefully with the stranger before him. "I always try to be cooperative with the authorities, but I did not get your name, *signore*."

"Ah, how remiss of me. My name is Chief Inspector Gianni Ravelli. Now, I just have a few questions, if you do not mind?"

Conti moved his head up and down slowly as if indicating that he indeed would cooperate.

"*Bene, bene, signore*. Now, just a short time ago a woman, a rather well-built woman, entered your establishment. Would you be able to tell me if she placed any telephone calls?"

"*Si, si*, this woman did indeed come in and she did make use of my phone," said Conti, who was now taking an increasing dislike of this oily-looking and insincere sounding so-called policeman. He had never trusted the authorities, any of them. The local arm of the law was a useless cretin who had only gotten the job because of family connections.

"*Bene, bene*. Did you happen to overhear anything this woman said?" the faux detective continued.

"Well, I really cannot say," hesitated Conti, who really didn't want to offer this creep anything, but he was also aware that he had to provide something. "She seemed to drop in a goodly number of coins, so the calls were probably long distance."

"I see, so you said she made… what was it, calls?"

"*Si*, she made two calls."

"Did you happen to hear what she may have said? Anything at all? Signore, I must remind you that this is a most important criminal matter."

"Criminal, you say? It's funny, this woman, this attractive woman did not look like a criminal," said Alberto Conti. By now, he did not believe for one second that the woman in question had committed or had been involved in any crime. It was more like a domestic matter and this inspector was out fishing.

"*Signore*, criminals do not always look like criminals," the man said patronizingly. "Well, if that is all you can remember, then. I thank you. Good day to you, sir." The detective turned on his heel and left.

Alberto Conti continued to stand behind his bar. His son, Tommaso, asked what that had been all about.

"Probably nothing. It was strange, however."

"Why do you say that, papa?"

"Well, you know, when the police interview someone they usually leave their card or a phone number where they can be reached. This man did neither." Conti would have to remember to mention this when the attractive woman returned—and return he knew she would. He had been able to overhear her say she would be back at the tavern in two days' time.

CHAPTER THREE - THE GIRLS

Barbara Danilo sat atop Mario Casso as she slowly impaled her muscled body on the man's rigid shaft. She was about to employ her full arsenal of sexual techniques upon this young stud of a male specimen. She could tell that Casso was absolutely enthralled with the sight, and the feel, of her spectacular bosom which sat firmly on her chest.

Mario Casso had never made love to a woman the age of Barbara Danilo. She had coyly hinted to him that she was past fifty, but he did not care. The woman was unbelievable, from her breasts, to her muscled upper arms, to her six-packed abdomen and her long legs. She was grinding herself with an increasing fervor, all the while with a slightly curved smile on her face. Casso was fearful he might not be able to fully satisfy Barbara's carnal desires, but he would most certainly try.

Later, Mario Casso had marveled at his lover's prowess, stamina, and endurance. He had driven himself with all that he had into Barbara's body. And she had responded in kind, her legs hooked up and over his back tightly as he pounded away. During their second session, he had entered her as she lay upon her elevated stomach. The scent of her shampooed hair had driven him completely wild; it had been so intoxicating. Barbara herself immensely enjoyed every minute of it and every inch of Mario Casso.

The girls were up early on Wednesday morning. There wasn't a cloud in the sky. It would be perfect. Rosetta and Barbara were able to slip past Signore Vito out of the hotel. Both felt sure that if the man had any inkling of their destination he would have someone follow them.

They arrived at Vento Beach by 10:00 AM, both wearing a bikini-style bottom. The piece was black, very little distinguished from panties. The Coppertone sunscreen was applied in copious amounts. Rosetta and Barbara then set to lay upon the olive-drab colored army blanket to soak up the sun's rays.

Rosetta noted a few beachgoers on this day. A few young women and a couple of aged men. They would have better served themselves, and the others, if they had fully clothed themselves. Barbara said with disgust,

"You would think those two would have the decency and self-respect to withhold from us the disgusting sight they're presenting. Look at those stomachs. It is as if they swallowed the globe. I don't think they can see their cocks when they have to take a piss," said Barbara with disgust.

"Now, now, my friend. They are entitled to the same privileges as us on this beach. We shouldn't look down on them," replied Rosetta.

"That is easy for you to say. Have you taken a good look at them?"

"No, thank you."

"How long do you plan to spend in the water today?" asked Barbara as she continued to scan the beach.

"I was thinking of trying to stay maybe up to three hours at a time. I want to catch some sun," Some seagulls were circling lazily in the azure blue colored skies.

"Do you think we'll see our acquaintances from last night? Mario had indicated that he planned to make an appearance here today. Of course, there will be no surprise, at least, in regard to his equipment. Rosetta, are you listening to me?" asked a pretendedly indignant Barbara.

Rosetta waved a hand in the air. "You don't have to fill me in on the details of your conquests. I really don't care. Bob is supposed to be here by some time tomorrow. He mentioned he would try and arrive by early afternoon. At least, that is his plan. Of course, as he said, he will have to schmooze his superior if he is to be successful."

"I just love that word, 'schmooze,' which is what ninety-eight per cent of the men in Italy do. Well, back to Mario. Perhaps, it was just too much for him. It was a rather strenuous session I will have to admit," Barbara went on.

After turning over for about twenty minutes, the girls decided to go for their extended swim. Both agreed that when they returned to Rome they would look to purchase waterproof dive watches so they could tell exactly how long they were in the water. Rosetta and Barbara swam and dove for what they later estimated had been in excess of three hours. As they walked back in toward the beach, Barbara turned to Rosetta and said, "You know, at least we're free up here," as she pointed at her breasts. "I really do like the feeling of being unfettered."

Rosetta only smiled and shook her head. Her friend was simply incorrigible. Barbara always had been, and always would be. It was an indelible element of her nature.

* * *

Bob Rossi was finally able to extricate himself from his duties in Rome and he arrived at the Hotel Brentano just after 4:00 PM on that Thursday. He asked at the front desk for his wife, only to be told by Vito, that the girls had not been seen for several hours. Vito did relate that he had heard a rumor that Rosetta and Barbara had been entertained by two handsome young men the previous evening. Bob had looked at the man with a feeling of revulsion, not believing for a second that his wife would betray him. As for Barbara, it was indeed possible, no, more likely probable that she would indulge herself in physical passion with an eligible younger man.

That same Thursday, Rosetta and Barbara ducked out of the Hotel Brentano before 8:00 AM and arrived at the secluded beach by 9:00 AM. Following their obligatory application of sunscreen, the two women laid down to sun themselves under another cloudless sky. The air was dry, not inundated with the usual clinging humidity. Within the hour, both dove into the water. They swam long strokes of the crawl, breaststroke, butterfly, and backstroke. It was again a sight to see Rosetta and Barbara steaming themselves through the punishing butterfly. Their muscled, tanned bodies glistened in the sunlight.

Watching from a distance was Mario Casso. Carlo Tresca had returned to his hometown of Milan. Casso could hardly contain the bulge he was experiencing in his black Euro styled bathing suit. He wouldn't dare try his hand in joining these two Amazonian creatures in the water. He might well drown. No, he would keep an eye out for the moment they returned to their blanket. Then he would approach and engage Barbara. Casso wanted another night in the sack with this breathtaking woman.

And that was precisely what Casso did when Rosetta and Barbara emerged from the Ligurian water. It was just after noontime. The two walked from the receding water and looked like goddess apparitions to him. Water cascaded down their bodies. Rosetta noticed Casso lurking near some of the abandoned barbed wire and quietly informed her friend.

"I was wondering if he would show himself again," said Barbara as she shook some of the seawater from her frizzled hair. "Well, it will be fun to tease him just a little."

"That is up to you. But, remember, you're supposed to make that follow-up call to Stefano Lucca," intoned Rosetta. She was anticipating her husband's arrival that afternoon.

"No, I haven't forgotten. I'm just going to have a little fun with my young friend. I'm going to lure him into the water and then pretend to drown him," Barbara teased. There was a fiery delight in her eyes.

"Barbara, you're free to do as you wish, but I'm only your sidekick," Rosetta said as she started drying herself off with her beach towel. "I can't wait to see Bob. I have my own evening planned for him. If you know what I mean?" Rosetta winked at Barbara.

"You naughty girl. Would you like for me to give you any tips for the boudoir? Feel free to ask. There would be no charge."

"No, thank you. I think I know just what to do. Thank you for the offer." Rosetta winked and resumed her reclined position on the blanket. "Oh, here he comes. Be nice."

Barbara looked up and took in Casso in his Euro suit. He wasn't as impressive physically as he had appeared the night they had shared in bed. He could do to add some muscle tone to his arms and legs. No wonder Italy had lost the war, if Casso was an example as to who had marched forward into battle. "Mario, good to see you again. I thought I might have scared you off after our night together."

Casso twisted his head deferentially, nearly blushing. "No, no, it is just that I have had some business to attend to. You know how it is."

"Of course, darling. I was just teasing you. Do join us. You remember Rosetta?"

"*Si*, of course I do. A pleasure to see you again, Rosetta," Casso acquiesced as he took in the full measure of this other remarkably built and attractive older woman.

Rosetta raised herself up. "Nice to see you again Mario. Yes, please join us. It will be nice to have a man around," she teased.

For the next two hours, Mario Casso stayed with Rosetta and Barbara. He was, indeed, lured into the water by Danilo. At one point, she had dived below the surface and did not come up for a couple of minutes, leaving a concerned Casso to wonder if she may have met with misfortune. He was treading water, becoming more frantic by the second, when he was practically tackled by Barbara. She had made a stealthy approach, similar to one a great white shark would have made. Casso felt the impact of her body across his chest as he was driven under. Momentarily losing his breath, he took on some water and began to gag when he was finally able to resurface. Barbara, nearby, threw back her head in laughter. Of course, she raced over to Casso and feigned her deepest concern.

Back on the beach, Rosetta had remained and had looked on with bemusement as Barbara had toyed with and teased the unfortunate young man. But who was she to interfere. Her thoughts drifted to her husband. She would truly entertain Bob in bed. They had not had sex in more than a week. Bob was a most considerate and consummate partner. He seemed to know just about every right move to make. He knew how to bring out the best that Rosetta had to offer as a woman.

The girls left Vento Beach just after 3:00 PM. Barbara had wanted to leave enough time so that she could make her follow-up call to Stefano Lucca. Barbara put her foot to the pedal and the women literally flew back to the Hotel Brentano. The sports car roared to a sudden stop outside the hotel entrance. As Rosetta emerged from the vehicle she was greeted by the obsequious Vito.

"Ah, *buon giorno, signora.* I do hope that you and your friend have had a most pleasant day," he gushed.

It was too much, too thick, for Rosetta, who could barely bring herself to respond to the man. "*Si, si,* it was, signore…"

"Eh, Vito, *signora.* I am most glad to hear of it. Oh, I have some very good news for you. Your husband arrived this afternoon. He has been most anxious to see you. If I might add, he did seem a little disappointed that you were not here to greet him. I did try to allay some of his fears," Vito went on in that annoying and chattering mannerism of his.

Rosetta was glad to hear that Bob had arrived at last. She murmured a brief thank you to Vito and then brushed past him. Strolling through the lobby was Bob himself. Upon seeing him, Rosetta rushed over to embrace him.

"I'm so glad that you are here. I've missed you so," she burst forth. Rosetta wrapped her arms around Bob's head and brought her lips to his in a passionate kiss.

"It took a little doing, but I'm here."

"*Bene.* How are the children and mama?"

"Everyone is fine. Your mother is watching them, at least, as much as one can with two teenagers."

"*Si,* I do wonder whether Ariana will listen to my mother," Rosetta said warily. "Ariana is a concern. Sometimes, I do not think I even know her anymore."

"Do not worry so much. If there is one thing I know is, is that Ariana loves and has deep respect for your mother," Bob said soothingly, trying to alleviate Rosetta's fears. "Now, why don't we try and enjoy the rest of the afternoon."

* * *

"Come on, come on Ariana. What are you waiting for?" insisted an increasingly impatient Angelo Tomma.

"I don't know. I'm not sure I'm ready," replied an anguished and nearly half-dressed Ariana Rossi. The girl had discarded her blouse and now was covered only by her bra. It afforded a birds-eye view of her fulsome breasts to Tomma. He had long envisioned engaging himself with them and now he was so close to doing so.

"I can't. I…I…just can't. Please Angelo, I'm not ready. You have to understand," the girl pleaded.

"I understand perfectly. What? Am I not good enough for you? Is that it?" Tomma sneered down at the trembling girl before him. Tears were falling down her cheeks. This only seemed to make Tomma angrier. "Okay, have it your way, miss prissy. I've been very patient with you. Believe me. And for what? To be rejected by a little girl who has tried so mightily to pretend she is a woman," Tomma practically screamed at Ariana, who was now openly sobbing.

Ariana clutched at a handkerchief, trying to dry away some of her tears. Her face was bathed a deepening scarlet. Her chest was heaving, her fulsome breasts seemed only to grow larger to Angelo Tomma. He had to admit that he was getting turned on. If only he could direct Ariana in the direction he wanted. "Look, Ariana, I'm sorry. I didn't mean to offend you. I did not. But, we have been fencing around this issue for some time and …" Tomma's voice trailed off and had softened in its stridency. He was no longer shouting.

"This issue, you say. You mean sex, don't you, Angelo? You just want to get your hands on these hooters," Ariana fired back as she looked Tomma straight in the eye. At the same time, she cupped her breasts in her hands. "You only ever wanted to get me into bed."

"No, no, that is not true, Ariana. I swear it on my mother," he pleaded back.

"No, I think you're lying. I've seen almost from the first how you've looked at my mother whenever she was around. Oh, you always tried to be coy about it, but I saw the way you would look when she bends over."

Angelo had to admit to himself that he had always been impressed and aroused at the sight of Rosetta Rossi and her impressive frontal physique. Tomma now brought his mind to the moment at hand. He had had enough of Ariana and her shyness and her little girl ways. All right, have it your way, but this was it.

Ariana knew at that very moment what Angelo Tomma now meant to her. Nothing. Absolutely nothing. She knew it. What her mother had been trying to get through to her for so long, almost from the very moment she had been introduced to Tomma, was unequivocally true. Ariana had not seen it then, or just refused to see it. It had been her show of defiance before Rosetta. Ariana knew she would have some fences to mend with her mother, but she thought she would be forgiven.

* * *

Barbara Danilo excused herself from Rosetta and Bob in the hotel lobby and then proceeded on her way to make her follow-up call to Stefano Lucca. The drive to Alberto Conti's tavern was relaxed for Danilo, as she did not see a need to risk her neck by driving at breakneck speeds. Following her at a discreet distance was the vehicle driven by the faux carabinieri inspector. She arrived at the tavern and came to a halt in a cloud of dust. Barbara glanced in the rear-view mirror to make sure her hair looked reasonably fashionable. She also checked to see how much grime she might have picked up on her face during the journey.

Alberto Conti was standing behind the bar at his usual spot as Barbara strode through the door. The woman, once again, looked positively breathtaking: the frizzled hair, the striking clear blue eyes, the firm face, and the magnificent figure. It was most remarkable, particularly since Conti guessed that she must be in her fifties. He motioned to Barbara to approach the bar. She wondered what this could be about.

"*Scusi, signora*, but I was wondering if I could have a word with you?"

"*Si, signore*," she responded.

"*Bene*. I just thought I should tell you that the other day, when you stopped in and made some phone calls, a man posing as a member of the

Carabinieri approached me for some information. He said it involved a criminal matter. Now, I am not making any judgment, I assure you, but I thought you would want to know."

"Grazie, signore…?"

"Oh, excuse me. I should have introduced myself to you. I am Alberto Conti, the proprietor of this establishment." Conti offered his hand to Barbara, who returned the handshake. The man was suitably impressed with the woman's grip.

"Eh, grazie, Signore Conti. Did this so-called inspector leave a name by any chance?" Barbara asked with one arched eyebrow.

The woman had a distinct presence to go with a spectacular body.

"He did. He said that he was Inspector Gianni Ravelli. There was something else as well."

"And what was that?"

"He did not leave a business card or where he could be reached should I discover anything new. I thought it to be rather odd."

"Indeed, signore Alberto," Barbara agreed, and proceeded to extract a fifty lire note from her handbag.

"Oh no, signora. That will not be necessary. I am only too glad to glad to let you know," said Conti in a self-deprecating manner. He placed his hand up as if to figuratively push away the proffered money.

"No, please, I insist. You have done a great favor. And," Barbara said as she proceeded to remove another fifty lire note," this is if I can ask to use a private phone you may have here. What with the strange things we have been discussing, I would appreciate a degree of more privacy." Barbara then tilted her head and leaned forward, offering Conti a more complementary view of her.

It seemed as if Conti would refuse the request and the money, but he relented. "I do not see why you cannot be accommodated, Barbara." Conti discreetly took the two fifty lire notes and stuffed them into his shirt pocket. He then guided Barbara to a small room located behind the bar. It looked to be where the tavern keeper did his personal business. Conti instructed her on how to place a long-distance call. He did not ask of the destinations of the calls. He did not want to know.

53

In the next moment, Barbara was connected to Stefano Lucca. The private detective had been expecting her call, and it had not stopped him from entertaining a client. This happened to be a young woman named Paulina Rubio. It seemed as if Mrs. Rubio had reason to believe that her fifty-five-year old husband was going to try and get rid of her. He had had the gall to suspect that she, Paulina, had been unfaithful to him numerous times during the one year of their marriage. The word going around the Eternal City was that Paulina Rubio was known as the gadabout goddess.

The goddess in question was seated across from Lucca, leeringly licking a swizzle stick as she sampled a Campari and soda. Lucca had been discreetly eying his potential client. Short, bob-style hair, full lips, soft brown eyes, and breasts that would not quit. The phone rang and Lucca lifted the receiver, all the while admiring Mrs. Rubio. "*Si, pronto*. Ah, Barbara, I have been expecting your call."

"And, I trust that you have come up with some information," Barbara said, cutting right to the chase. She had no time for phony pleasantries on this day.

"Oh, well. Yes, I did indeed come up with some interesting information. It seems as if your hotel clerk was only recently installed at the Brentano some three weeks ago. Previously, he was at one of the parent company's establishments in Venice."

"M-m-m, that is interesting. Any idea as to why he was assigned to the Brentano?"

"There is. Now, Barbara, you know that I have always tried to comply and fulfill your requests." Barbara knew what was coming. "I simply cannot provide…" There followed a pregnant pause.

"Ever the businessman," Barbara said icily. "All right, Stefano. You know full well I have always paid you with money, and with, on occasion…" she paused, "with my body. How much will this information cost me?"

"Now, Barbara. I do not have a fee set in mind yet. Let us just say, I will require some future remuneration."

"All right, Stefano. Now, give. Let us cease fencing around," Barbara said as her eyes rolled. She could not help but think of her and Lucca in bed together at the Hotel Bernini Bristol for those two glorious days. The man had been a good lay. But now it was time for business.

"Well, it seems as if the hotel group was approached by someone working on behalf of someone else working in the Vatican. Can you believe that?"

"For the love of God. Doesn't the Church have something more important than pursuing us? I mean, Rosetta and me," Barbara hissed into the phone. She felt a sheen of perspiration break upon her face. Droplets of dew started to run down her chest. Her top was becoming more revealing in the overheated back room.

"Well, I do not know about the continuing interest by the clergy."

"Who is it? Do you have any names?" asked Barbara.

"I'm still working on it. As soon as I know more I will let you know," Lucca replied as he gazed out past Paulina and through his office window. It was a splendid view of the old Roman fort, Castel Sant'Angelo. "And, I thought you also might like to know that your oily clerk at the Brentano has been reassigned. It's being arranged as we speak. There is no additional charge for this service."

"That's good news, Stefano. Not that I care as to where this Signore Vito is being sent. I know Rosetta will be pleased. She couldn't stand the man any more than I could."

"I think it is a place called the Trengano, something or other."

"Where is that?"

"It's in some backwater town, as I understand it. The infernal reaches would be akin to it." "

That should be worth a little extra, Stefano." Barbara couldn't resist the dig.

"Now, now, Barbara. Let us not quibble over a little thing like money. As I just said, the reassignment is gratis. In any event, with this Vito character gone, you and your friend Rosetta will be free to holiday to your hearts' content."

"*Ciao*, Stefano. And *grazie*," Barbara said with probably her most sincere statement to Lucca.

She hung up the phone and as she walked out of the tavern, caught Alberto Conti's eye. She mouthed the word "*Grazie*" and then quickly walked out. Barbara looked about in the remaining bright sunlight of the day. She noticed a white Lancia parked along the side of the road, its driver pretending to be engaged in reading something, perhaps a map. *Well,* she thought, *I think I'll have a little fun.*

Once out in the lot, Barbara slung herself into her car and took out her sunglasses. She inserted the key into the ignition, the powerful engine roaring to life. She disengaged the handbrake, pressed her left foot onto the clutch pedal, then placed the gearshift lever into first and roared off. Barbara placed her foot to the floor of the accelerator pedal and the vehicle's rear wheels responded by throwing back gravel and pebbles.

Gianni Ravelli started up his car's engine as soon as he saw Barbara peal out and tried mightily to keep up but he soon realized he would be doomed in his effort. His prey was easily pulling away and within a couple of miles, he had lost her. He slammed the steering wheel in frustration, sweat starting to pour down his brow. "Damn it!" he shouted out loud to himself. "I am going to get that bitch, so help me God!" What could he tell his client? 'Oh, I just happened to be given the slip by a middle-aged woman?' No, he knew he wouldn't do that. Not in 1940s Italy where women were still considered inferior to men. He would be a laughingstock. He would have to come up with something far better.

Barbara Danilo looked back into rearview mirror to see that she had shaken off her pursuer. She smiled. It had been relatively easy… perhaps it had been too easy. If this fake inspector could be eluded this easily, well then, he was clearly overmatched. Barbara decided she would wait until the following morning to tell Rosetta and Bob about what she had learned from Stefano Lucca and about her car duel. She would let them enjoy their evening of domestic bliss.

After she had gone a few more miles, Barbara eased up on her driving speed, there was no further need for her to drive as if she were entered in the Mille Miglia race.

* * *

Following a relaxing and leisurely dinner at a nearby seaside restaurant, Rosetta and Bob had strolled hand in hand along the shore. Bob was growing impatient; Rosetta could tell by his fidgeting. She knew he wanted to get back to the hotel and to make mad and passionate love to her. Rosetta, too, was eager to go to bed with her husband.

Bob Rossi watched, enthralled, as Rosetta slowly and lingeringly removed her articles of clothing. First came her blouse, revealing her magnificent bust. Next, her bra came off. Bob's breath caught in his throat. Rosetta then removed her skirt and panties. Finally, she kicked off her sandals. She then cupped her breasts and made a cooing sound toward Bob.

What followed was nearly two hours of unbridled sexual passion as Rosetta and Bob hurled themselves at one another. Their first sex had seen Bob ride Rosetta. The next time had Rosetta riding Bob as if she were a wild and bucking bronco. Rosetta felt that she and Bob had not had enough sex in the past couple of months, what with all of the activities they were both engaged in. But tonight, they were more than making up for lost time.

The couple proceeded to take breaks between sessions until they felt fulfilled and exhausted. Both lay back in bed with looks of contentment on their faces.

"So, mama is looking after the children?" asked Rosetta.

"*Si*, er, yes, she is. I think they're in good hands."

"I still worry about Ariana. She has been so… difficult of late," said a worried Rosetta.

"It's probably just a phase she's going through," replied Bob, who offered to share his cigarette with Rosetta. She declined.

"That's what they always say. 'It's just a phase she's going through'. But what if it isn't? What then? It's that bum, Angelo Tomma. I knew he was bad from the first instant I saw him. I swear he used to practically leer at me. I could always feel his eyes crawling all over me. I would feel sick!" Rosetta went on. She was nearly tempted to reach over and grab Bob's cigarette.

"Now, now, Rosetta. I know how you feel. That Angelo character has always made me feel uneasy as well. I agree that he's probably a bad egg.

But I also think that Ariana will eventually see through this guy. I trust she'll do the right thing."

"Bad egg, you say? I think he's a complete asshole. There, I said it, and I mean it!" Rosetta nearly shouted.

Bob didn't reply. He snuffed out his cigarette in the glass ashtray and then leaned over and cradled Rosetta until they both fell into a restful sleep.

Friday dawned cloudy, the sky spitting a light drizzle. It would not be a good day for the beach. In any event, the water was choppy, not at all conducive to swimming or diving. During breakfast in the Brentano's restaurant, Barbara informed Rosetta of her findings and events of the previous afternoon.

"So that's why Signore Vito has suddenly disappeared," said a now pleased Rosetta. "I couldn't stand that man from the instant I first laid eyes on him. I'm so glad. But who may have sent him here, and why?"

"Well, as to who sent him here, Stefano Lucca is still working on it. And he will. Stefano is one of the best private detectives in all of Rome, in fact, Italy. He has many sources, many connections. He'll find out. As to why, I think that's obvious. Someone, and I think I know who, is out to discredit you, if not destroy you." Barbara left it at that as she buttered a roll with real butter. A reintroduced luxury to Italian dining tables.

Bob Rossi, who had joined the girls in mid-conversation, intoned, "Rosetta and I have discussed this matter. I think, as you have intimated, that someone or some group has an innate fear as to what your gymnasium stands for. Personally, I think it's all balderdash, but nevertheless, to *someone* you two girls are a threat. In any event, with this Vito character out of the way, we should be able to all relax a little, at least for the next couple of days."

* * *

The following day was the polar opposite to Friday. Sunlight, brilliant rays of sun, cascaded down on the town. Rosetta and Barbara, along with Bob, went to Vento Beach. Bob drove them all in his rental car, a small and unimpressive Fiat. Rosetta would not have grip the door handle as she would have had if Barbara had taken the wheel. They arrived at a more crowded Vento. Rosetta and Barbara stripped down to their black colored briefs. They were topless. Bob himself donned a white Euro suit. He was not sure how he really felt about his wife displaying her endowment. This was Italy, Europe, and it seemed perfectly acceptable. And yet, he did not like for others, particularly men, eying his Rosetta. He felt as if some could not help but leer at her. As to Barbara, Bob well knew that she didn't care one whit.

All three strolled languidly down to the water from their blanket after they had sunned themselves for a short time. Barbara set out first as she swam overhand strokes and then taking in a large breath of air, dove under the water. She didn't surface for several minutes. Bob was captivated. "What lungs!" he exclaimed to himself.

Rosetta swam away from her husband and, then, she too dove under and began to swim for a couple of hundred yards. Bob would not even consider an attempt to match the women's exploits. He knew he could not even come close to them.

Rosetta and Barbara returned to the water a couple of more times throughout the remainder of the day. They both spent from one to two hours at a time in the water. Bob could not help but admit to himself that Rosetta and Barbara were more like fish. Maybe comparing them to sharks would have been a more apt comparison. They were both completely at home in the embrace of the sea. In a way, he envied them. Or was it something else?

* * *

Upon her return to Rome, Rosetta settled back into her routine. During the week, she continued to perform her duties with the American military mission by day, and, for several nights she spent her time at the gym working out and overseeing the other women. Of course, she had administrative duties to perform as well. She was ably assisted by Barbara Danilo and another older woman, Maria Franchi.

Maria had never made any pretense about working out. She was pushing sixty years of age, and while she did not have an athletic build to speak of, by any means, Maria seemed content to remain slightly overweight and out of shape, until one day when she was in the office alone with Rosetta. The pair were going through some of the paperwork.

"Rosetta, I've been thinking. By that, I mean I've been giving some thought to something new. For me, it would probably be considered revolutionary."

Rosetta broke from her concentration on her work and looked over at Maria. She thought she was going to be asked about some routine matter. Instead, she was about to be pleasantly surprised, almost shocked. "Yes, Maria. What is it?"

"Well, would you mind if..." Maria hesitated. Perspiration broke out on her face, even though it was not that warm in the room. "I... I would like to join you and the other girls in working out. I would like to do something for myself. I see how you all seem to be enjoying yourselves, giving yourselves a sense of purpose beyond the same day-to-day routine. I mean, look at me and what do you see? A frumpy old woman. I want something different for myself. Can it be done?" Maria looked down at the floor, as if in embarrassment.

Rosetta said gently, "Maria, of course it can be done. You shouldn't feel ashamed. I would be more than happy to see you join us in our activities. Tell you what I'll do. I'll devise for you a simple beginning routine. We'll see if it suits you and if you like it. If so, then we can progress from there. What do you say?" Rosetta finished brightly.

"*Bene, bene*. I think I would like that."

"*Bene!* Then it's settled. We'll begin this week."

"Oh, Rosetta, there is something else. I haven't mentioned it, but I overheard your daughter, Ariana, speaking to one of the other girls. Something about her joining in some workouts here."

"Did she?" marveled Rosetta.

"I hope I haven't spoken out of turn. I mean, beyond my place," Maria said.

"No, no, you haven't. I'm glad you told me," Rosetta said as she privately hoped that maybe Ariana was slowly coming around. What had once seemed to have been an unbridgeable chasm was now closing if, at least, just a little. What was more, Ariana had not mentioned Angelo Tomma's name for quite some time. Perhaps Ariana had finally moved on from that loathsome character.

* * *

By the fall of 1946, the weather had begun to turn grayer, the brilliant sunshine of Rome had begun to diminish from its usual intensity. On a Saturday, Rosetta Rossi was in the gymnasium and from her office window, she looked down upon some of the women. *Her girls*, she thought, as they went through a variety of exercises. Ann Carter was seated on a bench as she worked her way through a set of 200-pound bench presses. The muscles on her arms glistened from the sweat she generated. Ann was fast developing a world-class body. She was nearly at the level of Rosetta herself, and that of Barbara Danilo.

Rosetta then looked over and took in Barbara Diala, a short but powerfully developed specimen in her own right. Barbara was performing some 40-pound arm curls from a split position on the gym floor. Diala was still in the process of psychologically recovering from her own detritus of the war. Her husband had been killed as a result of an Allied air raid on the island of Pantelleria, near Sicily. Alfonso Diala had been serving with an Italian army unit on the island when he met his end in 1943. Barbara was left to raise two teen-aged sons on her own. One of them, Alfredo, had disappeared into the hills surrounding Rome just prior to one of the German round-ups in late 1943. She never saw him again. Her other son, Damaso, age sixteen, had taken up with an underground unit. He survived the war, but now lived with a woman of questionable repute somewhere in the Piedmont region. Barbara seldom saw him now. Even the thought of speaking to one another was a rare occasion. People on the outside never saw the residues of a war. Most just assumed that people merely picked up from wherever they had been before a war. It was never that easy, or that simple.

Rosetta was very proud of what Barbara Diala had been able to accomplish. She had turned her body into a virtual block of granite. Her chest was more than 38 inches in diameter. Her thighs had muscle on top of muscle. Barbara Diala had also turned into a remarkable swimmer, now able to swim laps in the pool for more than two hours at a time. She had also begun to accompany Rosetta and Barbara Danilo when they ventured to the nearby sea to free dive.

Diala could now dive down to more than a hundred feet beneath the surface and remain under for more than four minutes. Rosetta privately worried that maybe Barbara Diala saw some need to push herself to the point of recklessness.

Rosetta now checked her chart. Barbara Dwaretz and Barbara Danilo were due in soon to begin their own workouts. She herself would go down to the floor soon for her own conditioning. Rosetta had planned to work out for several hours. Just then, she noticed Ariana walk out onto the floor. She was dressed in a skin-tight black leotard, which seemed to accentuate her own impressive frontal physique. Ariana had been working herself very hard for the past few months and her body was developing quickly. She now possessed some real definition in her upper arms and thighs, and her stomach was taking on a very flat, washboard appearance. Rosetta silently marveled at what she now saw… and slowly smiled to herself. At last, at long last, Ariana had turned her back on Angelo Tomma and had turned her own life around.

* * *

The year of 1946 turned into the year of 1947. In a way, it represented the year two in the rebirth and recovery of Italy. Things were slowly moving forward economically and perhaps, equally important, spiritually for the country. Everyone seemed to have a brighter outlook on almost everything. There was still much to do before Italy could be said to be back on its feet, but this was a good start.

By late June, the weather had become absolutely gorgeous and the sea was as glorious, as well. Rosetta, Barbara Danilo, and Barbara Diala drove out from Rome during the last weekend of the month. Their destination was the seaside resort town of Nettuno, located just to the southeast of Anzio along the Tyrrhenian Sea coast. Anzio had been the site of an epic battle between the Germans and Allied forces in 1944. The Americans and British had invaded Anzio in January with the express purpose of driving on Rome, a scant thirty miles away. It was hoped this would cut off the German forces locked in battle with the Allies at Monte Cassino. It failed to turn out that way largely because of the timidity and overcautiousness of the American general in command. From January to late May, the two sides had torn at one another in a virtual death struggle. On two occasions, the Germans nearly pushed the Allied units into the sea.

Today had dawned bright and sunny and clear. It promised to be perfect weather for the three women when they free dove. Some of the depths reached down to more than three hundred feet, if one went just past the shelf of the sea floor that skirted the coast of Nettuno.

The girls had arranged for the rental of a small boat which they would use to convey themselves to their dive site. The boat was of wood construction and was about fifteen feet in length. There was no motor, but a pair of oars were supplied for their use. One of the women would have to row out from the Nettuno pier for nearly a mile. Rosetta volunteered. The return trip would be left to the two Barbara's to sort out. Rosetta kept her black tee shirt on over her bathing suit, as she didn't want to incur a burn before she even went into the water. She settled herself onto the center bench seat and took hold of the oars. The Barbaras both helped to push the craft off from the dock.

Soon, Rosetta was able to adapt to a smooth rowing routine, her strokes being executed with a minimum of effort. The oars hardly making a ripple. Barbara Danilo was seated in the stern of the boat. She wore a trim black suit, one that she had personally designed. Considered scandalous by some, it came up well past her hips. The front dropped downward into a sharp vee.

Barbara Diala was seated in the front, sunglasses down, the Nettuno shoreline nestled in the background. This Barbara wore a white one-piece suit of a cut a little more conservative than Danilo's. This would be Diala's first time to this particular dive site.

"Easy, Rosetta, easy. You'll wear yourself out before we even begin to dive," chided Barbara Danilo, her sunglasses down, shielding her bright blue eyes.

Rosetta continued steadily, each stroke as powerful and sure as the preceding one. Maybe she was trying to impress her friend with her rowing prowess and stamina. A little over an hour later, they arrived at their spot. Barbara Danilo dropped the weighted anchor over the side. The rope length had been calibrated to about one hundred feet. It settled itself upon there sea bed eighty feet down.

Rosetta and Danilo would dive first. Barbara Diala would remain on the surface wearing a snorkel mask. It would be her job to keep an eye on the two women as they dove down. Rosetta removed her tee shirt and took hold of her black outlined goggles. She smoothly dropped herself into the calm and placid water. Barbara Danilo did the same. Rosetta took in a huge breath of air and then jack-knifed herself over. She rapidly began clawing her way downward. Attached to her wrists were two instruments; one was a waterproof dive watch, and the other on her right wrist, a depth gage. Danilo wore the same instruments.

Rosetta and Barbara continued their downward course to the bottom. The water temperature was becoming slightly cooler, but not to the point of being uncomfortable. It took them a little more than two minutes to reach bottom. They were exactly forty-five feet from the surface. Each of them moved about slowly and easily as both felt that they each were in possession of a good amount of air in their lungs. The girls were moving along what was termed the shelf. Just beyond this, the sea floor dropped off precipitously. It was said by some locals to go down to another 200 feet in some places. This had all been explained to Barbara Diala the night before.

Rosetta and Barbara spent nearly another two minutes before deciding they should surface. This would be done in stages in order to prevent becoming overcome by the bends. Once back on the surface, they took in large gulps of air. They had been under for more than six minutes. Not bad for their first dive.

"Barbara, why don't you take your dive now. I'll watch you," said Barbara Danilo. "Don't worry, you'll be alright."

"*Si*, okay," said Diala as she now placed her own goggles on her face. When she was ready, she took in as much air as he could and dove under. Danilo observed her swimming down steadily. She seemed to be doing fine.

Barbara raised her head from the water and said to Rosetta, "I'm going down again. I think I should join her. After all, this is her first dive here."

"Are you sure? I mean, we just returned to the surface," Rosetta said guardedly. She thought Danilo might have an ulterior motive of going far deeper than one should. Always having to prove herself. Always.

By this time, Danilo was already on her way down. She was moving effortlessly as she continued at a steady pace. She soon joined Diala at the bottom. Danilo indicated by sign language for Diala to surface. She herself was going to try and go down deeper, exactly as Rosetta had feared.

Diala began her ascent, but was under no distress. Danilo, meanwhile, had plunged herself downward just past the shelf, and was going to what was called the unknown. She looked at the watch on her left wrist. She had been under for almost four minutes. Barbara then looked at her depth gage. It told her she was now at more than sixty feet under. She was now pushing the envelope. But then again, it always seemed she had to. By now, Barbara Diala had surfaced and she began to gesture and tell Rosetta what was happening down below.

"It is all right, Barbara. I think I know what our friend is up to. I'm going down. I have a bad feeling about this." Rosetta placed her goggles on and went over into the water. She sucked in as much as air as she could muster and dove under. Rosetta remembered to move steadily, not to overexert herself. She desperately hoped that Barbara had not run afoul of anything and was in trouble. Rosetta soon reached the shelf and swam along its edge. There, not quite fifty feet away, she saw her friend. Danilo seemed to be in good shape. Rosetta swam over to her. Barbara suddenly noticed her friend and gave her a thumbs-up and a toothy smile.

Rosetta signaled to Barbara to go up. Enough was enough. Barbara indicated her agreement and together, the girls slowly made their way to the surface. Breaking water, Barbara said, "You worried about me, Rosetta?" She said this coquettishly, removing her goggles and batting her eyes.

"You're damn right I was. I just knew you would go to beyond the shelf! Barbara, really! Why do you always feel that you have to prove yourself? One of these days..." Rosetta's voice trailed off, but not the glare on her face. There, she had said it. Perhaps it was her building frustration, but had always truly felt this about Barbara Danilo.

"One of these days? You mean you might not be there to save me. Why don't you just come right out say what's really on your mind," Barbara responded icily.

In the middle of this spat sat Barbara Diala, who quickly attempted to mitigate the escalating tension. "Girls, girls, please. There's no need to fight. We're supposed to be out having a good time. We're supposed to be—"

"Oh, shut up, Barbara," hissed Barbara Danilo and Rosetta in near unison. Danilo's blood was up. "Just shut the fuck up!"

Barbara Diala sat back in the boat in stunned silence. She never would have imagined Barbara Danilo using language like that in speaking to her.

Rosetta looked at Diala and thought she might be about to cry. She then swung her gaze back to Danilo.

"I'm sorry, Barbara. I truly didn't mean it. I really didn't," Danilo said in a near pleading tone.

Diala turned her head back and muttered, "Go fuck yourself, Barbara."

The day was ruined. Rosetta was now really upset. She was pissed, but didn't say another word. The three women eventually calmed themselves down and stayed at the site for another hour. But things had changed. Each one was now looking at the other in a new and different light. This was especially true between Rosetta and Barbara Danilo.

Silence reigned on the journey back to the pier. When it came time to drive back to Rome, Rosetta took the keys. There would be no hair-raising travel with her behind the wheel. Hardly a word was spoken between the three. There was a distinct chill in the air, and it wasn't from the weather.

CHAPTER FOUR -
DISCOVERY

The men gathered around the threadbare table were not there in attendance of their own volition. All were there because of different, but no less compelling reasons. The unofficial chairman of this little eclectic group was Marco Dubnik, a middle-aged Slovakian hailing from somewhere in the vicinity of Bratislava. It had always seemed amusing to Dubnik, as everyone just assumed that any Slovakian must be from Bratislava. There was nothing amusing for the men gathered in this dusty, nondescript room, in this shambling, tumble-downed building situated on Via Bembo in Venice. Their location was not very far from the world-renowned and famous Rialto Bridge in the virtual heart of this picturesque city.

"Gentlemen, I've asked you here for the express purpose of informing all of you of certain developments. I do believe you will find them... rather enlightening," said Dubnik.

"You had better be right, Marco," began the foreboding-looking Cesare Puglio as he directed his gaze at Dubnik. Puglio took in the receding hairline and aquiline shaped nose of the Slovakian. He also noted the cold, grey-green eyes of the man. "I was forced to break off a rather important engagement."

"You mean you had to leave your current *paramour*, Cesare," offered the third man of the group. He was none other than Fabrizio Valpone, the reputed crime boss of the Cosa Nostra chapter of the Piedmont region. "Believe me, I do understand. But I think I would have remained with my own cuckhold."

Puglio didn't bother to reply. He wouldn't attempt a riposte to Valpone. The man could easily take it the wrong way, and that could well result in dire consequences for him.

"Gentlemen, please, if I may continue," pleaded a now urbane sounding Marco Dubnik. "I have asked for this meeting because I have recently come across some information that could prove significant for all of us. And by significant, I mean from an economic stand-point."

"You have our attention, Marco. I assure you," replied Valpone, taking the liberty of speaking for Puglio as well. It was clear to all that he was the main figure, the one that Dubnik would have to impress.

"*Bene*. My source tells me there is a gold shipment lying in the waters of the Gulf of Genoa. Specifically, it is rumored to be somewhere in the vicinity of Varazze."

"Gold? And how much is rumored to be there?" questioned a suddenly alert Valpone, his craggy face showing interest for the first time. Valpone was always intrigued when the subject of gold came up. "And you say you have a source?"

"*Si*, Don Fabrizio, I do, but I cannot reveal this person's identity at the moment. To do so could well compromise this person's very existence. However, I can assure you this source can be vouchsafed without question. Now, as to the gold. It seems there was a shipment in June of 1944 from Rome, and its likely destination was Genoa. The means of conveyance was an old tramp steamer. My source is still trying to determine the identity of this vessel. We hope to have it soon. In any event, the amount of gold this vessel was carrying is believed to be substantial. I do think it would worth our time to pursue this."

Cesare Puglio asked, "And how did this so-called tramp steamer meet its demise? I assume it was sunk, either by a submarine or a mine?". He felt himself to be safe in posing the question.

"We're not quite sure yet as to how this boat met its end. That's not particularly relevant at this point," replied Dubnik.

"What is being done to ascertain the validity of this gold, Marco?" interjected a now increasingly interested Fabrizio Valpone.

"I'm putting together a team to look into this matter."

"And you will need some funding, am I correct?" asked Valpone, his lupine eyes boring their way into Marco Dubnik's.

"*Si*. Er, there is that, Don Fabrizio." Dubnik hesitated. He felt his normally pale face reddening. He thought he was becoming short of breath and yet had to maintain his equilibrium. He could not afford to blow things now.

Fabrizio Valpone said now, "Well, Marco, what you've told us is somewhat intriguing, I must say. However, I will need to hear some things of a more concrete nature before I commit myself and my resources to this endeavor. When you've done so, contact me again.

You know the usual method. But do not use Pietro Novella." He then reached forward to refill his glass of Pinot Grigio wine. This particular bottle was from one of his vineyards, a point of special pride for the Don.

"*Grazie*, Don Fabrizio, *grazie*. I will follow-up with more detailed information for you, and for you, Cesare. It is, and will remain, my top priority." Marco Dubnik felt relieved to have gotten it all out. Hurriedly, he excused himself from Valpone and Puglio and left.

"Well, what do you think, Cesare?" asked Don Fabrizio.

"I think it may be promising," replied Puglio, now employing the honorific title to Valpone.

"All right, we'll keep in touch. If your gang should come up with anything, you will, of course, let me know."

"Of course, Don Fabrizio. You know you can rely upon me."

"Cesare, one more thing. Who do you think Dubnik is fronting for?" Puglio stood up with a dumbfounded look on his face "Come now, Cesare. The Russians? No, too direct. Perhaps the East Germans?" said Valpone. "Yes, indeed."

* * *

"How did it go?" asked the cold, leaden voice.

"I think we may have a partner," replied a guarded Marco Dubnik as he sat in his comfortable suite at the Palazzo Steen. His room provided him with a fabulous and breathtaking view of Venice. The hotel was one of the finest and prettiest of the Grand Canal palazzi. Its interior was extraordinary in its Gothic-Moorish appearance and decor. Dubnik was not ensconced there for the view he was provided, nor for the amenities of the establishment.

"You think? What was your sense? I know that your antennae are quite sensitive in such matters. Is that not true?" the voice questioned.

Dubnik was not quite sure as to the identity of the man on the other side of the long-distance line to East Berlin. All that he had been provided with were instructions and a number to call following his meeting with Cesare Puglio and Fabrizio Valpone.

"Well, Valpone appeared to be quite interested. As to Puglio, I was quickly able to establish he is to be a minor figure. The true muscle in this equation is Valpone. I think I know just how to handle him. You know, how to string him along."

"I would not try to be too clever in this case. Valpone is not a man to be trifled with."

"I realize that. But I do believe that with just a little more prompting and some well-placed bait, we can reel Valpone in," continued Dubnik. At no time during their conversation did either man refer to themselves by any given names. That was verboten.

"All right. You seem to know best. Keep me posted on any new developments. And, and I mean *any* developments. I don't care how trivial they may appear to be. Is that clear?" the cold voice questioned.

"*Yawohl*, sir," replied Dubnik, nearly bringing himself to click his heels together. He had noted that his telephone companion had almost let slip his name. Dubnik hung up the connection and sat back to contemplate his next move. It was time for him to make contact with his secret connection. He knew these men to be reliable. They had never failed him before.

* * *

"Barbara, Barbara," an exasperated Mauro Guzzo said to his bedmate.

"Well, what was I to do?" feigned a seemingly distraught Barbara Danilo. "I mean, we'd been having a lovely day and then Rosetta just started up. She actually thinks I'm jealous of her. But, in truth, I think she is jealous of me. Being objective, I have a better build than she does, despite being more than ten years older. I can lift more weights, and I'm a superior swimmer and diver."

"You don't have to sell me, Barbara," Guzzo said, laying back against his pillow. The two of them had just concluded a spirited romp of sex. Guzzo had managed to keep up his part, but just barely. For the life of him, he didn't know where this woman's sexual drive or athleticism came from. Barbara was now sitting up as well. Guzzo offered her a tumbler filled with Jack Daniels whiskey. It had recently become Barbara's drink of choice. Undoubtedly, an influence given off by the Americans. Guzzo spied her magnificent tits mounted firmly on her chest. They were, in and of themselves, things of wonder.

"*Grazie*," Barbara said as she took the glass. "And then, that little pipsqueak, Barbara Diala jumped into the—"

"Discussion?" interjected a bemused Guzzo.

"*Si, si*, the discussion, so I basically told her to fuck off. I don't think it was out of place, do you?"

"Well, I'm not sure. However, haven't you and Rosetta encouraged these other women to stand up for themselves... to not take things lying down?"

"Sure, go and take that little bitch's side," Barbara grumbled. "Still, maybe you're right. We've tried to instill some..., how would you say... omph. But what right did Diala have to say, 'Fuck you, Barbara?' I mean, really."

"I think that maybe all of you girls may have spent too much time together. It was probably just a matter of time before something like this would happen," Guzzo offered reasonably.

"Perhaps, perhaps." she conceded. She seductively fingered her glass, while at the same time eying Guzzo's member. She detected its arousal, smiling to herself. There would be more carnal relations, and they were imminent. "Oh, listen to this. While we waiting to get into our car for the trip back to Rome, the little one started up again. She practically challenged me to a fistfight right there in the lot. I looked at her and said, 'Go ahead, Barbara. Go ahead and take the first shot.' I would have kicked her puny ass to Rome and back. While all of this was transpiring, what was Rosetta's reaction? You know, I think she was secretly hoping things would escalate into a full-blown fight. Diala and me mixing it up."

"I don't believe that. That's not the Rosetta I know." He could feel himself becoming more aroused. "I think you should apologize to Barbara. Be the bigger person. I mean figuratively."

"Perhaps you're right," Barbara said as she put down her glass and turned back to Guzzo. Her left hand took hold of his manhood.

"When will you see Barbara next?" he asked a little breathlessly.

"Probably tomorrow. Rosetta will be taking some leave. She says she needs to get away. And, get this, despite all that has just gone on, she will be leaving me in charge."

"Well, that should say something. What about Bob Rossi? Will he be going along?"

"I don't think so. Rosetta indicated that he probably can't get away at this time. I think he may be sticking around to keep an eye on me." Barbara then began to increase her stroking pressure. She was handling Guzzo's cap as if it were a gearshift knob, placing it into first gear. Barbara had decided that enough small talk had gone on and now proceeded downward.

* * *

Rosetta Rossi arrived at the Hotel Brentano exhausted and when she looked at herself in the rearview mirror, she saw a picture of nearly complete dishevelment. Grime had combined itself with sweat, now caking her face. Long gone from the Brentano was the oily and unctuous Vito. In his place now stood a lovely and attractive young woman of about twenty-five years of age. Her name tag identified her as Silvia. She possessed almond-shaped, hazel colored eyes, complemented by soft auburn hair that ran straight down along her face. Rosetta thought the young woman was exquisite. She reminded her of Ariana.

"*Buona sera, signora*. Welcome to the Hotel Brentano, "said Silvia amiably.

"*Buona sera, signorina*," replied Rosetta.

"I see that you will be staying with us for one week. I hope that everything will be to your satisfaction. I see that you have been one of our frequent guests. We will try to meet your every expectation."

Rosetta thought the girl might be laying it on a bit too thickly and at this moment, she was tired and only wanted to be ensconced in her room. She informed her that she only wanted to be shown her room, which was actually on the fourth floor. European hotels didn't list the ground floor as the first. Americans often found this confusing.

As soon as the bellhop delivered Rosetta's bags to her room, she went straight to the bathroom and began to draw water from the tap. Moments later, she stripped off her clinging, sweat-stained clothes and settled herself into the warm, hot water. Rosetta proceeded to wash herself with the face cloth she had brought along with her.

After she had dried herself off, Rosetta settled into a red leather armchair and sipped a French cognac. The amber-colored liquid went down her throat soothingly. Tomorrow, she would head out past Vento Beach. Rosetta had already made arrangements to rent a small boat. A local man, Pasco Borrelli, would operate the craft. Borrelli had performed a number of services for Rosetta during some of her prior visits. Yes, tomorrow she would swim and dive solo in waters well off from Vento Beach. It would be just her and the sea. She really needed this holiday. It was early July and Rome had once again become suffocating. Not only the temperature, but also the tempestuous relationship she now found herself in with Barbara Danilo. *Yes,* she thought to herself, *we have all become too close, too clinging.* A break had been badly needed for all of them.

"Pasco, I would like for you to take the boat a little beyond the promontory over there on the right. It should be to a point a couple of miles away," Rosetta instructed Pasco Borrelli, who was seated astern of her. Rosetta had placed herself in the bow of the small boat. Sunglasses set over her eyes, she wore only her black one-piece bathing suit. In her hands she fingered her diving goggles. Rosetta had already strapped on her dive watch to her left wrist and the depth gage on her right.

A swarm of seagulls flew by overhead, impervious to the human interlopers below. They didn't appear to be in any type of formation, as would be seen with geese. The gulls resembled more of a gaggle. The sea was pleasantly calm and gentle, perfect for Rosetta's planned day. She had already checked on the projected water temperature. Again, perfect. Rosetta had also gone over some nautical charts that she had brought with her. She thought she had a good idea as to the depths she would encounter. The charts had been procured by Bob, courtesy of the US Navy.

Borrelli sat unobtrusively and calmly guided the craft. He genuinely liked Rosetta and had always enjoyed working for her. She never looked down upon him and his apparent low station in life and she had always paid well, and on time. Besides, she was a stunning woman. She possessed a superb body. She more than had *La Bella Figura*.

"All right, Pasco. I think we're at about the right spot," Rosetta said. The coastline could barely be seen in the distance.

"*Si, signora*. I will throw out the anchor," Borrelli said, and he proceeded to grab hold of the twenty-five-pound anchor attached to its rope. He hoped it would reach the bottom.

Rosetta placed herself over the side and affixed her goggles. She then proceeded to remove her suit from her body. "Pasco, I would appreciate it if you will look after this for me,' she said as she handed up her suit.

Borrelli could barely bring his eyes to the suit as he took hold of it. He spied a quick glance at Rosetta in the water, only her frizzled blonde head visible. "*Si, si*, I will."

"And, Pasco? I trust you will be discreet."

"You can count on me, *signora*," Borrelli said as he continued to look away. After all, who was he to judge. If the woman wanted to swim bare-ass naked, then so be it.

"*Bene*. I plan to stay in the water for about two hours. Is that all right?"

"*Si*," agreed Borrelli. What could he object to. He watched as Rosetta Rossi started to swim off. He could not help but notice her fulsome and powerfully developed buttocks. Rosetta was swimming smooth and even strokes of the Australian-crawl as she cut through the water. As she swam on, she would periodically breathe out of the corners of her mouth: right, left, right. She preferred to breathe primarily out of the right side.

Rosetta had swum for about several hundred yards even further away from the shore. The waves remained low and not very challenging. There was little current to contend with. Rosetta pulled up, treading water for a couple of minutes, then took in as much air as she could and jack-knifed herself over. Her muscled legs and feet slid silently into the water, leaving no wake. Rosetta swam downward with powerful strokes. The water exhilarated her, her body feeling completely relaxed.

Rosetta kept on driving herself to the sea floor. When she finally reached it, she noted she was nearly forty feet beneath the surface. She looked about along the seabed. It was predominantly sandy; some small rocks appeared here and there. The area looked nearly pristine. She moved about languidly and easily. Rosetta was aware that she would have to be deliberate in her movements this far down as the oxygen in her bloodstream would be a little thinned out. Rosetta checked her dive watch and saw that she had been under nearly three minutes, but she still felt fine, strong. She knew well she possessed a good set of lungs. She always seemed to feel as much at home in the water as she did on dry land.

After spending another minute at the bottom, Rosetta decided it was time for her to surface. After all, she had just begun her day. Breaking water, she took in air and went onto her back, floating. Rosetta then began to backstroke her way on the surface. This was perhaps her favorite stroke, as it afforded her the ability to look up into the sky and to relax, more so than the other strokes. She also really liked the butterfly. With her patented three-stroke underwater routine, it could be said that this was what set her apart from other swimmers. Not many individuals, men or women, could perform her method of being able to stay under for three full strokes before needing to surface on the fourth to take in air.

For the next hour or so, Rosetta swam a series of different strokes, then decided to dive once again for the bottom. After she surfaced, she noted a black dot in the sky. It was approaching her position from the west. The object was closing, not rapidly, but nonetheless closing on her. Rosetta turned and paused in the water, shielding her eyes form the sun's glare. By this time, the aircraft was nearly upon her. Rosetta could now tell it was a US Navy PBY patrol aircraft, painted a variety of blue hues.

"Hey, guys. Get a hold of that," cried out co-pilot Ensign Craig Jarrett. "My, my, what a beautiful sight for sore eyes. Are they deceiving me, or is that a woman swimming in the nude?"

"Yeah. Look at that. Man, oh man. Lordy," cried out crewman Mike Mannix.

"Gentlemen, I think we should go and take a closer look. This is definitely something we need to get a better look at," said pilot First Lieutenant Jeff Ward.

The PBY was nearly overhead when Rosetta looked up, smiled, and waved. Her breasts were now fully exposed to the plane's crew.

"Oh, man. What a set of hooters. I'm telling you, the guys back at the base are never going to believe this," continued a near goggle-eyed Mannix.

"Mr. Slattery, would you kindly get a fix on our position. For future reference, of course," Ward directed to the plane's navigator.

Meanwhile, Rosetta turned over and went into an overhand crawl. She noted that the plane was turning around, undoubtedly for another look at her. When the aircraft had leveled out, Rosetta dove under the water and began swimming the breast-stroke. She was about three feet under the surface. Onward she swam.

The PBY crew had noticed her dive and were following her progress. All were impressed with the mystery woman's underwater prowess. "Man can she stay under. She's like a fish. I mean, did you see those flapjacks? Wow!" Mannix continued to cry out.

"Easy, Mannix, easy. I wouldn't want to hear that you'd blown your load over this… this destination," deadpanned Ward.

Rosetta continued for what she guessed was a thousand yards and, then she had to surface. She looked up and saw that the navy plane was circling again. These guys wanted another look. All right, she decided, she would give it to them. As the PBY was almost on top of her, Rosetta looked up and cupped her breasts and bounced them up and down.

Jeff Ward thought he might well lose control of the aircraft. He actually swore that his vision became a little blurred, but he was able to hold on.

Rosetta continued looking up and saw the PBY waggle its wings. It flew on. It would not circle back this time. "I hope you enjoyed the show, boys," Rosetta said as much to herself as to the few seagulls that now filled the air.

* * *

The next day dawned cloudy, but patches of clear sky could be seen to the west. The forecast called for the skies to clear, but the clinging humidity was set to remain. Rosetta decide she would forego any diving on this day. She would instead go to Vento Beach for a day of leisure, where she would lay about and sun herself. Of course, she would periodically take to the water. It had almost become a source of lifeblood for her. She could not explain it; she just had to immerse her body in the glove of the sea.

Rosetta had dismissed Pasco Borrelli for the day, but not before she had paid him for his unused services. This was deeply appreciated by the elderly man and his estimation of her only grew more. She would need him for the following day, when she planned to swim and dive for a more extended time than she had already done. Yes, the sky was clearing rapidly, the air still warm. The sky was starting to turn to a deep rich blue. Rosetta applied gobs of Coppertone sunscreen to her body when she heard over her left shoulder.

"*Er, scusi, signora*, but would you require any assistance in applying the sunscreen to her back?"

Rosetta turned and looked to observe a handsome and well-turned out young man smiling down at her. She thought he might well be in his late twenties. The man had a close-cropped head of dark blond hair with twinkling hazel-colored eyes. A thin-lipped mouth and an aquiline shaped nose completed his face. The young man possessed a superb body, muscular upper arms and slightly developed thighs. The midsection was sculpted into a near six-pack. Clearly this specimen was not from the local area, where most of the people did not have the time, nor the place, to engage in required work-outs. Rosetta had the immediate sensation that here before her was just another hunk of Italian manhood out for a good time.

"*Si*, I would appreciate it, er…"

"Carlo. Carlo Deluca at your service. Ahh… *signora*, I did not notice your ring. My apologies," offered Deluca. He took hold of the offered sunscreen and began to apply it to Rosetta's back. She noted that Deluca had long, probing fingers. She felt as if she were undergoing a massage. It titillated her to the point that she felt herself begin to blush.

"*Grazie*, Carlo, *grazie*. That feels good. Would you like for me to return the favor?"

"*Prego*, and, yes, I would. That is if you do not mind?" said Deluca. He had been more than impressed with this forty-something's body. He had taken measure of Rosetta's deeply-knotted back. "I must say, *signora*, that you possess a superb body. How have you managed to achieve it?"

"Vitamins and clean living," deadpanned Rosetta as she began to coat Deluca's own impressive back with Coppertone. "No, seriously. I work out at a gymnasium I operate in Rome. We have a group of women who work out as well. You might say we are, or have been, trying to recover ourselves after the war."

"Well, whatever it is, it seems to have worked for you. By the way, if I may ask, what is your name? And, would you mind if I joined you for a little while?"

"My name is Rosetta. And, no, I would not mind you sharing my company for a… little while," Rosetta offered back as she took Deluca's offered hand.

"*Bene, bene*," said an enthused Carlo Deluca, dressed only in a skimpy white Euro suit. He lay down on his back.

The next couple of hours went by, with Rosetta and Carlo taking to the water. Rosetta did not engage in any strenuous swimming, as she did not want to show off. She did observe Deluca to be in pretty good shape, and who could hold his own in the water. The last time the pair emerged back onto the beach, Carlo reached for one of Rosetta's hands. She did not reject it.

"Rosetta, would you mind joining me for dinner this evening? I hope that I am not being too forward," said Deluca.

Rosetta, lying on her stomach, looked over at the young stud and said, "No, I would love to go to dinner. But *Signore* Deluca, I must forewarn you.

It can only be for dinner, nothing more," Rosetta said as she arched her right eyebrow. "

"*Si, si*, of course. My intentions are strictly honorable. Of that, I can assure you," Deluca said as he moved his hands to signify his innocence.

"Hmm, I think I've heard that before."

The pair then settled back on Rosetta's blanket, and Carlo Deluca began to formulate in his mind how he could best approach his task of trying to ferret information out of this engaging and stunning woman.

"So, you come here to Vento Beach for some relaxation? I have heard the Americans use the expression 'Charge my battery', or something to that effect. Am I correct?"

At first, Rosetta didn't reply, but carefully eyed her upcoming dinner companion. She was slowly becoming more convinced this man was not only after her body, but he was artfully and craftily probing her for information. "*Si, si*, I like to come here for purely holiday purposes whenever I feel the need to get away from Rome. Don't get me wrong, I love the city. I was born and raised there, but, well, you know."

"I understand. Tell me, when you go to the beach, you sometimes... I mean, you do not always go just to the beach, you, you..." Deluca began to stumble.

"You mean I don't go strictly to the beach. No, Carlo, I do not. For instance, yesterday, I swam and dove for more than two hours. And tomorrow, I plan to do more of the same," Rosetta replied carefully. She didn't want to provide the man with too much information. She wouldn't reveal her destination. "Also, I usually prefer to dive alone. I hope you understand. I don't not want to sound abrupt.," Rosetta reached over and patted his hand.

Later at dinner, Carlo said carefully. "But tell me, isn't that a little dangerous? You never know what you may encounter. Have you seen anything of note during your dives?"

"Of note?" asked Rosetta coyly.

"*Si*. I mean, well, you know. Maybe treasure? Antiques, artifacts, that sort of thing." Deluca probed on while he appeared to be looking away he was observing Rosetta out of the corner of his eye.

"I haven't seen anything of particular note on my dives. I'm sorry if this disappoints you," she replied as she tooled around her veal parmesan. She looked directly into Deluca's brown eyes. He shifted his own from her face to her notable cleavage. Rosetta was wearing a white, deep-necked blouse. This was topped off by a pearl amulet which hung from a twenty-carat gold chain, resting in the chasm of Rosetta's twin peaks.

"Rosetta." Deluca now reached for Rosetta's hand. "I know you have set strict boundaries concerning our evening, but is there any way you might reconsider?"

Rosetta slowly withdrew her hand from his. She would let him down easily; she would not cut him off at his knees.

"I mean, your husband would not have to know," Deluca nearly pleaded his case. How he so desperately wanted to bed this woman.

"No, Carlo, he would not have to know, but I would know. *Grazie*, Carlo, and I want to thank you for a most pleasant evening. I would now like to return my room for some badly needed rest."

* * *

"I am afraid we'll have to forego lovemaking this evening, my pet. I think I'm coming down with a cold. My throat is scratchy and dry. I feel terrible," lamented a pale-looking Barbara Danilo to her *paramour*, Mauro Guzzo.

"That's all right Barbara. I think I'll be able to get by for this evening. You do look a little sickly. Are you hungry? I could pick up a couple of panini from one of the street vendors, if you'd like."

"Perhaps later. Right now, I'm really not that hungry. Do me a favor, would you Mauro?"

"*Si*, what would you like?"

"Could you make me some tea? I think I'm going to have to put on some of that God-awful chest rub. I hate the way it feels," said Barbara as she made a distasteful looking face.

"As you wish, my dear. By the way, have you heard from Rosetta? I mean, how has she been getting on during her holiday?" Guzzo asked as he puttered about Barbara's kitchen. He was having a hard time finding the tea kettle. Her kitchen was in what could be characterized as ordered disarray.

"*Si*, I have, now that you mention it. Rosetta called me last evening from the Brentano. She seems to have settled in nicely," Barbara informed him as she reclined back upon her settee. "Mauro, are you having trouble finding my teapot? I'm not surprised. I'm afraid my housekeeping has fallen by the wayside of late. I never seem to be able to find the time for it."

"No, I just found this rather elegant looking ceramic one. Now, what were you saying? I mean what did Rosetta say?"

"Oh, you know, the usual things about nothing. Bland pleasantries, etcetera." Barbara felt her eyes becoming heavy and starting to fill with fluid. Yes, her cold was getting was worse. She might well need more than tea.

"Well, it was nice of her to call you. How did she sound? I mean, how was her tone?"

"Oh, you know, she was pleasant enough. I think she was trying to smooth things over between us. I want you to know I was touched by her. I mean by the sincerity I heard in her voice. So much so that I decided to break the ice and told her I was deeply sorry about our little spat out at Vento Beach."

"And what did she say to that?" asked a now interested Guzzo.

"She said that our little rancorous episode had bothered her, and that she knew my apology was heartfelt. It meant a lot to her."

"I'm glad to hear it. You see, sometimes one has to humble oneself, even when you think you shouldn't have to. A friendship such as the one between you two girls is not something to be trifled with."

"I suppose so," Barbara said wistfully, her nose now starting to run. "How is the tea progressing? I think I'm starting to sink into oblivion."

"Any minute now, my pet. Oh, by the way, I almost forgot to mention it," continued Guzzo as he bustled about with the tea implements. "I had an interesting conversation with Enzo Cardinale yesterday."

"Who is this Enzo fellow?"

"He used to be on staff with Corriere della Sera. We go back many years, to even before the war. He does some occasional freelance work for me now. Anyway, Cardinale mentioned to me about a rumor."

"A rumor?" said a now interested Barbara Danilo.

"*Si*, a rumor about some missing gold in or around the Vento Beach area," Guzzo rolled on.

"Gold, you say? I have never heard of a cache of gold in that area," Barbara said as she now sat up, her interest in the topic piqued.

"Well, as I said, it's just a rumor. It seems as if the Germans tried to ship a quantity of looted gold from Rome aboard some kind of old tramp steamer. Apparently, this vessel ran afoul of a British submarine and was sunk somewhere in the Genoa area. That's all Cardinale could relate." Guzzo sat down in a chair next to Barbara.

"Did he say who his source was? Can we get any more information?" asked Danilo, her mind now working in overdrive.

"No, it was just pretty general stuff." He personally didn't think there was much credence to this so-called gold mystery.

"Perhaps I should mention this to Rosetta," continued Barbara as she gently fingered an ivory amulet that rested comfortably in the reservoir of her bosom.

"Oh, I think it could wait. You don't have to tell Rosetta right away. I think it can certainly wait until she returns to Rome.

* * *

"Personally, I don't think she knows anything. That is my considered opinion," mused Carlo Deluca as he reclined back into his armchair, sipping a double espresso.

"Well, I'm not interested in your 'considered opinion,'" spat back a concerned Marco Dubnik.

The third man, Herve Villot, remained silent. Villot could best be described as a taciturn, humorless man. Dubnik thought him to be about twenty-four or twenty-five years of age. The man was reputed to have superior skin-diving skills, or so said Dubnik's German contact.

The three men were seated in a corner of the bar located on the ground floor of the Hotel Excalibur. The venue was about three blocks from Genoa's venerable waterfront. Villot thought Dubnik had a thing for old, aristocratic hotels, in which important meetings were to be held. This was the third one

Villot had had with the cold visaged Dubnik, and all had been held in the same type of setting.

"What makes you so sure she doesn't know anything?" pressed Dubnik. Villot sensed a heightened anxiety on his fellow conspirator's part. It surprised him, as he had always thought the man was devoid of a pulse rate.

"Well, I was very discreet, of course, while I was engaged with Signora Rossi. But I want to tell you. Che bella," said Carlo Deluca as he pressed two fingers to his mouth. "I mean, the frontal artillery on this woman. What cannons!"

"Never mind that bullshit, Deluca. What did you ask her?" Dubnik was in no mood for frivolities.

"I was very… very circumspect, if I might say, in that I asked her if she had observed anything while she had dived off Vento Beach. You know, in a casual way. And I watched for her reaction. And get this, Dubnik, while I was discussing this matter I took hold of her wrist. I wanted to see if I could detect an elevated pulse rate. Clever, don't you think?"

"And did you, Dottore Deluca?" asked a sneering Herve Villot, at last finding his voice.

"Quiet, Villot. And did you, Deluca? Did this Rossi woman give off any indication that she might be holding something back, that she knew more?" asked Dubnik.

"No. As I said, I don't think she has any idea about any gold. What more can I tell you?"

Dubnik sat back in his club chair pondering what he'd heard and wondering what his next move should be. "All right, Villot. Get your gear together. I want you to keep an eye on this so-called wonder woman, as Deluca has so avidly told us about. Do you understand?"

Villot asked, "You mean you want me to shadow her the next time she should dive near Vento Beach? If I think she may be onto something, what do you want me to do?" Deluca thought he might have detected a sinister sneer within the man's voice.

"If you think she may have found any gold, then, deal with her, then and there," Dubnik said as he drew his right hand under his chin and mimicked an ichh sound. "You may want to bring along an accomplice, and not Deluca, if this woman is as formidable as our friend makes her out to be."

"I can take care of the matter myself, believe me. Just leave Signora Rossi to me and my very capable hands and you will have no further trouble from her."

"You might do well to not be so over-confident, Villot," murmured Carlo Deluca as he continued to sip from his second espresso. "This woman is more than a fish in the water. I tell you, I've seen her. She's a veritable shark. I think she's as much at home in the ocean as she is on dry land."

"Don't worry, Deluca. If the situation should present itself, I will take care of her."

* * *

Thursday morning opened to low, scudding clouds, which were predicted to move off thereby revealing nearly perfect pitch blue skies. Rosetta awakened to discover that the teeming humidity of the previous days had dropped considerably. She contacted Pasco Borrelli to arrange for her transportation to her selected dive point for the day. It would be about two miles off the coast, near the coastal town of Saverna.

At 9:00 AM, Pasco Borrelli was ready and waiting to take Rosetta to her destination. He had made sure that he would have sufficient water and rations to last for the better part of the day. Who knew how long this Amazonian woman would stay in the ocean on this day? He shook his head. Just then, Rosetta appeared and greeted him cordially. She always seemed to be in a good mood. Borrelli saw that she was adorned in a loose fitting white blouse, but he was still able to pick out her impressive breasts. Rosetta settled herself in the center of the boat, just ahead of Borrelli in the stern. The old Italian turned to start the small outboard motor. After three pulls of the starter rope the engine caught, a blue flame rose from the exhaust port. Off they went, Borrelli maintaining a low, easy speed of not more than five knots.

Rosetta gave him instructions as to exactly where she wanted to go. Borrelli silently nodded his head. By 10:00 AM, they had arrived and Rosetta removed her blouse, tossing it on the seat. She dipped her hand into the water. *Not too bad*, she thought. This day she would retain her white bathing suit. The water seemed a little cooler than two days ago. Rosetta secured her goggles to her face and checked her watch and depth gage. Then, in one quick motion she leaned over and out of the boat. She then took off by diving under the water. After about a hundred yards, she surfaced and looked back at Pasco Borrelli. She smiled and waved at him. He gave a languid wave in return. Borrelli found himself thinking that, though he was old, he was still a man and he couldn't help but be intrigued by this sea creature.

Rosetta had informed Borrelli before she had left the boat that she planned to spend about three hours swimming. Now he watched Rosetta as she took in a large breath of air and turned her body into the water, disappearing from his sight. She plunged downward, utilizing the breast-stroke style. The water felt clean and refreshing to her body. Soon, Rosetta was at the bottom. The chart had indicated that the depth in this area should range from thirty to forty-five feet.

Everything looked rather commonplace as she gazed about. Rosetta did notice some debris: broken wooden boxes, cast-off earthenware, and she began to recall back to some of Carlo Deluca's questions from the night before. Could there be? Might there be?

Rosetta had been under for some four minutes when she decided to surface for air. Slowly, she glided her way to the surface.

Looking about, she saw Pasco Borrelli off in the distance. Continuing her gaze, she looked in the opposite direction and thought she might be seeing another small boat moving slowly about. Rosetta paid it no mind and began to swim off, this time effecting the butterfly stroke. She swam on for about three hundred yards and then returned in the opposite direction. Pausing for several minutes, she gathered herself and then jack-knifed over and swam downward. The depth at this point was reported to be in the thirty to forty-foot range.

While on the seabed, Rosetta began to notice a more organized nature to the debris. She saw more broken crates, and then what appeared to be the wheel used to steer a vessel. She swam over to it and examined it closely. It appeared to be made from mahogany and had once been polished to a high gloss. Now, it had been delaminated to a dull, grayish state. Some of the wood fibers were fraying. Rosetta moved on and was about to swim over to another area when she spied an object. In the paling light of the water, it still resonated a glitter.

She moved over to it. Brushing some sand away, she saw that it was a gold brick. Her eyes alighted as she cleaned off more sand. On one side was a numbered designation, and in the lower right corner a small swastika had been engraved.

Rosetta looked at her watch and saw that she had been under for three and half minutes. Not a problem for her as she looked over to her right. She swam over and found a couple of more bars. Unbeknownst to her, Rosetta now had a visitor. Herve Villot had been in hiding behind one of the few boulders present in this part of the Ligurian Sea. He was following the instructions of Marco Dubnik. That is, to observe Rosetta Rossi and, as to what she might find. Villot did not think the woman had seen him yet. He could not help but notice that she had apparently stumbled upon might well be the gold that Dubnik had mentioned during his briefing to him and Carlo Deluca. Villot would now be able to kill two birds with one stone. First, he would dispatch this impudent woman, and second, he would bring a sample of the gold to Marco Dubnik. And he would relay its location.

Rosetta continued being mesmerized by the gold brick she held in her hand. Her mind recalled Carlo Deluca's subtle probing of her diving activities. Suddenly, she looked up and saw a shadowy dark figure. Rosetta estimated the figure at less than a hundred feet away, moving toward her at a quickening pace. Could this be just a coincidental appearance by another diver? She began to have a feeling of dread. There was something dark and menacing about this figure.

Villot unsheathed his dive knife from its scabbard on his left wrist and placed it in his right hand. He began to swim more quickly toward his prey. Rosetta could now see that the man had an object in his right hand, a knife of some kind. He was moving more deliberately toward her. He was going to kill her.

Villot now saw more fully Rossi's voluptuous figure and a small smile crept across his face. He appreciated the magnificent figure he saw before him and realized with some regret it was a pity he would have to kill her.

Rosetta was now faced with a decision. Should she flee the area? No, she did not think she could reach the surface before she would be overtaken by her assailant. If she stayed to confront this man, would she have enough air to be able to disarm him and, possibly, kill him? *Well*, she thought, *I'm about to find out*. What would be the best way for her to defend herself? Rosetta had hardly ever been in any fights on dry land. Perhaps once or twice when she had been a schoolchild, but certainly not in a knife fight in the ocean.

Villot approached until he was about ten feet away from Rosetta when he paused, as if he was now unsure how best to proceed. He hesitated, as he had fully expected this woman to flee in panic when she finally noticed and discerned what his intent was. Rossi was now virtually face to face and then incredibly, she moved in to engage Herve Villot.

Rosetta had decided that her best course of action would be to advance on her adversary. This man would never expect this. Just before it seemed Rosetta would make contact with Villot, she scrunched her body up and delivered a kick from her right foot. The blow glanced off Villot's left shoulder, but connected with the left side of his head. Stunned, Villot dropped his knife and before he knew it, the woman had her left arm around his throat. The woman was unbelievably strong. With her right hand, Rosetta tried mightily to rip off Villot's dive mask. After nearly a half minute of struggle, she succeeded. Next, she tried to remove his mouthpiece.

Herve Villot was now nearly blind. Who was this woman? She was going to end his life. His only thought was to get away. This did not seem likely as Rosetta had tightened her vise-like grip around his head. Both were now on the sea floor. Rosetta was running out of air. She thus made the decision to release her attacker and make her own escape.

Villot, upon being released, was able to swim away as fast and as far as he could. Not once did he look back. He knew he would have to conjure up a good and convincing story for Marco Dubnik, who would clearly not be pleased when he heard that the woman had gotten away. At least, he was pretty sure she had. Then again, he would tell him the news about the location of the gold. That should please Dubnik, or he hoped it would.

Meanwhile, Rosetta had begun her ascent to the surface, desperately hoping she would later be able to ascertain the location to Pasco Borrelli. She also hoped that Pasco himself had not run afoul of any misfortune. Finally, after what had seemed like eons, Rosetta broke the surface and took in as much air as she possibly could. She tread water, still stunned at what had just taken place not that far below. She felt a sting on her left shoulder and when she turned to look, she noticed blood seeping from a wound. Her attacker must have nicked her during their grapple. Rosetta slowly regained her bearings and began to look around her for some sign of Borrelli— anything. Taking in the angle of the sun, she set off toward the east. This seemed to be the right direction. Rosetta swam slowly in the breaststroke fashion. After what she guessed was about one-half mile, she thought she saw a small boat. Her exhausted mind fervently hoped it was the one. She approached the boat and saw a figure crouched in the rear seat, seemingly asleep. "Pasco, are you asleep?" Rosetta shouted as loud as she could.

Borrelli jerked himself upright and looked in the direction of the woman's voice. He knew it had to be Rosetta's but he was surprised, as he had expected her to have remained longer in the water. As she swam closer to the boat, he noticed a trickle of blood seeping from her shoulder.

"*Signora*, are you all right? What has happened?" asked a now frightened Borrelli.

"*Si, si*. I think I must have accidentally cut myself. Please, help me into the boat." Rosetta wouldn't reveal to the old man what had transpired in the depths. Rosetta reached up and Borrelli took hold of her and helped heave her in. Rosetta reached for a towel and held it to her shoulder, stanching the blood flow. She would live. "Pasco, you must get me to shore quickly. *Subito*! *Subito*, Pasco! It's very urgent."

"*Si, signora*, I understand." Borrelli started the outboard motor and quickly sped away.

Rosetta huddled in her seat, clutching at her shoulder. She lifted the towel and noticed that the cut kept bleeding. She would probably require stitches. And that would probably involve the police.

CHAPTER FIVE-
THE FORTUNE

*ignora*, you expect me to believe that you were attacked by an underwater frogman?" asked an incredulous Giuseppe Carbonara as he reclined back into his

"That is exactly what I expect you to believe," exclaimed an excited Rosetta Rossi. She was seated across from the young Carabinieri lieutenant, trying as best she could to explain her recent harrowing experience off Vento Beach.

"Let me get this straight. You say you were swimming off the coast or, you were diving, is that correct?" Carbonara asked, slowly becoming intrigued by the story unfolding from this attractive and beguiling woman. He noted her frizzled, blonde hair coupled with her determined eyes and mouth. He could also see her well-developed upper arms.

"That is correct, *Tenente*. I've frequently swum and dived in these waters. This morning, while I was minding my own business, I was suddenly attacked by this knife-wielding mad man. Let me show you his handiwork." Rosetta slipped up the sleeve of her upper right arm. A gauze pad was taped to her shoulder, blood seeping through it. Rosetta slowly removed the gauze, revealing a smooth knife cut about two to three inches long. "Do you think this supports my claim, *Tenente* Carbonara?"

The young policeman stood up from his chair. "Hmmm, but how do I know you did not get this cut from perhaps having cut yourself during your dive?"

"Do you honestly believe I would fabricate a story, a fantastic story, and then come here to waste your time?" asked an increasingly perturbed Rosetta Rossi.

"I think you may require some medical attention. Do you wish to see a doctor before continuing with your deposition?"

"No, I don't. I think I can hold out and tell my complete story." Rosetta felt herself beginning to calm down. She also thought Carbonara was starting to believe her story.

"*Bene*, I will call in the stenographer to take down your testimony," said Carbonara. He reached down and touched his intercom button. "Maria, would you be so kind and come in to take Signora Rossi's deposition?"

A minute later, a tall, thin, and thoroughly attractive young woman stepped into Carbonara's spartan office. Rosetta thought she must be all of twenty years of age. She somewhat resembled her own daughter, Ariana, from her hairstyle to her nearly angelic face. Rosetta could also clearly see that the young woman possessed a well-endowed physique.

Giuseppe Carbonara took Rosetta through the events of the morning, beginning with her entry into the water. She did not bother to describe what type of suit she had been wearing, and Carbonara did not seem interested.

"Well, *signora*, can you describe your assailant? I mean, beside the fact that he was wearing a black skin-diver suit."

"*Si*, his hair was dark in color and probably on the curly side. He had gray-green eyes. His build was sort of athletic."

"How were you able to tell about his hair?" questioned Carbonara, his eyes piercing into Rosetta's.

"Well, as we were grappling together I was able to tear off his mask, and I could see some of his hair."

"I see. Did he have any distinguishing features or marks that you can recall?" continued the young lieutenant. He was fully engaged in his questioning of the woman before him. His earlier self-doubt was slowly ebbing away.

"Let me see," pondered Rosetta. "Now that you mention it, he did have a mark, a scar, on the left side of his face. It was rather jagged in appearance. But that's all I can remember. Do you think it will help?" Rosetta asked.

"Perhaps, perhaps, *signora*," Carbonara said as he again sat back and steepled his fingers. "I will have Maria type up the report. You can then review it, and if it's correct to your recollection of the events, you can sign it. I think that in the meantime you should have your wound looked at. I'll see to it that you're escorted to the nearby medical facility. After this, if you would like, I can have you escorted to where you're staying."

"*Grazie, Tenente*. That sounds good. And thank you for being so understanding and kind." Rosetta's eyes met the lieutenant's stare but now she added an appreciative and heartfelt smile.

* * *

The three men were huddled together in the room Marco Dubnik had reserved at the same hotel where they had previously met. Only this time, they would not be enjoying a casual espresso in the hotel bar. This time, Marco Dubnik was spitting fire. "What do you mean she got away? Oh sure, you were so confident, so cocky, Villot! And what happened? Tell me." Dubnik felt like hurling his mineral water into the Frenchman's face.

"Maybe the old girl was just too much for our commando extraordinaire. I warned you not to take this woman lightly. And now we see the result of your foolhardiness and ineptitude," needled a chuckling Carlo Deluca.

"All right, Deluca, enough with the sarcasm. The question now for all of us is how do we proceed?"

"Well, Marco, I was able to see that the Rossi woman apparently uncovered some gold bars," stammered a humiliated and mentally beaten down Herve Villot. He was trying his best to recover the smallest shred of his dignity. Villot looked out the window of the room to a sight of doom. Dark, overhanging clouds now gripped Genoa. It seemed as if at any minute the heavens would thunder down.

"Do not try and take credit for a disaster, Villot," said a now calmed down Dubnik. "Yes, it is true, we apparently now have a confirmation, if you will, of our goal. It is likely this may very well be connected to the Moschilo cargo. Where is this Rossi woman now?"

"I believe she has skedaddled back to Rome. It seems she was injured while you were wrestling with her, Villot," said a bemused Carlo Deluca.

"Do we know if she made a police report concerning the incident with our friend?" Dubnik asked.

"Yes, a police report was generated by the local Carabinieri commander. I have a source with the police," responded Deluca with a note of pride.

"Villot, how good a look did this Rossi woman get of your face?"

Herve Villot sat in his chair, carefully formulating his response. He could not reveal that the woman had been able to pry off the dive mask from his head. Dubnik might well assault him right there and then. He could well-imagine words of condemnation and derision: *Villot you stupid fool! You let this unarmed woman disarm you of your own weapon and then tear off your mask? How could you? It would have been better off if she had terminated your life, as well!* Instead, Villot again tried to claim credit for confirming the gold.

Carlo Deluca broke the silence that had descended upon the eclectic group. "Marco, if I may suggest something. Perhaps, I can find out when Rosetta Rossi will return, and then engage her again. You know, in an innocent, by chance meeting."

"Yes, perhaps, you could do that. For the moment though, I'll have to come up with something more substantive for my... for *our* partners. That is, beside the gold. In any event, Villot, I want you to disappear for a while. I want you to lay low, to be practically non-existent. Do you understand?" pressed a dark scowling Dubnik.

Herve Villot did not immediately respond, but merely nodded his head as he looked down at the thickly carpeted rug beneath his feet. At that moment, he wished he could have dug a hole through it.

* * *

The two men were seated at one of the outdoor tables of Trattoria Morgana on Via 146 Mercenate, enjoying the sights of a number of pretty and attractive young women as they strolled by. Mauro Guzzo thought a couple of them were going to approach him and his companion, Stefano Lucca. They did not. Guzzo had always enjoyed the atmosphere of Morgana, and its food. The veal piccata was amazing and which he was now indulging, along with a bottle of Ruffo Chianti. This quintessential Roman restaurant had opened its doors in 1935, and was an instant success with the city's *cognoscenti*. It had also acquired and impeccable reputation for its outstanding service.

It was a pleasant, rather dry day, unusual for Rome during the month of July. A few low-hanging clouds lingered in the skies above the men. "Well, Guzzo, I think it was a wonderful idea to meet here. You know, I do not believe I have ever dined at Morgana before today," gushed an effusive Stefano Lucca as he continued to make short work of his sole *francaise*. He too, was indulging in the Chianti wine. Guzzo thought this an odd choice of Lucca. He should have gone with a white vintage, but whatever. It had been Lucca's choice.

"You don't know what you've been missing. I've enjoyed dining here ever since it opened in 35'," replied Mauro Guzzo. He broke off a piece of fresh Italian bread. Its aroma wafting up to and into his nostrils.

"I can see why, Guzzo. Would you mind if I called you Mauro? You can call me Stefano."

"I don't see why not," replied Guzzo affably.

The two men continued with their mid-day meal and just after their table had been cleared in preparation for dessert and coffee, Stefano Lucca leaned forward. "I have learned of some interesting developments, Guz... er, Mauro."

"Really?" asked Mauro Guzzo as he sat back in his chair.

"*Si*, and they have to do with our two friends."

"Rosetta and Barbara, correct?" asked Guzzo. He reached into his inside jacket pocket and removed a pack of Marlboro's. He tapped the pack to expose a couple of cigarettes and selected one, bringing it up to his lips.

Stefano Lucca placed his Ronson lighter up toward Guzzo and lit it for him. "*Grazie,*" said Guzzo.

"*Prego,*" responded Lucca who returned the lighter to his pocket. "As I was saying, I have come across some new things. I think the girls would be well-advised to be cautious on two things. The first is their little athletic club. The Church, and by that, I mean in the person of Cardinale Maggione, is dead-set against it. The whole idea of women grunting and straining themselves with great weights and developing their bodies is preposterous and inconceivable to them. They see it as dangerous. It's no place for women of the standing of Rosetta Rossi and Barbara Danilo," Lucca stated in a direct and serious manner.

"And the second point?"

"Ah, yes, the second point. Signora Rossi's apparent discovery of some gold near the Vento Beach area is very intriguing," Lucca said. The waiter was serving them Tiramisu and double expresso coffees in elegant demitasse cups. The crest on them reminded Guzzo of the House of Savoy, the former royal family of Italy.

"Intriguing? In what way?" asked Guzzo cautiously. He feared what he thought he was about to hear from the lips of Stefano Lucca.

"All I can say is that the word is going around that this so-called 'gold cache' was part of a shipment sent by the Germans from Rome to some point past Genoa. It was shipped on an old tramp steamer that had been commandeered by the Germans. This was some time in 44'. I think it must have been around the time Rome was falling to the allies." He paused and Guzzo thought Lucca did this for a more dramatic effect.

"Go on."

"*Si.* Something happened to this vessel. The…" Lucca pulled out a small notebook and flipped it open. "Ah, yes. This vessel, the Moschilo, went down. It has been surmised that it either hit a mine or was torpedoed by a British submarine."

"Why British?" asked a now more than curious Mauro Guzzo.

"Because at the time in question, the British and their submarines were quite active in the Med. The Americans, not so much. In any event, I think

Signora Rossi and Danilo would, or should, take caution. Maybe they should not pursue this gold matter any further."

"I may as well try and spit into the wind, Lucca. I think you and I both know these two women will not shy away from what you have revealed. They, especially Barbara, will not heed your advice," mused Mauro Guzzo. He could well imagine Barbara's reaction when he told her of his conversation with Lucca. "Back off he said. I say fuck off. There is no way either Rosetta or myself will be intimidated."

"Well, it is just a word of advice… and caution."

* * *

Pasco Gonevento stood nervously outside the door to the office of Cardinale Ernesto Maggione. He knocked lightly and then he crept inside. Maggione was seated behind his massive, oversized oaken desk, busily working his way through a blizzard of correspondence. He did not look up as Gonevento nervously approached.

"Ah, *scusi, Cardinale*, but I was wondering if you would have a minute of your time to spare?" asked a near shaking Gonevento.

Maggione still did not look up, but merely said, "*Si*, what is it, Gonevento?" The abject coldness and downright rudeness caused the quaking novitiate to shake even more uncontrollably. "Well, you see Cardinale the matter is rather important."

Still, Maggione did not look up from his desk. "Well, what is it? Can't you see that I am a busy man? I do not have all day," continued the dispassionate Maggione. Only now he looked up at Pasco Gonevento.

"Well, you see, my contact has informed me of a new development. The woman…Well?"

"Out with it, man. Why are you prevaricating? You know, I at times wonder if you are a man who is up to the task at hand."

"As I was saying, your eminence, this woman, this Rossi woman, seems to have possibly stumbled across something quite significant," Gonevento stammered on. He was now openly perspiring, beads of sweat ran down his pale and gaunt face.

"Yes? Significant, you say? Well, what is it? Gonevento, for the love of God, I don't have all day," shouted an increasingly frustrated Ernesto Maggione who had now returned his attention to his paperwork.

"*Si, Cardinale.* You see… she has apparently uncovered some gold bullion and—"

"Gold? Gold, did you say?" Maggione had cut off Pasco Gonevento. "How do you know, or more appropriately, how does your source know" asked a now interested Maggione as he directed a stern gaze at Pasco Gonevento.

"Well, it seems as if the Rossi woman was swimming in the waters off Verrazze, and discovered this gold."

"Is there anything else?" Maggione questioned.

"No, that is all, I'm afraid."

"Well, I must say that is interesting. Anything else that you can relate?"

"All I have been able to learn is it seems as if a gold shipment was lost off the coast during the war. The Germans were shipping it from Rome to some point in the vicinity of Genoa. I believe this occurred some time in 1944, that is when the Germans were abandoning Rome to the Allies," Gonevento rallied. He was beginning to calm down. He could feel his blood pressure returning to some degree of normalcy. Maybe he could get out of Maggione's office without being completely flayed of his skin.

"All right, Gonevento. It appears as if we may have something to go on. Follow up on this. I will need something more substantive. Now, is there anything else?"

Well, Excellency, there is a matter concerning financing. That is, my source has indicated that he is in need of some additional…"

"Yes? Some additional money?" Maggione said.

"*Si, si, Cardinale,* some additional money. You see, my contact has incurred some unanticipated costs and—"

"Yes, I see. I sense a shakedown. All right, what additional money do these people want?" leered the venomous voice of Maggione.

"Well, well…" stammered Gornevento.

"Gonevento, prevaricating again, are you? Really, just tell me what the figure is. I call this extortion by these men."

"The sum is five thousand lire, *Cardinale*," said Pasco Gonevento, who could hardly get the words out of his quivering mouth. The perspiration was returning. He had to get out from Maggione at that very moment.

"For the love of God. Five thousand lire, you say?" asked an incredulous Maggione.

Gonevento would have sworn that he saw steam coming off the skull of his superior. "*Si, Excellency*. What do you want me to tell him?"

"You can tell them to go to hell for all that I care," shouted a thoroughly enraged Ernesto Maggione. "No, no. All right. This information about a gold cache is good, but I will not allow your so-called *source* to hold me for ransom." Maggione began to calm himself down. Who did they think they were and, who did they think they were dealing with?

"Then, you agree? That is, you agree to their request for the added money?"

Maggione sat quietly for the moment, contemplating his next course of action. "*Si*, I will consent to this request, but only this time. Go and see Father Correnti. Tell him that I have authorized for the 5,000 lire to be drawn from the appropriate Vatican account. I want this to be done as quietly and as surreptitiously as possible. Do you understand, Gonevento?"

"I do, *Cardinale*. I will see to it at once," said a now breathing easier Pasco Gonevento.

"Then, go to it. Now, is there anything else? And I pray to God that there isn't."

"No, I believe that covers everything, Excellency." Gonevento continued to stand like an automaton in front of the domineering Maggione.

"Then, go and get this done." He paused. "There is one thing, Gonevento."

"*Si, Cardinale?*"

"I want… no, I demand that henceforth information he provides has some real teeth to it."

"Yes, I will be sure to let him know this," said Pasco, who privately worried how he would ever be able to do this with a menacing character like Marco Dubnik. Quickly taking his leave of the glowering cardinal, Pasco Gonevento departed.

Cardinal Ernesto Maggione continued to sit in silent and agitated contemplation as to what had just transpired in his office. He was still in the process of calming himself down. *This is having all of the earmarks of an East German operation behind it. Well, we, or I will just have to see how things play out*, he thought.

* * *

She figured she had about two more hours in which to prepare herself for her evening out with Rosetta Rossi. Barbara Danilo was just finishing an exhausting day of reviewing sales accounts of some of the local Maserati dealerships in the greater Rome area. Business was slowly picking up, ground was being gained, or regained, which would be a better way of putting it. Ever so slowly, Italy was making a comeback and with that, the fortunes of the Maserati company were also beginning to flourish. The war had devastated just about everything having to do with Italian commerce. Along with that, the venerable Italian auto builder had endured great economic discomfort. But that was slowly receding. *Thank God*! thought Barbara. Italians were just starting to purchase some of the finest automobiles produced by any manufacturer. And, a number of American servicemen and government officials were also buying Maseratis.

Barbara and Rosetta were set to dine at one of the newer culinary establishments in the city. Pastiche was an avant-garde sort of place, at least in terms of its atmosphere and some of its dinner courses. It was an open and airy venue with a modern, clean look. Formica covered most of the surface areas, and with its gleaming stainless-steel appliances and fixtures, it gave off the look of a new day, a new Italy. Barbara thought she would indulge herself in a light repast for her meal. It was a Friday and tomorrow she would work out for several hours in the gym hefting weights on a variety of the apparatuses. In the afternoon, she would go to the pool for a couple of hours of grueling laps. Barbara was fanatical about maintaining her physical prowess. She felt as if she were at the peak of her physical powers, but still she felt as if she could push herself and her body even further.

Barbara poured herself a glass of Galliano as she drew hot, steaming water into the bath. She stripped off her clothing, which had taken on a clammy feeling even though the day had been rather pleasant. The notorious Roman summer heat and humidity had finally taken a turn for the better. As she stood naked in front of the floor-length mirror, she glanced at her body. Her breasts were larger than ever and firm. They really projected themselves off her chest. Her stomach was not only flat, it was packed with well-fortified muscle. Her upper arms were in the form of pile-driving pistons. And her legs: long, lean, and bulging.

After a sufficient amount of water had filled the tub, Barbara stepped in and sat down, luxuriating in its welcoming warmth. As she did, her mind drifted back to just a short time ago, to a time during the war when Italy was in the throes of the mighty cataclysm between the Allied forces and the Germans. She had always regretted not having taken a greater and more direct role in the work of the legendary Escape Network, set up and run by the Irish monsignor, Hugh O'Flaherty. Rosetta Rossi had harbored numerous British and American prisoners of war who had been in hiding from the Nazis and specifically from the SS and Gestapo. In addition to having placed herself and her children at great risk, Rosetta Rossi had run numerous errands for the group. Several times she had nearly been apprehended by the Gestapo. Rosetta had carried secret and sensitive information and oftentimes, large amounts of cash. If she had been caught, it would likely have meant incarceration, or even worse, perhaps torture and death. Rosetta Rossi had been one of the true heroines of the resistance movement. It had been her way of devoting herself to something, some cause, to take her mind off her memory of her husband having been killed in action in North Africa in 1942.

For Barbara, having already lost her own husband to rectal cancer before the war, those years of conflict could have been characterized as years of drifting. True, even though she had contributed vast sums of money to the resistance cause, she had done little beyond that. Of course, there had been her mission in early 1944. It had been the result of a request from Rosetta in which Barbara had been tasked to try and find out information as to the whereabouts of a priest who had been apprehended by the Nazis. The priest,

Father Gugliemo, had been discovered to have had compromising information and a large sum of money on his person. Rosetta's people had been in fear that the man was being tortured, but did not know where he was being held. Barbara was to find out where the Nazis were holding him. She had then contacted an Italian lawyer she had long known. The man worked closely with the Fascist Grand Council in Rome. Rosetta had not come out directly, but Barbara had intuitively understood she would be required to sleep with this man if she hoped to be successful.

Following a delightful meal prepared by Alberto Coppolino, Barbara Danilo took the lawyer, more than ten years her junior, to school. That is to say, she humped the ever-living daylights out of the man. She used nearly every conceivable weapon from her extensive carnal inventory. Barbara had mounted Coppolino, performed fellatio, taken the missionary position, and then to conclude her sexual escapade, positioned herself to receive her lover for a back-door entry.

As Barbara warmed herself in her tub, she began to unconsciously finger herself. She distinctly remembered how Coppolino's well-developed body and more specifically, his elongated penis had penetrated her vault. How she had fiercely gripped his plunging body with her own magnificent legs. She had marveled at the man's physical stamina and endurance as he ravaged her body.

Coppolino had promised Barbara he would try and find out the location of the priest, but he did not promise her anything definite. A few days later, Coppolino quietly informed Barbara that the man was being held at the city's notorious Regina Coeli prison. And there had been more. Father Gugliemo was scheduled for execution in two days hence. Barbara duly passed this on to Rosetta, who, in turn, conveyed it to Monsignor O'Flaherty. The Irish priest, disguised as an SS officer, infiltrated his way into Regina Coeli the night before Coppolino's execution and heard the battered man's last confession.

* * *

"Rosetta, you look absolutely ravishing!" gushed Barbara Danilo in an exaggerated, semi-falsetto voice.

"Buona sera, Barbara. But, please be careful how you address me. You know, some people may get the wrong idea about us," Rosetta replied modestly. She was dressed rather casually in a khaki colored skirt that was cut just below her knees and a white, frilly, deep open-necked blouse. An ivory amulet at the end of a twenty-carat gold chain hung down.

"Oh, who cares what some other people might think. Let them entertain their own perverted thoughts. I personally, do not give a damn," replied a defiant Danilo. Barbara had chosen to wear an ensemble that consisted of a deep V-necked black blouse, matched to a flowered purple skirt. Her legs were sheathed in a fine nylon mesh, as were Rosetta's. Rosetta noted that Barbara had opened a good amount of her chest for public consumption. It seemed as if the two women were in an open competition as to whom could out duel whom.

The sky was still light, darkness would not descend until a couple of hours later. High, cumulonimbus clouds floated by, almost dancing along in their flight to some unknown destination. A waiter soon appeared at their table to take their drink order. Both girls would share a carafe of pinot grigio, accompanied by bottled carbonated mineral water. The city may have been eternal, but its water supply was still abysmal. No sane person would dare consume it. It was bad enough for bathing in, as it had a heavy deportment to it.

"I'm so glad you suggested that we dine, and here at Pastiche. It is so eclectic, so divine. Don't you think?" enthused Barbara who slinked back and stretched out her legs. Passers-by walked within feet of their table. Neither woman paid them mind.

"Well, I was just thinking it might be a good idea. After all, we do have to unwind at some point," evinced Rosetta.

"*Si*, I agree. I'm going to the gym tomorrow for a heavy workout, then to the pool for some laps."

"Good for you. I'll be at the gym working out as well," replied Rosetta. "I have to keep my strength up. By the way, have you seen

Maria Franchi of late? She is really getting into the swing of things. I am very impressed."

"Yes, I have. But now, to other… things, such as your episode out past Vento Beach. I was completely thunderstruck the other day when you first told me. I have to say, 'good for you', Rosetta. I mean, being able to disarm this man, and with a knife. To send him on his way, and on one breath of air," Barbara said with admiration as she looked directly into Rosetta's eyes.

"You know, you should have seen the look on his face, at least what I could see of his leering eyes. Maybe he was distracted by what I was wearing, I don't know. In any event, I had to take advantage of what little I had." Rosetta continued to sip her wine while Barbara munched on one of the breadsticks the waiter had brought to their table.

"Well, I must say, it was impressive. Personally, I would have tried to break his neck."

"I did, at least until I began to run out of air. Phew." Rosetta blew out a burst of air from her soft-pink colored lips.

"And to discover gold. By the way, I mentioned this to Mauro and he said he has heard that it may be connected to a Nazi shipment that was en-route from Rome to some point past Genoa. It seems as if the Germans had used an old tramp steamer and tried to spirit the gold on the sneak. For some reason, the boat went down," breezed on Barbara. She thought she noticed a gentleman staring rather intently at the two of them, but had been concentrating on her. He had to be. Barbara then returned her attention to Rosetta.

"Does he know how this vessel met its end?" "

"Speculation has it that it was either because of a mine or a submarine may have torpedoed it."

"Mmm," mused Rosetta. "I think I'm going to do a little research on the matter. This has started to intrigue me."

"Indeed, I would think it would. Rosetta? See that man over there, the one by the railing? I think he may have set his sights on us, or at least, one of us," said Barbara as she arched her right eyebrow.

"And who should I think he is concentrating on? I don't have a clue," feigned Rosetta in mock indignation.

"Want to have some fun?" Barbara asked as she leaned closer to the table. Her blue eyes flashed.

"Not for me, Barbara. Now, as to this gold."

"Well, I would not return to Vento Beach alone," Barbara replied. Her attention again returning to the mystery man by the railing.

"I most certainly will not. If and when I do return, you shall accompany me."

"*Grazie*, Rosetta," Barbara said as she now leaned toward Rosetta. "By the way, have you mentioned any of this to Bob?"

"No! Are you crazy? He would have me committed. At the least, he would forbid me to return there. It's been bad enough convincing him that swimming in the nude is a perfectly acceptable and permissible activity. I was able to steer him away from his puritanical American thoughts concerning modesty." Rosetta sipped her drink. "Not to change the subject, but how are you and Mauro getting along?"

"You know, it is funny you ask. I can almost say he may be turning me into an honest woman." Barbara laughed lightly, now turning her interest to the label on the wine bottle.

"Is that a bad thing?"

"No, I suppose not. But as I said, he has *nearly* turned me, not completely, mind you. I do like him a lot, and his body and lovemaking skills are something to behold. Why, just the other night, he was humping me from the back door and—"

Rosetta held up her right hand as if she were stopping a speeding automobile on the autostrada. "Please, Barbara, you don't have to go into any detail concerning some of your sexual techniques or…your exploits. After all, I could relate to you some of my own stories on Bob and me humping away."

"Oh, no, Rosetta. You can feel free to expound on this matter with me any time. Besides, I might be able to pick up a thing or two."

Rosetta shook her head. "No, that could never happen. I think you're probably picturing some techniques that haven't even been invented yet." Rosetta sat back and smiled wickedly at her friend. Secretly, she did wonder if Mauro Guzzo, or any man, could ever tame this wild and unbridled woman. At that moment, the waiter dutifully arrived back at their table and took their orders: veal piccata for Barbara, sole lambrusco for Rosetta.

"Barbara, I mean it. I'm going to really look into this gold, this cache. I have to find out more about it," Rosetta said. Barbara noticed a fervor in the timbre of her voice.

"And I'll try to pump more information out of Mauro when I hump him. I also think I'll contact my old private eye friend, Stefano Lucca. It couldn't hurt."

As the women dined, the sun slowly began to set in the Roman sky. Nearby, the man who had been staring so intently at Barbara Danilo quietly paid his waiter and got up and left the restaurant. Gianni Ravelli had work to do, and certain interested individuals to contact.

* * *

"Mauro? Mauro Guzzo?" asked a tentative Bob Rossi.

"*Si*, at your service, *signore*. And to whom do I have the pleasure of speaking with?" asked back an overwhelmed Mauro Guzzo.

"I do not believe you know me. My name is Bob Rossi. Rosetta Rossi is my wife."

"Oh, yes, Barbara has spoken of you. It's a pleasure, *signore*. How can I be of assistance?" Guzzo continued looking down at some of his notes concerning a story he was working on. It was about yet another scandal connected to the current Italian government. It was a similar and pervading theme: local building contractors having to pay out extortions to unsavory characters in order to earn the right to conduct business.

"Well, it is about… how can I say it?" Bob Rossi was stammering, unsure of himself as to whether he should even bother a man like Mauro Guzzo. It was not at all in character nor to what he had once been just a short time ago as an officer in the U.S. Army. Rossi, now, wouldn't have been at all surprised if Guzzo just hung up the phone on him.

At his end, Guzzo was becoming increasingly impatient at his caller. But the man was the husband of Rosetta, someone he deeply respected and admired. "As I said, Bob, what can I do for you?"

"I was wondering if we could meet. You know, for a friendly drink. There is something I would like to discuss with you that involves my wife and Barbara," continued Rossi, who felt himself regaining some of his composure. The butterflies in his stomach were beginning to quieten down.

"Of course, Bob. I would very much like to meet with you and discuss your concern. As I said, Barbara has spoken of you. She likes and admires you. So, when would you like to get together?"

"I was hoping it could be as soon as possible. I do realize you are a busy man, but could it be tomorrow, say around noon?"

Guzzo made a show of pretending to look through a calendar as he replied, "Let me see. Tomorrow? Hmm."

"It doesn't have to be tomorrow," hastened an anxious Bob Rossi. He was starting to become a little unglued once again.

"No, I'm afraid tomorrow wouldn't be suitable. I'm working on a deadline article now. However, I think I can schedule something for Thursday. Yes… say around noon, you said?"

"That would be fine, and I really appreciate you taking the time," Rossi said.

"*Bene*. And now, where would you like for us to meet?" asked Mauro Guzzo, who for the first time began to feel somewhat amiable.

"Well, I was thinking of Harry's American. Would that be good for you?"

"*Si*, that sounds splendid. All right, I will see you on Thursday at 12:00 noon at Harry's. Let me make a note of it or else I'll most certainly lose track and then you would be left hanging high and dry. Isn't that how you Americans say it?"

"More or less. Okay, I really appreciate it, and the drinks will be on me. Oh, and *ciao*, Mauro."

"*Ciao*, Bob," replied Guzzo. *More than the drinks will be on you, my friend*, Guzzo thought. What had struck him the most about his conversation with the man had been the tentativeness in his voice. It had been as if Rossi was very unsure of himself. Not at all what Guzzo would have expected from a former American army officer. And one who was now involved in tracking down fugitive Fascists and Nazis. On top of that, this had been a man who had once had to adapt to a furtive type of existence for several months, as he had been hidden from the Germans in Rome during the war.

* * *

Herve Villot was tinkering with some of his dive equipment when his phone jangled in its cradle. Villot stopped what he had been doing and went over to answer it. "Hello?"

"Villot, I think we need to talk," came the cold, emotionless words of Marco Dubnik.

"Eh, Marco. What, no hello? Where are your manners?" joked a suddenly jovial Herve Villot.

"Don't be a smart ass with me, wise guy. We have to talk, and you know what it's about. What have you been doing? My patience is wearing thin," continued a thoroughly displeased Marco Dubnik.

"Well, you did tell me I should lie low for a while, didn't you? Besides, the Rossi woman has not returned and—"

"I'm not interested in the woman at this time, only in so much as it relates to our main goal. I am only interested in the…" Dubnik hesitated.

"Gold?" offered Villot.

"I have repeatedly told you, my misguided and sometimes foolish friend, not to speak over the phone in such direct terms. But, yes, you are correct. By the way, what have you been doing? My partners have been growing a little displeased at our, or your, lack of finding more of the, let us say, treasure."

"I have told you that I have been down to the area two or three times but I've not found any further evidence as to more… well, you know, more of what I saw the woman uncover." Herve Villot was beginning to enjoy his little *tête-à-tête* with Dubnik. The man who thought himself to be so superior, so smug. A big secret agent during the war. Big deal.

"Well? I expect you to try again, but discreetly, and soon. If you feel you can't do the job then I will find someone else. Do I make myself clear?" Dubnik growled as he played with a Walther PPK sidearm. The blue-gray steel of its stock resting comfortably in the palm of his left hand. He well

106

might have to use it and soon on Herve Villot. The Frenchman was not one to be trusted. At least, not trusted to any appreciable degree. Something was not quite right with the man.

"All right, I get the message. But let me also remind you of some money that should have come my way by now," Villot couldn't resist putting the needle into Dubnik.

"What do you mean? You've been paid, and rather well," fired back Dubnik as he tightened his grip on the Walther.

"Well, what I mean is that what I've been paid has only been sufficient for the first two dives I made. But I have equipment costs, boat rentals, et cetera. You know how it is, my friend."

"Listen to me, Villot, do not try to extort any more money out of me. This could result in an unfortunate circumstance for you."

"Mauro, you've been watching too many Hollywood movies, or maybe it has been French movies. I sometimes get them confused. You know, just the other day, I was at a cinema and I saw movie starring Fernandel. And do you know what? Fernandel said almost the exact same thing you just said. Talk about—"

"All right. How much do you need?"

"That is more like it. You see, it's not so hard. I think about five hundred Francs will be sufficient for now," Villot said.

Marco Dubnik's blood pressure was rising. He was glad Herve Villot was not in the same room as him. He may've been unable to contain himself and would have just shot the impudent Frenchman right then and there. "All right, I'll wire the money to you."

"No, no, my friend. I don't want anything that could be remotely traceable. No, I suggest we meet. You know our usual rendezvous, the one we have used on the last two occasions."

"All right. I'll meet with you there on the Friday, the 13th," Dubnik said.

"An interesting choice of date, my friend." Villot chuckled.

"Why do you say that?"

"Well, it *is* Friday the 13th. I hope that it will be fortuitous for the both of us."

"Just be there." Marco Dubnik slammed down his phone.

"Swine. Asshole. Pig." muttered Herve Villot as he returned to his work.

* * *

The time was just past five o'clock, and Mauro Guzzo had been able to stem the tide. He had calmed down the nerves of his editor about meeting the deadline for the bribery scandal. The phone jangled on his desk. Guzzo puzzled over whether he should ignore it or answer it. It could be a lead. The instrument kept up its bleating. Guzzo made his decision and picked up.

"Hello?"

"Mauro Guzzo? *Ciao*, this is Rosetta Rossi and I was wondering if I could have a minute of your time?" Rosetta asked tentatively.

"Of course, Rosetta, it is so nice to hear from you. You know I always have time for you."

"*Grazie*, Mauro. I may call you Mauro?"

"*Si, si*, of course. There is no need to be formal. What can I do for you?"

"Well, I was hoping to be able to meet with you, and also with Barbara. It's rather important."

Now Mauro Guzzo's interest was piqued and he sat down in his chair. What could Rosetta Rossi want to discuss with him? And, with Barbara. "Well, what is it you would like to discuss?"

"I'm afraid it's not a subject I would feel comfortable speaking about over the phone. It is one that should be done in private, that is face to face."

Guzzo began to silently drum the fingers of his left hand upon the plate glass that sat atop his desk. "I see. Well, we could make arrangements to meet. How about if Barbara and I stop by your apartment one evening?"

"No, no. I don't want to trouble my husband. At least, not yet," came the agitated reply to his suggestion.

"Well, then, how about if we meet at Barbara's home?" asked Guzzo hopefully.

"That would be fine. When could we meet?"

"Could we arrange something for, say next Monday about seven?"

"*Bene*, I think that will be fine. I do appreciate you agreeing to meet, Mauro."

"Think nothing of it, Rosetta. After all, we are all friends, and you are a close and dear friend of Barbara's," enthused back Guzzo.

"*Grazie*, Mauro. Well then, I will see you and Barbara on Monday. *Ciao*," Rosetta said with a sigh of relief.

"*Ciao*, Rosetta. Until Monday." Mauro Guzzo hung the phone up. He sat back further into his adjustable office chair, courtesy of the Americans. Maybe one day he could be using things actually made in Italy. The chair now voiced its displeasure in a loud and drawn-out screech. Here he already had an appointment with Bob Rossi on Thursday. And now he was to see Rosetta on Monday evening. Clearly, the two had not discussed things beforehand. And both had acted rather surreptitiously. Guzzo brought his hands together in the shape of a tent. He wasn't at all sure what Rossi male wanted. He thought he had a more definite idea about Rosetta's request. It must be something to do with the gold she had stumbled upon in the waters off Vento Beach. Guzzo was also fairly sure Rosetta had not yet mentioned it to her husband.

Mauro Guzzo stood up and reorganized some of the sundry items that littered his desktop. He would have to make sure he did not let anything slip when he met with Bob Rossi.

CHAPTER SIX -
DEVELOPMENTS

B ob Rossi arrived at Harry' American Bar a good half hour before his noon appointment with Mauro Guzzo. As he sipped on his espresso coffee, one of the customs he loved most about Italy, he reflected on how far he'd come in his life. Rossi had grown up dirt-poor and had lived a hardscrabble life in the steel-making town of Clairton, PA, a suburb of Pittsburgh. His father had been employed off and on at one of the steel foundries, and during the Great Depression, mostly off. Bob Rossi had been one of five children born to Robert Senior and Helen Rossi. Sports had been the virtual one redeeming feature of life for Bob Junior. It had been how he had gotten by; schoolwork had often been of secondary importance and priority. Rossi's ability on the football field had led to his admittance and scholarship to Penn State as a tackle on offense and a hard-hitting linebacker on defense. Bob Rossi had especially loved playing on defense, when he could really lay into an opposing ball-carrier. It was when he could release many of his pent-up frustrations and get away with it.

Following graduation from Penn State, Rossi kicked around in a variety of low-paying, low fulfilling jobs. He'd tried out and failed to make the roster of the Pittsburgh Steelers. Football had taken him only so far. No, he would have to make his way in the world another way.

In 1937, Bob Rossi decided he would join the US Army as a Second Lieutenant. The army at that point was in a sorry state of affairs. After the war to end all wars, America and its leaders had turned away from its military. So much so that the US Army had even fallen behind Portugal in armed strength. That he had been able to be promoted to the rank of captain by the time of Pearl Harbor had been nothing short of miraculous.

By February 1943, now newly promoted to major, Rossi found himself in battle at the Kasserine Pass in Tunisia. His unit was up against the battle-hardened troops of Field Marshal Erwin Rommel's Afrika Corps. Rossi soon found himself a prisoner of war before he'd even known what hit him. Eventually, he was transferred to an Italian POW camp near Naples. In late 1943, he was able to escape and with the assistance of civilians, he was spirited to Rome. He became one of the hidden members of Cardinal Hugh O'Flaherty's escape organization. The cardinal was the de-facto head of a vast network committed to aiding and assisting Allied prisoners of war from the Germans.

"Scusi, *signore*, would you care for another espresso?" asked the kindly and attentive waiter, a neat small-statured young man who waited patiently as he held a small platter to his chest.

"*Si*, I would. *Grazie*," Bob Rossi said as he broke from his memory.

The young man nodded his assent and went off for another cup. Rossi looked about Harry's Bar, famous among the cognoscenti of Rome. Harry's had it all, serving chateaubriand, lobster salads, cocktails, and of late, American style hamburgers. From the vantage point of his outside table, he was able to catch a glimpse inside at the gleaming brass-work and dark-stained woodwork. He was glad he had chosen it for his rendezvous with Guzzo.

Mauro Guzzo arrived promptly at 12:00 noon. This normally would have been considered a small faux-pas if he had been meeting another Italian. In Italy, it was thought of as fashionable and even proper to be late for an appointment. Guzzo immediately recognized Rossi, even though the man was dressed in civilian attire. Rossi's hair was in the clipped, short-cropped military style. His bearing was upright, not languid in any sense.

"And you must be Bob Rossi? I am Mauro Guzzo," said the Italian as he stepped forward to shake Rossi's hand.

Rossi rose and shook Guzzo's offered hand. "Yes, er, *si*, I am. How did you know?"

"It was just a guess on my part," replied Mauro Guzzo as he sat down. The waiter had returned, bringing Rossi's espresso.

"What are you drinking, Mauro?" asked Rossi as he almost spilled his coffee as he took it from the waiter.

Guzzo paused as if giving great weight to his decision. "I think I will have a Campari and soda. That is what I will have."

Again, the waiter silently nodded and strode off.

"I'm glad you chose Harry's, Bob. I have always liked the… what is it? Ah, the *bonhomie* of it. In any event, it's finally nice to meet you. From Barbara, I have heard so much about you."

"Mostly good, I hope," Bob Rossi said in a somewhat guarded and deferential tone.

"Indeed, all of it. By the way, do you mind if I smoke?" Guzzo asked politely. He removed a pack of Marlboro cigarettes from his jacket pocket.

"No, no, I do not mind."

"*Grazie*. Barbara is always trying to get me to quit. She says it's bad for my health. I always mean to, but I just can't bring myself to do it. You know what I mean?" Guzzo asked as a cloud of smoke billowed up from his first puff.

"I do indeed know what you mean. Rosetta says just about the same to me, word for word." Bob Rossi sat back and took in some of the measure of Mauro Guzzo. He knew the man was considered a legend among the Italian news corps, and he was also aware of the man's deep and personal loss of his wife and only son during the war. Yet, the man had a relaxed air about him, an affableness, as if he did not have a care in the world. Bob liked him immediately.

"Well, I hope that I'm not too direct, but you did mention that you had a matter of some importance to discuss with me," said Guzzo as he continued smoking. By this time, he had been served his drink.

"I do and I appreciate your taking the time to meet with me. I know you are a busy man."

Guzzo noted that the man's fingers had started to twitch. He saw that Rossi knew that he knew.

"Not too busy. Well, really, I have all sorts of deadlines that I am hopelessly behind on. No, that is not quite true, I am just pulling your leg. Is that not the correct expression?" asked Guzzo as he threw his head back in laughter.

"Yes, er, *si*, that is the correct expression," Rossi said, smiling. "Well, you see, I am a little concerned about Rosetta. I have asked her about it, but all she will say is that it is nothing. That I am imagining things. I don't know what it could be. It's just a feeling I have."

Guzzo took this in and contemplated as to whether he should reveal what Barbara had told him about the gold, and Rosetta's near-death experience. He quickly decided not to. Barbara had advised him not to. Should Guzzo tell Rossi about the gold, it would in all probability set the man off his rails. He had to be careful as to how he replied. "Well, I'm not aware of anything untoward. That is, anything in which you should feel apprehension about. I am sure it is nothing."

"It is just... I don't know. You simply know when something is up between a man and woman. Something I cannot put my finger on," Rossi continued, almost as much to himself as to Guzzo.

"Bob, look at me. If I hear of anything, believe me, I will let you know. Don't worry, my friend." Guzzo paused. "Did you have any other... ah, concerns?" asked Guzzo paternally.

Bob Rossi sat staring down at the table, as if he wanted to permeate through it. "No, I don't think so."

"*Bene*. I do have a suggestion, perhaps. While we're here at Harry's, why don't we partake of a lobster salad. It is absolutely superb, trust me. You know, Bob, we all have to eat."

"Yes. Yes, I think that is a great idea, Mauro," declared a suddenly brightening Bob Rossi. A broad smile crossed his wide and pleasant face.

* * *

It was just past 5:00 PM and Mauro Guzzo was buried under an avalanche of balance sheets and random lists of data. Assisting him had been a young staff member of Corriere della Sera, Paula Augusto. Guzzo had been staring absentmindedly at the stunning young woman. She thought he must be enamored with her twin peaks. Not as impressive, nor as developed as Barbara's, but quite spectacular in their own right. Augusto would not be the last young woman who would go to bed with a man who could help advance their career. When the phone rang, it was a relief to Guzzo and the young woman as well.

"Hello?" answered the journalist phlegmatically.

"Mauro! How are you, my sweet?" Barbara Danilo oozed into the phone.

"Barbara, how nice to hear from you," responded Guzzo, who was now looking between his fact sheets and Paula. The young woman blushed slightly and then self-consciously brought cover to her chest.

"I was wondering, dear, if we might enjoy the evening together. After a gorgeous dinner, of course. I would make the night unforgettable for you."

Guzzo rolled his eyes up into his head at the dramatics of the woman he had become intimately involved with. "Now, Barbara, I'm sure you would indeed make the evening memorable, as you almost always do. However, I am swamped with this extortion story. I'm afraid I'm going to have to take a raincheck. Oh, by the way, your friend Rosetta is seeking an audience with the two of us for tomorrow evening. It nearly slipped my mind."

"And what did you tell her, my good friend?"

"I told her it looked to be quite doable. And Barbara, we are going to meet at your place." Guzzo couldn't resist a little dig at his paramour.

"You bastard. Well, I don't have anything on the burner. All right, Mauro. Did she say what it was about?" asked Barbara as she played her fingers through a men's skin magazine. One never knew when one could pick up another tip for the bedroom.

"No, not specifically, but I suspect it has directly to do with her discovery. And, get this, I just had lunch the other day with Bob Rossi. It was all rather mysterious, I must say," Guzzo continued as he again stared at the young and very attractive young woman in front of him. On the phone was an older woman, but who was more than spectacular in every way in matters of sex. The quandary he was in.

What was a poor man to do?

"All right, it will have to be until tomorrow night. I'll just have to find some way to entertain myself tonight. Perhaps I'll call Ann Carter and we can go swimming for a couple of hours at the Metropole Pool."

"*Si, si.* you see, you just solved your own problem," said a quietly relieved Mauro Guzzo. "Now, my pet, I really have to return to my work."

"Yes. By the way, is that young assistant, what is her name… Paula? Is she assisting you?" asked a suspicious Barbara Danilo. She had been trying to sound as if she didn't care, but in truth she was a little jealous. Barbara could just picture Mauro humping the daylights out of this, this Paula woman.

"*Si*, she is, but it's not what you think. I do believe you may be a little jealous. Yes, you are. How quaint, and…" lingered Guzzo. "*Ciao*, Barbara."

"*Ciao*, Mauro. I can promise that once Rosetta leaves tomorrow night, I will make you forget all about this Paula."

"I look forward to it. *Ciao*," Guzzo hung up and then turned to Paula Augusto. "Sometimes, I think she actually believes she invented sex. She tried to sound as if she were kidding, but she seems to have this idea that you and I are going to… oh, I shouldn't actually say it." Guzzo was turning slightly red in the face.

"That we are going to have sex. Would that be such a bad thing Mauro?" Paula finished for him as she leaned forward.

The woman rose up from her chair and turned and went to the door and locked it. She next started to disrobe. Her blouse and bra came off first, revealing a pair of exquisitely formed breasts. Next came her black skirt and panties. Finally, she kicked off her low-heeled pumps.

Mauro Guzzo thought he was going to come in his own pants. After what seemed an eternity, he hurriedly removed every vestige of his clothing. Paula Augusto advanced toward him as he moved around from his desk. They swiftly embraced. Guzzo suddenly grabbed the woman and pinned her against the desk. The pair were going to fuck until both were completely satisfied and fulfilled.

* * *

Barbara Danilo arrived minutes before 7:00 PM that same evening at the Metropole swimming venue. She had, of course, driven her way there at a breakneck speed through the Roman streets, her blonde hair blowing in the wind as she guided her flaming red Maserati sports car.

As Barbara approached her locker, she saw that Ann Carter had already arrived. The young Englishwoman was doing some stretching exercises, her tight-fitting black bathing suit enhancing her continuing physical development. "*Buona sera*, Ann," Barbara said, greeting her friend.

"*Buona sera*, Barbara. How are you?"

"Oh, pretty good. I'm glad you could join me this evening. It seems as if Mauro is too involved with his work," Barbara said as she stripped down and got herself into a new white bathing suit. Privately, she had wondered in the past if Guzzo was in fact a little too involved with this Paula Augusto woman. Barbara had met her on a couple of occasions and had clearly seen how attractive the Italian was. She could turn any man's head. Barbara tried to push away the thought of Mauro and Augusto engaging in a sexual tryst.

"It was a great idea, Barbara. I hadn't planned on doing anything in particular. It will be good to swim for a couple of hours," Ann said pleasantly. She had ceased her stretching and now waited for Barbara.

"*Bene. Andiamo!*" commanded Barbara as she led the way to the pool.

Barbara and Ann noted that only a couple of other people were lazily swimming laps. Both women affixed their goggles to their faces to ward off the sting of the chlorine from their eyes. They moved to the center lanes of the thirty-meter long pool, paused, and then dove in.

For nearly two hours, Barbara Danilo and Ann Carter swam lap after lap. They had begun, as they almost always had, ten laps of the overhand crawl, followed by ten laps each of the breaststroke, butterfly, and backstroke. Each set was culminated by swimming ten laps underwater. The girls and paused for ten minutes after they had swum for about one hour for a brief respite from their exertions. Barbara had noticed that despite several attempts, she had been unable to shake off Ann. The Englishwoman had come a long way. She was now a force to be reckoned with in the pool, as well as in the gym.

As Barbara and Ann were preparing to shower, Barbara turned and proposed to Ann, "I'm thinking about taking up scuba diving lessons. What do you think?"

Ann paused and gave thought to the idea. "I think it might be a good idea. You can count me in. Have you mentioned any of this to Rosetta?"

"No, not yet. It's just a thought. You know, we could consider this as a new endeavor."

* * *

"I don't like being deceitful, and that's what I'm feeling right now," said an anguished Rosetta Rossi as she opined to Barbara Danilo and Mauro Guzzo. "I mean, I don't like going behind Bob's back, but in this case, I felt I had to."

"We understand, dear," said her friend Barbara. "What can we do to help?"

"Well, Barbara, as you well know, I have been… well, I have become obsessed with this gold. And my encounter with that man who tried to kill me…" Her voice trailed off.

"Rosetta, this is not advice, but only a suggestion. At some point, you may well have to confide in your husband," Mauro Guzzo said, speaking for the first time. Cigarette smoke curled up from his right hand. Barbara looked over at him which said in effect: "Keep on smoking those things and see how far they get you." But she remained silent.

"I know, but at this time, I cannot. I know he would instantly forbid me to go any further." Rosetta kneaded her hands together as if she were cradling rosary beads.

"Maybe, you should just forget about this gold," said Guzzo.

"I can't do that, Mauro. It drives me. It consumes me. I don't know how else to explain it." Mauro Guzzo and Barbara looked at one another as if in bewilderment. Neither one seemed to know what to say next.

117

"Well, Rosetta, the summer season is approaching its end. Let us think over this issue over the winter. We, or you, can revisit it in the spring with perhaps a new outlook. It will be 1948 and who knows?" Barbara offered brightly, her vibrant and lucid blue eyes alighting.

"You know, that may well be a good idea," Guzzo quickly chimed in. "I tell you what, Rosetta. I will keep researching on my own at the paper. Maybe something new may come up." At that, the discussion came to a close and the three of them resumed sipping their tea. Rosetta silently agreed with Barbara's suggestion.

* * *

The next night duly saw Mauro Guzzo fully engaged with Barbara. Barbara felt every inch of his elongated penis penetrate her. Guzzo, atop her back, nuzzled her lilac-scented hair, sending waves of increased passion throughout his body. He brought his hands under her chest, fondling her breasts. Barbara absolutely loved what was being done to her. Her face was a taut mask, but not of one experiencing pain, only pure intense pleasure.

"Well, Mauro, I do hope my performance was more enjoyable for you than Signorina Augusto's," Barbara threw out in a casual way. She now lay in bed beside Guzzo. "And don't tell me that you don't know what I'm talking about. I've been around the block a few times, and with many men."

Guzzo was sitting back and for some reason found himself staring at a gold-faced wall clock. For once, following sex, he was not smoking a cigarette. He knew better than to try and fence with Barbara. "All right, it happened. What do you want me to say?"

"Nothing at all. I appreciate that you didn't express outrage and swear to the heavens that I was mistaken. But Mauro, really. Don't you think she's a bit too young for you?"

"Yes, I suppose you're right." Guzzo sighed resignedly.

"You know, I've been unable to say this, but I think I've really fallen for you. I really mean it. It's more than the fantastic sex we have. I've developed genuine, deep feelings for you." Barbara gripped Guzzo's right hand tightly.

"I'm glad to hear you say that, Barbara. It makes me feel good. And despite my having strayed, well… I do believe I've fallen in love with you. As you said, it's more than the sex. I love being with you. I can't wait to hear or see what you'll do next."

Moments later, Barbara turned to Guzzo and said, "Mauro, I find this to be a tender moment. It should be savored by us." She then turned her back to him and reached to turn off the bedside lamp.

* * *

"Can you believe it? The bastard never showed. Here I was at that God awful, stinking quayside bar and I waited and waited, and…" Marco Dubnik hit his flailing hands fully into his lap.

"I am not surprised," replied an enigmatic Carlo Deluca. He had joined Dubnik at a slightly more upscale establishment than the one Dubnik had just described. Low-scudding clouds flitted across the sky outside. Deluca was enjoying the aroma of his double espresso.

"What do you mean?" asked Dubnik.

"Well, I guess you haven't heard. It seems as if our erstwhile colleague decided he would consume a large amount of alcohol, and then decided to drive at high speed. Mind you, this was done in the dead of night. Apparently, he tried to take his vehicle around a hairpin turn and—"

"He didn't make it," finished Dubnik. Suddenly, he thought about what they would do now. Villot was the only one who had some inkling as to where the gold cache might be. And now?

"No, Marco, he did not. Herve Villot, formerly of Commando Francaise, hero of Ouistreham. And now, kaput," continued Carlo Deluca, who was simultaneously lighting a Marlboro cigarette. How he loved these American cigarettes. "The question is what do we or, more to the point, what do you do now? I don't think some of your German friends will be pleased, not to mention your client in the Vatican."

"Never mind about the bloody Church. They are of no consequence. As to my other clients, Germans and the Don, as you so eloquently put it, well, that is a matter that will have to be handled a little more delicately," said

119

Dubnik as he bit off his words. A nervous tick was formulating by his right eye.

"I think we should continue to monitor the activities of Rosetta Rossi and her friend Barbara Danilo, to see if they can lead us to where we want to go. They'll probably do nothing further this year. After all, it will soon be 1948," said Deluca.

"You're probably right," mused Dubnik, seemingly distracted. He looked outside the bar's window at the random people scurrying about. "I'll get in touch with our new source at the Hotel Brentano."

"You have a new source there?"

"Yes, just because Signora Rossi was able to get rid of Signore Vito doesn't mean I'd be unable to follow up with a new contact," replied Marco Dubnik in a self-satisfied tone. "Yes, my new informant is a lovely *signorina*. You see, Deluca, if one spreads around enough cash, almost any man, or in this case, any woman, can be bought. Yes, you are probably quite right. There is little likelihood of anything new developing before the end of 1947."

"I'll keep my eyes and ears attuned to anything that may arise, as well," said Carlo Deluca.

"Just try and be as circumspect as possible. Don't overplay your hand. We have to stay on top of things."

* * *

Rosetta Rossi arrived a few minutes before her scheduled 10:00 AM meeting at the Biblioteca Nazionale Centrale di Roma (Rome National Central Library). She stood facing the building characterized by some as an iconoclastic monolith that had been designed by a gaggle of disaffected architects. Rosetta looked up at the imposing edifice, subconsciously straightening out her dress and walked up the stairs.

In front of her stood an assemblage of desks representing a variety of functions. Rosetta looked around until she saw an Information sign in the far-left corner of the hall. An unusual place, she thought, to locate the very sign a newcomer would need. Rosetta walked over to the desk where she observed a disheveled looking young man wearing thick-framed black eyeglasses. The man did not look up as Rosetta stood before him for what seemed to her to have been several minutes. Her irritation began to build at the impudence and downright rudeness of the young man.

Rosetta cleared her throat. "Harrumph! Excuse me, if it is not too much trouble," she muttered. Rosetta wanted to reach down and grab this little snot and give him a good thrashing. She felt she could easily do it.

The man continued to ignore her. Undoubtedly, he had secured the position through a political connection or through some family friend. "Excuse me!" Rosetta nearly shouted. "But I have an appointment, *signore*. Would you mind extending to me the barest courtesy by just looking at me?" she declared as she began to feel her chest heaving.

Finally, the youth looked up from his copy of the daily newspaper. It was with a look of disdain, as if he had been disturbed to have had his attention taken from the news. "Yes? How may I be of assistance to you, *signora*?"

"If it is not too much trouble, young man, I would appreciate it if you could tell me where I can locate the office of Signorina Stefania Andino." Rosetta could barely hide the contempt she felt for this peremptory and ignorant piss-ant of a man.

"*Si*, she is on the first floor," the man replied in a tone that said, *You are bothering me.*

"Would you be so kind as to tell me where on the first floor I can find her office?" retorted an enraged Rosetta, who was now about to reach down and grab this punk by his necktie and thrash him to within an inch of his life.

Resignedly, the man said, "Go up the stairwell you see on the right," he pointed. "At the top go the stairs you will do down the corridor to your right. Once you have done that," the man paused, and Rosetta was sure he was about to roll up his eyes. She thought he was allowing her to digest the information, as if she were a simpleton. "Once you have done that," he repeated, "go down the hallway until you come to the third door on your left."

"*Grazie, signore*. You have been most helpful. And I might add that it would do you well to extend a little common courtesy in your day-to-day dealings with the public." Rosetta bit off her words as she turned abruptly on her heels. The impudent shit gave off a phht sound.

Rosetta immediately turned and rounded on the man. "What was that?"

"Err, *niente, signora*. I was just trying to clear my throat," the man said sheepishly, keeping his eyes from meeting hers.

Rosetta looked down at him and saw that he was beginning to perspire a little. She turned and walked off. As Rosetta ascended the stairs of the grand library, she called up in her mind what her research of the building had revealed. The venue was one of the two national libraries in all of Italy. Its mission was to collect and preserve all publications in Italy, and the most important foreign works as well. They were to be made available to anyone. The library's collection consisted of more than six million printed volumes, two thousand incunabula, eight thousand manuscripts, and untold thousands of drawings along with countless miscellaneous items.

Moments later, having duly followed her directions, Rosetta stood in front of the door of STEFANIA ANDINO. The name was highlighted in muted golf lettering. She knocked lightly on the door and heard a soft feminine voice say, "Enter." Rosetta turned the handle and walked in. Before her sat an attractive dark-haired young woman. She appeared to be in her mid-twenties. The woman looked up. "Signora Rossi, I've been expecting you. I am Stefania Andino. Please, come in and have a seat."

Andino stood and extended her right hand to Rosetta. "Thank you," Rosetta said, shaking her hand. "I'm so glad to be able to meet with you, Signorina Andino. I do so much appreciate your taking the time. I know that you must be very busy." Rosetta smiled and took the seat opposite the young researcher. The chair groaned and squeaked. "I do hope this isn't an indication that I may have put on some weight recently."

Andino gave off a light pleasant-sounding laugh. "No, no, not at all. I can assure you you're fine and from what I can see, a woman who is in superb physical condition." The young woman's left hand now displayed her gold wedding band. "I'm never too busy. After all, that's what we at the library are assigned to do." Stefania Andino gave off an almost reverential look to Rosetta. Here was a young woman, quite unlike the rude young man at the information desk, who knew how to treat a visitor such as Rosetta... with the respect and dignity she deserved.

"I must say, you are far cry from the young man who sits at the information desk."

"You mean, Angelo? He is a horse's ass. Pardon my language. *Signora*, he is the perfect example of one having the right connections. I believe his uncle was some big shot in Mussolini's army. In any event, how may I be of assistance to you? You were rather sketchy about what you might be looking for during our phone conversation," said Stefania Andino as she coolly looked at Rosetta.

"I didn't mean to be obfuscatory on the phone with you. May I call you Stefania?" The young woman nodded assent. "I am interested in a particular ship, more like a tramp steamer that was sunk, or at any rate, went down somewhere off the Ligurian coast just past Genoa. This happened, we, or I believe, some time around the German evacuation of Rome in June 1944."

"I see, I see," mused a pensive Andino, her brow knitted in concentration. "Well, I'll take you to some archival material. I must confess to you that things are still in a state of disarray. We're trying to put things back together, or, at least in some sense of order because of the war."

"*Grazie, signora*. You know, I did not mean to insult you just a minute ago. I mean you look quite young to be married. Perhaps, that is because I am showing my age," Rosetta said.

"No, that is quite all right... may I call you Rosetta? You see, Alberto and I were married in a rather hurried affair in 1944. Ironically, it was in June 1944. In any event, we were married. I was twenty and Alberto was nineteen." Andino halted and a tear started to fall down her right cheek. "I am sorry, but I'm becoming emotional. You see, right after the wedding, if you could call it that, Alberto was dragooned into captivity by the Germans. He was sent to a labor camp in Austria and...and..."

"I would understand if you did not want to continue," said a heartfelt Rosetta. The pain in the young woman's voice was palpable and heartbreaking. "I did not mean to intrude on something so painful."

"No, no, it's all right. Some say it's therapeutic to discuss difficult and unpleasant things with another person. Rosetta, I think you are the right

123

person for me to share my story with. However, we are cutting into your time for research," Stefania Andino said apologetically.

"No, please, take your time, Stefania."

Well, where was I? Oh, yes, Alberto. He was taken to Austria. I'm not sure as to what he may have seen or heard, but he has not been the same ever since. I mean, before he had always been carefree and lighthearted. Now, some days, he can hardly seem to stir himself. He can't seem to hold a job, which is difficult in any event, what with the current state of the country. I do not know…" continued an anguished Stefania Andino.

Rosetta took this in and silently contemplated. "Sometimes when I am feeling a little sorry for myself, I come across a Stefania Andino, and I am ashamed." Rosetta vowed to herself that she would do all she could to help this young woman, and her husband. It was a vow she was determined to keep.

"Ah, Rosetta, let me take you to the archives I have mentioned and you can begin to perhaps clear up some to the mystery that has confronted you about this mysterious vessel."

* * *

Some time during the following week, Rosetta Rossi and Barbara Danilo were seated in the comfortable armchairs in the office of Stefano Lucca. On this particular day, the weather was certainly nothing to write home about. It had begun with a light drizzle coating the streets and alleys of the Eternal City. Now, it had turned to an outright downpour, with water cascading down the window panes of Lucca's office overlooking the Castel Sant'Angelo.

"I'm so glad you girls could meet with me this morning. I only wish it was under better conditions," a gracious Stefano Lucca said, greeting the women.

"Grazie, Stefano," Barbara responded drily. "Now, you said you had some interesting information for us." Barbara leaned backward.

"Indeed I did. But first, may I offer you girls some refreshment?"

Both demurred by shaking their heads. They wanted him to get on with it.

"Well, then, yes. I have found out some rather… pertinent information. First, your athletic activities and your holiday excursions to Vento Beach have come under the auspices of Cardinale Maggione. His direct subordinate is one Pasco Gonevento, a novitiate Priest. This man is in direct contact with a man known as Marco Dubnik. Mr. Dubnik has been employing the services of two associates. One of them has been identified as Herve Villot. The other has not been I.D.'d as yet, but we are working on it."

"And just who is this Dubnik character?" asked Barbara as she crossed her nylon-sheathed legs. It stirred Lucca as she knew it would.

"A mystery man. During the war it was rumored that he at one time acted as an Allied agent. At another, he was working for the Germans. Some even said he may have been spying for the Russians. If that were so, you would have had a case of a man working as a triple agent."

"And now?" again from Barbara.

"Now it's rumored Dubnik may be working for the East German secret service. A rather nasty organization."

"The East Germans you say?" questioned a now perturbed looking Barbara.

"Eh, well, I meant no offense, Barbara. In any event, these seem to be the primary people we are dealing with. I can assure both of you that my team of operatives will continue working diligently for you."

Barbara said, "You don't have to sell us on your services or your capabilities, Stefano,"

To this point in the conversation, Rosetta had been a silent witness to the back and forth between Barbara and Lucca. She could clearly discern the kismet that may have previously existed between the two, that is, in bedroom activity. Rosetta was also well-aware of the teasing Barbara liked to employ on occasion when she dealt with certain men.

"If I may interject, Stefano. How much will it cost us to continue to utilize your services?" asked Rosetta.

"Well, I can't give you an accurate figure at this time. I'll have my secretary put together an accurate projection," Lucca responded as he continued to direct his gaze at Barbara's chest. Lucca could now barely contain himself. Rosetta thought the two of them might go at it right then and there on his desk. Lucca tore his eyes away.

"Now, is there anything else I can do for you at this time? I am afraid I'm engaged in several other projects."

"I am quite sure you are, Stefano. Just do the best you can. Oh, Rosetta," Barbara said as she leaned forward and lightly touched her sleeve. "Should I mention about what we'd been talking of just before our meeting?"

Rosetta leaned back and tilted her head to one side. "That's up to you."

"What is this?" asked a now curious Stefano Lucca.

"Well, I have grown quite bored of late with my current position of regional sales representative for Maserati. Therefore, I am going to propose to them that I'd like to become one of their test track drivers."

Lucca stretched himself back into his groaning swivel chair and threw his head back in convulsive laughter. "Barbara, I am not laughing at you, believe me. I'm almost never surprised when you tell me something. And how do you think the dinosaurs at Maserati will react to your, ah, proposal?"

"Just like I expect them to react. They'll puff out their scraggly chests, tut-tut and pftt. Still, I won't be deterred. I will not," stated a defiant Barbara Danilo.

"I *have* told her that she's crazy," offered Rosetta as she shook her head dolefully. "However, I have learned by now that when Barbara puts her mind to something, then somehow, some way, she will find a way to do it."

"Undoubtedly, she will. You know, Barbara, you'll probably have to win over their chairman of the board, Marcello Mastrani, and that will be tough."

"I think I know a way I could use to overcome any resistance on the part of Signore Mastrani." All present knew what she meant by that statement.

"In any event, I wish you well in your endeavor. As I was saying, I will continue looking into this Dubnik character, the East Germans, Cardinale Maggione, and so on," concluded Stefano Lucca.

"You are ever the raconteur, Stefano, but you will always be a dear fellow," said a smiling Barbara.

* * *

126

"Yes, I am sure by your description of them. These are the two women that I had observed earlier this year," said the erstwhile Carabinieri inspector, Gianni Ravelli.

"Mmm," mused Marco Dubnik. "That's interesting. All right, they're obviously digging for more information. I mean, Stefano Lucca is probably one of the best detectives in Rome. All right, Gianni, keep tabs on these two women, but I also want you to shadow Lucca. Even if that means bringing in additional resources."

"Well, you know what that would mean. Would you be willing to pay for these 'other resources'?"

Marco Dubnik could feel his blood pressure rising. Always about the money. "Yes, yes, do not worry. You and your associates will be well taken care of. Haven't I always looked out for you, Gianni?"

"Oh, sure you have. You know, my friend, I heard a rumor about the demise of... oh yes, Herve Villot."

Dubnik immediately cut off Ravelli. "Don't concern yourself over that matter, do you understand? It's of no consequence to you." With that, Dubnik hung up.

To Ravelli, he had clearly struck a nerve with Dubnik. Perhaps, in the future it would be a nerve he could exploit.

* * *

The following day, Barbara Danilo was making her pitch to Maserati's Director of Testing and racing, Pietro Roberti. She had prepared herself for this moment very diligently and carefully. She was well aware of the impression she had to make on Roberti. Barbara had calmed herself as she sat in her office in Rome and placed her call to Maserati headquarters. "*Ciao*, Barbara. *Viene qui*?" gushed Pietro Roberti.

"*Ciao*, Pietro, I am well. And how are you?" asked Barbara politely. She was twisting the cord of the phone around her wrist.

"*Bene, bene*. What can I do for you on this fine day?" Roberti asked, coming straight to the point.

"Ah, well," began Barbara as she felt herself beginning to hesitate. No, she just had to go for it. "Pietro, I've been thinking about something for a long time. It's something I've always wanted to do, and I know I can do it."

Roberti remained silent on his end of the line before he said, "Yes, Barbara. What is it that you would like to do?"

Barbara would just come right out with it. "Pietro, I would like to become one of Maserati's test drivers. I know I can do it. I would just like to be given a chance. What do you say?" She nervously awaited the man's answer.

To her relief, Pietro Roberti did not laugh or try to make a mockery of her proposition. "Well, that's certainly interesting, Barbara. Tell me, I know you said you can do it and why you can. I mean, what are your qualifications?"

"I realize I don't have an engineering degree, per se, but I've driven many Maserati vehicles over the years. Some, in fact, at the test track in Bologna. Besides, I know the product line inside and out. And I do have a degree, even if it is in marketing and accounting. On top of that, I have the drive and will to succeed," Barbara said, completing her effort at persuasion.

Roberti replied evenly and smoothly. "I will tell you what I will do, Barbara. I'll broach the idea to my colleagues here, and I will also contact Marcello Mastrani. You may well have to convince him yourself of your desire."

"Thank you, Pietro. I do believe I know a way to convince Signore Mastrani, should it become necessary."

"I do believe that you do, Barbara. I should caution you that Mastrani is a tough nut. *Ciao*, Barbara." Roberti thought to himself that Danilo did not have a chance.

* * *

On the following Wednesday evening, Barbara Danilo would personally meet with the enigmatic and flamboyant Marcello Mastrani at his plush villa on Via Gregoriana, virtually in the shadows of the iconic Spanish Steps. That day Barbara had set aside completely in order to prepare for her rendezvous with the most powerful man of the company. Everything had been scrutinized down to the last detail: hair, make-up, lipstick… right down

128

to the underwear she would don beneath her deep V-necked black shift dress. Its length fell to just above the knee. Although considered somewhat unfashionable at the time, Barbara did not care. She wanted to display as much leg as possible.

Marcello Mastrani was seventy-one years old, but did not resemble anyone of that age. He was not especially tall at 5' 9", but he was exceptionally fit. from the top of his gleaming shaved head to the tips of his toes. Marcello Mastrani was a physical fitness buff, as he possessed a wide and developed chest, a rock-ribbed mid-section, and powerfully defined thigh muscles. He was known to be quite accomplished in the boudoir. Following the death of his wife more than ten years before, Mastrani had often been seen escorting a bevy of younger, glamorous women about Rome and Italy.

Barbara realized she might likely have to entice Mastrani into the bedroom and display her own physical and sexual attributes. In a way, she secretly hoped it might come to that. This was despite her feeling that she had developed something special and meaningful with Mauro Guzzo.

She arrived just after 7:00 PM, having taken a taxi from her home to Mastrani's palatial mansion. Looking up at it from the street, Barbara took in the breathtaking majesty of the building. Composed largely of granite blocks, wide-mullioned windows, and more than one hundred feet in length. There were two floors, topped off by a black-slated roof.

Danilo walked up to the double front door and firmly shook the lion-headed escutcheon. After waiting for several moments, the door was opened. Standing before her was a cadaverous looking older gentleman, replete with black tie and tails.

"You must be Signora Danilo," the man said politely. The voice did not match the outward appearance. "I will inform Signore Mastrani of your arrival."

Barbara stepped into the large living room area. It almost took her breath away. She looked around the room and saw that it contained what could be considered a veritable museum in its own right. Every piece imaginable of artwork, tapestry, and antiquity was contained within this one room.

Having waited for several minutes, Barbara decided to seat herself. Moments later, the man of the house bounded into the room.

"Ah, Signorina Danilo. I'm so glad you could join me here in my home." Although he smiled at her, his eyes had remained flat, emotionless. It was rather cold to Barbara and inwardly she began to tremble.

"*Grazie, prego, Signore* Mastrani. It is indeed my pleasure. I know you are a busy man and for you to take the time to meet with a subordinate is most kind." Barbara began to feel overheated and speaking too fast. She was, strangely, nervous.

"Please, *signorina*. Let us dispense with the formal titles and address ourselves as Marcello and Barbara," Mastrani suggested affably.

"*Si*, why not?"

"Please, sit. Would you care for an hors d'hoeuvre? Perhaps I can offer you some refreshment? I am going to indulge myself with some Ouzo."

"No, no. I am fine as far as food is concerned," Barbara said as she glanced down at a couple of platters containing several cheeses, crackers, and shrimp and changed her mind. "I'll take you up on your offer of the Ouzo."

"*Bene, bene*," replied Mastrani as he proceeded to pour two generous dollops of the Greek libation into cut-glass tumblers.

"I must say, this is one of the most stunning rooms I have ever seen. I am most impressed. Not to speak of your home itself," Barbara said as she continued to look about her.

"*Grazie, prego*, Barbara. I do what I can. I feel that as a man of great wealth, I should occasionally indulge myself. Do you not agree?" Mastrani handed Barbara her drink. "

"I do indeed," Barbara said affably as she thought that Mastrani had indulged himself several times over.

"*Bene*. Enough with the banal pleasantries. I understand that you wish to become a test driver for my company. When I heard from Pietro Roberti of your request, I will have to admit that I was quite astonished. After all, it is quite unusual, if not considered improper, in Italy today." Mastrani then gestured for Barbara to join him on his couch.

Barbara went over and could feel an immediate magnetism emanate from the man. He exuded presence as he sat in his open-necked black shirt and tan, woolen slacks. His only adornment was a gold chain that encircled his neck.

"Well, Marcello, I believe I can best characterize myself as a maverick sort of a woman. I like to take chances. I fear nothing. I believe I can offer services to the Maserati firm that will be an asset."

Barbara could not help but notice that the man was beginning to develop an erection. This was going to happen sooner than she had expected. She would go for it, then and there. Barbara moved herself closer to Mastrani, not quite touching him, but close enough so that she could see his chest beginning to rise and fall at a faster pace.

Mastrani put his drink down. He had already decided to allow Barbara to become a part of his stable of drivers, but he wanted to drag things out a little, to tease Danilo just a bit more. He wanted to bed this vixen right then. Normally, he was the one in control, but Barbara Danilo had cast her seductive powers upon him. In one swift motion, Marcello Mastrani was on Barbara. He flitted his tongue into her waiting mouth. She eagerly responded in kind. He then placed his hand inside her dress and began massaging her left breast. He felt her hardened nipple, arousing him to an even higher level.

Barbara, meanwhile, had placed her hand on Mastrani's crotch. He was very hard. She pondered to herself as to whether to perform fellatio upon the man or whether to wait and let things play out a little further.

Mastrani quietly suggested they retire to his first-floor bedroom. Barbara followed him as they ascended the magnificent and opulent staircase, French kissing as they went. Mastrani stopped in front of the second door on the right. He took hold of the short-handled knob and twisted. A soft metallic click sounded. The pair entered through the doorway and the door clicked shut. Mastrani and Barbara tore off their clothes with animalistic abandon. Mastrani then virtually attacked Barbara in the center of the room, his mouth and tongue taking hold of Barbara's. She had briefly taken note of his body. Huge, piston-like upper arms, a ribbed mid-section, and bulging large thigh muscles.

On this night, Mastrani decided he would dispense with much of the foreplay he normally would employ. He pinned Barbara to the mattress and as he did so, she took hold of his manhood and slid it between her legs. Mastrani began a slow rhythmic movement, which quickly shifted into overdrive. He felt

Barbara hook her own magnificently developed legs around his plunging body, and he felt her squeeze them, and then squeeze them even harder.

Barbara Danilo felt every ounce of her lover's power. She liked the way his penis felt inside of her writhing body. Strangely, she now found herself in a new position. Usually, she was the dominant partner, but not tonight. She conceded that Mastrani was dominating her physically. In fact, the man was absolutely pulverizing her. Finally, Mastrani could contain himself no longer and he ejaculated into Barbara. Both had climaxed simultaneously.

The pair was now resting side by side in Mastrani's huge king-size bed. Barbara had accepted his offer of a Gaulloise cigarette. Secretly, she cringed. For one thing, she did not smoke anymore because of her workouts, and secondly, the French brand had to be one of the foulest things ever devised by man.

Barbara looked over at the bedside clock and saw that it read 10:00 PM. Mastrani was just returning to the room with two more Ouzos. She loved looking at the man's bald pate and his superb body. *Seventy-one?* she thought. *I will have to ask him his secret.*

"Marcello?" Barbara asked.

"*Si?*"

"I think I would like to go for a swim."

"*Si, si*, that sounds like a good idea. *Andiamo*, we go," Mastrani said as he put the drinks down. He then bounded out of the room, closely followed by Barbara. As the couple walked down the stairway, Mastrani reached down and pinched his lover on her left buttock. Barbara responded by cooing in his ear and pinching his own right butt. "You know, Barbara, I have always liked aggressive women, and with you, I think I have found one of the most aggressive ever."

Once they were at the edge of the pool, Barbara immediately dove in, swimming underwater rapidly. Mastrani quickly followed. He swam all out and soon was just behind Barbara's flailing legs. He dove down on her, driving her body to the bottom. His hands gripped her breasts. He then turned her around and began kissing her. Barbara eagerly responded, and soon they surfaced.

Mastrani was all over her. Finally, Barbara was able to break from his embrace.

"Marcello, I would like to swim a little. There will be plenty of time for additional rounds of sex." And with that, Barbara took in a big breath of air and dove under. Marcello Mastrani reluctantly acceded to her wish and followed suit.

Barbara and Marcello swam underwater laps, although he had surfaced after completing ten of them while she went on to finish twelve. The couple swam for more than an hour. Barbara had been suitably impressed with Mastrani's fitness, as he had been able to stay with her throughout. At last, Barbara ascended the pool stairs and Mastrani followed her up. He then went over to the cabana where he proceeded to pull out two four by four foot mats of the kind used by gymnasts. Mastrani placed them side by side on the pool patio.

Barbara came up to Mastrani and embraced him. Their bodies glistened in the moonlight cast down. Feverish French kissing ensued and was soon followed by the pair floating down to the mats.

"Marcello?" she asked.

"*Si?*"

"I would like to propose a bet. If I should succeed in besting you, then you will nominate me to be one of your test track drivers. What do you say?" Barbara asked while she looked directly at Mastrani.

"An interesting proposition, my dear. I tell you what. I agree.

Then, let the games begin," she declared. Barbara tried to pin Mastrani down, but he proved to be too quick for her and too strong. He then went through the requisite foreplay ritual before he entered her again. Mastrani was humping away at a high pace when Barbara instinctively felt him begin to slow. Perhaps his age was finally revealing itself. "Marcello, it's all right. I'll finish for us. Let's roll over together."

Mastrani had to reluctantly agree to what Barbara suggested. It literally killed him to have to submit to a woman, even one as extraordinary as Barbara Danilo. The pair rolled and Barbara rose up from Mastrani like a veritable Phoenix. She bucked atop him like a wild bronco, her fulsome breasts bouncing and swaying out of control. At last, Marcello Mastrani shuddered his release into Barbara.

CHAPTER SEVEN -
FULL SPEED

Sunlight filtered its way through the room as a gentle breeze swept its way in through the partially opened casement windows. Barbara Danilo awakened in a groggy state; it had been a remarkable night. She had thoroughly enjoyed her romp in the sack, and the mats, with Marcello Mastrani. Barbara was still amazed at the man's strength and endurance for a man of his age.

Next to her lay Mastrani, lightly snoring away. Barbara looked over at his exposed back, its heavily muscled surface. She knew she would have to make another decision soon as to which man she should cast her lot with. On the one hand, there was Marcello. Barbara had found him to be an absolute bull in bed, but one with a deft hand. She had to admit if she opted for him, he would no doubt continue with his affairs with younger and more glamorous women. In the other, Barbara felt almost certain that Mauro Guzzo would be totally devoted and committed to her. She remembered what Rosetta had once told her: "You know Barbara, a relationship is more than just the fulfillment of carnal desires."

Mastrani began to stir beside Barbara. She decided that when her man awakened she would entice him into another round of sex. But this time, she would allow him to dominate her. "What time is it?" muttered Mastrani.

"A little after eight, Marcello."

"Well, I must say, that was quite a night, wouldn't you say?" asked Mastrani as he stretched out his arms above his head. He looked over at Barbara and thought she looked completely refreshed, and ready. The gleam from her crystal blue eyes told him she wanted to resume with more sex. And he, the gallant gentleman that he was, would only be too happy to comply. First, though, he excused himself so he could go and brush his teeth.

Barbara had already done so and had made sure to lubricate herself as well. She was sitting up, fully naked and exposed for Mastrani to take in when he returned. She heard the tap water shut off and Mastrani walked back into the bedroom. Barbara thought he must have worked himself up because she now saw a man fully erect.

Marcello Mastrani got back into the bed and immediately engaged Barbara. This time, he would utilize more extensive foreplay.

When Barbara silently indicated to him that she was ready, he entered her and began a slow and rhythmic pace. This was quickly accelerated to the point that he was once again pounding away at Barbara. She gripped his body fiercely with her legs. Minute after minute, Barbara took on this raging bull until he finally climaxed. She hoped that Mastrani would feel good about his performance.

"Marcello?" Barbara asked in a soft and demure voice.

"Yes?"

"What would have happened if you had won our little contest last night?"

Mastrani did not answer at first, but then said, "What do you think, Barbara?"

"That is precisely what I thought."

"Now, this is what you shall do. First, I will instruct my staff to provide you with train transportation to Bologna. You will be staying at the exclusive Hotel Belvedere. I want you to be there by Sunday. On Monday, you are to be at the track by 8:00 AM sharp. I will contact Roberti to have him make all of the necessary arrangements," Mastrani concluded.

"*Grazie*, Marcello," cooed Barbara as she ran a finger around one of Mastrani's nipples.

"Prego," he responded.

"Do you know what type of model I will be given to drive? I'd like it to be one of the top of the line vehicles, such as the 8CTF. I have to be able to really prove myself."

"I'm not sure, but I'll see that Pietro Roberti is made aware of your preference. Do not worry, I have every confidence in you. You will succeed with flying colors."

"I think you may have mixed your metaphors, Marcello. I'm only kidding," Barbara said playfully as she lightly punched his arm.

Marcello chuckled. "I also want to say that if you should at any time in the future feel the need for a good thrashing in bed, you may feel free to contact me."

"*Bene*, Marcello. I will keep that in mind."

* * *

Some time later, back in Rome, a more mundane and routine event was about to take place, but don't ever say that to Maria Franchi as she stood over the bar containing the near equivalent of three-hundred pounds. Maria had chalked up her hands and adjusted her weight belt. She had been working hard, very hard, of late and her body was now proof positive of that. Her upper arms now had good definition, as did her upper body and legs. In fact, it was upon them she would primarily rely on to hoist the weight set before her.

Maria closed her eyes and squatted. She took hold of the bar and paused. In one herculean effort she raised herself up and took up the weight into her hands and arms. The bar bent slightly downward, Maria's face was now twisted into a tight grimace; her eyes flashed. She held the weight for the requisite five seconds and then let it drop onto the floor. Maria Franchi raised her arms in triumph. She had done it.

Ariana Rossi, who had been spotting for Maria, raced up to the older woman to offer her congratulations. Maria demurred, or at least pretended to do so, but secretly she was very pleased. All the work, sweat, everything, had been worth it. Maria Franchi was developing a first-class body, and it was being done it at sixty years of age. She was also pleased that she and her husband were once again having incredible sex. After years of going through rather desultory motions in their bedroom, the flame had been rekindled, and this flame was growing.

Maria Franchi was not yet through on this day. No. Now she placed herself on the bench-press apparatus. Ariana was again spotting for her. Maria took hold of the one hundred and fifty pounds of weight and brought it down to her chest. Once, twice, and so on, she performed five repetitions. Ariana noted how much the woman's muscles had developed. As Maria bench-pressed, her face again wore a grimace, beads of sweat poured out from her skin. Maria's upper arms glistened. She was exerting every ounce of her increasing strength. During the dead-lift, Ariana had been more than amazed as she observed Maria's body. Every muscle was taut, those in her upper arms and legs bulged outward to the maximum.

Later that night after they had enjoyed a light and leisurely repast of cheese and antipasto, accompanied of course, be a liter of wine, Maria determined she would take her husband to the woodshed—figuratively in bed, that is. Franchi nearly attacked Alberto, and after having fondled him to attention, she straddled him in one quick motion. The move had surprised Alberto, but secretly, he had not minded. Alberto, after some initial reluctance, had to admit he liked the new Maria.

* * *

Bob Rossi was working at his desk at the AMGOT mission during the early morning hours in early September. He was trying very hard to direct his attention to the tasks at hand, and yet he could not help but think of his own personal situation. Not that he thought that his marriage was in trouble, but of late, he had become increasingly concerned. No, it was more than a mere concern. How had things happened between himself and Rosetta? Something was wrong. Very wrong. Where just a short time ago the couple had engaged in frequent and joyous sex, this had almost come to a stop.

Rossi was sure something had happened to Rosetta during her last trip to Vento Beach, but she refused to offer up anything in the way of an explanation. It had to have been something ominous, almost traumatic. Now, his tortured mind had turned to something that a short time ago would have been completely ludicrous to him. What if Rosetta had taken on a lover? Maybe some of the influence of Barbara Danilo had rubbed off on her. Danilo had always been something of free spirit. To hell with tomorrow, live only for today.

Rossi stopped his perusal of his paperwork, it could wait. He looked over at his card file on the left side of his desk. He reached for it and began thumbing his way through it. Should he enlist the services of a private detective? He ruled out using Stefano Lucca. The man was an intimate, in more ways than one, with Barbara Danilo. If Rossi went to him, it was a sure thing that Barbara would be in the know. And then soon after, so would Rosetta.

"Mmm," he murmured as his finger stopped at the name of Robert Anderson, a former colleague of his when both had been in the army together. A short time ago, Anderson had been in need of a private investigator when he felt strongly that his wife was seeing someone else on the side.

"Good morning, Bob. This is Bob Rossi."

"Hey, Bob, how the hell are you? It's been a while. What are you up to these days?"

"Oh, not much. Staying pretty busy. And you?" continued Rossi guardedly. Bob knew that Anderson was still working with the American mission in Rome.

"Eh, you know how it is. Pretty much the same. Hey, I've finally been able to start divorce proceedings against that two-timing bitch of mine. Hey, get this. She had been, and probably still is, shacking up with this greaseball lawyer here in Rome."

"I'm sorry to hear that. I'm glad for you in that you can begin to move on. It's probably been tough on you," lamented a well-meaning Bob Rossi.

"Don't you know it."

"Well, Bob, the reason I decided to call you is because I have a... a little problem," Rossi said. He wasn't sure whether he should go on with Anderson. "Uh,, do you happen to recall the private detective you used...?"

"I don't believe it. Don't tell me the you suspect Rosetta of anything?"

"Well, I wouldn't necessarily say that, but..."

"I just can't believe Rosetta would betray you. I mean, you and I both know you're not much to look at," Anderson said with a nervous laugh, "but I'd swear that woman worships you."

"Well, sometimes things change. But I would appreciate it if you could provide me with the name."

"Yeah, sure, ol' buddy. I don't even have to look it up. His name is Giorgio Finalmente. Pretty funny, huh? I mean having a name like that. Final." Anderson's cackled laughter punctuated the line.

"Oh, yeah, right." Bob Rossi laughed, but he did this without a smile.

"Hold on, I have his number right here. By the way, the man is very good. Very discreet, and he won't rob you blind," continued Anderson as he gave out Finalmente's number.

After Bob Rossi had hung up from Anderson, he fingered the paper with the phone number on it. He also let his mind drift back to when he had first met Rosetta Consento. Rossi, who had been taken prisoner in North Africa, following the American debacle at Kasserine Pass, and was eventually sent to a prisoner of war camp near Caserta, Italy in 1943. Some time during the fall of that year, Rossi and several other Americans effected their escape and melted into the hillsides. Bob Rossi and two other men were able to make their way to an area just outside of Rome. It was there, fortuitously for them, they made contact with a group of Italian civilians. These brave souls were working in concert with an escape organization led by the indomitable Irish monsignor, Hugh O'Flaherty.

Several days before Christmas, Bob Rossi found himself in the well-furnished apartment of Rosetta and her two children. It was for him, love at first sight. The relationship between himself and Rosetta had begun rather cautiously. Bob Rossi tried desperately to maintain some sense of decorum and a degree of separation, but it was of no use. He had been completely smitten with this unbelievably lovely and vivacious Italian woman.

For her part, Rosetta really had no interest in kindling any type of relationship with Bob Rossi, or with any man. The death of her husband less than two years before was still fresh in her mind, and was still too painful.

By February of 1944, Bob Rossi was no longer being hidden in Rosetta's home. Numerous British and American POWs were often routinely moved from one location to another so as to stay ahead of German surveillance. But the two still frequently came into contact with one another. It was during a sunny afternoon when Rosetta's children had been away and Bob Rossi had been unable to contain himself, or his urges. He had been sitting alongside Rosetta and he kept finding himself staring at her face and her body. The moment had come. Rosetta too, succumbed. The pair consummated their new relationship in bed for more than an hour. Rossi had been more than amazed at the raw energy and passion that burned within Rosetta. It had been as if she had waited for this one moment to become a total woman once again.

* * *

Monday morning, 13 September 1947, dawned bright and crisp with barely a wisp of cloud cover. Barbara Danilo had arrived promptly for her 8:00 appointment. She had thought it had been fortuitous that the date was not Friday the 13th. Waiting for her at the Maserati test track in Bologna was Pietro Roberti and a gaggle of company representatives. Barbara could not detect any air of condescension from the men as they had greeted her.

Pietro Roberti informed Barbara she would have to undergo a physical exam that would be conducted by a physician employed by Maserati. Barbara felt no undue concerns as she knew she was in great shape. Probably better than anyone the doctor had ever previously examined.

Indeed, this was confirmed by Dottore Massimo only moments later. The physician had even complimented Barbara on her overall physical condition. She was in better shape and possessed a better body than almost all the women Massimo had ever examined in his lifetime. Barbara thanked the elderly man and smiled to herself. And, why not? She had worked very hard to get to where she was.

When Barbara returned to the track, Roberti introduced her to Ludovico Scalifi, "Ludi," Maserati's top driver. Scalifi bowed before Barbara and then took her hand and kissed it as though he were a gallant knight and she a damsel in waiting. It made her inwardly cringe a little.

Scalifi informed her she would be fitted in the best available protective clothing a white jump-suit like type of coverall. Somewhat heavy black boots would adorn her feet. Danilo would have her ensemble topped off by a white polo-styled helmet, along with black-trimmed goggles. And, it was advised she wear a handkerchief tied around her nose and mouth.

Ludi Scalifi then pointed out to Barbara the vehicle she would be driving, a Maserati 8CTF, a white open-air roadster. The car had garnered many laurels for the firm in races throughout Europe. In 1939 and 1940, American Wilbur Shaw had captured the Indianapolis 500 behind the wheel of an 8CTF. The same vehicle had secured victories for Maserati at the 1938 Italian Grand Prix and the 1939 German Grand Prix.

The 8CTF was a powerful race car that utilized a 2991 cc engine. It produced the equivalent of more than 250 horsepower. Danilo carefully looked the sleek vehicle over. She knew Scalifi and the other company executives were also watching her closely, undoubtedly hoping to see some sort of indecision, perhaps panic. But she did not, and would not, flinch. Barbara was determined above all else to prove these chauvinists wrong.

Scalifi patiently pointed out to her some of the technical details and handling characteristics of the race car. Barbara listened carefully and attentively to the briefing. She had to get this right the first time. There would be no second chance. Then, she was directed toward a dressing room where she could outfit herself.

At last, the moment, her moment, had arrived. Barbara closed her eyes in the dressing room. She did her best to calm herself down. She looked into the mirror and realized she would be making a statement not only for herself, but for all the women of Italy. Most of whom were looked down upon as second-class citizens by a still male-dominated society.

Finally, Barbara was ready. She strolled out toward the track. The Maserati people had done their best to provide her with a comfortably fitting coverall as was available. The one she was wearing still felt a little tight, especially under her arms. Still, Barbara thought this only enhanced her physique to the assembled company personnel.

Barbara had earlier been instructed by Roberti to take the 8CTF around the track for five laps, and only five. She paused for a minute alongside the vehicle. The Maserati cognoscenti were probably thinking, or hoping, that she would chicken out at the last minute. No way was that going to happen. Barbara climbed into the car and buckled herself up with the leather-lined seat and shoulder belt. She started up the powerful engine and heard the throaty roar and then hum as she let it idle. Danilo was now in her element. She felt it as surely as the blood that coursed through her veins.

Barbara gripped the steering wheel with her left hand while she simultaneously reached for the gearshift lever with her right. She applied a steady pressure to the accelerator with her right foot. Her left foot engaged the clutch. Almost immediately, the Maserati seemed to take off. It was a clean getaway. Barbara made sure not to let the car fishtail as she started forward. It was a smooth and clean break.

As her vehicle moved forward, Barbara eased in the clutch and shifted out of first gear and smoothly moved into second. She did this repeatedly as she increased the speed to the 8CTF. Soon the first curve appeared, and Barbara eased off of the throttle for just a fraction. She expertly guided the car down low at the bottom of the bank and held it steadily and firmly. She did not apply the brake at any time. This was a cardinal rule to even the most inexperienced of drivers. Never apply the brake upon entering a turn or when exiting one.

The 8CTF responded to her deft touch and Barbara felt herself as being as one with the machine. They were in complete and perfect synchronization. Down the straightaways she roared and was a soon hitting speeds in excess of 150 mph. As each lap followed, Barbara kept pressing the envelope. On her fifth and final lap she pushed the car to its utmost, and it responded. She had gone past 160 mph.

The Maserati personnel were all stunned as to what they had just witnessed. This woman had not been intimidated in the slightest. In fact, it had been as if she had taunted all of them. *See, and you all thought I was just a woman. What could I do? Well, there it is! In your face!*

As Barbara guided the car to a stop she caught sight of Pietro Roberti. Earlier, he had informed her almost in passing that should she incur any injuries, she would be responsible for any medical costs. Privately, she had scoffed at the idea. If she had been injured, she would have contacted Marcello Mastrani. Barbara was pretty confident the chairman would have more than gladly covered any such expenses.

Barbara shut down the engine and got out of the car. Pietro Roberti strode up to her, a broad and genuine smile creased his pleasant face.

"Bravo, Barbara! Bravo! I must say that was an impressive performance."

"*Grazie*, Pietro. *Mille grazie*," responded a pleased and radiantly smiling Barbara Danilo as she removed her helmet, her frizzled blonde hair unfurling out into the wind.

"Now, just a word of caution. I cannot guarantee you this will lead to a spot on our Maserati test team. I will inform Chairman Mastrani of your performance," continued Roberti as he now kissed Barbara on both of her cheeks.

"I understand, Pietro. I just want to thank you and all your people for just giving me the chance to show what I could do. I must say this car is a real beauty. It performed beautifully. You know, I felt as if I were one with the machine itself."

* * *

A roadside cafe sat nestled alongside the foothills of the town of Arenzano, just outside Genoa. Though it was mid-September, the weather was damp and cloying. A low drizzle filled the air as two men sat under an awning of the Taverna Rosso. Neither one had any real desire to be there, or to be seen together. The two war-time colleagues, at least for a limited time, sat perched, sipping mid-morning espressos. One of them, facing the street directly constantly craned his neck about, eyes swiveling back and forth. There was a distinct resemblance to a bird.

"I don't see why you had to meet with me here," said a disturbed and unhappy Gianni Ravelli.

143

The man's constant flicking about of his head was beginning to disturb Marco Dubnik. He eyed his companion carefully. "Ravelli, I don't care as to whether you see a need. In my view, I thought it was time that we better coordinate our actions. After all, we're supposed to be working together," said Dubnik patronizingly. He took a brief sip of his coffee and then a drag from his Pall Mall cigarette. "Now, I realize that you consider yourself somewhat of a free-lancer, but nevertheless, you are still beholden to me. You do see it that way, do you not?"

"Marco, we go back a little, but I'm not a flunky of yours, nor should I be treated as one. Now, what is it that you see a need to coordinate that is so important?" Ravelli, at last, sat back and appeared for the first time to be relaxed.

"All right, here it is. I want you to become more engaged directly with these two women. Rossi and…?"

"Danilo."

"Yes, yes, Danilo."

"You say more engaged. In what way?" probed Ravelli.

"I mean, we, or I, need more information on the shipment that was being carried by the Moschilo."

"And you really think these two are your best chance?"

"At present, they have to be. After all, we know that Rosetta Rossi took hold of at least one gold bar. I believe it may well be connected to the shipment. I am convinced she knows more. A lot more. I think you should focus on her, or her family." Dubnik said this in a monotone, but he felt uneasy. He felt as if were losing control of the situation. Not good for a controlling operative to be in.

A loud, smoking Vespa motor scooter rattled by their table. A plume of blue smoke rose in the air. Bloody Italians and their conveyances.

"All right, Marco," said Ravelli in a lowered voice as he leaned forward. "I'll have to move my center of operations to Rome. What about the situation in Genoa?"

"Forget about that for now. I don't anticipate these women of coming back here for the rest of the season. Yes, you should be in Rome," concurred Dubnik.

"By the way, I have heard through the grapevine that you recently fell into some bad luck. One of your associates met a sudden and violent demise."

"Never mind that," said a shaken Marco Dubnik. "That is none of your concern. Is that clear?"

"I seemed to have touched a nerve. I am sorry, Marco. Good help is increasingly hard to find these days. All right, I will relocate to Rome. Oh, by the way, there is that little problem of money…"

"Never mind that, you know you have always been compensated, and rather well at that," Dubnik spat out. All these characters he was associated with always pressed him about money, and more money. Well, it was only to be expected from this assembled list of roguish personalities.

* * *

Meanwhile, a vicious downpour was descending upon Rome. Rosetta Rossi and Barbara Danilo were seated outside the office of Stefano Lucca.

"I take this as a bad omen, Barbara. The last time we were here it was raining cats and dogs. That is the expression Bob uses."

"*Si*, it was, but I don't take it as bad sign. By the way, how is my dear Robert?" Barbara asked her friend.

Rosetta sat beside her, but didn't immediately reply. She wore an expression of emotional pain. She shook her head.

"Rosetta, you know full well you can talk to me at any time. We've known one another for far too long," Barbara continued. She desperately wanted to help her friend, but did not know how at this moment.

"I think I may be losing him. We sometimes barely speak to one another. I know I should tell him about what happened at Vento, but I just can't bring myself to find the words."

"You have to. You'll have to reach inside of yourself and find a way," Barbara said, who now sought a course to change the subject. "By the way, I'm going to contact my old friend, *Comandante* Tenente Enzo Stefani about us taking scuba lessons. How are things progressing as far as acquiring the dive equipment?"

145

Rosetta continued to sit quietly, looking down at her hands which she had twisted together nearly into knots. Finally, Barbara leaned over and touched her hand. Rosetta looked up and murmured, "Oh, yes, well, Bob has made some good progress in getting all the equipment we'll need for our expedition. The Americans have been good to us. We now have enough air tanks, dive masks, suits and fins, but still are in need of two more regulators and breathing hoses. We're supposed to be getting them soon."

"There. You see, Rosetta? You're at least communicating a *little* with your husband. Things must be improving." Barbara smiled brightly.

"*Si*, perhaps just a little," said a doleful Rosetta.

At that moment, Stefano Lucca's secretary appeared before the two women. "Signore Lucca will see you now. Right this way." She led them into Lucca's office.

"Barbara, and Rosetta, what a pleasure it is to see you both again. I only wish the weather was better, but…" exhumed a smiling Lucca.

"*Grazie*, Stefano, *grazie*. By the way, what is the deal as to why we were kept waiting for more than thirty minutes outside of your office?" asked a smiling Barbara, her right eyebrow arched.

"I am so sorry to have had you wait, but I am currently involved with a rather ticklish situation. I'm sure you would understand," Lucca said as he sat back down. The smile had quickly faded.

"Another situation involving a jilted spouse, Stefano?" asked a dubious Danilo.

"No, no, nothing like that."

"*Bene*, you told me over the phone you had some new information for us."

"*Si*, I did. Well, first off," Lucca paused as he cleared his throat, "I have found that our Marco Dubnik has acquired a new friend, or associate. His name is Gianni Ravelli, but that is just an alias. His real name is Heinz Dornhoeffer."

"German?" asked Barbara.

"No, but you 're close. This fellow hails from Liechtenstein."

"Liechtenstein? I once holidayed in the capital city of Vaduz. Charming place."

146

"Yes, well, as I said, this fellow Ravelli worked with Dubnik during the war. It is rumored the two were involved in some sort of operation in Latvia, or maybe it was Yugoslavia."

"What sort of operation?" asked Barbara.

"I was getting to that." Lucca's tone was terse.

"I'm sorry to have interrupted you, Stefano," apologized a chastened Danilo.

"That is quite all right. Anyway, this operation was rumored to have been about gold. Not much is known about this Ravelli, or Dornhoeffer character. He, too, may have been a shady operator. Who knows?" Lucca threw his hands up.

"A double agent?" Rosetta piped in.

"As I have said, but I believe he is a man to be watched. Oh, incidentally, I was able to trace this guy to your stay at the Hotel Brentano when you two had been to Vento Beach."

"And how were you able to do that?" Barbara asked in an exasperated manner.

"Well, yours truly contacted the taverna from where you had made your phone calls. It seems as if the last time that you left, this Ravelli fellow had tailed you, but as you related, you were able to quickly lose him. Well, it seems as if our erstwhile detective rented his vehicle. He probably didn't want to risk any potential police involvement should he have stolen a vehicle. But what was really foolish was that he had signed his own name. That is, he had used his Ravelli name. One thing led to another, and here we are," Lucca concluded.

"Interesting," said both Barbara and Rosetta simultaneously.

"Stefano, you will of course continue to bill me for your services?" asked Rosetta.

"Of course, I will as I have always done. I have not put together a current billing statement as yet, but…"

"Don't screw her, Stefano," warned Barbara Danilo, a scowl crossing her face.

Lucca feigned shock. "I would never do such a thing, Barbara. I am stunned that you would even hint at such a gross thing."

147

"What about this other associate of Dubnik you'd previously mentioned to us? Have you made any progress on that?" again it was Rosetta who had spoken.

Maybe, thought Barbara, *Rosetta is starting to come around.*

"No, I am afraid I haven't. Rest assured, I'm continuing to work on this matter. As soon as I come up with anything, I will let you know."

As Barbara and Rosetta began walking down the stairs from the first floor of Lucca'a building, Rosetta turned to her friend. "I was glad to hear you hadn't crashed your car at the Maserati track and broken some bones."

"There was no way that could happen, Rosetta. No way. I have to tell you it was one of the most exhilarating moments of my life. At times, I felt intuitively connected with the car. There is really no way to adequately describe the experience."

* * *

Former Lieutenant Commander Enzo Stefani of the Italian Supermarina, now employed by the U.S. Navy in its on-going salvaging efforts along the length and breadth of the Italian peninsula, was sitting in the living room of his small home located near Anzio. His wife Angelina was seated nearby, busily knitting away on some afghan blanket. Both Enzo and Angelina were listening to a Sunday afternoon broadcast of some symphony. Stefani was hardly listening to the music, nor did he pay much attention to his two children as they ran in and out of the house. He only hoped that when the kids ventured outside they would be careful. There was still much damage about as the town, as well as the entire Salerno area, was still in the process of digging itself out of the ruins left by the war.

No, Stefani's mind was drifting back to the time of September 1941, when he had been a member of the naval attack team in its operation against the British navy in their supposedly impregnable fortress of Gibraltar Harbor. Three two-man teams, riding aboard specially designed torpedoes, entered the harbor and placed their explosive charges against the hulls of three ships. The results had been spectacular, as two freighters and a Royal Navy tanker were crippled.

148

Subsequently, Enzo Stefani was involved in the planning of another two-man PIG torpedo attack in the harbor of Alexandria, Egypt in 1942. The British battleship, Queen Ann, was sunk as a result.

Those had been heady days for Enzo Stefani and the Supermarina. In 1942, he was promoted to the rank of *Comandante Tenente* (Lt. Cmdr.), but by that time, the end was in sight for the fortunes of Italy. It would be only be a matter of time as to when she would have to quit the war. Her partnership with Nazi Germany had been an unmitigated disaster. Defeat followed defeat for the Italians through 1943. First was the Axis loss of North Africa in May, followed by the Allied invasion of Sicily. This resulted in the fall of Benito Mussolini, il Duce, as the head of state. Upon his being informed by King Victor Emmanuel of his end, he was also told that at time, "You are the most hated man in Italy."

In September 1943, the Americans and British landed on the Italian mainland. The Americans at Salerno, and the British at Reggio de Calabria. Italy immediately sued for peace. Her long national agony was over. Enzo Stefani's war was over as well.

For the past year, Stefani had been able to gain employment with the US Navy in its efforts to clear the country's coastal waters, harbors, and bays of sunken shipwrecks and mines. It was a herculean task. It was something that Stefani relished and he was very grateful for the work. It allowed him to regain some sense of self-worth, and it provided him with a living. There was food on the table and his family had a roof over their heads.

And now, just a few days ago, he had been contacted by an old friend, Barbara Danilo. The woman seemed to know just about everyone in the country. At least, those that were of any consequence. She had mentioned that she and a group of equally physically fit women were anxious to learn about scuba diving. Danilo had not said much beyond that. It had made Stefani curious as to why women would want to take up a pastime which could be dangerous if even the smallest of mistakes were made.

Enzo Stefani offered to travel to Rome to meet with the girls in late September, even though Barbara had insisted they could travel to Anzio. But Stefani had remained firm; he would stop to meet them. And besides, he wanted to see Rome. He would take Angelina, who unbelievably had never once been to the Eternal City. It was all the more remarkable as Anzio was less than thirty miles from Rome. Stefani knew that some people, like Angelina, were absolutely petrified at having to leave their villages, even if it were to be for only a short time. It was parochialism to the extreme. The children would be left in the care of his mother-in-law. It was always a good thing for Stefani when he could put distance between himself and Margareta Santagata.

* * *

Barbara Danilo and Rosetta Rossi had agreed with Enzo Stefani to meet at Orlando's Brasserie on Via Capo d'Africa, virtually across the street from the fabled Colosseum. The hulking monolith was one of the last vestiges of the city's high point in history. Stefani had made sure to arrive before the two women. Orlando's would not ever be considered a fancy place, and certainly not pretentious. It admirably served its main purpose: to provide good food and at a reasonable price and to provide impeccable service. It would never be considered a tourist trap. Massimino Orlando would have spun in his grave if it had done so.

Enzo Stefani sat at his sidewalk table and sipped on his carbonated mineral water. He gazed absentmindedly at the people passing by. Most of them appeared to be business people scurrying about. It was good to see Italy beginning to regain some of her footing. Some of the passers-by were street peddlers, but they were usually shoved away by patrolling police. Stefani also spied some tourists about, oblivious to their surroundings, looking lost with maps in hand, desperately trying to orient themselves. A goodly number carried cameras strung about their necks. Americans were perhaps the easiest of all to pick out.

Around 12:15, Stefani turned to see Barbara and her friend, Rosetta, approaching Orlando's. Barbara, as expected, wore a low-cut cream-colored blouse. She had never been bashful. Rosetta was a degree more modest in her attire, but not by much. What a contrast they presented in comparison with his Angelina. They were avant-garde. Angelina was 19th century.

Barbara rushed up to Stefani as he stood up to greet her. They kissed one another on each cheek.

"Enzo, I must say it is so good to see you again. You are looking well" gushed Barbara. "Enzo, may I introduce you to my old and very dear friend, Rosetta Rossi." Stefani took in the full measure of Rosetta and was immediately taken, not only by her attractiveness and her obvious physically good condition, but by something else. The woman commanded presence.

"It is a pleasure to finally meet you, *Comandante*. I've heard so much about you," said Rosetta, as Stefani bowed slightly and took her hand to bestow a light kiss on it.

Stefani was momentarily tongue-tied as he continued staring at Rosetta. Finally, he was able to clear the lump that had formed in his throat and murmur, "Eh, *prego*, *signora*. Barbara has spoken most fondly of you and very highly. It is indeed a pleasure to meet you at last." Stefani would likely have volunteered to go to the end of the earth to meet Rosetta Rossi.

"I think he likes you, Rosetta," Barbara needled as she took a light poke at Rosetta's arm.

Barbara!" hushed a coloring Rosetta.

As the two sat, Barbara asked about Angelina and the children. Stefani replied with the usual platitudes about being well and fine. Barbara had once met Angelina and had found her to be shrewish and rather dowdy. If she had ever found the time, she might have made a serious attempt at bedding the handsome Italian naval officer.

"You know, Rosetta, this man was a real hero during the war. He along with some of his compatriots attacked several British warships at Alexandria and Gibraltar in these… two-man submarine torpedoes. What were they called, Enzo?" Barbara asked as she leaned forward toward Stefani. She always enjoyed teasing men who were hesitant or shy.

"PIGs, they were called. But that was in name only, I can assure you. They were some of the best naval weapons Italy ever developed," said Stefani self-deprecatingly.

"Indeed, they were," answered Barbara.

"As you said, Enzo… may I call you Enzo?" asked Rosetta. She was warming up to the man more and more by the minute. Maybe it was something more.

Enzo Stefani nodded as he looked at Rosetta. He loved the sound and lilt of her voice. She unknowingly exuded an earthy sexiness. Quickly, he snapped himself out of his clouded state of mind.

"*Si*, I hope to have all of the dive equipment within the next week or so. Later today I'm going to check with my husband to see how things are going. By the way, I am assuming that you have some experience with the American navy's scuba gear?"

"I do, *signora*, er, Rosetta. I have used it extensively in the past six months as I have been assisting the navy's salvaging operations here in Italy. That was an excellent question, by the way," said Stefani, who just couldn't help himself from staring at the woman. He was completely enthralled by her.

"*Bene, bene*, then. We shall contact you again very soon. We can then make more concrete arrangements as to our training at the Metropole pool. I also just want to thank you again for agreeing to take the time to train us."

"You are most welcome, Rosetta. I do have one question for the both of you, and it is, why do you wish to become scuba divers? I mean, don't get me wrong, but it's rather unusual for women, certainly Italian women, to want to undertake something like this. It is or it rather can be dangerous."

It was Barbara who spoke up. "We are tired of being taken as second-class citizens within our own country. Let me tell you something about this woman," as she pointed at Rosetta. "Did you know that during the war this woman put herself, and her family, in extreme danger when she hid numerous American and British prisoners of war? In addition, she performed some hair-raising surveillance of Fascist and German commands and senior military personnel. Rosetta displayed more balls than most of the men that I know. That does not necessarily include you." Barbara sat back and crossed her arms underneath her breasts.

"No, no, I meant no offense. It was just something I was curious about, that's all," Stefani answered defensively. Clearly, these two were a rare breed apart anywhere, let alone 1947 Italy. A thought began to cross his mind. Perhaps, just perhaps, he might be able to engage them with his own Angelina. Maybe they could provide the impetus to bring his wife out of the shadows she now lived in.

* * *

Seated several tables away lurked the ubiquitous Gianni Ravelli, aka Heinz Dornhoeffer and his associate, one Carlo Ragazzo. The two men were furtively sampling a Charcuterie platter containing cheeses and cold cuts. Dornhoeffer was immaculately tailored in his Giorgio Bertoni custom suit. A Bertoni creation had become something of an artifact, or a mark of dubiousness. During the war, Bertoni had been one of il Duce's most ardent and enthusiastic supporters. Following his conviction in June 1946, Bertoni now sat in a Milan jail cell for his crimes of collaboration and malfeasance.

Carlo Ragazzo did not possess the financial resources. nor the wherewithal, to dress in the finery of Ravelli/ Dornhoeffer, but one would not have described him as dressing in threadbare clothing. One would have better characterized him as resembling a bird of prey. The man possessed a hawk-like face, especially the shape and length of his nose. The eyes complemented the rest of his bird-like visage in their piercing sharpness, as if they missed nothing. They seldom had.

"Did you get a picture of them, particularly the man?" asked a pensive and not so happy Gianni Ravelli.

"I did. It was really quite simple when you have the proper equipment," answered Ragazzo smugly, hinting at the miniature camera hidden in the upper lapel of his suit jacket. "I've been meaning to ask you about some remuneration coming my way. I have expenses. I cannot live on air. This has become more of an issue of late, ever since you requested increased surveillance of the subjects." Ragazzo surreptitiously indicated with his dome-shaped head.

"Do not worry. You will get paid. Haven't you always?" an angry Ravelli softly snarled. His own face now resembled someone who had consumed some bad fish.

"*Si, si*, I have been compensated, but the last payment was more than two weeks late."

"Look, don't try to hustle me. You will get paid. Don't forget, we all have our problems. Consider yourself fortunate in that you have a job. Many of the people one sees out and about do not."

CHAPTER EIGHT -
TRANSITION (1947-1948)

Following their mid-day rendezvous with Enzo Stefani, Barbara and Rosetta had hailed a cab to take them back to Rosetta's apartment.

"He likes you, Rosetta, he really does," Barbara remarked as she looked outside the taxi, taking in the Romans scurrying about on the streets and boulevards. It was a long overdue and welcome sight. The veil of doom and uncertainty that had fallen on the city in the wake of Fascism's evisceration was lifting like a departing fog.

"Pfft," Rosetta sputtered in reply. "I don't think so."

"Are you kidding me? You mean you couldn't see how he looked at you? He hung on your every word. I really shouldn't say this, because I really like Enzo, I mean, I admire him for what he and some if his former navy men accomplished, but in truth, his Angelina is really just a plain and dumpy woman. One who is in fear of everything. Did you know that she has never, ever, been to Rome? Can you imagine? Barely thirty miles away. And do you know why? She is just like so many women of her ilk. They just cannot bring themselves to leave their village. Some of them are in fear of even going over the next hill from their village." Barbara turned to face Rosetta.

"I think you may be just a little too harsh, Barbara. I certainly can't make a judgment, as I've never even met the woman. And I don't want to place any false ideas or misconceptions into Enzo's head. I'm grateful for the fact he's going to teach us how to scuba dive."

Barbara had noticed the cab driver glancing more and more frequently at the two of them in his rear-view mirror. She leaned in toward Rosetta and whispered, "Rosetta don't look, but I think our driver is getting his jollies by staring at our artillery. Want to have some fun? Let's pretend we're lesbian lovers. What do you think?"

Rosetta cast a quick glance at the rear-view mirror and, sure enough, the man was helping himself to another eyeful. She whispered back to Barbara, "You can never resist the temptation to seize an opportunity to have some fun. I'm not going to stop you, but don't expect any assistance on my part."

Barbara nodded and then replied aloud, "*Si*, I'm really looking forward to tonight at the Club La Bamba. It should be a good time. There's no telling what or who we might find there." She winked at Rosetta who in turn just rolled her eyes and shook her head. She wore a wry smile on her face.

At the mention of 'Club La Bamba' the driver's eyes widened. The notorious club was known far and wide as a hangout for lesbians and gay men. After this, the man no longer had any further interest taking in any more views of these women.

* * *

Fall was coming to the Eternal City. The air was drier, its stifling summer humidity having departed. Fewer people could be seen lingering around the Colosseum, the Palatine Hill, or the Giardini del Quirinale. It was a rather appropriate backdrop for the meeting between Stefano Lucca and Mauro Guzzo. Both men were seated on a bench set alongside Viale Domus Aurea. Across the street stood the site of Nero's Golden House. To the left of the men loomed the immense shadow of the Colosseum itself. Pigeons loitered about with their incessant bobbing of their heads, looking for any scraps of food cast off by foolish tourists. No sane Roman would do such a wasteful thing.

Mauro Guzzo remembered of how the pigeon population of Rome had practically disappeared during the war. If veal and pork dishes had virtually vanished from people's dinner tables and all that was left, they, one might say, had been supplemented by the venerable and disgusting bird.

"I'm glad you could meet with me today, Mauro. I thought it might be time we met," announced Stefano Lucca affably. The private investigator was leaning toward Guzzo. He was wearing an off-white not quite khaki colored trench coat opened at the collar. Its lapels blew out with the rustle of the wind. Naturally, he was smoking one of his foul-tasting and foul-smelling Gauloise cigarettes.

"*Si*, I am glad you asked me as well. I must say, I found you to be somewhat surreptitious when we spoke," replied Mauro Guzzo, who for once was not smoking a cigarette. He wore a dark brown woolen sweater accompanied by tan wool slacks. His legs were crossed, his Salvatore Ferragamo calf-skinned loafers highlighted.

"Well, let me get straight to the point. I think that Barbara and her friend, Rosetta Rossi, may be getting into something that is over their heads. And by that, I mean dangerous," continued Lucca, his eyes boring into Guzzo's.

"Well, I know the Church and some other rather influential people here in Rome are not too happy about their little athletic club, but—"

"Forget that, Guzzo. That's child's play. What I am talking about is far more dangerous. Sinister and unsavory characters are entering the picture," Lucca paused for effect. "Look, I'm a private detective and supposed to maintain some degree of confidentiality concerning my clients, and Barbara and the Rossi woman are clients. Nevertheless, I felt I could no longer remain silent. Barbara, I know, is a free spirit. She always has something to prove. Believe me, I know. And I am sure that you would acknowledge this as well. I am counting on Rosetta Rossi to instill some level of commonsense. Do you understand?"

Mauro did not reply right away as he contemplated what Stefano Lucca had just told him. "This time, I am not so sure that it's Barbara who is the impetuous one. From my perspective, I think it may well be Rosetta who is the driving force. Were you aware that Rosetta Rossi was attacked by a mysterious skin-diver off Vento Beach not too long ago? She told Barbara

157

she'd been able to fend off her assailant. As to Barbara herself, what can I say? She has a mind of her own and will do whatever she's determined to do. She's headstrong, and always has been. I don't think I could influence her and, by extension, Rosetta Rossi to put aside or to forget about this gold thing. I am assuming you know about that and that is what you have been obliquely referring to?"

"*Si*," said Stefano Lucca as he nodded. "Yes, I know. And, you mentioned Barbara's wild streak. She, or rather Rosetta, informed me of Barbara's attempt to become a Maserati test driver."

"So you know what I am up against," conceded Guzzo.

"*Si*, I know, and believe me, I understand," replied Lucca. He didn't mention anything about Maserati's chairman of the board, Marcello Mastrani, and rumors of dalliances between him and Barbara. It would break Guzzo's heart.

* * *

It was October before Rosetta Rossi had procured all the scuba equipment that would be required for herself, Barbara, Ann Carter, and Ariana. On an overcast Saturday, the four women were assembled before former Lt. Commander Enzo Stefani. Along the edge of the Metropole pool, he looked them over and what he observed he was more than impressed with. All of them were in superb physical condition. In fact, the musculature each of them displayed was more impressive than could be found on most military men he had seen. Even Ariana Rossi effected a superb and well-toned body. She was slightly taller than her mother, but her upper body was fully developed. Also like her, she was large breasted, the glands mounted firmly on her chest. Her upper arms and thighs looked as if they could pulverize anything, human or inanimate, placed between them. Stefani called them to attention.

"A moment, girls, if you please," Stefani commanded as he clapped his hands together. "*Bene*. Let me say that it's a privilege to be here today to help instruct you all on scuba diving. Just out of curiosity, does anyone know what the acronym SCUBA stands for?"

"*Si*, Commander, I do," piped up Ariana. "It stands for self-contained underwater breathing apparatus!"

"Indeed, it does, Ariana. Very good."

Ariana allowed herself a small smile, but secretly she was more than just a little pleased.

Her mother, Rosetta, could not help but allow herself a grin. How far Ariana had come within the past year. All had once seemed lost, the gulf between them all but unbridgeable.

"Very well," continued Stefani. "Normally, I would require you to show me your competence and stamina in the water. For example, you would have to tread water for about one hour. And then, I would have you swim several laps in the pool. I can clearly see that all of you are in peak, physical condition. And, two of you," Stefani looked directly at Rosetta and Barbara, "have already proven yourselves as being very adept in the water."

Both Rosetta and Barbara blushed slightly at the compliment. The young Englishwoman, Ann Carter, continued to stare straight ahead. Stefani noticed and hoped he had not offended her.

"*Si*, well then. Let us proceed. I would like to explain some of your scuba equipment and their functions." Stefani picked up a dive mask. "This is the dive mask which, as you can see, contains this black rubber flap at the base. This will allow you to clear any water which may accumulate inside the mask. The mask has a snorkel tube attached to it. Some divers prefer to wear it for snorkeling purposes. Others don't like to use it when diving. They feel it interferes with their diving. It is up to you as to whether to use it or not," Stefani paused to let some of this sink in. All the women were paying rapt attention to his presentation. There was no kidding around; all of them were there to learn. Even Barbara Danilo, who could be well expected to crack a joke or two. But not today.

"Very well, we shall continue. These are, of course, diving fins," said Stefani as he held up a pair in his right hand. "They are self-explanatory. This is your weight belt. I will show you how best to place it upon your bodies as you outfit yourselves. And now, we come to the *piece-de-resistance*, the air tank. This piece of equipment will literally be your lifeblood. It is the most critical apparatus you will use," Stefani went on patiently. He showed them the tank itself with its gaseous mix of oxygen and nitrogen, the regulator and the air hose and mouthpiece.

"*Bene*, I don't want to overwhelm you all with too much detail. Feel free at any time to ask me a question. All right, I would now like each of you to don your equipment and we shall proceed." Stefani carefully watched how each of the women placed the various items on. He was surprised to see that Ariana had finished first. She seemed a natural for scuba. Rosetta and Barbara soon finished. The English-woman put on her equipment diligently and correctly. There would be no need to worry about any of these women.

For the next two hours, Enzo Stefani instructed and corrected them in the art of scuba diving. All performed well. In fact, better than he had expected. None were above any corrections he had suggested to them. Stefani concluded the session with a lesson on how to assist a fellow diver in distress. He told them he hoped none of them would ever have to carry out these measures in real life. However, it was imperative that each of them learn what had to be done in the event of an emergency.

Stefani would continue with the scuba lessons for the next several weekends. By that time, he had no doubt all the women would become totally proficient in all aspects of underwater diving.

* * *

In many ways it was to be a new beginning for Bob Rossi. For the past few months he had begun working for the American Graves Registration Command (AGRC). The organization had been created in 1945 and was responsible for the location, identification, and interment of remains of American military personnel who had fallen in battle in World War II.

For more than one hundred years, the United States military had been committed to the recovery and identification of its war dead. Improvements in the process had been on-going since the Civil War and on through the Spanish-American War. It had continued through the First World War where it had achieved unprecedented success. The unit had confirmed the need for a special service to perform the task of graves registration if the dead were to be recovered quickly, thereby maximizing identification.

Bob Rossi was now intimately involved in the recovery and concentration of isolated and unrecorded burials and unburied remains. European search and recovery missions were being accomplished by area sweeps, each of which was carried out in three phases. Rossi had been designated to be a member of a phase one team. These three-man teams were tasked with visiting communities in a given area and handing out posters which described the search and recovery operation. These men would also urge local people to come forward with any information they might have regarding places that might contain American dead.

The solid, block-style black telephone jangled on Rossi's desk. He reached for it unconsciously with his left hand while simultaneously scanning a document with his right. "Rossi, American command center."

"Ah, Signore Rossi, *buon giorno*. This is Georgio Finalmente. Would you have a moment?"

Bob Rossi straightened up in his chair. The paperwork he had been so engrossed with only a moment before now forgotten. "Yes, *si, si*, I have," responded Rossi, his heart starting to skip a beat. He felt a nervousness he hadn't experienced since he had been in battle in North Africa.

"Ahh, Bob, I think that we should meet. I don't want to alarm you, but I think you may be pleased by what I have to tell you. I suggest we meet some time this week. Let us say at a cafe. What do you think?" asked the detective.

Almost at once Bob Rossi felt a feeling of immense relief, yet one of anxiety. On the one hand, Finalmente wanted to meet with him personally. On the other, he had what he thought was good news. What to make of that.

The two men agreed to meet two days hence at 10:00 AM at Ruffino's, a small, out of the way cafe on Via Gregoriana. At first mention of it, Rossi had a twinge of panic, as this was not that far from his and Rosetta's home on Via Frattina. But he agreed to meet there with Finalmente at the appointed hour.

Georgio Finalmente saw that Bob Rossi must be clearly anxious as he joined him at Ruffino's and upon learning that the American had already been there for half an hour. He hoped he would be able to assuage the man's underlying fear. Although Rossi had not come out directly and said it, he had conveyed the idea that he thought, or at least strongly suspected

161

his wife might be having an affair. After the two had exchanged greetings and pleasantries, Finalmente came straight to the point.

"I know you didn't say so directly, I have the distinct feeling you suspect your wife may have been having an affair. I can put that suspicion to rest, Signore Rossi. I could never find anything to support this. And believe me, I employed every trick I knew." Bob

Rossi was visibly relieved at this news. His face started to break out into a broad smile. This was quickly dashed by the detective's next words.

"However, I did uncover some interesting information concerning your wife during her excursion up the coast earlier this year." Finalmente paused for effect. He also chose the moment to light a cigarette and to order a double expresso from the passing waiter. Bob Rossi declined on both counts. "Yes, as I was saying, I was able to find out from the local magistrate that one day when your wife was diving or swimming, she was attacked by a frogman-like figure. It seems as if she may have discovered something significant. At least, that is what the police superintendent suspects."

The news more or less confirmed what Rossi himself had long suspected and feared. He was relieved but he was also very upset with Rosetta for having gone diving alone. He had advised her to at the least be accompanied by someone like Barbara Danilo. She should never have gone out by herself. Rossi thanked Finalmente, told him his check would be in the mail, and sat back, contemplating how he would approach his wife about this development. Should he even approach Rosetta, or should he wait for her to tell him herself?

* * *

"How was your day, dear?" asked Rosetta in a soft, lilting voice as she stood by the sideboard.

"Oh, you know, just another day," replied a cautious Bob Rossi. He didn't dare reveal a thing about his rendezvous with Georgio Finalmente. To have told Rosetta anything, or even hint at the fact he had hired a private detective would have doomed their already fragile relationship.

In the early evening light that remained, Rosetta continued to linger by the sideboard. She wasn't sure as to how she should proceed with her conversation with her husband. How had things come to this, when she had to be so cautious and tentative in the midst of a casual conversation with the very person she was ostensibly the closest to.

"Rosetta, I have been giving a lot of thought to…" Bob stalled. Rosetta stood in abject fear as to what she thought she was about to hear. "I think it is best that I leave it to you. What I am trying to say…" again Bob hesitated. "is when you decide to tell me what may have happened at, you know, when you last went up to Vento Beach, I will let you decide when you shall tell me."

Rosetta knew the moment had come. She would have to tell Bob about her being attacked. She could no longer keep it hidden. "Bob, I've been terrible. It hasn't been fair to you for all of these weeks, these months." Rosetta paused, trying desperately to find the right words and to say them in the right way. Perspiration broke out upon her worried face. "You see, when I was swimming at Vento I was… I was attacked by a frogman. I guess that's the best way to describe my assailant. I was able to fight him off. I knew you would be furious with me. You have said many times not to go alone." Rosetta gripped the sideboard tightly with both hands. She started to feel herself sway, her head was becoming light-headed. She thought she might well keel over.

Bob sat silently for the moment, almost blurting out that he already had known of the attack. Instead, he said, "I only wish you had told me earlier. It seems as if a wall has gone up between us. Something that has never happened before in the time we have been married."

"I know, and I was wrong to have done this to you. It wasn't your fault at all. I know this has hurt you very deeply. You have to forgive me," Rosetta implored, her eyes nearly tearing up.

"You know, I am not against you going up there and swimming and diving," Bob waved his hand in the air, "but next time, please go with someone, such as Barbara. It would make me feel better. Okay?"

"You're right. It won't happen again." Rosetta reached over for the bottle of Mt. Blanc cognac and poured generous helpings into two cut-glass crystal tumblers.

"I'm glad you weren't hurt. You were lucky." *My, she is breaking out the good cognac,* marveled Bob Rossi. "This is turning out to be a special occasion."

"Indeed, it is. And after we have had our drinks, we shall indulge ourselves in rapturous and pleasurable sex," said Rosetta as she handed a glass to Bob.

He took it and together they toasted one another. Rosetta moved next to Bob on the sofa, put down her glass, and moved right next to him. She looked straight into his hazel-colored eyes and kissed him softly. Bob responded. Rosetta then inserted her tongue and reached down to touch his crotch. He was coming to a rapid boil. She stood up and taking his hand, led him to their bedroom.

"What about Ariana and Marco?" asked Bob.

"Don't worry, my love. Both will not be back home for some time," Rosetta husked in his ear as her hand tightened within his.

Rosetta began disrobing slowly. She removed her blouse and bra, knowing this would stir her husband. Bob marveled at the sight of her magnificent breasts. Her stomach, because of her strenuous workouts, was a flat surface that rippled with horizontally aligned muscles. Next, off came her skirt and panties. Rosetta's thighs were ripped heavily. The muscles bulged.

Bob was rapidly hardening and almost tripped over himself as he took off his trousers. This elicited a small laugh from Rosetta as she patiently waited. She teasingly knew she was increasing Bob's desire.

Both came together and embraced. Fevered French kissing was followed by a long and patient foreplay. Rosetta allowed Bob to linger over her mound and when she was ready for him, allowed him entry. All the passion and tension and drive, just so recently absent from their lives, had suddenly returned. Both madly wanted and desired one another. As Bob drove himself into Rosetta, she spoke the words she had been unable to utter for a long time.

"I love you, Bob. I love you and giving my all to you now." Rosetta gripped her husband fiercely.

Rossi, heavily engaged in his maniacal assault upon Rosetta's body, was able to pause by her right ear," I love you, too, my dear. I always have."

"I know, I know," oozed a falling Rosetta. She then brought her powerful legs up and took hold of Bob's body like she never had before. She squeezed her thighs for all she was worth. And Bob responded in kind by increasing his pace. For Rosetta it went on and on as if there would be no end.

* * *

"I'm so glad you could join me here this evening, Barbara," said an enthused Marcello Mastrani.

"It's my pleasure, Marcello," replied a buoyant and bright Barbara Danilo as she peeled off her clothes. "I must say that was a very lovely meal. It was just right. Not too light and not too heavy." Barbara was alluding to the fact that they would be engaging themselves in some heavy sex.

Mastrani laid back on his sumptuous and ornately trimmed king-sized bed, one made personally for him and his amorous activities. He was already naked and primed for action. He avidly observed his paramour for the evening as she had disrobed. The woman's body was positively breathtaking and stunning at the same time. Her rock-hard stomach. The flare of Barbara's powerfully developed thighs. Mastrani had to admit, she was better in bed than nearly all the younger women he habitually consorted with.

Barbara joined him in bed and they soon set to work. Mastrani immediately took control of the situation and paid expressed attention to the foreplay he used for this occasion. When he knew Barbara was ready, he slowly and lingeringly entered her. Soon, he was humping madly and rapidly. Mastrani welcomed the feel of Barbara's legs around his plunging body as she brought them to bear.

"Marcello, you are truly a wonder to any woman. I have to say that you are the best lover I have ever had," Barbara said as she shared a cigarette with her lover. Barbara never smoked with the exception of a night that involved heightened carnal fulfillment.

"You are being too kind, my love," Mastrani said deprecatingly. "I have to admit that you are one of my best lovers. And I really do mean it. Your passion and intensity, your strength and stamina, are something to behold."

"Marcello? I have to tell you something," Barbara halted for a moment. "I think… I think that I'm falling in love with you."

"No, my sweet, I do not think so," replied a now pensive Marcello Mastrani. "I think you're in love with my body and the sex we have in this bed. But that's not true love," he continued. "I think it might be best if you returned to Mauro. He can provide what is best for you and what you really need from a man."

Barbara laid back, remaining silent, and then nodded her head, as much to herself as him. "Yes, yes, perhaps you are right. I hadn't thought of things in that light before."

"*Bene*. You know, despite all that I have here," Mastrani spread his hands. "I'm really a lonely man. It's not easy to possess all that I have here through the company and then to maintain a life with some semblance of normality."

Barbara did not speak again for a while. She got up from the bed and went over to the sideboard table in the room where she poured out two glasses of Ouzo and brought them back to Mastrani. They toasted one another. Barbara luxuriated in the taste and the feel of the liquid as it went down her throat.

Mastrani excused himself and proceeded to the small lavette off to the side of his bedroom. Undoubtedly, Barbara thought to prepare himself for another round with her. When he returned, she thought he appeared to be slightly flushed in his face. She soon put this out of her mind as he got back into bed and enveloped her.

Sex this time around was much more animalistic. Mastrani virtually attacked her body and she willingly surrendered herself to the assault. At her moment of supreme climax, Mastrani poured more of himself into Barbara's body. She had clamped her legs around his torso and squeezed for dear life. Barbara had to admit to herself that she was holding on.

Finally, Marcello Mastrani released himself and let out a loud bellow as he ejaculated. Barbara felt his rage throughout her entire body. Suddenly, Mastrani just stopped. He did not move. He was just lying atop Barbara, who was at a complete loss as to what had just happened.

"Marcello? Marcello? What is it?" she practically screamed out loud in alarm. After struggling to free herself from under him, she turned to look down. His face was a blank mask, his eyes open, but unseeing. "*Oh, my God*! He's had a heart attack!" Barbara screamed to herself. Immediately she started CPR, first by breathing into Mastrani's mouth and then after no response, she began pushing down on his chest with both of her hands. Thirty times for thirty seconds. Nothing. The man was dead.

Quickly, she grabbed a bed sheet and wrapped it around herself and called out, "Arturo! Arturo! Come here, quickly! It is an emergency!"

Barbara then heard a soft knock on the bedroom door and Arturo De Giovanni's bald head appeared. "You need something, *signora*?"

"*Si, si*, I do indeed. I think Signore Mastrani has had a heart attack. I tried to revive him, but nothing," Barbara said as a palpable fear gripped her. She was sitting on the side of the bed and moved her hands in a helpless gesture.

"*Si*, I can see that, *signora*," said a distraught and shaken De Giovanni. "All right, I will take care of everything. Do not worry. I suggest that you dress and I will have you driven to your home. I will contact the authorities."

* * *

Within the hour, Carabinieri detectives had arrived at Marcello Mastrani's villa following De Giovanni's frantic call. Chief Inspector Aldo Moretti perused the scene before him. A white bed sheet covered the remains of Mastrani. Moretti lifted one corner and observed traces of semen along the penis and inner thighs. The inspector noted the impressive physique of the famous Italian magnate. It was truly impressive for a man of Mastrani's age. But in the end, it had not prevented him from succumbing to what looked to have been a massive heart attack. Mastrani's face had frozen into what Moretti took to be one of perplexity. How could he, Marcello Mastrani, have a heart attack?

"Inspector, this looks to be rather straightforward," said Moretti's assistant Lieutenant Luigi Cardoso. "Subject had apparently been sexually engaged with a… Barbara Danilo," continued Cardoso as he consulted his notepad.

"Mmm… it would appear so, Cardoso," murmured Moretti, who now surveyed the bedroom with a renewed scrutiny. Nothing appeared out of place. A tangle of bedsheets and covers cast about. *Mastrani must have had a good time for himself with this woman*, the inspector thought to himself. There was nothing that made it seem as if something untoward had occurred. Everything pointed simply to two people having engaged in sex. For one of them, Mastrani, it had resulted in his last act. "Did De Giovanni have anything to add? Any indication of a struggle of any kind? Did he hear of any shouting or raised voices?" continued Moretti.

"No, Inspector. he did not."

"I only wish he hadn't dispatched this Danilo woman so soon. I would like to ask her a few questions."

"He only said he had wanted to spare or to minimize what had transpired for the woman."

"Mmm, that was admirable on his part. Luigi, I would like for you to go and see this…"

"Barbara Danilo." "

"S*i*, Barbara Danilo at her home tomorrow. You know what to ask her. Let's see if there is any additional light that can be shed on this event," Moretti said as he swung his arm in a wide arc.

"*Si*, Inspector. It shall be done."

"Oh, Luigi, let's keep as tight a lid as possible on this for as much time as possible. When the news hits the streets, the press will run wild. You can just imagine a man like Mastrani meeting his demise while having had sex. I only hope he had a good last ride here tonight."

* * *

"You can just imagine what was running through my mind. I mean, only moments before we'd been humping away as if there were no tomorrow.

Mastrani was really giving it to me, and then poof, he was gone." Barbara Danilo was explaining her night with Marcello Mastrani to Rosetta Rossi.

Rosetta was sitting in Barbara's elegantly decorated living room, sipping on espresso and munching on some anisette cookies. She could scarcely believe the story that Danilo was relating to her. Of course, she had had to embellish it with a comment on the ferocity of their liaison. No matter, it had been a stunning story.

"I can't believe it, Barbara. He was… well, he was past seventy, but from how you've described him, it still seems inconceivable. But why did Arturo De Giovanni virtually throw you out of there?" Rosetta's eyebrows knitted closer together.

"He said he would take care of everything. He wanted to spare me any further indignity. I think that was how he put it," she said, not quite believing it herself. "That's probably why the police, the Carabinieri, want to talk with me today. In fact, a Lieutenant Cardoso is due at any time. He said he had a few questions to ask of me. All routine, of course,"

"Well, I'm sure it is. I don't think they could possibly believe you had a hand in his death," replied Rosetta.

"I suppose you're right, but what if they do suspect something? Maybe I should have gotten a lawyer before I agreed to sit down with this Lieutenant Cardoso." Barbara sat back, now questioning herself. "I tell you, Rosetta, I still can't believe it. One moment we're screwing like animals, and the next, well, he's dead. I guess he just came to the end of his run."

Rosetta still sat transfixed and was at a loss as the passing of the great Marcello Mastrani. Gone, just like that. She knew he'd been over seventy years of age, but still, it was a shock. "I'm stunned. I don't know what else to say. I think I would have screamed to the heavens if it had happened to me."

"*Si*, I still can't get over it. Poor man. He was so vibrant. And Rosetta, it was the best sex I've ever had. And that takes some doing."

"What do you think it may mean as far as you driving for Maserati?" Rosetta questioned. "Do you think they'll still let you?" Privately, Rosetta was hopeful it would mean the end of her friend's hair-brained idea. But she would not ever say it to Barbara. The woman had really set her heart on it.

"I don't know. I honestly do not know. Undoubtedly, some within the Maserati hierarchy will see this as an opportunity to squash it, and me," Barbara said as she now bounced around the spacious room.

Rosetta glanced around and although she had been to Barbara's home many times, she always marveled at the furnishings and artwork the woman had acquired. The home was not overly ostentatious, but it was truly elegant. Most of the rooms were painted white, and yet they didn't reflect a sterile atmosphere.

The doorbell chimed, announcing a visitor to see Barbara Danilo. "Oh, that must be Lieutenant Cardoso of the Carabinieri," Barbara said.

"Do you wish for me to leave?" asked Rosetta.

"No, no, please stay. I think I may need you for moral support." She went over to the mirror situated next to a china hutch. Barbara wanted to make sure she looked her best for the detective.

"*Signora* Danilo, it's a pleasure to meet with you. I only wish it were under more pleasant circumstances," apologized the youthful detective.

"Oh, I understand, *Tenente*. Please, call me Barbara, and this is one of my oldest and dearest friends, Rosetta Rossi,". She liked what she saw and felt in the young man. Dark wavy hair and a rather pleasant face with a firm set to his jaw. Barbara also noted how well Cardoso filled out his tan woolen suit.

"This is really just a formality, you understand. It shouldn't take long."

"Please, do sit down. I want you to feel comfortable. Can I offer you anything? Perhaps some tea or a libation?"

Cardoso began to feel himself color. The woman, despite her age, oozed sexuality. "No, no, I am... well, I am fine," said a now flustered and momentarily tongue-tied Luigi Cardoso. The sheer electricity and vibrancy that radiated off Barbara Danilo caused the hairs on his arms to stand up. Indeed, she must have provided Marcello Mastrani with quite a send-off. The young man took in Danilo's hairstyle, her crystal blue eyes, and her impressive cleavage.

For the next twenty minutes, Luigi Cardoso had Barbara describe her last night with Marcello Mastrani. Rosetta sat by quietly as she listened to Barbara relate her testimony to the detective. Occasionally, she confirmed some point or two that Barbara had made.

"Well, I believe that covers about everything for now," concluded Cardoso.

"You don't think someone in higher authority may have a preconceived idea in relation to me, do you, *Tenente*?" asked a now cautious Barbara Danilo.

"No, no, you should not consider yourself as someone who is under suspicion. I think this is simply a case of… well, a case of an older man here who had an unfortunate end. I thank you for your time, *signora*. I will see myself out." Cardoso got up to leave but paused just before he got to the door. "Ah, *signora*, it may come up that I will have some follow-up questions. But do not be concerned. This is strictly routine."

* * *

The two men were ensconced in Pietro Roberti's plush office at Maserati's test track in Bologna. It was late in November and the weather had started to turn a bit chillier and darker in the northern Italian city of some seventy-five thousand. Low scudding clouds crisscrossed the skies outside the windows of Roberti's office. Seated across from Roberti was Ernesto Forti, the newly installed chairman of the board.

Roberti and Forti were engaged in some routine business matters when the subject of Barbara Danilo came up. "Now, Pietro, about this Danilo woman. Do we really want or even need a woman as a test driver here at Maserati?" questioned a skeptical and none too pleased Ernesto Forti.

Roberti looked across his desk at the sixty-five-year old man, being careful to couch his words. How could he best frame things to Forti? After all, Barbara Danilo had proven herself to him and to the other Maserati drivers and personnel. She was good and she belonged. "Well, sir, Marcello Mastrani did sign off on her being accepted. And she did prove that she could handle our vehicle expertly. I mean, I was there to witness it. I have to say that it was a most impressive performance."

"Ehh, *si*, Mastrani accepted her. Probably because she'd been fucking his brains out. The woman practically, no, maybe she did kill him on the night that he expired," said an unimpressed Forti.

171

"Well, sir, how do you want to handle things? Do you wish for me to just flat-out tell her that she can't become a driver, or?" Roberti let his words hang in the air. He began to notice a knot forming in the pit of his stomach.

Forti remained rooted in his chair, his face impassive, giving off no visible clue as to his thoughts. "No, I tell you what, Pietro. Tell her that I've been giving it a lot of careful consideration and have decided I would like to see her behind the wheel for myself here in Bologna. Tell her the I'll allow her to drive again at some time in the new year. Let us say around... oh, I don't not know. Let's say in March or April. While I'm here, why don't you go ahead and call her."

Roberti nodded and placed a call to Barbara Danilo at her office in Rome.

"Ahh, Pietro, so nice to hear from you. How are you, dearest?" cooed Barbara in a near falsetto voice.

Roberti thought the woman may be mocking him. He was glad Forti could not hear her end of the conversation. "I am well, Barbara. The reason for my call is to tell you that our new chairman, Signore Ernesto Forti, has decided that he would like to see you drive again for us here at Bologna, some time in the new year around March or April. What do you say?"

"Well, Pietro, I'm a little disappointed to hear that. I do suppose I should be glad that Signore Forti didn't flat out turn down my request to be a driver. Does he not believe I'm qualified? Did I not show you my competence and ability just a short time ago?"

"Yes you did, my dear Barbara. Believe me, I have backed you up all the way. It's just that Signore Forti wants to take a little more diligent approach to this matter. You can understand that, can you not?"

"Ernesto Forti is seated in front of you right now, is he not, Pietro?" asked a now slightly peeved Barbara Danilo. She broke a pencil in two she had been holding.

"No, no, Barbara. Believe me, things will work out for you. So, is next year all right with you?" asked Roberti defensively. Forti continued to look on impassively.

"Yes, I suppose it is," conceded a deflated but accepting Danilo.

"*Bene, bene*. You will see it will be for the best. Just remain patient."

"All right, Pietro, as you say. Thank you for having the courtesy to call me with the news. *Ciao*."

* * *

Rosetta and Bob Rossi invited many of their close relatives and friends to their New Year's Eve party on the thirty-first. The year of 1947 was coming to a close. For the holiday makers, it represented the ushering in of a new year. Memories of the war were slowly receding into the background of their lives. The new year would hopefully bring forth a further renewal of hope and confidence.

Around 11:00 PM, Rosetta had become engaged with Captain Phillip Anderson of the British Army. The captain was also the boyfriend of Ann Carter. The two had been dating for the better part of the year. Rosetta observed he was of medium height and build. Brown, somewhat wavy hair sat atop his head. Clear blue eyes and a narrow aquiline nose characterized his face. In short, he was a most handsome young man. The Italian woman had been pleased to see the contentment and joy the relationship he had brought Ann.

"How much longer do you anticipate being posted to Rome, Captain?" asked Rosetta pleasantly.

"That's rather hard to say. I think it will probably be through 1948. At least, that's what I'm hopeful for," Anderson replied as he held a glass of champagne in his right hand.

"Well, that's good news. I'm sure that will be pleasing to Ann."

"Yes, I'm sure it will be," Anderson agreed as he scanned the crowded room. He was probably looking for Ann.

"You know, and I surely don't have to tell you, but she is a fine young woman. You're fortunate to have found her. And, of course, she is lucky to have found you."

"Yes, and don't I know it. I didn't think it would ever happen again for me." Anderson had a wistful and almost pained look set upon his face. "You see, I was married once before and… well," the young man hesitated.

Rosetta imagined he was about to tell her of it not having worked out. But the next words Anderson told her left Rosetta stunned.

"You see, my first wife, Nancy, was killed during a German bombing raid over Coventry in 1941, and that was not all," Anderson stammered, tears were welling up in his eyes. "You see, we had a little girl, Pamela. She was only two years old and…and…"

Rosetta's heart broke at the anguish and pain that resided within this man. She didn't know what to say. What could she say? So many people, so many families, so many friends had been lost. "I am so sorry, Captain. I didn't know. I don't know what to say. So many of us here tonight have suffered because of the war. I lost my own husband in North Africa. To this day, I have still not gotten over it," Rosetta said as she, too, felt tears come to her own eyes. She reached out and touched the younger man's sleeve and gave it a gentle squeeze.

Barbara Danilo had been standing nearby and had overheard the conversation between Rosetta and the British captain. When she heard the part of the man's mention of the deaths of his wife and small child, she had winced. It seemed as if there would always be remembrances and sad, pitiful stories of what had happened to this one or to that one of their family members or friends.

Later, after Phillip Anderson had left Rosetta to join Ann Carter, Barbara had sidled over to her friend. "You know, Barbara, I don't think I'll ever not hear the end of such heartbreaking stories. People who have never been through a war, those who have never suffered the loss of a loved one, or those who have never witnessed the life blood flow out from another human being's life can ever understand."

"Yes, you're right. But we do have to move on, do we not?" asked Barbara in a soft, compassionate voice. She gently embraced her friend and then brought her champagne glass up to Rosetta's in a silent, unspoken toast. The two women, lifelong friends, noticed the clock on the wall and saw that only thirteen more minutes remained to 1947. The subject of gold had receded for the moment, but would resume itself in 1948 when the women would dive.

CHAPTER NINE-
STATUS QUO

The year 1948 began in much the same way that 1947 had ended. Rosetta Rossi continued her day-to-day work for the Allied Military Government of Occupied Territory (AMGOT), performing largely translational services for those civilians still in need. Her husband, Bob, had now continued his own duties for the Graves Registration Command. This often required him to travel throughout the length and breadth of the Italian peninsula. Still, he always tried to spend as much time as possible with his adopted family in Rome.

"We're going to be losing Barbara Dwaritz soon," said Rosetta to Barbara Danilo as each worked out on a piece of weight-lifting apparatus on the gym floor.

"I suppose we had to expect this would happen," lamented Danilo. She was seated on a bench, arm-pressing forty-pound weights in each hand. A light sheen of perspiration bathed her face and body.

"*Si*, that is true. She feels she has to be with her people in the new Israel. I can't say I blame her. I'd probably do the same thing if I were in her place," replied Rosetta, who was going through repetitions of one hundred-pound arm-curls set on a bar. Her arm muscles tightened to their maximum each time she curled the bar up to her chest.

"She will be missed. The poor girl has already been through the mill, what with the war and all," continued Barbara.

"That is true. She has lost just about all her family in the Holocaust. Those Nazi bastards." Rosetta spat out the words, as if she had encountered a bitter taste.

"Hey, Rosetta, look over there. Look at Franchi. She's been hefting some impressive iron of late, don't you think?"

Rosetta paused for a moment from her workout to gaze at Maria Franchi on the other side of the gymnasium. The woman was just finishing up some leg-press curls. The thigh muscles on Franchi's legs bulged in the half light. She next proceeded to a horizontal bar about seven feet off the ground. Maria Franchi then began a series of two-arm pull-ups. She would go on to run through a series of one-arm pull-ups.

"Good for her. And to think less than a year ago this was a woman who was so shy, so meek. I'm really glad for her," concluded Rosetta with real pride and admiration in her voice.

"Yes, yes, she has indeed come a long way. And she tells me she has also improved her sex life with her husband. I'm proud to say I may have had a hand in that," Barbara said as she continued with her own heavy lifting.

"You would, Barbara. You would."

"Speaking of one's sex life, I take it things have improved for you and Bob?"

"Indeed, they have. It seems as if a great weight has been lifted off the both of us. We're even having sex several times each week," Rosetta said.

To Barbara it sounded flat, nearly unemotional. She wondered if Rosetta was just glossing things over. "Only several times?" teased Barbara. "I'm just kidding. That's *molto bene*, Rosetta. *Molto bene*!"

* * *

Late March was a peculiar time of year for those in residence in Genoa. Peculiar in the sense that one was never quite sure whether winter had truly relinquished its grip or that spring had taken hold. For Marco Dubnik, prospects were in a confused state of flux. He was unsure as to whether he was moving forward in terms of locating a definite fix on the Moschilo's gold, or whether he was merely standing in place.

It was not a good position to be in for a person such as himself. Dubnik felt he was once again being cast in the role of a triple agent, much as he had been in the Second World War. He had the Germans, his, more or less direct masters on the one hand, and the personages of Fabrizio Valpone and his erstwhile associate, or lackey, in Cesare Puglio. The third element if one could call it that, was the presence and involvement of the Church. Dubnik considered *Cardinale* Maggione a minor irritant, but one that had to be accounted for and factored into the eventual equation.

Marco Dubnik was sitting in a plain, black-leathered armchair in his third-class *pensione*-style hotel and pensively reviewing his options. Should he go forward in pursuit of this heretofore elusive gold? Or should he fold up operations and tell all interested parties there was nothing to the rumor of a vast gold cache. It just might satisfy Valpone and his Mafia associates. And he could well disappear into the vast and deep woodwork of European political circles.

Marco Dubnik's main concern and problem would come about where the Germans were concerned. The East German secret police equivalent was virtually identical to a previously sinister and deadly operation, the SS and its Gestapo subsection. High-ranking police personnel were aware of what Dubnik was up to, and two of those individuals had a direct stake in the operation's outcome.

Shadows began to fall in the late afternoon Genoese sun as Dubnik silently contemplated his options. In his mind, he was compiling a matrix of pros and cons concerning the gold. That infernal commodity. What was so bloody alluring about it? He was also desperately trying to rack his brain as to what he could possibly take from his previous espionage experiences in Yugoslavia and Italy just four short years before.

In a clearing near the Italian-Yugoslavian border just to the east of Trieste, a group of about one hundred civilians were gathered. SS and Wehrmacht troops surrounded them, awaiting further orders as to how these alleged partisans, as the Germans viewed them, were to be dealt with. It did not matter that more than twenty children, ranging in ages from three to sixteen were scuttling about. To Sturmbannführer Horst Gregor, it did not matter one wit. All were to be executed. There would be no mercy.

Standing nearby was a shadowy figure, one not completely trusted by the Nazis, nor by the Yugoslavs. And certainly not by the Allies. He was a man with virtually no friends in the world, and that was all perfectly fine as far as Marco Dubnik was concerned. For here was a man who had never known his father. His mother had been a twenty-something Slovenian at the time Dubnik had been conceived. He had grown up in a series of foster homes. Some had been kind, and some had been oppressive. By the time he was fourteen, the man of the house had already brutalized him on numerous occasions. This ogre had been the same toward his own children.

Gradually, Dubnik sidled himself beside the Nazi officer. He took in the profile of Horst Gregor who continued to impassively stare at the gathering below. Gregor wore a steel helmet atop his head. The man's nose ran straight down his face almost to a point. The chin was square and firm. Gregor's field-gray uniform was crisp and immaculate, as if he were ready to step on to the parade ground, not for an impending execution.

"Do you think they suspect that something may be amiss, Herr Major?" questioned Dubnik, deliberately using the address one would have normally used for an army officer.

"It is not my concern, Dubnik, as to whether they suspect something may be 'amiss', as you say," said Gregor. If he had taken any offense at Dubnik's use of the term "major," he did not display any displeased expression. "I will say, that was a rather clever maneuver on your part. Or should I say, sleight of hand."

"Oh, it was really quite simple. I merely proposed to them, or should I say some of their leaders, that it might be worth their while to cooperate."

"Cooperate, indeed. Clever, yes… it was very clever on your part, was it not?" The SS man turned to face Marco Dubnik. "Yes, cooperate, by sprinkling some honey and the bees took it."

"Yes, it has proven to be quite successful, you would have to agree. I simply had it conveyed to the village elders that it would be in everyone's best interests to have them hand over their valuables, gold, whatever, and it would be seen that they could go on… well, living. It would just be in a different place."

"Yes, living. It is amazing what a person will do to go on living for just another day, or week, or even for only a few more hours. You know, I have seen this very same thing in the Warsaw ghetto. Can you imagine? We had Jews turning on other Jews just to give them the illusion that they could go on living. At least, for just a little while longer. Fascinating."

Dubnik didn't reply. Even though he had not personally witnessed the ghettoes of Warsaw or Lodz, he had heard many stories about them. Gregor had referenced some Jews acting as police who had more than ably assisted the Nazis in gathering up their fellow "chosen ones", and then in maintaining order as those poor souls had been forcefully pushed onto the death trains bound for Auschwitz or Treblinka, or any number of God forsaken places contained within the far-flung Nazi empire.

"I think the time has arrived to put an end to this. Are you going to stay and witness our event?" asked Gregor in an imperious manner. "Or are you to exit with undoubtedly some vital task to perform?"

"*Nein*, Herr Major, I will stay," Marco Dubnik said as he cast a mournful look at the ground beneath his feet.

"Yes, there is nothing quite like the sight of some blood being spilled, or the gore of pieces of arms and legs after they have been torn off bodies, and today we have a treat. We have some small children among the gathering," glowed Horst Gregor.

Dubnik looked at the Nazi with bitter contempt and disgust. Why not just put these people out of their misery and be done with it. No, men like Gregor had to revel in their cruelty and wickedness. Men like Horst Gregor were nothing more than evil, malevolent psychopaths. Gregor held the power of life and death over these poor unfortunates. Somehow, Marco

Dubnik had cast himself outside the circle of responsibility for the impending execution of these "unfortunates."

* * *

No, thought Dubnik. There was nothing to be gained by going down that road. He rose from his chair and began to pace about the room. Other thoughts, other memories came to the fore in his mind. It seemed as if his entire life had been lived in the shadows. Until now, it had suited him nicely, his personality, who he was, perfectly. But Marco Dubnik was now entertaining doubts. Such silly things as giving up a life of intrigue and treachery, for a more sedentary one. Maybe he could have a family, complete with a doting and devoted wife, attractive of course. And there could be several children running about.

When the final collapse of the Third Reich had come, Marco Dubnik had been able to merge himself within the tide of stateless wanderers. He had been able to seek and obtain protection from the liberating Allied armies. Only Dubnik's protection came from the Soviet Union, that is, indirectly. Based on his wartime contacts amongst both the Americans and British on one side, and those from the East Germans, and an organization of theirs that would become almost as synonymous as the Gestapo had been. An organization that would one day be called the Stasi.

Dubnik continued with his pacing even as he unconsciously picked up speed. His daydream was only broken when he brushed up against an end table. A glazed figurine toppled over and crashed to the wood floor.

"I think we, or I, shall have to engage Signora Rossi more intensively. Surely, she will go back to Vento Beach on holiday." Marco Dubnik was certain of it. He figured he would have to direct Carlo Deluca to reenter the picture and to have him engage this intriguing woman. Surely, a man of Deluca's self-reputed talents as a lady's man should be able to penetrate this Rossi woman and come up with something quite substantive.

* * *

"Excuse me, Major, have you noticed those two guys back there?" asked Sergeant Mike Summers. "I heard them say they were reporters with some Italian newspaper. Uh, Corriere del... something."

"Corriere della Sera, Sergeant," finished Bob Rossi. "What is so unusual?"

"Well, those guys must have photographic memories. I mean, I've seen them for nearly an hour and I haven't seen them taking a note. Strange, don't you think?"

Rossi turned his attention away from the clipboard he'd been holding and took a sideways glance back up the hill at the two men Summers had indicated. The men suddenly started acting suspiciously, with nervous hand gestures and twisting and turning their bodies about. Rossi thought they resembled figures caught in the throes of the St Vitas dance.

The two erstwhile reporters were in fact hired hands of Gianni Ravelli, assigned to shadow Rossi. The American, now employed by the American Graves Registration Command (AGRC), were researching a field north-northwest of Anzio. The very area the two men were standing in had once been the site of vast carnage and destruction, and the loss of many American lives.

Rossi bent to his work once again. He was determined to find some kind of confirmation as to the existence of a squad of men. Virtually all of them had hailed from New Bedford, Massachusetts, a former whaling city that clung to the southeastern coast of the state. According to Rossi's notes, many of these men had either been relatives of one another or close, lifelong friends. Rossi would find something, anything which would provide some type of confirmation for the surviving relatives of these men. He would help to provide some closure of some kind for those still grieving.

* * *

It was now mid-April and Rome was basking in the luxury and splendid warmth of a rapidly approaching spring. Not a cloud floated through the blue and luminescent sky. For Rosetta Rossi, it was a time of personal warmth. She was still fixated on the gold treasure she knew existed off the Ligurian coast. Rosetta just knew and felt it in her bones.

Rosetta's other problem was of a more personal nature, and it was directly centered on her relationship with her husband. After their thaw-out at the end of 1946, clouds had soon developed between her and Bob. His new position with the Graves Registration Command had taken him across, it seemed to her, the entire Italian peninsula. She had admired, and still did, his dedication and zeal he had brought to his new posting. Rosetta knew only too well that Bob was trying, often desperately so, to locate the remains of missing men. She knew what it would mean to these men's families and friends back in the states.

Only now Rosetta was facing the prospect that her own marriage was resting on tenterhooks. The mad and passionate lovemaking had turned into moments she could count on one hand in a month. Tying in with this was Rosetta's feeling that Bob was just not bringing any kind of urgency to their passion. Sex had become a rather placid and sedate affair. She could not bring herself to want to cling to his body.

On this fine morning, Rosetta once again ascended the steps to the Biblioteca Nazionale Centrale and to the office of her newly acquired friend, Stefania Andino. She had been to the library several more times since her initial visit in the last year. So far nothing of any substance, nothing really tangible, had presented itself in her continuing research of the suspected missing gold. She figured that this visit would once again yield no real fruit.

Stefania Andino greeted Rosetta with an effusiveness that matched the Roman sky. "Ah, Rosetta, how good it is to see you once again," said the bright-eyed and enthusiastic young woman.

Rosetta looked at Andino and noticed that the girl had changed her hairstyle. It was now a bit shorter and was dyed a light shade of brown. Maybe things were picking up in Andino's own personal life.

"*Buon giorno*, Stefania. It is good to see you again."

"*Si*. Ah, well, I'm pleased to have to tell you I've made some progress on your project since your last visit," gushed a smiling Andino. Her whole face was lit up and appeared almost cherubic.

"You have?" asked Rosetta tentatively. She just could not allow herself to become too hopeful. She also secretly hoped Stefania Andino would be able to show her something with somesubstance.

182

"*Si, si.* Let me show you," continued Andino as she pointed to a small table where a leather-bound volume rested. "This is a publication from the British government's Ministry of Defense. Specifically, it relates to Royal Navy operations in the Mediterranean Sea for the years of 1942 to 1945."

Rosetta sat down on one of the plain brown wooden chairs that adorned the table. She studied the volume set before her, wondering what it would reveal.

"As I was saying, this volume also contains information of British submarine actions in the 'Med' for these years in question. And here on page one hundred fifty-two, you can see there is a description of one particular British submarine, the Conqueror. On the night of 30 May 1944, the Conquerer took a bearing on an old Italian steamer. The vessel was not the type that was much to speak of. Nevertheless, as I found out, and as you can see here," the young woman pointed with her right index finger of that she was speaking of, "this vessel has been identified as the MS Moschilo and it was carrying a manifest of several types of items. Among them was a consignment of gold bars the Nazis, it was believed, had looted from throughout Italy and perhaps from some other countries as well." Andino now paused to let her words sink in, but Rosetta could feel the electricity that exuded from the woman.

"Amazing. Simply amazing," was all Rosetta could think of and utter to the librarian. "Then at last we have something rather definite, something more tangible. We have not been chasing figments of our imagination. At least, not of my imagination."

"Indeed, Rosetta. Indeed. And, in addition, let me point out that here there is a description of the submarine, her crew complement, her capabilities, and her captain. His name was Lt. Commander Alan Stone."

But Rosetta had once again settled into a daydream, or nightmare, as she returned to her problems concerning her husband. She hungered for Bob to want her once again. He had to desire her once again for her body. It was rather funny to her in a strange way of Rosetta being up in the air, so to speak, her mind scattered all over the place. She didn't think that had ever happened with Paolo. Maybe it was because she was now married to an American. No, that was plain silly.

Rosetta couldn't even hear Stefania Andino as she continued to expound further points of interest relating to the Moschilo, the British submarine, and a myriad number of other details. Maybe Rosetta should just divorce the man or, at least, separate from him, the Church be damned. What did they know of what really went on between a man and a woman? Old, ponderous white men who always seemed to relish in telling others what was best for them; that they were all knowing.

Finally, Rosetta heard the unceasing ticking of the wall clock of Andino's office. She looked up at it as if she were mesmerized by the continuing revolutions of the second hand. All of a sudden, Rosetta uttered, "No, no, I cannot do it!"

Stefania Andino looked to Rosetta, startled. "Pardon? Rosetta, are you all right?" Andino asked cautiously. She noticed beads of perspiration forming on Rosetta Rossi's face and upon her upper chest.

"Oh, oh… I was just thinking of something else. You were saying?"

* * *

Several days later, Rosetta received an unexpected visitor in the person of Stefano Lucca. She had just arrived home from her AMGOT job and had just settled into her black leather Natuzzi couch. It was still a prized possession of hers. She and Paolo had personally selected it just before the war. It always brought back his memory.

The buzzer rang out in its shrill tone, momentarily startling Rosetta. She hadn't been expecting anyone. Who could it be? Going to answer the door, Rosetta paused briefly to check herself in the oaken framed wall mirror. *Eh, pretty good,* she thought to herself.

"Ahh, *buona serra*, signora. I hope you do not mind, you see, I happened to be in your neighborhood and I thought I would stop in," enthused Stefano Lucca.

"No, no, of course not, Stefano. Please, come in." Lucca looked somewhat disheveled, his overcoat rested rumpled upon his frame. She also noticed dark bags under his eyes, as if he hadn't slept well of late. "May I get you something?"

" Ah, well, perhaps some mineral water?"

"*Si*, of course. The tap water is completely unsuitable for drinking, as you well know. I wouldn't give it to a dog," Rosetta found herself prattling on. Unusual for her, a woman known for her succinctness.

"*Grazie*," said Lucca as he sat himself into a nearby armchair. "Your husband is not home?"

Rosetta said with a curtness that startled the listening Lucca, "No, he's not. I think he's on one of his assignments. I really don't know where he is at the moment." She paused a moment, calming down. "Do you have something for me? I mean, perhaps, some information?"

"*Si*, I do, Rosetta. And it has to do with your situation at Vento Beach. Specifically the steamer that went down. As you know, it was sunk by a British submarine in late May of 1944." Again, the man's exaggerated manner betrayed him. Whenever Rosetta and Barbara had spoken with him in the past, Lucca had always been, well, sure of himself. He had displayed the demeanor a patient might feel in the presence of a doctor, or of a client discussing a matter of great import with his solicitor.

"Yes, Stefano, we have suspected that the Moschilo might have met its end because of a submarine. Have you found anything else, something that might shed greater light on things?"

"I believe so. You see, I have found out, courtesy of a colleague of mine in Britain, that the captain of the submarine, a..." Lucca consulted from a small notepad." Ah, yes, a Commander Alan Stone, did not say that he had been aware of any particular manifest aboard the vessel at the time of his encounter with her. He had only been following orders, and those orders had been to sink anything moving in his assigned patrol sector."

Rosetta sat back, but then suddenly popped up. "Oh, I've forgotten your mineral water." With that, she got up and went to the sideboard where some chilled water rested in a glass urn-like container. She didn't mention that she already knew of the British captain.

"*Grazie, grazie*, Rosetta," enthused Stefano Lucca as he took hold of the proffered glass. "Yes, my British colleague also found out that Commander Stone had considered destroying the Moschilo by gunfire.

After all, in his opinion it would have been a waste of a valuable torpedo on such a small and harmless hulk."

"Then why did he in fact use a valuable torpedo?" asked Rosetta as she resettled herself in the Natuzzi.

"The captain did not say so. As we know, a torpedo was used. Stone said that it blew the poor Moschilo to kingdom-come. The captain did express his regret."

"Why so, Stefano?"

"Well, he figured that the crew, at least, were most probably Italian. And with Italy being out of the war, officially, at least, well…"

" I understand. Is there anything else?"

"No, I believe that covers about everything I have for now. Of course, if any new developments happen I will notify you or Barbara right away. Give my best to her when next you see her. Please, don't get up, Rosetta. I will see myself out. *Ciao*."

After Lucca's departure, Rosetta went to retrieve her notes from the Central Library. She was particularly curious now to find out more about the crew of the Moschilo.

* * *

On the last Saturday in April, the day did not dawn bright and clear. Low scudding, cumulonimbus clouds dotted the sky. Barbara Danilo did not dwell on whether this might portend ominous developments. She had just finished donning her tight-fitting white driving suit, her athletic figure highly accented. Barbara was alone, gathering her thoughts, and focusing on the task before her. She knew she would be up to the challenge. Try as she might, she could not quite shake off the thought she was only there to prove herself again because of one man, Ernesto Forti.

The newly installed chairman of the board stood alone, apart from the other high-ranking Maserati notables. Smoking a long black Partagas cigar, Forti stood imperiously. His time had come after having waited patiently for so many years. Forti continued to stand alone, his somewhat corpulent figure fitted within a black camel-haired overcoat. He carefully and artfully eyed Barbara Danilo and in his bones felt that this forward, avant-garde, woman would indeed have to prove herself once again to Pietro Roberti and his assembled engineers, and to Ernesto Forti himself.

"Are you ready, Barbara?" Pietro Roberti asked, the only Maserati man to approach her.

Barbara replied coolly as she tightened her black leather gloves on her hands, "*Si*, I am, Pietro. Let's get this show on the road,"

Roberti noted the steel-like glint in her crystal blue eyes. They openly breathed fire. He only hoped she wouldn't push the envelope beyond the point of no return.

Barbara gathered herself in the driver's seat of an identical 8CTF model she had driven previously. She took in the instrument panel, the intoxicating scent of the fine-grained leather upholstery. Barbara breathed in deeply. She was ready to again and become one with the machine. She would become master over this vehicle. It would submit itself to her will.

At last, all was ready. Barbara tightened the goggles that covered her royal blue eyes. She started up the ignition of the powerful 250 horsepower engine of the 8CTF. She let the vehicle warm up for several minutes before she placed the stick shift into first gear. Danilo pushed the clutch in with her left foot, and with her right she began a slow acceleration.

Barbara drove the Maserati around the banked, oval-shaped Bologna track for a couple of laps, and then roared down the straightaway, accelerating to maximum speed as she crossed the start line. In an instant the 8CTF was hers and the car knew it. Barbara sped around the track, lap after lap, hitting speeds no other Maserati driver had ever reached before.

Even as she went into the deep-banked turns, Barbara hardly slowed the big car down. She knew, deep within herself, she had done it. Her drive today had been even better than the first time. Ernesto Forti could not deny her chance to drive for Maserati. Or would he?

* * *

Throughout April and May, scuba diving lessons had shifted from the Metropole pool to the open ocean at a point near to the beach resort of Nettuno. Former Lt. Commander Enzo Stefani had chosen a site which he felt would help facilitate the transition from a controlled environment to the real world of diving.

Stefani tried as best he could to relate to the women what they could expect when each of them dove. He didn't think they would be shocked, and certainly not afraid of what they might encounter: waving grasses of the primeval forests, schools of fish, as if armies from another planet, and perhaps a shark or two. No, he didn't think so as all, with the exception of young Ariana, were experienced free divers. Enzo Stefani continually stressed the art of decompression, staging slowly to the surface at intervals of ten to fifteen feet at a time. He pointed out the need to rest adequately after each ascent so as to prevent the accumulation of nitrogen in one's bloodstream.

Neither Rosetta, nor Barbara had intimated in any way to Stefani the purpose of their taking scuba lessons. The former frogman had always felt that the women may have had an ulterior motive. He would provide these women any and all instructions which would aid and assist them in whatever pursuit they had in mind. The sea was a vast and open chasm. One not readily at home for most humans. It was not the same as being on terra firma, where a misstep was often just that. Errors and mistakes in the clutches of the deep could well result in one not seeing the next light of day.

On one weekend dive session the group was taking a break when Stefani sidled his way next to Barbara Danilo. "I'm not quite sure what you and your compadres may have in mind, but I just want to caution you that a dive, any dive, can be fraught with danger. This can be the result of simply being in the water, let alone if one is involved in what could be considered nefarious. And by that I mean a person having heard, perhaps, even caught a glimpse of something valuable. Do you understand?" asked Enzo Stefani, evident concern hidden within his voice.

Barbara looked up from the oxygen tank she had been adjusting directly into the man's eyes. "Enzo, we're merely trying to learn the right and proper scuba techniques. We've chosen you to teach us because you're the very best. You don't have to worry about any of us taking any undue and unnecessary risks." With that, she stood up and walked away from Stefani and joined her three confederates who were laughing amongst themselves over some private joke.

The Italian watched the confident and proud woman walk away and thought to himself, *there is the smell of gold or some such riches. The vultures come flapping as if to a dead body and sometimes, there are dead bodies.*

Before each dive instruction, Stefani would emphasize the constant need to check the pressure in the oxygen tanks and to check their regulators. He also kept reminding the four women of any exertion underwater would cause a greater and quicker discharge of nitrogen into their bloodstreams. This made the danger of the bends that much greater.

All four of the women had proven to be dedicated and committed. There had been no fooling around, no horseplay. Every one of them would have proven to be more than capable of serving in the Italian navy, or any other navy.

* * *

"I'm afraid I can't do it, Rosetta," exclaimed an excited Barbara Danilo. "I just can't get away for late June or… whatever for July. At least, not just now." Barbara had finally been accepted into the driving ranks of Maserati by Ernesto Forti. The venerable and stately chairman had at last given way to Pietro Roberti and others. Besides, thought Forti, having a woman might well result in a boost for the company in terms of image and more importantly, in terms of sales.

Rosetta Rossi faithfully sat at the other end of the line. She had fervently hoped she along with her friend would have been able to get away from the upcoming and stultifying Roman heat for a brief period.

"Say, I have an idea. Why don't you ask Ariana to join you? She's certainly more than capable of holding her own in the water," suggested Barbara, who was quietly filed her nails while she held the phone to her ear.

"*Si, si*, I think you may have something there. I hadn't thought of it," conceded Rosetta.

"Eh, it was just a thought. It'll give the two of you a chance to re-enhance the mother-daughter dynamic, don't you think?"

"Indeed it would. And to think that just a little over a year ago the two of us had stood poles apart. And now?"

"Well, Rosetta, they say that time usually heals all wounds, or at least many."

"Yes, they say it does," replied Rosetta wistfully. She immediately thought of Bob and their relationship. Although things had improved somewhat in their bedroom, there was still a way to go.

* * *

It was a hot, steamy, and sultry day in early July when Rosetta Rossi and her daughter Ariana departed from Rome. Both women were adorned in open-necked white blouses; Rosetta wore a khaki-colored culotte type of skirt while Ariana was dressed in a rose-colored culotte. The women rode the state-owned train out of the city's main train station out to Genoa. There they rented out a red Lancia convertible roadster. The men at the car rental agency ogling the clearly revealed physiques of Rosetta and Ariana. Both picked up on the sententious vibe immediately. The expressions on their faces said: "Let's get the hell out of here!" Rosetta took the wheel of the Lancia and set off at a more measured and leisurely pace than they would've experienced had Barbara Danilo been driving. The top being down caused the gently blowing wind to craft its way through the hair of the girls. The rolling verdant hills surrounding the towns of Vernazza, Montecossi, and Levanto seemed to melt as if upon a canvas backdrop. Palm trees gently swayed from their firmly rooted trunks, lending a tropical air. At last, the cloying, suffocating Roman climate was being left behind.

It was just after 6:00 PM when Rosetta swung the Lancia onto the grounds of the Hotel California, a small, not well-known hostelry that catered mostly to young travelers. It was a place with not too much in the way of amenities, but offered lodging at a reasonable price.

Rosetta had chosen the hotel, situated mid-way between Varazze and Savona because she felt that the Hotel Brentano had become just a little too familiar for her.

Rosetta and Ariana awoke early on Tuesday, they had much to do before they set out for the waters beyond Vento Beach. The services of Pasco Borrelli had long been secured by Rosetta. Although Borrelli performed a variety of tasks for the surrounding community, it always seemed as if when Rosetta Rossi came calling he was always available. To some around the Vento area he was at her beck and call. It made no difference to this kindly old gentleman. He was long past the age where he would care in the slightest at what some of his fellow citizens thought of him. Besides, the woman had never been unreasonable to him in any of her requests, and she had always paid in advance.

On this day, Rosetta had asked Borrelli to acquire one hundred feet of one-half inch diameter rope. In addition, he had been tasked with finding an anchor or a weight of some kind. Also, he had to come up with some kind of flotation device which could be secured to the rope. If these requests seemed unusual or bizarre to the old Italian, he gave off no indication to Rosetta.

Finally, at almost 11:00 AM all was ready and Rosetta and Ariana joined Pasco Borrelli in his fifteen-foot skiff. Rosetta wore a black one-piece suit, Ariana had chosen to wear white bathing suit of a similar cut.

Borrelli guided the small craft away from Vento Beach and toward the more open ocean of the Gulf of Genoa. The outboard motor wheezily put-putting away. A low blue cloud hovered over the motor, an indication of a slightly too rich mixture of the fuel. Rosetta noted that it had always acted this way.

The water was calm and was at low tide. Flocks of seagulls filled the azure blue sky above. Rosetta already knew the water temperature should be just about perfect for their planned swimming and diving.

"Mother?" asked Ariana as she slid herself next to Rosetta.

"*Si?*"

"Mother? Well, uh, would it be alright if we swam in the nude?" Ariana asked tentatively. She should have felt awkward asking such a question to the woman who was, after all, her mother, but strangely she didn't. Rosetta

191

had certainly never been a prudish woman with her two children. By the same token, she was not a loose one in the figurative sense. Ariana had seen her mother naked many times either upon her entering or exiting the bathtub. Rosetta had never allowed for either of her children to see her having sex with her two husbands.

"If you wish, Ariana. We can do it. You won't feel awkward?"

"Mother, I've seen you naked before and I know when you and Barbara have been here on prior occasions you've dispatched yourselves of your suits. It won't shock me," Ariana said in a low toned voice. It was in an octave appropriate for a low-budget spy movie.

"Then, we shall do so," Rosetta said. "Pasco, do you remember the site we were at last year? You know, the one where my… little incident occurred?"

"Ah, *si*, signora. I believe that I do," replied an impassive Pasco Borrelli. He needed no further instruction. He corrected his course slightly to the southwest. As this little conversation had played out, Ariana drew a scowl across her face. She had never heard anything before about her mother having had an incident. The word connoted something ominous. What other secrets could be in play? This, her mother and stepfather's difficulties of late. Ariana shivered slightly, despite the warmth of the surrounding air. She failed to notice the various species of birds in flight or the blue-green tinted water they were now sailing through.

Rosanna now realized she had inadvertently let slip her secret, something she had long and painfully kept hidden from her husband. And now she had revealed it to her daughter unwittingly.

Pasco Borrelli had by now maneuvered the boat to the approximate location where the signora had had her "experience" the year before. He could just make out the distant promontory, Monte Cavaldo lay some two miles in the distance. Borrelli figured they were now in about thirty to forty feet of water beneath them. He shut down the motor and then dropped the twenty-pound anchor over the stern.

Rosetta and Ariana placed their diving goggles on their heads. Rosetta also placed her dive watch on her left wrist and the depth gage estimator on her right. Her trusty dive knife was strapped to her right calf. She, followed by Ariana, then went over the side of the craft. Rosetta removed her black bathing suit. Ariana followed in kind. Pasco Borrelli dutifully took receipt of them with a phlegmatic look on his face.

"Pasco? I think Ariana and I will probably spend about two hours in the water," Rosetta said.

"*Si*, I understand, signora," Borrelli said as he prepared himself for his period of solitude. He was long used to the practice. Maybe he could spend the time in silent contemplation. He could review in his mind episodes he could recall over past decades. Those from the war, he would not bother with.

"Ariana, I think we'll swim out about a hundred yards this way," Rosetta pointed, "and then we can dive there for a while. Let me know at any time when you want to return to the surface. Don't push yourself. Okay?"

"*Si*, mother, I understand," Ariana said as she affixed her goggles to her face.

Rosetta, too, set hers in place and together, the two women swam off.

Borrelli glanced at the two Amazonian women and took in their gleaming backsides. They resembled seals to the old man.

Rosetta treaded water. "I think we'll begin our diving here." And with that she took in a huge lungful of air and jackknifed her body over. Her long, muscled legs receded into the water, resembling the prow of a sinking ship as it coursed its way to the bottom.

Ariana followed her mother's action. She could clearly see Rosetta's powerful body as it went downward. Ariana privately allowed for a thought of how spectacular her mother looked. A woman who had worked mightily to hone and craft her body until it was now at its apex.

Soon, both women were on the sea floor. Rosetta looked at her gauge and read a figure of forty feet, which equated to about six or seven fathoms. She signed to Ariana, who nodded. Ariana again marveled at the skill of Rosetta. It was a profound skill, as Rosetta had nothing else to rely on but two lungfuls of air and her own strength and calm courage. Her mother was at one with the sea. Ariana only hoped she could closely emulate her.

The two women had been down for about three minutes. Nothing of much interest had displayed itself as Rosetta and Ariana groped their way along the floor. Here and there were some small stones, an occasional boulder, scraps of refuse.

Rosetta looked over at Ariana and signaled it was time for them to surface. She didn't want to push things too far on Ariana's first dive. Both women rose up from the depths. their bodies glistening in the sunlight that filtered through the water.

"*Bene, bene,* that was good, Ariana," said an enthused Rosetta. She was clearly pleased with her daughter's own skill and ability.

"*Grazie,* mother. The water feels good. I thought it might be colder, but as it is, it is just right."

"Eh, *si.* Why don't we move over a little toward the shore. I'll let you lead this time. Okay?"

"You're entrusting me, I see," said Ariana in a mocking tone.

Rosetta and Ariana now swam about seventy-five yards in the direction Rosetta had just pointed to. Ariana gathered herself and rammed as much air as she could into her lungs. She dove over, her legs executing a maneuver that was a virtual carbon copy of her mother's minutes before. Rosetta was deeply impressed as she gathered in her own supply of air and dove her body into the gulf's welcoming waters.

Ariana and Rosetta swam down through schools of fish, some Rosetta identified as striped bass. Even a couple of sea turtles made an appearance as the women approached the sea bed. Again, both divers encountered more man-made detritus. Ariana motioned to Rosetta and swam off in the direction she had indicated.

Rosetta immediately recognized an object sticking up from the sandy bottom. As she got closer, she could tell it was unmistakably the rusting gun barrel of a machine gun. Only its barrel protruded up into the water. The stock of the weapon remained encased in the sand. Rosetta moved closer cautiously, simultaneously removing the knife from its scabbard on her lower right leg. The blade's surface gleamed in the water. She began to scrape away sand and gravel from around the gun, clouding the water around it.

Suddenly, Ariana moved close to Rosetta and touched her on her left arm. The girl's face showed fright. Rosetta turned and saw the menacing form of a modestly sized blue shark, about six to seven feet long. Her breath, as it was, caught slightly, and she momentarily turned her attention away from the gun. Rosetta now remembered something else Enzo Stefani had briefed them on. Sharks were often just curious when they encountered humans. This was not always the case. Stefani had instructed the girls that a display of combativeness would often result in a shark deciding to give up interest and just move off. Again, this was not written in stone.

Rosetta gripped the knife firmly in her right hand and boldly advanced on the shark. She proceeded to wave the weapon back and forth in a slashing motion, as she gritted her teeth. Rosetta desperately hoped this would work, as she could think of nothing else to turn to. And to her great surprise, and to Ariana's immense relief, it did precisely that. The shark suddenly darted off into the nether reaches of the ocean waters.

Rosetta now checked her dive watch and decided it was time for them to surface for a recharge of their air supplies. She also thought that they might well be quite near to the wreck of the Moschilo. Signaling Ariana, both women slowly ascended toward the surface, pausing about fifteen feet up to help equalize the air pressure in their bodies. This would help prevent an onset of the bends.

"Ariana, I want you to swim over to Borrelli and have him come over with the boat," Rosetta said. "I'll remain here treading water. It appears as if he is about five hundred yards away."

"Mother, how can you remain so calm? I thought I was going to have a heart attack seeing that shark," said a now calming down Ariana. The girl was amazed at not only her mother's skill as a diver, but her own courage as well.

"Never mind that. There are things we have to do. Go and swim over to Pasco Borrelli and have him come here."

Ariana dutifully swam off as Rosetta kept treading water. She periodically dipped her head into the water, lest their shark friend reappear.

"*Bene, bene.* Now, Ariana, toss over the line and as I go down pay it out slowly. I will secure the rope to the object we found. And Pasco, when I've secured the rope I'll tug on it two or three times. You'll then cut the rope and secure a marker buoy to it. Okay?" Rosetta was in full and complete command of the situation.

"Si, signora, but I don't think the authorities will like our placing our own buoy in the water," said a mystified Pasco Borrelli.

"Don't worry about that, Pasco. I'll assume full responsibility. One more thing. Ariana, would you please hand me my bathing suit?" With her swimwear now in place on her body, Rosetta took hold of the rope end, took in a lungful of air, and dove under once again. She drove herself down to the bottom. She moved directly to the machine gun and began looping the rope around the gun barrel slowly and methodically. Rosetta remembered an additional instruction from Enzo Stefani. When one was working underwater and especially deeper, it was paramount that a diver not expend too much energy, as this would only accelerate the generation of nitrogen in the bloodstream.

Rosetta finished looping the rope by tying two double sailor's knots, also courtesy of Stefani. She took a last look around and glanced at her watch. Four and half minutes. It was time to go up. She remembered to tug on the line to let Borrelli know it was also time for him to attach the buoy. Rosetta felt as if her heart were floating off her chest. In an instant, she thought of Bob and said to herself, *He is attracted to my sexuality, and yet he is repelled that I possess it and know how to use it.*

On the surface, Rosetta was pleased to find that Borrelli had done exactly as she had instructed him. Their own makeshift buoy was secure and very closely resembled some of the other government sanctioned ones floating nearby. Only if one looked carefully would one have noted that a small RR was present on its side. Rosetta thought it might be difficult to locate it once again. She then directed Pasco Borrelli to return them to shore. Enough had been accomplished for one day. She felt quite sure they were now quite close to the location of the MS Moschilo and its potential gold lucre.

The two women, mother and daughter, decided to spend the afternoon sunbathing and swimming off Vento Beach. They donned their respective bathing suits. It would not do nor help their cause for any potential prying eyes to catch them in an uncompromising position.

* * *

The next day, a Wednesday, opened gray and nowhere near as inviting as the previous day. Overcast clouded out most of whatever sunlight was available. Nevertheless, Rosetta and Ariana decided to set out to beyond Vento Beach. Today both would wear their suits as the water temperature had dipped. Not to the point where a swimmer would have developed icicles, but still.

By 10:00 AM, Pasco Borrelli had maneuvered his boat quite near to the buoy they had affixed the day before. Rosetta and Ariana took to the water and dove under. Ariana had been told earlier that morning by Rosetta they'd search a little more to the north of the point where they had located the machine gun. She was hoping for more tangible signs to manifest themselves that would direct them to the Moschilo.

As both women swam along the seabed, they both couldn't help but notice the abundant sea grass drifting upward. Ariana reached out to grasp some of the strands. It all seemed so peaceful here, so far removed from what was often found above the surface. Then she suddenly remembered the blue shark from the day before and how it had scared the daylights out of her. It was a telling reminder that danger could lurk from anywhere at any time.

As Ariana swam on, she noticed she was suddenly getting cold. Goose pimples manifested themselves along her arms. The skin on her fingers were turning white and pulpy. She didn't think she and her mother would be staying in the water for very long. No, indeed, it would be an attenuated day.

The two women dove and surfaced several times and Rosetta noted they had been swimming for nearly two hours. She was once again impressed by her own strength and stamina. After all, she was providing her own power and flotation. Swim fins were not being used. Still, Rosetta mused to herself this effort would require a capability that exceeded someone free diving. A diver needed more than just relying on one's own lung power. More so if any heavy execution were to be required.

"Mother, do you have any idea where the boat is?" queried Ariana, a worried tone in her voice.

Rosetta looked around and was quite surprised to find they must have drifted further away than she had anticipated. "I believe Pasco and the boat should be in that direction." Rosetta then pointed. "Yes, we should start going that way."

The past hour had seen a rise in the chop of the water. Now, the waves were increasing in their crests. The water was also getting colder. Rosetta proceeded to swim in the breaststroke style. Suddenly, she heard Ariana crying out. "Mother, mother, help me! Help me! I think I have a cramp!" screamed Ariana somewhere in the distance behind Rosetta.

"Ariana! Ariana! Where are you?" Rosetta shouted frantically. The sea was getting heavier and angrier.

"I'm over here! Oh, please, I think I have a cramp in my right leg," moaned Ariana.

"Keep calling out to me," Rosetta yelled back as she swam in what she thought was the right direction. About thirty yards away, Rosetta finally spotted her daughter just before she disappeared beneath the surface. Rosetta swam as she never had in her life. She could not bear to think of the loss of her daughter. She would never, could never, forgive herself. Rosetta kept on swimming and then Ariana surfaced almost right in front of her face.

"Oh, mother, it hurts," Ariana moaned again, her face distorted by the pain.

"Hang on. Let me see if I can massage the cramp. Hang on." Rosetta took in a deep breath and dropped. She probed Ariana's right calf muscle. It was knotted up, almost as if a golf ball had been implanted there. As calmly as she could, Rosetta massaged and kneaded away at the knot. Gradually, the cramp began to subside. Rosetta surfaced and found a more serene look on Ariana's face.

"Better. It feels better," said a relieved Ariana.

"*Bene, bene.* Now, place your arms around my neck and we'll swim back to the boat. I don't think it's too far away from us," Rosetta said. Almost as soon as the words had left her mouth, the sea swells picked up even more. The gods were already getting more upset and lo and behold, to any swimmer who tried to defy them.

After what seemed an eternity, but in actuality had been no more than ten minutes, Rosetta spied the stooping, bent figure of Pasco Borrelli. Only this time he was not sitting impassively as if asleep, he was fully alert and leaning over the port side of the boat. He saw them and immediately knew there was a problem. Borrelli saw Ariana with her arms draped around her mother's neck. He went to the stern and quickly started up the outboard motor. Thankfully, it started the second time he pulled on the starter rope.

CHAPTER TEN-
PAY DIRT

J ust at the moment Pasco Borrelli docked the boat, the heavens opened up. Large raindrops cascaded down upon Rosetta and Ariana as they gathered up their things. As they looked up, it seemed as if the entire sky had turned an ominous black. There would be no sunbathing for them at Vento Beach for the remainder of the day.

As soon as Carlo Deluca had left the reception desk at the Hotel California and was turning the corner to go to a stairwell, he spotted his subject out of the corner of his eye. After having searched several nearby hotels and hostelries, he had finally located Rosetta Rossi. He only wished he could have had more time to look over the woman. Deluca had been able to see that Rosetta had been soaked, causing her T-shirt to fully emphasize and enhance her bust. But this was not the time for him to accidentally bump into the signora. No, he would do that later.

Upon entering his room, he sat and reflected on what he thought was a rather clever plan of action. Two days before, Deluca had been able to hire the services of one Rudi Califano, a young, ne'er do-well playboy type. Califano had been a one-time on again, off again boyfriend of Ariana Rossi.

The young Italian had been rather easy to entice with an offer, as he had recently fallen on hard times. Money for Califano had become very tight. It would be Califano's job to engage Ariana, tie her up, so to speak, thereby freeing Deluca for the machinations he had planned for the girl's mother.

Through his stuntmen, Gianni had been able to find out Rosetta Rossi had taken her daughter with her to holiday in the waters of the Gulf of Genoa. Deluca had been expecting to hear that the friend of Rossi, Barbara Danilo, would have accompanied her. No matter, this had worked out for the better.

* * *

Rudi Califano had paid careful consideration to the instructions of his new-found friend Carlo Deluca as to when to approach the younger Rossi woman. Califano's assignment for that evening would be to entice Ariana for a drive along the gulf coast, and in between, a sumptuous dinner at a quaint sea-side cafe. This would clear the deck for Deluca to just casually run into Rosetta. He would again charm her, wine and dine her, and Deluca was fairly confident this time he would be able to bed the voluptuous and sensuous woman.

Things fell into place almost as exactly as Carlo Deluca had planned. The smooth and urbane, devious Califano had succeeded in getting Ariana Rossi to join him for the evening. The young woman had clearly been more than glad to see Rudi once again. It had been written all over the girl's face.

* * *

Well, thought a pensive Rosetta, *what shall I do with myself for this evening?* Surely, she was pleased that Ariana had just happened to run into an old boyfriend, one Rosetta hardly remembered. Ariana assured her the young man was really a very nice guy. She was very glad to see him again. Things with Califano hadn't seemed to click the first time.

Rosetta was troubled by one thing though. Why had this Califano fellow invited Ariana for a drive and dinner when the weather outside was still rather dreadful? She looked out her hotel window. It appeared as if things were slowly beginning to clear. Maybe she was just thinking too much, her maternal instincts coming to bear.

Seated discreetly behind a small palm tree in the hotel's lobby waited Carlo Deluca. Just before 6:00 PM, he looked up as Rosetta Rossi descended the ornate staircase. Her dress surprised him, as she wore a modest printed shift. It still highlighted her amply developed arms and legs and did not do anything to diminish in any way her outstanding figure.

Rosetta paused at the reception desk, exchanging a brief word with the clerk on duty. Looking around the lobby, she then left and walked out the front door. Deluca waited for less than a minute after Rosetta had left the hotel before he rose up from his red-leathered upholstered armchair. He took his folded-up newspaper, a two-day old edition of the Corriere della Sera, straightened his pale green paisley tie, and absentmindedly brushed back the side of his head with his right hand before walking out the front door.

Staying within the shadows cast by the descending night, Deluca followed Rosetta surreptitiously. The woman seemed to have no idea that she was being followed, and if she had, she clearly didn't care.

After about ten minutes, Carlo Deluca noticed his quarry was entering a small restaurant named Valentino's. The sign above the establishment contained an outline of the famed American 1920s movie star, Rudolf Valentino. Strange, thought Deluca, in that the name and the appearance of the place gave off the air of a cheap tourist trap. Not anything he would have expected from such a sophisticated and refined woman such as Rosetta Rossi.

Deluca began to frame in his mind his upcoming plan of action with Rosetta Rossi. He would casually kill some time wandering around outside Valentino's, perhaps smoke a cigarette or two while he did so. Then, he would casually enter and locate where Rossi was. He might get himself a libation at the bar, which appeared to be situated just to the right of the entrance. Deluca would then introduce himself to the woman as accidentally as possible. Above all, on this night he had to extract something tangible, something more valuable than what he had been able to do so far. Marco Dubnik and others would be more than dissatisfied if he, Carlo Deluca, came up empty-handed again. True, the evening might well gain him an engagement in bed with the woman, but at the expense of possibly later losing his head.

Carlo Deluca entered Valentino's around 6:30 and made his way to the small bar where he ordered a double scotch and soda. He wanted to lubricate himself a little, not too much… just a little. It would help him prepare better for when he made his approach to the woman.

As he savored his drink, Deluca looked about the bar and out into the main dining room. The place was crowded, but not with the patrons he assumed would be, that of the tourist trade. No, there were gatherings of mostly younger upward professional men and some women. They were representative of the new Italy. Or at least, newer than the ones he would have expected only a few years before.

Periodically, Deluca would check his Patek Philippe watch. When the time neared 7:00 PM, he decided the moment had arrived for him to make his move. He got up from his barstool and began to saunter toward the dining room. He did this in his most casual manner. It would not do for him to act hastily.

"Ahh… signora, how nice to see you once again," enthused a broadly smiling Carlo Deluca.

Rosetta looked up from her plate of veal francaise, startled. She took in the full length of the smiling, voluble, urbane gentleman standing before her.

"Ah, signore…?"

"Carlo. Carlo Deluca. Do you remember me?" Deluca asked coyly, his left eyebrow arched upward lending his face a quizzical look.

"*Si, si*, I do seem to remember now," Rosetta said haltingly as she racked her brain for a better recollection. Then it hit her. It had been the previous summer. The fog was clearing and she remembered things more clearly. This man, this Carlo Deluca, had previously struck her as being somewhat unctuous, not quite seeming to be what he had tried to present himself as. But now, he appeared to Rosetta in a different light. Perhaps it was due to Rosetta having consumed a half-liter of Vin Rose. Not used to drinking copious amounts of liquor, it might just be clouding her senses. "Please, Carlo, sit down and join me."

"*Grazie, grazie.* Ah, may I call you Rosetta?"

"*Si*, you may."

"Are you here on holiday with—" Deluca suddenly stopped himself as he had been about to blurt out Ariana's name. A nervous tic suddenly began to manifest itself around his right eye.

"Well, I am here on a holiday of sorts," Rosetta responded. She thought Deluca's abrupt stop may have been attributed to his assumption that Barbara would have accompanied her. "My daughter, Ariana, has joined me."

"Ah, that's nice. A mother and her daughter enjoying the beauty and serenity that are here in abundance."

"Eh, *si, si*, as you have so eloquently stated. Perhaps you would like to order something to eat, Carlo?"

"Well, you may have something there as I am a bit famished and—" Again Deluca cut himself off. He had been about to reveal that he had been driving all day to get to Vento Beach. Deluca gained the attention of a passing waiter and told the young man that he would like a small antipasto and a plate of calamari with hot pepper rings. "Just a little repast," Deluca said smoothly to Rosetta. He looked into her clear hazel-colored eyes and at her golden blonde, curled hair. The soft and gentle curls framed her face perfectly. He was also struck by the folds around her eyes that gave off an owled expression. Rossi's mouth had settled into a demure look. "Well... ah, Rosetta. Have you and your daughter done anything exciting with yourselves while you have been here?" continued Deluca.

"I'm not sure you would find anything that I'd tell you that would be considered exciting. Interesting, perhaps," Rosetta said as she began to feel more relaxed. This Deluca fellow seemed pleasant enough. In a flash, she thought of Bob and as she did, she clumsily dropped her fork onto the floor.

"Oh, Rosetta, you've dropped your fork," Deluca remarked as he simultaneously gestured to their waiter for another one. "Is anything wrong?"

Rosetta quietly regained her composure. "Ah, no, no. I was just a little clumsy. Please, you must forgive me."

"I see you've just about exhausted your wine. Shall I order another? Perhaps a full liter bottle?"

"Yes, that would be good." Rosetta wondered what was coming over her. She hardly ever drank this much wine.

"Yes, as we or as you were saying. I think you mentioned something about... interesting. In what way?" He sensed that Rosetta wanted to be wooed; she wanted to succumb. This was playing out nicely.

"Well, it was interesting in that both Ariana and myself were free-diving in the area and..." Rosetta halted herself, wondering how much she should reveal to this man. He was becoming more familiar and she was becoming more relaxed in his company, but still...

"Well, we like to dive. We, or I at least, like to test myself in terms of skill and endurance and we did come across something that appeared to have come from a boat. You know, one that may have sunk or... had been sunk." Rosetta began to feel herself sway a little, her words slurring as she spoke.

This was getting very interesting for Carlo Deluca. He would now carefully probe this intriguing and beguiling woman. But it would be done very craftily. After all, this was what he did and what he had always been known for. The ability to schmooze anyone, be it man, woman, or child.

The couple finished their meal and then Rosetta acceded to Deluca's suggestion to a slow stroll along the waterfront. At one point, he felt confident enough that he could take Rosetta Rossi's arm. She did not reject him. In fact, she squeezed his arm with her hand. Carlo Deluca felt her body melt its way into his. Yes, it was indeed more than possible, even probable that he'd soon be taking her to his bed. Something within her, something deep within her body, was troubling her. It was something he could and should use to his advantage.

After almost an hour, Carlo guided Rosetta to a small tavern. Several sidewalk tables were occupied by mostly younger couples lost within themselves. They paid no mind to this older pair. Deluca managed to find a table that was unoccupied. Carlo asked Rosetta what she would like to drink and she breezily suggested Remy Martin cognac. For the next hour, they both consumed their drinks.

Rosetta felt as if her head were swimming. She couldn't remember the last time she had had this much liquor in one evening. She didn't feel as if she were drunk; feeling not much pain, yes. At some point, she reached a decision she wanted to be conquered by Carlo Deluca. She wanted to feel his body, and for him to feel and experience her own body.

Over the course of the next few hours, Rosetta allowed her body to be assaulted by Carlo Deluca in almost every way imaginable. She found him to be an ardent and accomplished lover. For his part, Rosetta Rossi was even more than he had ever imagined. From her full and spectacular breasts, to her rock-hard mid-section, and her legs were like driving and pulsating pistons as they enveloped his own plunging body.

It had seemed to Rosetta even through her alcohol induced mental fog—she had been reaching for a new height. She was realizing and fulfilling her sexual prowess and endowment. Deluca had pounded her body, and she had more than welcomed it. The feel of his elongated and driving penis had created in her cascading fire-works. She had been in the midst of a sexual frenzy. At last, when she had no longer been able to contain herself from climaxing, Carlo Deluca had roared to the heavens.

Just before midnight, the couple were lying entwined with one another, smoking a shared cigarette. The drinking of cognacs had resumed. Rosetta's head had cleared a little and she contemplated whether she should engage with her lover in another round. No, was she crazy? Hadn't what she had already done been enough? And who really was this Carlo Deluca?

Minutes later, she was startled by a loud noise from the next room. The young woman's voice instantly made Rosetta's blood run cold.

"Oh, Rudi, it's been a wonderful evening!" the words slurred out of Ariana's mouth. Clearly, she had had more than something to drink while she had been in the company of Rudi Califano.

Rosetta sat bolt-upright. The cigarette she had been holding in her right hand had burned down nearly to her fingers almost causing her to drop it into the bed.

"Well, I guess someone has been having a good time tonight," said Carlo Deluca. Of course, he knew that it was his erstwhile confederate who was in the next room with Rosetta's daughter. He only wished that Califano had kept the girl out on the street until past midnight as he had earlier instructed. Well, Califano had never been the brightest bulb on the circuit. All in all, things had come to near perfection. Carlo had gleaned additional tidbits from Rosetta during their tryst in bed. Deluca could now reliably inform

Marco Dubnik that maintaining surveillance of Rosetta Rossi would most definitely lead to the gold.

"Ahh… I have to go now," stammered Rosetta.

"Now, Rudi, you have some protection, haven't you?" came the leering and taunting question of Ariana Rossi.

"Of course, what kind of young man do you think I am, *signorina*," came the smooth and soothing practiced voice of Rudi Califano. He didn't sound as if he had consumed anywhere near the amount of alcohol as Ariana.

All of this was heard through the virtually paper-thin walls of the hotel. Rosetta got up quickly from the bed, causing a loud squeaking sound. She gathered up her clothes haphazardly and threw them on. She struggled to put her bra on, then decided to just chuck it into her handbag. She had no need for it now.

Watching this sat a bemused Carlo Deluca. He got up and moved toward his lover. "I will help you," he said softly into Rosetta's ear. "It has been a wonderful evening. Will I see you tomorrow?"

Rosetta continued throwing things on and straightening out herself as best she could. "I…I… don't know. Umm, thank you for the evening. You've been most kind." Rosetta did not even turn to face Deluca. She just reached out for the door handle and in a flash stumbled her way out into the hallway.

Carlo Deluca allowed himself a small smile. The night had indeed been quite fruitful. He had garnered some valuable information as to the location of a potentially large gold cache. And, he had bedded a voluptuous and sexy woman. Deluca also smiled as he heard Ariana and Rudi Califano thrashing about in raucous foreplay. The young woman seemed to have the same ability as her mother in fulfilling the carnal needs of a lover. "Ohhh… Rudi. I love the way you feel inside of me," moaned Ariana. The bed beneath her squeaked and groaned with increasing intensity.

* * *

"Mother, would you mind if I went with Rudi today? He'd like to take me up into the hills, as he put it," breathed a now recovered and lucid appearing Ariana.

Rosetta sat muted in her chair. Hotel guests were sauntering into the small dining alcove of the Hotel California.

"Mother? Have you heard me?" repeated Ariana. A look of impatience had now taken shape upon her face. Had her mother guessed at Ariana's own night of debauchery with Califano? No, probably not, but still…

"Uhh, *si*, I heard you. No, no, I don't mind," said a subdued Rosetta. How could she forbid her daughter to be with Califano when she herself had spent the night in the arms of another man. Never before had Rosetta betrayed either of her two husbands.

"I know we were supposed to have had plans for the beach today, but…"

"No, believe me, it is all right. A young woman should be with a young man, and not always with her mother. Just be careful."

"Oh, of course, I will. What do you have planned for the day?" asked Ariana.

"Oh, I do not know. Perhaps I will just lay around the hotel, do some reading."

* * *

It was mid-afternoon and the sunlight blazed its way through the double windows of Carlo Deluca's room. Rosetta Rossi sat straddled atop the Italian operative. Her breasts heaved and swayed above Deluca. His smooth, uncallused hands fondled and kneaded them. He was deeply penetrating what he considered to be a love goddess of a woman. He couldn't ever get enough of Rosetta Rossi.

As Rosetta humped away atop Deluca, she slowly began to focus on what the hell she was doing. *This has to stop!* screamed its way in and around her brain. What was this incredible pull of this Carlo Deluca? She didn't seem to be able to break free from the orbit she was trapped in. This orbit that revolved around Carlo Deluca.

* * *

THE WOMAN WHO SWAM IN THE NUDE

"I thought it best if I spoke with you directly, Barbara," began Stefano Lucca in his most gracious and professional manner. The information his detectives had uncovered had been more than just significant, it had been explosive. The meeting was once again in his spacious office overlooking the Castel Sant' Angelo.

"Why don't you just cut the shit, Stefano." Barbara had felt that something big had come up. Stefano Lucca had almost never behaved in her presence before as he was now. Lucca had always treated her and Rosetta in a manner that better resembled a casual conversation.

"As I was saying. My men have uncovered some things." Lucca gestured with his right hand, as if were weighing something of great import.

"Stefano, please, you can come out with it. I'm a big girl, you know." Barbara began to feel more and more uneasy.

"Well, as you know, your friend, Rosetta, and her daughter were up at your hangout near Vento Beach. I'll just come out with it." Lucca again hesitated. "My men were able to observe Rosetta in the company of a man over the course of two days." Lucca paused as he consulted some notes set before him on his glass-topped desk. "Ah, *si*... This man has been identified as Carlo Deluca. He's the third man. If you remember when I briefed the two of you last year, I had uncovered a triumvirate of Marco Dubnik, Herve Villot and an unknown associate. Well, we now know who this third man is."

"Well, she was seen with him, bad enough at first glance. Do you think it could've been a coincidence?" asked Barbara, fearing the worst.

"Well, ah, no. You see, my men, of whom I trust implicitly, have come up with something more. They believe, and I concur, that there is a strong likelihood that Rosetta and Carlo Deluca conducted... carnal relations," Lucca concluded as he sank back into his leather reclining chair.

Barbara looked directly at Stefano Lucca. "And you think... you think...yes, I see." Beyond the obvious of Rosetta having had an affair with anyone, let alone a nefarious character like this Deluca, could well ruin her reputation with the Church and with Cardinale Maggione. He would dearly love to have this information, this dirt. He could ruin her.

"Indeed, and I have more."

"What? Could there possibly be worse news?"

Lucca pursed his lips, paused, and reached for a cigarette from the wooden case on his desk. He lit it with his silver lighter, the smoke drifting up into a haze above his head. "I'm afraid so. You see, while Rosetta was being entertained by Deluca, her daughter was being entertained by one Rudi Califano."

"Who is he?"

"A small time operative in the rackets. Signore Califano was once a boyfriend of sorts of Ariana Rossi. And he, too, just happened to show up at the same time as—"

"Carlo Deluca," Barbara finished his sentence. "And this Califano was in the employ of Deluca for the purpose of tying up, if you will, the girl while Deluca himself operated on the mother."

"*Si, si,*" conceded Lucca, who continued smoking. He offered to Barbara, but she declined. "I thought it better to speak with you first. Would you like for me to speak with Rosetta? Discreetly, of course."

Barbara shook her head dolefully. "No, Stefano, I think it would be better if I were to do it. I think it can be done better by a woman. No offense to you."

"None taken," he quickly interjected.

Barbara sank into her chair as she contemplated what Stefano Lucca had just revealed to her. She knew that Rosetta and Bob had continued to have problems within their marriage. And although Rosetta had not exactly come right out with it, Barbara had strongly suspected that these problems were deep-seated in the bedroom. Now, her friend had apparently sought solace and fulfillment for her libido in the arms of another man. And not just any man, but one intimately involved with others who were after the treasure of the Moschilo. The now deceased Herve Villot had tried to kill Rosetta in the waters off Vento Beach.

* * *

Two days later, Rosetta was seated in a wicker chair in the garden patio behind Barbara Danilo's stately home. A pitcher of iced tea rested upon a glass-topped table. Barbara had taken a liking to the American drink. She thought it the perfect beverage to assist one in warding off the stifling heat and humidity that was Rome in July.

Barbara had just poured glasses of the tea when she finally sat down and placed her gaze on Rosetta.

"As I was saying, Barbara, I couldn't wait to speak with Enzo Stefani when I got back to Rome. When I told him of our discovery of the machine gun, he told me based on my description of the weapon, it sounded distinctly like a German MG42. He said it was one of the best weapons of the war. And, that by that time in 1944, Italian boats were being armed with them." Rosetta stopped her chatter when she noticed Barbara continuing to stare at her. She had said nothing while Rosetta had prattled on. "Why do I have the distinct feeling that I'm about to hear bad news. Am I correct?" A pit was forming in her already queasy stomach. She was still in the internal process of passing the stone of her having had sex with Carlo Deluca.

"Rosetta, you are one of my oldest and dearest friends. And the best way is for me to come right out with it," Barbara said, yet she hesitated before she continued. "Yes, well… it has to do with your recent trip up to Vento Beach. I spoke with Stefano Lucca the other day and he and his men have found out some… interesting things."

"Go on," Rosetta's guard was up. She knew she was about to hear what she had been fearing most for the past few days.

"Yes, well, do you remember when we spoke with Lucca last year and he mentioned about three men being involved with our little enterprise?" said Barbara,

"Yes, I remember. Go on, Barbara," soothed Rosetta, who now began to feel the ground beneath her start to sway.

"Yes, at that time, he had been able to only identify two of the three men. One was of course, Marco Dubnik, and the other had been… Villot, or something."

"Yes, I remember." Rosetta was now certain that Barbara was going to go on and say that the third man was none other than Carlo Deluca. The sky was darkening for her, even though there was a bright blue sky above.

"This third man is none other Carlo Deluca. And—"

"Stop! Please, Barbara, just stop."

"Rosetta, I'm your friend and I would like to help you. I won't judge or condemn you," continued Barbara. She would not mention the other item of Lucca's news concerning Ariana. It would absolutely crush her. Rosetta was a strong-willed woman, but even she had a threshold for personal pain.

"Barbara, what can I say? It was a moment of weakness. It was stupid, I know that now."

"Well what's done is done. You can't turn back the clock, as they say." Barbara now reached over and placed her right hand on Rosetta's arm. "Are things that bad between you and Bob?"

"More than you would ever know," Rosetta said as tears welled up in her eyes. Rivulets of them started to run down her cheeks.

"Oh, dear, you poor thing." Barbara got up and walked behind her friend. She leaned forward and placed her arms around Rosetta's neck, her breasts nestled themselves behind her head. Barbara did this out of her deep and abiding love for her friend. Straightening up, Barbara now knelt next to Rosetta. "Rosetta, you're going to have to confront this head-on. I'm not trying to tell you what to do, but the longer this festers, the worse it will become. You'll have to have a heart-to-heart talk with Bob. I think you know what may well happen if you don't."

"I know, I know. You're right. Do you think my affair with Deluca may make its way to Cardinale Maggione?"

Barbara thought for a moment. "No, I do not think so. Marco Dubnik is after the suspected gold that may be on board the Moschilo. He will want to keep tabs on us. Most likely, he'll continue to string out Maggione through that messenger boy, Gonevento."

"I hope that you're right. As to my own personal problem, well, you're probably correct there as well."

"By the way, where is Bob now?" asked Barbara as she resumed her seat across from Rosetta. She now extracted a cigarette from a case. She offered one to Rosetta, who accepted. The two women lit up. Smoke rings swirled their way into the air above their heads. No doubt, it was an ironic moment for the two of them, as neither one hardly smoked anymore. It was too much of a detriment to their health and their physical activities in the gymnasium and in the water.

"Rosetta, you have to find a way to get Bob back into your bed. Believe me, sex is the most powerful and effective antidote for dealing with… with problems between a man and a woman."

* * *

Several days later, Bob Rossi was sitting in the black leather couch when Rosetta walked in. It was just after 7:00 PM. "You look lovely, dear," Bob said courteously.

"Thank you, but I really don't look so lovely. It was kind of you to say," Rosetta replied as her face flushed. She brought her hands up to her hair as if to straighten it out. She felt that the words between them were stiff and sounding rehearsed.

"No, really, I mean it." There was genuine tenderness in his voice. Rosetta called to mind the words of Barbara, *you're going to have to confront this head-on.*

"Rosetta?" Bob got up from the couch and moved behind his wife. His powerful arms enveloped her abdomen. He possessed the unmistakable scent of musk. It was turning her on. She couldn't help it. "Dear, I haven't been a good husband to you of late, and I want to apologize. Will you forgive me?"

Rosetta felt the heartbreak and anguish in his voice and she visibly winced. She thought that her own heart would break as well. Why did two people create so much pain between them? How had it happened? Rosetta turned to face Bob. She had been unfaithful to him. What could she say?

"I love you, Bob. I always have, but it has been my fault as well. I've kept things from you when I shouldn't have. And…everything."

Bob took out his handkerchief and daubed at Rosetta's eyes. Gradually, her tears began to subside. The passion had been building slowly, ever so slowly. Both of them knew and felt it. Bob leaned down and kissed Rosetta's waiting lips and tongue.

Lightly flaming scented candles set upon a side table outlined the writhing bodies of Rosetta and Bob Rossi as they made mad and passionate love over the course of the next two hours. Rosetta submitted her body to the repeated assaults of her husband. She could feel the electricity running through her entire body. When Bob entered her the first time, it had seemed as if it were the same as when they had had sex together the very first time.

Bob had driven himself deeper and deeper in the throes of complete ecstasy. He'd wanted to keep going, a night without end. He'd always known he was deeply in love with Rosetta. For the life of him, he had not been able to figure out where their passion for one another and their marriage, had gone off the rails. Well, he felt as if he were back in the engineer's role, full steam ahead.

Rosetta, on her part, reveled as she thrashed beneath the weight of her husband. Her muscled thighs gripped with a ferocity she had never known before. Bob had been inside of her for a good while when he, and she, simultaneously climaxed.

A short time later, the pair copulated again. Only this time, Rosetta straddled Bob as she humped herself into a total frenzy. She and Bob simultaneously massaged her heaving breasts. The two smiled and at one point, even broke out into laughter as they had continued to hump away. Bob Rossi again mentally questioned himself. *How could I ever have doubted this woman? How could I? I must have been out of my head.*

Rosetta's own mind had lapsed into memory of just a short time ago, when she had sometimes nearly shuddered at the very sound of her husband's voice. They both had mutually proclaimed their love to one another several times during the courses of their sexual jousting.

The night of passion was concluded with Bob again driving himself at full force. Rosetta felt every impulse of his tempered rage. Bob took in the scent of honey shampooed hair. It spurred him on and at the very moment of his maximum ramming speed, he ejaculated.

* * *

In the last week of July, Enzo Stefani was in earnest discussion with Rosetta Rossi, Barbara Danilo, and Bob Rossi. The quartet had gathered in the living room of the Rossi's. Windows had been thrown open to provide

214

the barest modicum of relief from the suffocating heat enveloping them in the early evening.

"In my opinion, I think you should execute your little operation some time in September," Enzo Stefani opened cautiously. The former Italian navy commando was seated by himself facing the Rossi's and Danilo. "To conduct your search in August would, in my opinion, be unwise."

"Why is that, Enzo?" questioned Barbara as she leaned forward.

"Because, as you all well know August is a time when virtually everyone flees Rome and every city throughout Italy, and I see no reason why the coastal area of the Gulf of Genoa can't be expected to be crowded with some of these very holiday people."

"Yes, yes, I think you are right, commander," offered Rosetta graciously. Seated next to her, her husband sat with his hands clasped together with Rosetta's. For the evening, she had dressed more conservatively than her friend.

"Anyway, as I was saying, you should plan things for some time in September. I've been looking over the list of equipment you will need and in what quantity. I also think you should restrict yourselves to using only three divers. Perhaps Ariana could act in a reserve capacity in the event one of you three should become ill or… something," Stefani said. He did not expound upon the or something. "So, I recommend that you have a total of twelve to fourteen air tanks at a minimum. That way you'll be able to conduct two dives per day over two days. After that, you'll have to have the tanks recharged. I see the you have the requisite number of regulators, masks, fins, suits, etcetera. Let me see…" paused Stefani. "I think that covers just about everything. Oh, wait, yes, you have two first aid kits, morphine, sulfanilamide, and syringes. Bob, I see that you're certified in first aid and CPR resuscitation. Mmm… let me see." Stefani pondered.

"Did I not tell you," piped up Rosetta. "I found a boat to charter, the DiMarlo, out of Genoa. I have all the required paperwork and I think the captain and crew are more than qualified and capable for our purposes. Of course, Enzo, I would feel better if you were able to confirm this for us.' Rosetta sat back proudly. Bob clasped her hand tightly, as if to say, well done.

"I will, Rosetta. Good job on your part. Eh, well I do know that you women have all worked very hard and have prepared yourselves well. I know you will do fine, but remember, don't push yourselves. Never try to do too much" Enzo Stefani looked at Rosetta and Barbara intently. "If you should be down at forty to fifty feet, stay under for only thirty to forty minutes. This will be especially true if you should be exerting yourselves. And if you should find yourselves at, say seventy to eighty feet, remain under for only fifteen to twenty minutes. You must always remain calm and work methodically. Nitrogen build-up in the bloodstream could well prove fatal." Stefani had always pounded that point home. It was more than a cardinal rule for him.

"Enzo, you don't want to join us?" implored Barbara as she batted her eyes at Stefani.

"No, I think that all of you are more than capable. However, if something should arise, something unexpected, don't take chances. You should contact me immediately. Oh, yes, Rosetta I see that you have secured the requisite paperwork from the government so that you can conduct the dive. Good."

"Enzo, please accept our thanks. I don't think we could've even realistically contemplated pulling this off without your help and assistance," Rosetta said, who seemed to be melting herself into Bob's side.

Barbara Danilo had been closely watching the dynamics being played out between the Rossi's during the evening. She was secretly pleased for them. They had been down a long and perilous road. They now seemed to be on their way to a better place. It reminded her of her own rekindled relationship with Mauro Guzzo

Enzo Stefani self-deprecatingly tilted the side of his head in silent acknowledgment and gratitude.

* * *

Once again, Pasco Gonevento stood outside the chambers of his superior, Cardinale Ernesto Maggione. The young priest knocked lightly in a foreboding sense of trepidation and a building reservoir of contempt for the man. For months, Gonevento had had to suffer one indignity after

216

another. He could never get over Maggione's absolute and utter crudeness in the way he treated Gonevento. Here was supposed to be a man of God, a member of the cloth, a servant of the people?

"Enter!" came the command from Maggione.

Pasco Goneconto did as he had been ordered. He brought himself up until he stood just before the cardinal, mute and filled with loathing.

Maggione kept his attention directed to some document, occasionally writing a notation in its margins with a quill pen. Gonevento looked down and had never been able to get over the fact that Maggione still actually used a genuine quill-feathered pen. He supposed the man just liked the fact he had to dip the point into a reservoir of ink. Such pompousness, indeed!

Maggione still had not looked up. "Well, Gonevento?"

"You sent for me, Cardinale?" stammered Gonevento. He began to shift his weight from one foot to the other, his disgust only building. Maybe he would be unable to restrain himself from striking the man.

"Yes, I did," said Maggione, still looking down, still being contemptible. "I want you to direct word to your contact that we will be suspending a need for their services for the time being." Only now did Maggione look up. A look of barely concealed loathing was cast across his face.

"Err... may I ask why, Cardinale?" asked the young priest, a palpable fear taking shape within his body.

"No, you may not. Let us say that I have my reasons."

"As you wish, Cardinale."

Maggione returned his attention to the document. "Well? That will be all, Gonevento. You have no further need to stand before me like a dummy."

Pasco Gonevento nodded and turned on his heel and thought of a single word, *Swine!* There would be a special place in hell for the likes of Ernesto Maggione.

Maggione looked up and almost as much said to himself, *I think I may have to turn to my own contact deep within the East German secret police.*

* * *

Dawn on September 8, 1948 opened brightly for the four women of Rosetta Rossi's dive team. They were gathered on a Genoese dock set amongst some abandoned warehouses. Despite the building sunlight, there was a sense of coldness about like a shroud. Rosetta could intuitively feel it. All were ready to board their vessel, the venerable MS Di Marlo. The boat was captained by Paolo Marchetti, another Italian navy man from the war. Marchetti had once commanded one of the fearsome MAS motor torpedo boats in action in the Mediterranean, mostly against British naval forces. His crew of five men were also all veteran one-time navy men. They were all professional and all knew what they were doing.

Rosetta Rossi, Barbara Danilo, Ann Carter, and Ariana Rossi had all trained diligently, especially during the months of July and August. During the first two weeks, they had dove four times per week: Tuesdays and Thursdays, and both days on the weekend. The last two weeks of August had been confined to Saturdays and Sundays.

All of them were ready and itching to go. Rosetta had mentioned, and Enzo Stefani had concurred, that all the women were trained to the highest degree possible. They were as finely honed as a razor-sharp knife. She had been concerned they may have over-trained and would act irresponsibly if a chance arose. Still, it was now or never.

The DiMarlo plowed its way onward from Genoa and through its gulf waters. Scattered flocks of seagulls flew overhead. All in all, everything seemed set for a good day. Rosetta was hopeful they'd be able to locate the wreck of the Moschilo on that Saturday and failing that, find some semblance of it by Sunday. Failure to do so would force them to recalculate their prospects. They would have to return, and that would mean they would need more money.

Much of the girls' equipment had been courtesy of the US Navy and some of it from discarded stores from the war. The dive suits had been a tricky proposition, in that all four women possessed substantially larger frames than was found on most women. Men's large-sized dive suits had been found to be most suitable, as it were, for them.

Additional funding could be partially filled by Barbara Danilo from her own ample bank accounts and investments. Danilo had assured Rosetta she was sure she could pressure some kind of monetary commitment from Maserati if needed.

Following the women's prayer meeting on the DiMarlo's after deck, each one made herself ready. All the equipment had been checked and rechecked. It was time. Rosetta looked over at the slightly bent figure of Pasco Borrelli. She thought it would be fortuitous to their project to have the old man on board. Indeed, with his intimate knowledge of the area and its waters, it would be doubly so.

Incredibly, they were able to find the buoy marker that Rosetta had placed earlier, still tied to the German machine gun. They had all agreed to dive first just to the east of it. There had to be something more from the sunken Italian steamer that would reveal itself.

Rosetta Rossi cast a final look at her compadres and dropped herself into the water. Small pockets of air bubbles filled her view out beyond the portal of her dive mask. The water's temperature did not seem too cold to her. All three of the women had chosen to dive without head coverings.

Rosetta's curled blond hair flowed out as she waited for Barbara Danilo and Ann Carter to join her. Seconds later, Barbara descended into her view. She flashed an upward sign with her thumb. Rosetta gave her own thumbs up. Then, Ann Carter dropped downward. She was only distinguishable from her companions because of her straightened blonde hair.

The three women descended down toward the ocean floor. Rosetta took a reading of her depth gage, which registered around forty feet. Light filtered down through the water to the women, but they would still need their powerful light torches for additional illumination.

As the women swam on, all noted the current was not particularly strong. A few sea turtles paddled away from them, not at all unduly disturbed by the presence of the dark-figured swimmers in their midst. They all proceeded deliberately, clearly mindful of Enzo Stefani's recurring words. Stefani had also recommended to them that if they indeed located the hulk of the Moschilo they were to proceed very cautiously. There could well be beams or broken pieces of the hull covered with coral and shellfish and small projections of all kinds. Brush up against them and one could easily cut her breathing tube. The ex-Italian commando had also spoken of monsters of the deep. Fish that were dangerous for any diver to encounter. However, he assured them most fish were more likely to be as wary of the diver as she was of them.

Rosetta led the way by having placed herself in the center. Barbara was positioned on her left flank about ten to fifteen feet away. Ann Carter was to her right in the starboard position. Rosetta switched on her torch, which only slightly improved her vision. She thought it would have provided better illumination.

All of the women were well-aware and made a constant check of their respective air supplies. Nearly twenty-five minutes into their dive, Rosetta spied something ahead about twenty-five feet away. She swam toward the perceived object and when she got there, she saw quite clearly it was the helmsman's wheel of the very ship they were after. In bold gold and black highlighted letters, was the word MOSCHILO. She immediately waved over Barbara and Ann.

Barbara slapped a hand to Rosetta's right shoulder. Ann Carter, a thumbs-up and a toothy smile. It was as much of smile as the Englishwoman could muster through her dive-mask.

The three women moved on, continuing in an easterly direction. Rosetta checked her air supply; about ten to fifteen minutes left. Almost at that very instant, she saw Ann gesticulate wildly. Dead ahead rested the upturned remains of the MS Moschilo. It was plainly evident she had slipped beneath the waves of the Gulf of Genoa. The Moschilo had somehow corkscrewed herself over and then become embedded in the soft sands of the sea floor.

Rosetta observed that some wooden boxes had been scattered along the bottom. She and Barbara swam over to some of them. Barbara reached down and took hold of a gold bar. Imprinted along one side was a swastika and an identification number.

Rosetta grabbed hold of another bar, and then signaled to Barbara and Ann that they should surface. The day had been beyond their expectations. They had found the Moschilo, and they now had tangible, unmistakable proof of a cache of gold. At least there was some gold. As to how much, who could tell? They would dive again in a couple of more hours. Some rest and recharging of their own internal batteries was now in order. Rosetta took out a small marker buoy from her waistband and tied its string around one the crates. She then let the buoy rise to the surface.

Shadowing the DiMarlo at a safe and inconspicuous distance was a thirty-foot black-hulled craft. On-board stood Gianni Ravelli and three skin divers. Their head man was Albero Conti, nephew of crime boss, Fabrizio Valpone.

"Do not approach our target too closely, Mondari," commanded Ravelli to the erstwhile captain of the boat. "I do not want to give ourselves away, if we can help it."

"Do not worry, Signore Ravelli," said Alberto Conti with an air of the utmost confidence. We know what to do."

"Are you sure you have enough with only three divers?" queried Ravelli as he closely watched the activity on the DiMarlo through his Zeiss field glasses.

"More than enough. After all, we're only dealing with women, are we not?" leered Conti.

Ravelli took his eyes from his Zeiss and turned toward Conti. "Don't get overconfident, Conti. These are not ordinary women." Ravelli well-remembered hearing of the cautionary words of Marco Dubnik when he had informed Ravelli of Herve Villot's boast of being easily able to handle just one of these women, Rosetta Rossi. The woman had kicked his ass underwater. "I think you should get your men ready, Conti."

"I will know as to when we should get ready, Ravelli. Look, the divers are now just surfacing. And by the looks of things, they have found the Moschilo and maybe what she may have been carrying."

"Well, all the more reason for you to get ready now," fired back a now pensive and concerned Gianni Ravelli.

"No, I don't think they will dive again for at least another two hours. They will need to replenish themselves. We are talking about a dive operation, Ravelli. It's a little different from walking from one venue to another on dry land."

* * *

One by one, Rosetta, Barbara, and Ann Carter were hoisted back aboard the DiMarlo. Rosetta removed her mask and waved the gold bar in her hand. "Well, we found it, the Moschilo!

And some of her treasure?" exclaimed an excited Bob Rossi, a broad smile creasing his face.

"Yes, indeed, we have." Rosetta smiled back. "I think we'll rest for a couple of hours or so, and then go back down."

"The mother lode!" shouted an exultant Barbara Danilo. "It was quite a fucking sight, I'll tell you."

Bob Rossi turned to Barbara, slightly aghast at her use of an expletive. He had to admit he was still trying to get used to some, at least, of this new breed of Italian women and some of their newly found customs. "You've done well, dear," said Bob as he embraced his wife. "I'm so proud of you."

"Ehh, we've only just found the Moschilo and some gold. We'll have to go back down. I'm afraid we'll have to bring in the US Navy. The Moschilo is now resting over on its back. It may be too difficult for us to gain entry into it," Rosetta explained at length.

None of the women ate anything of substance other than some pieces of fruit. They were still too highly charged up from their electrifying first dive. Rosetta and Barbara would elect to wear dive hoods when they went down on the second dive. The water had turned slightly colder than they'd anticipated. Ann Carter chose not to wear a hood. Her golden blond hair would again flow forth.

* * *

"Signore Bob, I think you should have look at this," Captain Paolo Marchetti said cautiously as he pointed toward the black-hulled boat lying stationary about one-half mile away. "I've been watching this boat for a while now. At first I didn't give it much thought, but after watching things through my field glasses, I think it might be wise to pay more attention to it."

Bob Rossi took the proffered binoculars from Marchetti and looked at the craft occupied by Gianni Ravelli and company. "What do you think it means?" asked Rossi, trepidation and concern lined his voice.

"Who is to say?" Marchetti said with a shrug. "Just that we should bear things in mind when your wife and her friends return to the water."

By this time, Pasco Borrelli had sidled his way near to Marchetti and Rossi, but remained mute. He thought the black-hulled boat could well mean ominous things might be afoot. Gold. The lure of gold could result in many unfortunate things, both for the possessor of it and those in pursuit of it.

Just before 1:00 PM, Rosetta Rossi, Barbara Danilo and Ann Carter, sans hood, were ready to make their second dive on the Moschilo. Rosetta, as team leader, was the first to descend into the water. She was quickly followed by Danilo and Carter. The DiMarlo was by now anchored virtually just above the wreck. Bob Rossi had taken his wife aside only moments before, warning her of the presence of their visitor. Rosetta took the news in stride. Nothing could or would deter her now. They had all worked too hard and for too long.

Rosetta instructed Ann to act in the role of guardian as she and Barbara conducted a closer inspection of the boat and the gold. As Rosetta and Barbara approached the Moschilo, they turned on their torches. Small fishes fluttered about the shattered hulk seemingly oblivious to their human visitors. It was almost as if the women were being invited into their presence. Some crystallized growths could be seen along the hull.

Rosetta suddenly pulled to a stop. She motioned to Barbara with her pointed right hand. There, just beneath them, lay the presence of two skeleton forms. No doubt members of the crew. It made for a ghastly and forlorn scene.

Both women tried as best they could to put the picture aside and continue with their work. Broken wooden crates lay scattered about as if a child had tossed out the contents of a toy box. Gold bars had been their content.

Rosetta and Barbara both removed their knives from their scabbards and began to probe the soft sand that now provided the gravesite for the Moschilo. As the women worked below the surface, new developments were unfolding atop it.

"Signore Bob. I think our visitors are preparing for action," said Captain Marchetti laconically as he pointed to the black vessel.

"Yes, I see." Bob Rossi scanned the horizon with the Zeiss binoculars. "All right, Rufo, prepare the M-1s. I think we may need them." Rossi had issued the command as if were back on the battlefield. In a strange way, he

223

felt himself calming to the situation even though he was well-aware of the potential danger that lurked below for his wife and the others.

Michele Rufo went to the small cupboard-like compartment on the starboard side of the bridge and took hold of the M-1 Garand rifles. Bob Rossi had decided to take the precaution of bringing the weapons along just in case they might be needed. Rufo was another of the World War II Italian navy, having served with Marchetti aboard his MAS torpedo boat.

"Eh, you see, my friend," said Alberto Conti to Gianni Ravelli. "Our friends are now about to dive again on the wreck, and as you can see, we are ready to go forth." Conti finished his little soliloquy with a flourish. He was clearly relishing the moment. He and his men would show these impudent women.

"Yes, I can see, Conti. Let me remind you once again not to underestimate these women. They are deadly, especially the Rossi woman," Gianni Ravelli said. Angst and an increasing anxiety began a slow build-up within his body.

"Do not worry, my friend. My associates and I will make short work of all of them." And with that, Alberto Conti completed his own preparation of his dive equipment. He and his two men would not be using spear guns. He thought them to be too new and unreliable. Conti and company would dispatch the women to a watery grave by use of knives.

"Ariana! Ariana!" Bob shouted out to his step-daughter. "Get your equipment on now! *Subito! Subito!*" Ariana, who was standing right next to Rossi, nodded her assent. She had been startled by his use of the Italian word for right away.

"You must go and warn Ros—your mother and the others to expect visitors," Bob said. He didn't feel as if he had to add the fact that these visitors would have ill will in mind. But he did anyway. "Ariana, you must try and get them out of the water immediately."

Ariana nodded and then hurriedly donned her scuba equipment. She cast a last look at Bob Rossi and gave him a thumbs-up, and then dropped into the water. As she descended through the water, Ariana suddenly remembered she had not placed her weight belt on. Well, no matter, what was done was done. It was too late now.

Swimming as determinedly and prudently as she could, Ariana could just about make out her mother and Barbara Danilo working together alongside the shattered vessel. As she approached them she thought they resembled blowfish what with their mouths clamped around their mouthpieces. It was an odd juxtaposition for Ariana, which she quickly put out of her mind.

Rosetta noticed Ariana's presence and instantly recognized the fact that something must be wrong for the girl to be now down amongst them. Ariana began gesticulating with her hands in sign language to her mother, who quickly got the message. Rosetta looked at Barbara, who also had understood what the girl meant.

Meanwhile, Ann Carter, positioned just above and to the right of the Moschilo wreck, spotted the approach of Alberto Conti and his two henchmen. She tensed for only a moment as she slowly extracted her dive knife from the scabbard hooked to her right calf. Ann Carter, who had never before been engaged in even a fist fight on dry land, was about to enter knife-fight thirty feet underwater, but she was ready and determined to do what had to be done.

Alberto Conti directed Robbi Penta to deal with the blonde-haired woman without the hood, the one whose hair was floating around her head. Penta acknowledged receipt of Conti's command, knife already in hand, and dove toward Ann Carter.

Carter prepared herself for her attacker. But she would allow him to make the first move. She thought she could detect a leer in the man's face, as if he thought the deed was already done. Well, she hoped she would be able to give him a little surprise.

Penta lunged at Carter with his knife extended from his right hand. Upon seeing this, Ann deftly shifted her body a little to her left and as Penta drifted by her, she swiftly sliced upward with her own knife, just catching her assailant's air hose. Not hesitating for a second, Ann thrust with the knife upward, setting off a cascade of air bubbles from around Penta's head. The man grabbed at his head with his two hands, violently shaking it from side to side.

Ann watched in silent fascination as the man began flailing in his attempt to reach the surface. As she contemplated going after him to finish him off, she caught sight out of the corner of her eye Alberto Conti going after Barbara Danilo. She immediately kicked her legs into overdrive to try and get to Barbara to help her from her attacker. It was no time to be cautious or worried about over-exertion.

Long anticipating this engagement with these Amazonian women, as Gianni Ravelli had put it, Alberto Conti dove on his target with a degree of alacrity. His sudden move on Barbara initially surprised her. The pair grappled with one another in a whirling, violent dance. Conti was surprised to find how strong this woman was. Twisting and turning, bubbles of air frothing the water, both knives they exposed flashed in the dull light muted by forty feet of ocean. Conti was finally able to obtain a grip around Barbara Danilo's waist. He plunged his dagger into her right shoulder.

The entry of the knife stunned Barbara who instantly screwed up her eyes and nearly bit off her mouthpiece. Blood filled the water around her and Conti. But before he could inflict another stab wound on Danilo, Alberto Conti felt the left forearm of Ann Carter close around his throat. Now he was truly surprised and shocked. Ann Carter increased the pressure around the man's throat as she brought up her right hand to tighten and secure her death grip. She drove Alberto Conti to the ocean floor. Ann only wished she hadn't dropped her knife on her way over to help Barbara.

As Conti was plunged downward, his last conscious thought was how could all of this occur… and how he managed to have succumbed to a woman.

Watching all of this play out was an absolutely stunned and shaken Ariana Rossi. She had just watched Ann Carter, the young Englishwoman, dispatch two men. Quickly regaining her senses, Ariana noticed her mother who had moved to assist Barbara Danilo, who was bleeding so profusely that Ariana feared Danilo might well bleed to death.

During the maelstrom between Ann Carter and two of the divers, Rosetta had been about to face off against the third man, Roberto Tosta. Withdrawing her dive knife from its scabbard, Rosetta had watched as her assailant approached, her body tensing for her own possible fight to the death. Suddenly, the man turned and took off, swimming as fast as he could. Roberto Tosta had no stomach for taking on Rosetta Rossi, or any one of the women they had been sent after.

Seeing her friend in distress, Rosetta swam over to the swirling blood that enveloped Barbara Danilo. She could see her friend was still conscious. It was vital that Barbara remain so and not go into shock. Taking off one of her gloves, Rosetta tried as best she could to apply pressure on the wound in Barbara's shoulder.

Ariana had debated as to whether she should go after the third attacker, but she realized she had also forgotten to take her own dive knife. Instead, she swam over to Barbara Danilo and tried to provide whatever assistance she could to her mother's own efforts to save Danilo's life.

CHAPTER ELEVEN-
SALVAGE/ MURDER

Slowly, Rosetta and Ariana brought Barbara up to the surface, breaking water about a hundred feet from the Moschilo. Ann Carter surfaced almost simultaneously and could see Captain Marchetti and his crewmen swinging into action to bring the boat closer to the women. She also saw the black-hulled craft move toward two men struggling in the water about two hundred yards off. Undoubtedly, the swine attackers who had tried to kill her and her two friends.

"What happened?" cried out Bob Rossi as he took in the scene of his wife and stepdaughter cradling a clearly in distress and wounded Barbara Danilo.

Rosetta shook her head as she and Ariana tried mightily to heave Barbara upward into the waiting strong arms of two of Marchetti's men. She and Ariana soon climbed aboard.

"I'm going back down to get one of the pieces of shit who tried to kill us!" shouted a defiant Ann Carter, who replaced her mouthpiece into her mouth and dove under. Rosetta tried to dissuade her, but it was of no use. Ann was determined to retrieve the body of Alberto Conti.

Back on the Moschilo's after deck, Bob Rossi quickly took command and control of the situation. He knew he would have to staunch the flow of blood from Barbara's wound and it would have to be done immediately. There was no telling how much blood she had already lost. Bob also had to prevent the woman from slipping into shock.

Taking hold of Rosetta's knife, he deftly cut away the rubber dive suit around Barbara's right shoulder. It was as if he were filleting a flounder fish. As Rossi tossed aside some of the neoprene rubber, Barbara's right breast had become partially exposed, but no matter, it had to be done. It was no time for false modesty.

"We'll have to apply pressure to the wound and we have to keep her conscious. I'll go first, then you, Rosetta, and then Ariana," commanded Rossi.

Just as soon as he had handed Barbara off to Rosetta, Rossi went to Marchetti's side. "How long before we can reach Genoa?"

Paolo Marchetti shrugged, but his reply was dead-level in earnest. "Perhaps forty to forty-five minutes."

"Push this boat to its limit. I don't care what the risk is. Also, radio our situation to Genoa. We're going to need an ambulance standing by the moment we arrive."

"*Si*, signore, it shall be done. Do not worry, we will get Signora Barbara safely back."

Bob Rossi looked back at Barbara Danilo as she lay prone and helpless on the deck. Occasionally, she thrashed her legs from side to side and moaned. It was a pitiful sound, but there was little else anyone could do. Rosetta kept applying a steady pressure to the wound by pressing gauze pads against it. Blood was still seeping thought the bandages, but Rossi thought it might be subsiding. He hoped and prayed the wound looked more serious than it actually was. He'd given Barbara a shot of morphine for her pain and applied sulfanilamide to the wound.

Not five minutes later just before the Moschilo set course for Genoa, Ann Carter surfaced with the body of Alberto Conti. Quickly, it and Carter were hauled aboard and Captain Marchetti gunned the engines of the boat.

Rosetta nestled herself within the framework of Bob's powerful arms as she recounted what had transpired beneath the surface. She spared him few

229

details in her description of the events and she paid great tribute and thanks to the work of Ann Carter. None of them would be alive had it not been for the young Englishwoman. Rosetta marveled at the woman's coolness and how she had been able to dispatch not one, but two attackers.

"Well, the main thing is you're all safe, save for Barbara's condition. But I think things appear to be stabilizing for her," Bob said as he continued to comfort and soothe his wife. He couldn't tell himself enough how grateful he truly was.

"I'm glad you didn't hesitate to send Ariana in to warn us," said Rosetta.

"It was not an easy decision to make, but I thought you might have killed me after you found out. After all, she is your daughter and… well, you know. I know how protective Italian mothers can be when it comes to their children."

"She's a grown woman, my love, and as much as I'm protective within reason, I would've been most disappointed if you'd forbidden her to go over."

Bob didn't reply, but he had been struck by Rosetta's response and reasoning. Clearly, as if he needed confirmation, these women were not at all what may have been considered typical Italian women; women who would be content to spend their lives within the succor of the indoor lifestyle.

It was just past 3:00 PM when the MS Moschilo chugged its way into Genoa's sprawling harbor, abuzz with the normal maritime traffic one would have expected in any major port in the world. Marchetti guided it back to the very same dock from where they'd embarked from only several hours before. Waiting for them was a white, red-crossed emblazoned vehicle.

By this time, Barbara Danilo had drifted off into a restless sleep. Ariana was now holding the compress on the wound in Danilo's shoulder. Two white-clad, burly men gently placed the wounded woman on a stretcher and maneuvered her off the Moschilo and into the ambulance. Rosetta Rossi, now dressed in civilian attire, climbed into the vehicle to accompany her friend on the short one and half mile journey to the city's main hospital.

"Your friend is very lucky, my dear," began Dottore Alberto Martino. He spoke patiently and soothingly to Rosetta Rossi. "The wound was approximately 1.85 inches in depth. Fortunately, the knife impacted mostly muscle mass in Miss Danilo's shoulder. You and your compatriots did a good job in stanching the blood flow and you getting her to medical attention quickly also helped."

"*Grazie*, Dottore, I'm very grateful for all you have done for Barbara, but I'd be remiss if I didn't mention what my husband did for her. He really took the lead," replied a thankfully relieved Rosetta.

"I'm afraid your friend won't be able to dive again any time in the near future. We have to guard against the onset of infection. But with the new wonder drug penicillin, we should be able to prevent it."

As Dr. Martino walked away from her, Rosetta thought to herself, *you will not be able to drive race cars for Maserati for a while either, my friend.*

* * *

Several days after the debacle in the waters off Vento Beach, a nervous and near shaking Roberto Tosto stood before Don Fabrizio Valpone in the spacious living room of his villa set in the hills above the town of Varuglia. The picturesque village was less than ten miles from Genoa.

"Tell me what happened, Tosto. Do not spare any details," snarled a furious Valpone. The Don had been more than upset upon hearing the news of the death of his nephew, Alberto Conti. He was now filled with a seething rage. Someone would pay, and dearly.

"Well… you see, Don Valpone," stammered a quaking Tosto. "Alberto had assigned each one of the three of us to go after one of the women divers. My target was the woman to the right of us. Alberto went after the next one in line, and so on." Tosto could feel his knees begin to shake and his legs turning to jelly. He thought he might well collapse.

"Go on. Why did things go so badly? Why is my beloved nephew dead?" roared Fabrizio Valpone.

"Well… well, you see, this other… this other woman diver, well, she wasn't wearing a dive hood. She had blonde hair. Well, Don Valpone, she first took out Robbi Penta by cutting his air hose. She then went after… after your nephew, who was, as I have said, going after the center woman." Tosto

231

paused, almost to help himself regain some sense of his equilibrium. He took out a handkerchief and mopped his brow with it.

"And this blonde-haired woman killed my nephew? How?" Don Valpone questioned. His black eyes continued to bore into Roberto Tosto's own unremittingly.

"Well, Don Valpone, she strangled him."

"Strangled him, you say?"

Tosto could see the anger building itself up again within Valpone. "This woman took hold of Alberto by the throat. Mind you, Alberto had inflicted a serious wound upon this other woman. Blood was all over the place and—"

Valpone held up a hand to silence the frightened Tosto. "And you, my friend, what were you doing while this melee was going on? Could you not have assisted Alberto in any way?" sneered Valpone, as he bit off his words.

"Well, you see, Don Valpone, a fourth woman diver entered the water and—"

Once again Valpone held up a hand to Tosto. "Oh, I see, a fourth woman entered the scene. And this, of course, tipped the balance irretrievably against you. You are worthless, Tosto. Completely worthless. Take him away!" bellowed Fabrizio Valpone.

"No, no, please, Don Valpone! I beg of you. I… I… we did all we could, but," Roberto Tosto was now openly weeping as he was hauled away by two of Valpone's burly henchmen. They knew what they were to do with Tosto.

"Carlo." Valpone motioned to his lieutenant, Carlo DeLuglio. "Find out who this blonde-haired woman diver is. We'll start with her and work our way to the other two, or, I guess it is now three other women. Yes, begin with this woman, the one who killed my nephew."

DeLuglio nodded his assent and left immediately to begin his assignment.

* * *

Marco Rossi was seated on a barstool at Cafe Fontana, a small, less than impressive tavern situated along Via di Coronari. It was nearly directly across the Tiber River and the Castel Sant'Angelo. The early September night was rather warm and sultry. Earlier, rain clouds had cleared off and yet, a lingering funereal air hung about.

Young Marco was reflecting on the rather dismal turn of events that had come to mark his life in recent months. Who was he, and where was he going? He had embraced several rounds of Scotch whiskey when he felt a bump to his right elbow. When he turned to face his neighbor, he slowly recognized that it was none other than Ariana's long lost former boyfriend, Angelo Tomma.

"Nice night, is it not?" he greeted Marco. "I haven't seen you in a while, Marco."

"No, it has been a long time…er, Angelo?" Marco struggled with his recollection of the man. He wasn't sure if it was because of time or whether it was due to the amount of alcohol he had consumed to that point. Perhaps it was a combination of both.

"Indeed, indeed. In any event, how are you, and how is Ariana?" Tomma asked cautiously while signaling the bartender for his attention. "What are you drinking, Marco?"

"Oh, nothing, Angelo. I think I've had enough for the evening." Marco turned to face Tomma more fully. It was strange, thought Marco, but now Tomma seemed to have emerged in a different light. Different from the picture Ariana had painted as a result of her last, for her anyway, frightening experience with Tomma.

"You know, Marco. I've come to realize I was not good to Ariana. In fact, I was an asshole. I have come to realize that now."

Probably too late, thought Marco silently. Well, he would listen to Angelo for a little while, at least. Then he would have to move on.

"I was wondering," Tomma resumed cautiously, if you might be able to put in a good word for me with Ariana. That is, if you would not mind."

"Good word, Angelo? I am not so sure it would do any good. I could try, but I can't promise you anything," Marco Rossi said, wishing he could extricate himself from Angelo Tomma.

"Well, in any event, I would really appreciate it if you could tell her that I believe I have changed for the better," continued Tomma plaintively.

Marco, again thought to himself that indeed Ariana had herself changed a hundred and eighty degrees in just the past year or so. What with her workout regimen and diving with their mother and the other women. He kept this to himself. "Angelo, I wish you well, but I'm afraid I'm going to have to call it a night."

As he got up to leave, Marco leaned in toward Angelo Tomma. "You were a foolish man and didn't treat my sister nicely. But, I am a forgiving man. When, and if, I feel the time may be right, I may put in a word for you. Do not get your hopes up. Ariana has moved on in so many ways from just a short time ago."

* * *

Slowly, Barbara Danilo began to recover from the grievous wound that had been inflicted upon her. Rosetta visited her as often as she could manage in the hospital. It was a hectic time for her, what with the gym's continuing activities and the recovery effort connected with the Moschilo.

On a sunny Sunday afternoon, Rosetta was sitting with her friend as they sipped minted tea. There was hardly a cloud to be seen in the azure, blue-colored sky. Seagulls and robins flittered about seemingly on gossamer wings.

"And how are our colleagues doing?" asked Barbara, who was now able to sit up in a chair. Her blue eyes were slowly regaining their character and definition.

"Oh, pretty well," answered Rosetta. "Although, I am a little concerned about Ann. You know, just the other day, she was telling me about the moment she killed the man who attacked you. It was rather an extraordinary thing in that she said she felt as if she almost enjoyed killing the man. It gave her a feeling of ultimate empowerment," said Rosetta as she looked wistfully out the window of Barbara's hospital room.

"Well, all I can say is that she saved my life. I thought I was going to die, but she showed up almost out of nowhere. I never realized Ann would have been capable of what she did. I will always be grateful to her."

Rosetta remained silent as she took a sip of her tea and nodded at Barbara's remark.

"By the way, not to change the subject, but how are things going in connection with our salvage effort?"

Rosetta seemed to brighten at Barbara's question. "Oh, pretty well, I think. Bob has managed to get the government involved. In fact, when he got word to them about our find, they immediately dispatched a naval vessel to keep vigil over the site. You know, to help prevent any interlopers from trying to move in and take advantage of things."

"Indeed. I'm a little shocked to hear the government we love to poke fun at has moved with any type of alacrity. Pleased, but shocked as well."

Rosetta nodded.

"Not only will I be unable to resume diving for the foreseeable future, but I'm afraid my driving at Maserati will be suspended as well," interjected a now unsmiling Barbara Danilo.

"You'll just have to take things a little more slowly. At least, for the time being. By the way, how is Mauro?"

"Oh, he's doing well. He was just here this morning. In fact, we were able to have a little roll in the hay. It was short, but sweet. You must have just missed him on your way in. As I was saying, we had sex, but I have to concede I'll need curtail my sexual activity in the future as well. Although, I do believe I can always give him a pretty good hand job. Provided, that is, I use my left hand." She threw her head back in unbridled and unrestrained laughter.

"Barbara, you will never change. And I thank God for that," Rosetta said as she, too, laughed. Indeed, Barbara must be healing quite well. She still retained her bright outlook on life. Nothing would ever diminish her spirit, her vitality. She lived to seize the day. Every day.

* * *

For the rest of September, Rosetta and Bob Rossi were almost exclusively engaged in obtaining additional support from the Italian government and assistance from the US Navy and its salvage capabilities. Bob was forced to take a leave of absence from his job and he used it to make full use of his contacts with the navy. Rosetta was able to persuade her

AMGOT superiors that her work with the Moschilo salvage effort was necessary and justified. After all, her involvement, the entire effort, everything, was for the purpose of giving back to Italy and those unfortunates who had had their life's savings taken from them. Some of those unfortunates had also paid with their very lives.

Soon, all was ready for a return to the Moschilo dive site. Rosetta and Ariana would dive and provide guidance to a team of US Navy frogmen. Six divers from the famed underwater demolition team that had been formulated by the navy in the Second World War. It had been the responsibility of these specially selected and trained men to scout enemy occupied beaches, and also to help clear away beach obstacles through the use of explosives.

The frogmen, Rosetta and Ariana, Bob Rossi, and Enzo Stefani were all aboard the APA Samuel Burrows, a veteran in its own right of the navy's brutal and savage Pacific campaign against the Japanese. The Burrows had been a survivor of several Japanese kamikaze attempts to sink her during the US Marines invasion of Iwo Jima in February 1945.

Today, the Samuel Burrows was on a different mission. On her decks lay three UDT small-craft boats, specifically designed to launch and collect navy frogmen. Two of them would be utilized by the navy divers. The other would be occupied by Rosetta, Ariana, and Stefani. The venerable veteran of Italian navy underwater campaigns in the Med had been persuaded by the Rossi's to assist them in the recovery effort.

One vital piece of equipment on board the Burrows was a powerful Caterpillar marine engine bolted down to the after deck. This would provide the power source for the operation of a giant vacuum unit. The one-foot diameter hose would be deployed over the Burrows starboard side and would be extended down to the Moschilo. The suction created would bring up the sand and soil presently encasing the wreck. This would clear the way for the divers to gain better access to the suspected gold within the hold of the Moschilo. Then, a sling would be brought into action to bring the gold the surface. Provided it was truly there. The sand vacuumed off the seabed would be brought up as well and filtered into a barge which had accompanied the navy ship.

Seagulls crisscrossed the soft Ligurian skies overhead accompanied by the occasional sea skua. Rosetta, Ariana, and Enzo Stefani held a final briefing with Bob Rossi, the team's unofficial dive manager. All was ready, all was set. The time had finally arrived for them to go down and retrieve a treasure trove of gold.

Rosetta set her mask in place and secured her mouthpiece. Ariana and Stefani did likewise. Making the sign of the cross, Rosetta jumped from the black raft into the waiting waters. She was the unofficial dive leader. It had been her vision, her drive, and her determination that had brought them all to this point.

Ariana and Stefani followed Rosetta over the UDT boat's side. Immediately they were joined by the navy frogmen. A cascade of air bubbles populated themselves around each of the divers' heads. Rosetta Rossi cautiously and methodically led the way downward to the waiting MS Moschilo.

As Enzo Stefani descended through the blue-green water, he was reminded of the first time he had dove and how, subsequently, he had always been amazed at the wonder he always seemed to experience. No monsters lurked about, only fish, and now humans were joining the underwater realm. It was Captain Nemo's world.

Rosetta pointed to the remains of the Moschilo with her torch and Stefani nodded. Visible were projections that might well have been beams, a recess that may well have been a bunk alcove. And, then Stefani's own light revealed the skeletal remains of a crewman. The veteran navy diver visibly recoiled at the sight. It was something one never got used to. The remains represented all that was left of what had been once a man. Who knew of the story of the life of this person who now called home a place at the bottom of the ocean.

Watching the scene unfold before her, Ariana could not begin to comprehend what was actually taking place. Although she was safely ensconced within a layer of neoprene rubber to ward off the cold, she instinctively felt a chill that went into and throughout every bone of her body. How ghostly, how utterly surreal, and yet, how transcendent. Here they all were in only about thirty or so feet of water, and yet it could well have been that they were on a construct on the far side of the moon.

The American navy divers had brought along with them their own powerful torch lights that while not exactly turning the scene into the light of day, a clear delineation of the Moschilo was chillingly beginning to be revealed.

Rosetta and Ariana watched these highly trained men go into action. All were canny professionals who knew their business. Rosetta realized her work was done. She had fulfilled her mission. Now, the only mystery that remained would be whether the Moschilo did indeed hold forth a hoard of gold or whether the yield would only amount to a few scattered gold bricks.

* * *

On that very day, Ann Carter paid a visit to the bedside of Barbara Danilo in Genoa. Truth be told, Ann had become deeply troubled in the wake of what had happened in the waters off Vento Beach. She was especially troubled by the fact she had felt a surging feeling of enthusiasm when she had literally choked out the life of the man who had attacked Barbara. Carter gave off an air of insouciant nonchalance, but just beneath the surface lay a curtain of deep and foreboding anxiety.

"I'm so glad you could come, Ann," Barbara said as she smiled at her friend. The pair were sitting at an outdoor patio area on the hospital grounds. It was a restful and peaceful setting.

"I'm sorry, Barbara. I should've visited you more often," apologized Ann, her eyes masked by her aviator-styled sunglasses.

"Oh, that's all right, dear. You don't have to apologize."

"No, you see, ever since that day… well, you could say that many things have changed. I… I…" Ann seemed to stagger, as if she were unsure of herself.

"Ann, please, look at me," said a now solemn Barbara as she reached out and patted one of Ann's hands. "I think I know what you're going through. Although I can't really say because I've never killed a man, or any person, but what you are experiencing can only be natural."

"I'd like to believe that, but I'm not so sure. You know, Barbara, I had never, ever once, been involved in a fight."

"You saved my life, dear. I'll never forget that for the rest of my life. You did what you had to do," Barbara said as she sipped her glass containing Jack Daniels mash whiskey. The liquor had been spirited inside the hospital grounds, courtesy of Ann Carter's visit.

"How long will it be before they release you?"

"Ironically, this is supposed to be the last full day I'll have to spend in this God-awful excuse of a hospital. They're discharging me tomorrow. Mauro will be coming to get me. I mean, the hospital and the staff have been great. And I have especially liked being in the care of Dottore Martino. A real hunk, if you know what I mean," Barbara said as she batted her bright blue eyes.

Ann nodded knowingly. "I am glad to hear that, Barbara.'

"And how are things going with you and Captain Anderson?"

"Uh… pretty well, I think. He's a nice man. He's gone through a lot himself, what with the war and his having lost his family," Ann said, looking down at the floor. She noticed for the first time she had placed different colored ankle socks on her feet. On the right was a white one and on the left was a black one. How could she have done that?

"I'm glad, but you should remember he's very lucky to have you. You have a good heart, Ann Carter."

"I think he knows that. And I am lucky to have him as well, especially right now."

Moments later, the two women said goodbye to one another. As Ann Carter was leaving the hospital, her departure was noted by none other than Dottore Alberto Martino.

"Yes, she has just left the hospital," gasped Martino into his phone in his office located on the hospital's ground floor. "How should I know how long it will take for her to get back to Rome. I would imagine not before five or six tonight." Martino listened attentively to the speaker at the other end of the line as beads of sweat appeared on his face and forehead. He was now regretting ever having gotten mixed up with this gang. But when you have a past of some ill-repute and you are currently in some monetary distress, you don't have a lot of options to turn to. "What about this Danilo woman? What is to be done with her?" Martino asked, fearing he would be assigned the task of killing Barbara Danilo right then and there. "All right, all right, I didn't mean to sound presumptuous or out of line. I'll stand by and await any further instructions."

* * *

By early afternoon, the UDT frogmen, under the command of Lieutenant David Edmonds were preparing to swing the giant vacuum into action along the hull of the Moschilo. Edmonds was an inspired choice to lead the navy's salvage effort, having been a veteran UDT diver with operations in North Africa and Italy.

Enzo Stefani went down to merely observe the proceedings. Rosetta and Ariana would remain aboard the Samuel Burrows. The Italian would serve in much the same role as would an emeritus chair would occupy on a university faculty. When the vacuum was finally in place, the navy divers began the suction process which would remove as much as possible the sand now encompassing the Moschilo's overturned hull.

Enzo Stefani watched the operation transfixed. No wonder Italy had had no chance against the combined forces of the United States and Great Britain. He continued watching as the divers worked calmly and methodically for more than an hour.

Then, one of the divers signaled to have the vacuum stopped. The command was given by the tugging of a rope that had been lowered into the water from the Burrows. Lt. Edmonds approached the Moschilo's shattered hull and reached out. It was almost as if he were gazing at an apparition and was bestowing reverence on the inanimate object now lying before him. Edmonds and his men completed their assessment and then ascended to the surface. Stefani followed them up.

"Well, what do you think?" asked Bob Rossi pensively.

The young navy lieutenant stroked his barely visible stubbled chin. "I think we're going to have to cut our way into the hull. It's a good thing we seem to have all the equipment we might need here on the Burrows."

"Yes, the Moschilo is, or was, a steel-hulled vessel. What do you think, Lieutenant? Perhaps a half-inch or so thickness?" Rossi inquired. Rosetta and Ariana had retreated into the background of the discussion. This was not of their provenance.

I think you are right, sir," replied Edmonds. "It's a little after two-thirty. The light will be fading soon. I think, if you agree, that it may be better if we wait until tomorrow morning to resume operations."

"I concur with your assessment, lieutenant. It is probably best and prudent that we wait," Rossi said.

* * *

It was just after 8:30 PM when Ann Carter found herself entering the outskirts of Rome. She was approaching the conclusion of a more than two-hundred-and-fifty-mile journey, most of it spent on the S-1 Autostrada. She was beyond exhausted as she motored her way through the Roman streets in her MG roadster, its top down, her golden-blonde hair flowing in the wind. Even though it was fall, it felt good to breathe in the cool air of the evening. If only the folks back in England could see her now, living the life of, *la dolce vita*, the sweet life.

Carter was driving down Via Ottaviano, heading directly toward Vatican City, when she noticed a black sedan that appeared to be tailing her. Thinking quickly to herself and trying not to panic, she decided to go on a little diversion before she headed for home on Via di Croce.

Taking a grip of the gearshift lever, Ann suddenly downshifted and hung a left onto Via Germanico, and then a right onto Via Cola di Rienzo. She looked into her rearview mirror to see that the sedan was still behind her. Ann had always felt at home in the city. In fact, Rome had become her *de facto* home for the past four-plus years. She was now just passing by the Castel Sant'Angelo, its outline framed by the surrounding street lighting when she decided to make a break for her apartment building.

Crossing the Ponte Umberto, Ann Carter pressed her right foot to the accelerator as he shifted into third gear. Racing down the main drag of Via Monte Breanzo, Carter thought she may have at last lost her pursuers. She allowed herself a breath of respite. She was now less than one-half mile from home.

Trying to locate a parking spot as close to her apartment as possible, Ann spied one just across from Piazza di Spagna. Not bothering to put up the top of the MG, Ann quickly got out and began walking. She had gone less than fifty feet when she noticed over her left shoulder two large burly men, dressed in topcoats walking rapidly behind her. Ann now wished that she had heeded the advice of Rosetta and Barbara when they had suggested that she obtain a firearm. Ann had scoffed at the idea as being unnecessary. How foolish she had been.

But now at that very moment, Ann Carter was alone and had the distinct feeling she was in desperate trouble. She paused for a minute and reached down to remove her shoes. She could make better progress. Almost immediately, Ann thought she was beginning to leave her pursuers further behind her. That was, until she stepped on a sharp-edged pebble with her right foot. Ann winced in pain and tried desperately to maintain her balance, but to no avail. Tumbling to the ground, Ann tried mightily to get back onto her feet. Before she realized it the men were upon her.

Sitting on the sidewalk, Ann Carter saw the men approach her. Quickly regaining her footing, Ann decided to go on the attack on the man closest to her on her left. She lashed out with a vicious karate-like kick that connected with the man's groin. He let out a howl as he swore in Italian the word for bitch. His accomplice, leering at the woman, moved in with his own assault.

After her karate kick, Ann had again lost her balance and was now her knees. She was trying to regain her footing when the second moved in and struck her with a mighty blow to the right side of her face. The force of the punch staggered Ann and she began to see stars and wondering if her jaw may have been broken. Still down on her knees, the man moved in again but Ann, despite her intense pain and the fogginess residing in her brain reached up with her right hand and secured a grip on the man's penis and balls. Ann Carter squeezed and squeezed and held on. The man howled and screamed as he somehow was able to extricate himself from Carter's grip.

Just as her head was beginning to clear a little, Ann felt the strike of a rubber truncheon that man number one had removed from a pocket in his trench coat. Ann Carter's head was now swimming in a maelstrom of fog, pain, and delirium. She didn't know how she would be able to get herself out of this predicament. She believed she wouldn't.

The first man, known as Carlo Vestri, was one of the low-level soldiers of Fabrizio Valpone's criminal empire. A heavy, lurking brute with a less than handsome face had been known to strangle to death chickens, and cats, and dogs in his youth. He soon gravitated to performing the same act, plus the occasional knifing and shooting on the enemies of Valpone.

Vestri removed a razor-sharp knife from his other pocket. When he reached down to Ann Carter who was now once again on her knees. Vestri pressed his left knee into the small of her back. This knocked the air out of Carter as she crashed to the ground. She had nothing left. She had fought with every ounce of her strength. Vestri took hold of her blonde hair with his left hand and with the knife in his right, swiftly drew it across the woman's throat.

Ann Carter's last conscious thought just before she was plunged into the ultimate darkness was, "I'm going to die. I wish I…"

* * *

The mantel clock was nearing the midnight hour and Carabinieri Chief Inspector Aldo Moretti was savoring a glass of zinfandel wine as he slowly paced in his living room. His wife, Francesca of more than twenty years had long been asleep. It had been a long, tiring day for the inspector; two murders, one so grisly it staggered his objective and professional sensibilities. The unfortunate individual had been identified as Marco Dubnik. Almost as the clock struck midnight, the phone which sat nearby on a small end table rang with what Moretti took to be an especially shrill sound. Reluctantly, he placed his wine down on to another table and went to retrieve the phone.

"*Pronto*," Moretti answered laconically as he unconsciously loosened the knot of his tie. It was a purple paisley one Francesca had given him last Christmas.

"Inspector, Cardoso here. Sorry to bother you at this hour, but something has come up that I thought you should know about."

"*Si*, go ahead," answered Moretti, who really did not want to hear about another case. He just couldn't handle another murder if that is what it was. As he listened to Cardoso, his blood began to run cold.

"Yes, sir. The body of a young woman was found behind some bushes along Via di Crice about one hour ago. The victim was youngish, perhaps thirty or so with blonde hair. She was also described as not looking Italian," Cardoso continued at length.

"How was the young woman killed?" asked Moretti cautiously. He thought it might well sound similar to the earlier murders he had been called to.

"The young woman's throat had been cut virtually from ear to ear. It was remarkably similar to the ones we saw earlier this evening," continued Cardoso straightforwardly. He was still in full police mode.

"Any idea as to her identity, Cardoso?"

"At this time, no. There was no identification of any kind on her. There is one other thing, Inspector…"

"And?"

"This woman must have put up a tremendous struggle. There was a deep laceration and swelling on the left side of her head and a deep bruise along the small of her back. From what the arriving officers said, she had a more than well-developed body. I mean this woman had tremendous musculature not seen in most women."

As Aldo Moretti listened to Cardoso, a thought came to his mind. Something concerning an athletic club, a gymnasium of some kind, organized by a group of women soon after the war. It had caused great angst among some of the leading members of the Church in Rome. It would bear looking into. He would mention this to Cardoso when they would meet the next day to develop a plan of investigative action. There might well be some connection to all these murders. "All right, Luigi, we'll meet at the station tomorrow morning and begin to put our heads together."

* * *

By 10:00 AM on a bright and clear October Sunday morning, the navy divers had already been in the water and at work on the Moschilo's hull for

244

nearly an hour. Calmly and professionally, Lieutenant David Edmonds directed his men as they cut a six foot by six-foot opening with the use of an acetylene torch. Once inside the hull, their flashlights highlighted a number of wooden crates, and among the detritus within the bowels of the once not so majestic steamer, lay scattered gold bars.

Around ten-thirty, the divers guided a large sling into the water. The sling was lowered from a crane mounted on the Samuel Burrows' deck. For the next two plus hours, crate after crate was removed from the Moschilo. There was no telling how much the haul would amount to, but it appeared it would be substantial, of that there was no doubt.

Rosetta, Ariana, and Enzo Stefani could not resist another glance at their quarry lying at the bottom of the Gulf of Genoa, and so they suited up once again and dropped into the waiting waters. As they descended, Rosetta and Stefani quickly discerned that the current thirty to forty feet below was running a little more briskly than it had been just the day before.

Stefani again marveled at not only the way the UDT men worked, but also at their state-of-the-art and abundant equipment. It had not been a wonder that America, and the US Navy in particular, had been able to fight a two-ocean war in the Atlantic and the Pacific. Mussolini and his Fascist lackeys must have been out of their minds to have ever contemplated taking on the Americans.

After a short break for a light mid-day lunch, the divers resumed their work. There would be no Italian style siesta observed on this day. The Americans were all business. The navy men and soon thereafter, Rosetta, Ariana, and Stefani had taken on new air tanks.

By 3:00 PM, the salvage work had essentially been completed. Enzo Stefani went down for a third time. Rosetta had thought the man to be foolish. What had been the point? And for what purpose? But she had said nothing. "Tenente, have you seen Commander Stefani?" asked a tremulous Rosetta Rossi.

The American officer looked about him. All his men were back aboard the Burrows. "No, I haven't seen him. You don't think that…" Edmonds didn't finish his sentence.

Rosetta was still in her dive suit. She grabbed her mask with the snorkel attachment and strapped it onto her head. Without so much as a glance she jumped overboard.

"*Mother!*" screamed Ariana.

Bob Rossi turned just in time to see his wife hurl herself overboard. Edmonds just stood and stared open-mouthed. Rosetta immediately swam downward toward the Moschilo. She dove with all her might. It was just like the time she had swum to Ariana to rescue her. She had tried to take in as much air as possible just prior to her entry into the water. As Rosetta neared the sunken wreck, she thought she could just make out something. She frantically hoped it would indeed be Enzo Stefani. There was no telling how long he may have been under, and possibly without air. He may even be badly hurt.

Rosetta moved closer to Stefani's inert body. She could see some small air bubbles emerging from around the man's head. Somehow, incredibly, the man had been able to retain his air hose in his mouth. As Rosetta looked closer, she could see a reddish laceration just above Stefani's right ear. He must have struck a beam or something with his head and then blacked out.

Reaching gently under Stefani's arms, Rosetta tried to pull him upward. To her, he seemed like dead weight. She thought to herself as to whether she should return to the surface for help or if she should grab some air from Stefani's hose. Rosetta took the mouthpiece from Stefani's lips and took in much needed air. She then placed it back into Stefani's mouth.

Again, with all her strength, Rosetta heaved at Stefani's body. It occurred to her to remove the air tank from the man. She did so. Now, she was able to make progress. She was glad now more than ever she worked out with weights and could swim seemingly forever in the ocean. Slowly, ever so slowly, Rosetta was able to bring up Enzo Stefani. She thought her lungs would burst, but she would get the former navy underwater commando to the surface. She would not lose him. Rosetta would do it for Stefani and his waiting family. She would do it because there had already been too many casualties associated with this venture.

Still struggling mightily, and herself virtually operating on fumes, Rosetta broke the surface of the water. Immediately upon seeing what was happening Lt Edmonds directed two of his men to jump in to provide assistance to the remarkable and redoubtable woman who had just rescued Enzo Stefani.

CHAPTER TWELVE -
JUSTICE

"I think he's going to be all right," Bob Rossi said as he leaned his weary body against the deck railing of the Samuel Burrows.

"I'm glad to hear that," said a completely worn-out, and weary Rosetta Rossi. She was standing next to Bob along the railing. "I'm going below. I need to change. I also think I need some coffee and perhaps something stiffer. I also want to check on Enzo to see how he's doing."

Bob nodded as he watched his wife move off. She still possessed that seductive feminine walk despite the ordeal she had just been through. He would never be able to cease being amazed by her. Not only for what she had just done, but had been able to do for the past four years. There had been her resistance work during the war, then her founding along with Barbara Danilo of the athletic club to help shattered women regain a sense of dignity and empowerment… and now this dive effort to recover an indeterminate amount of looted gold stolen by the Nazis.

Almost as if he had been reading Rossi's thoughts, Lieutenant Edmonds now stood next to him along the railing. Both men watching the beehive of activity going on throughout the ship. "You have a remarkable wife, Major. And your stepdaughter as well. You must be very proud of them." Edmonds had spoken from the heart, not at all trying to be solicitous.

"I know, Lieutenant. And I am very proud of them." Bob Rossi looked out over the increasing wave activity surrounding the dive site.

"They can serve with my men anytime, anywhere. Oh, I think I should mention that a PT boat is being dispatched to take you and your wife and the rest of your party back to Genoa. It should be arriving here at the Burrows within the hour. This will get you all back much quicker."

"Thank you, Lieutenant. I think Rosetta and Ariana will be most glad to hear that. I do believe it's time for us to depart from these waters. By the way, how much do you think the haul will be?"

Edmonds hunched his shoulders. "Hard to say, but I'd be willing to bet it could easily run to between one or two million. All in all, a pretty fair amount."

* * *

Inspector Aldo Moretti reconvened a mustering of the assigned Carabinieri detectives at 1300 hours on the Monday following the murders of Ann Carter and Marco Dubnik. "All right, Luigi, what have we learned?" asked Moretti as he poured himself a glass of mineral water. He made a face as he tasted what he thought was a stale liquid. Maybe Italians should come around to the American idea of using ice cubes.

"Inspector, I am going to defer to detective Monti," Luigi Cardoso said as he indicated to the junior detective Ernesto Monti.

Clearing his throat nervously, Ernesto Monti began recounting what he had been able to discover over the previous day. If he was showing signs of nervousness, it would have been understandable. After all, he was reporting to one of the legendary Carabinieri detectives, Aldo Moretti.

Moretti allowed the young man a moment to collect himself. He didn't want to appear to intimidate the youth. That would not be fruitful or helpful in any way. Moretti had seen too many young and upcoming detectives have their careers squelched by overbearing, odious superiors.

"Well, Chief Inspector, I was able to find out that the dead woman in question is English. And her name is, or was Ann Carter. She lived in an apartment on Via Frattina."

Moretti continued his patient listening but he hoped the hesitating detective would get on with things. "And how did you establish her identity?"

"Well, on a hunch, and this was after it had been noted that the young woman possessed a very athletic build that I did some checking. It seems as if this Ann Carter belonged to a gymnasium I had remembered hearing about." Again, Monti referred to his notebook before he resumed. "As I was saying, this club was co-founded by a Rosetta Rossi and a Barbara Danilo."

"And you have been to this club?" interjected Moretti.

"*Si*, Inspector. However, it seems as if these other two women are not in Rome at the present time."

"Where are they?"

"Well, and I got this from the woman who is acting in a sort of de facto capacity in running this gymnasium, her name is Maria Franchi, Rosetta Rossi has been off on some kind of dive expedition up around the Genoa area. The Danilo woman was just released from a hospital in Genoa yesterday," Monti said almost in one breath.

"Why was the Danilo woman in the hospital?" questioned Luigi Cardoso.

"The Franchi woman would only relate that Signorina Danilo had suffered some sort of mishap. She is due back in Rome sometime today."

"Good, good, Detective Monti," complimented Moretti. "Luigi, this Ann Carter, she had her throat cut, you said?"

Cardoso nodded.

"Eh, and this other apparent murder, Dubnik, you mentioned?" He was found with the same type of wound?"

"Yes, Inspector."

"And when was his body found?" asked Aldo Moretti who now opened a desk drawer and removed a silver-plated cigarette case. Moretti smoothly removed one and then closed the case with a soft metallic click.

Cardoso reached across Moretti's desk to light the cigarette, resembling a butler or a passing waiter in a restaurant. The scene reeked to one of the other assembled detectives, Pietro Angelosi. He had witnessed too many of these scenarios between Moretti and his sycophantic lapdog. Angelosi may have also been in a resentful mood as he had felt that several times in the past he had been passed over for promotion because of Luigi Cardoso. Angelosi had no need of a cigarette at that moment, for he was already smoldering, if only in a figurative sense.

"All right, gentlemen, good work. But let's stay on top of this. And, Luigi, let's try and keep this from the press for as long as possible. I would like to have us notify the Rossi and Danilo women before word eventually leaks out. That will be all, gentlemen," Moretti said, thus concluding the briefing.

Aldo Moretti settled back into his chair and lit another cigarette. He always seemed to smoke more when he had a tough situation on his hands. His wife was always after him to stop, or, at least, to cut back. Maybe he should reach out to his friend the journalist, Mauro Guzzo.

* * *

Deadlines, always deadlines, an increasingly despondent Mauro Guzzo inwardly moaned. He always seemed to be buried under an avalanche of them. At least that was how it always appeared to the veteran journalist. As Guzzo checked, rechecked, and cross-checked his facts on another one of Rome's interminable political scandals, a recurring thought kept luminating itself within his mind. It was more than a thought, it was something closer to a plea. One day, and that day could well be very soon, he would actually make the decisive break he had always aspired to, he would devote his writing to full-time murder novels. Scandalous, blood-dripping, lusting novels of murder, revenge, treachery, love, lust…

For the time being, Mauro Guzzo would continue to direct his attention to the matter at hand. After all, he was Corriere della Sera's chief journalist in the Eternal City. Even though the Milan based newspaper was not the most pre-eminent paper of record in Rome, its name and reputation still carried great weight. People, influential personages, be they be politicians, the clergy, businessman, the average every day citizen, all read the paper avidly.

251

By 5:00 PM, Guzzo had just about finished up another exhausting and mind-numbing day, and it was only Monday. He didn't know how he would make it through to Friday. The wall clock tick-tocked its way second after second for each minute, for each hour. He found himself actually listening to its sound. Suddenly, the phone rang. On the third ring, Guzzo summoned the strength to answer it. "*Guzzo*," he answered in true journalistic vernacular.

"Ah, *Guzzo*, *buona sera*," gushed an equally weary Aldo Moretti. "I was wondering if you might have a minute or two."

"*Si*, Aldo," replied Guzzo, who had always enjoyed an open, non-hostile relationship with the Carabinieri detective chief. "What can I do for you?"

"Well, I will come straight to the point. You may have already heard about a couple of murders over the past two days here in Rome. One in particular concerns a blonde-haired young woman. I would appreciate it if you could persuade some of your colleagues not to print any stories as I fear this may compromise our investigation. Can you accommodate my request?" concluded Moretti. He almost felt as if he had been pleading to the journalist. He knew Mauro Guzzo well and his recent tragic family past. He knew the man to be fair and honest; a scrupulous person of integrity. Moretti didn't usually make such requests to members of the Italian fourth estate, but in this case, he had felt compelled to do so.

Guzzo sat and listened quietly to Moretti's request before he replied. "I think that's a reasonable request on your part, Aldo. I personally have not heard of the tragic demise of this young woman, but I'll see what I can do to still some of my fellow journalists from getting any stories out. I can't promise you anything, if you must know."

"I do, Mauro, I do. This is a very tragic case. This young woman, who is not Italian, was killed in a most savage and brutal manner..." Moretti could not finish the sentence.

"How, may I ask, did she die?"

"Her throat had been cut virtually from ear to ear."

Mauro Guzzo leaned back into his chair, thinking this had most likely been a young and charming woman. Someone with her whole life ahead of her. But no longer.

* * *

The Rossi family was now speeding back to Rome, having decided to take the train from Genoa. Upon their return from the Samuel Burrows via PT boat to Genoa, they had spent that Sunday night on one of the four-star hotels in the city called the Splendide. Bob Rossi thought they were all entitled, especially Rosetta and Ariana, to at least spend one night of luxury in premier lodging.

During the course of their train ride, Bob and Rosetta occasionally chatted between themselves, often holding hands. Ariana spent most of her time reading or else napping, reflecting on what had transpired down below the waters of the Gulf of Genoa.

Rosetta felt as if she were reconnecting with her husband on several levels. They had worked together well as a part of a team. She beneath the surface, and he aboard the ship. Bob had impressively taken charge when they had brought up the grievously wounded Barbara Danilo. He had not panicked, not that she would have expected him to. Bob had displayed the tenets and professional coolness he had learned as an officer in the US Army. On another level, Rosetta could feel love, real love, and not just in a physical sense in the bedroom, but in normal, everyday routines.

Onward the FSC train sped toward Rome and their home. But not one member of the Rossi family, not Rosetta, not Bob, nor Ariana, had any idea of the news that awaited them once they did set foot inside their home.

* * *

Mauro Guzzo was driving Barbara Danilo back to Rome following her release from the Genoese hospital she had been confined to. As the open road of the A-12 Autostrada unfolded before them, Mauro still not knowing of Aldo Marchetti's news. He had to bring his relationship with Barbara to a head. There could be no longer be any beating around the bush. The time for fencing around the issue had to end. Would their relationship move forward? Or would it stagnate and eventually wither and die?

Guzzo slowed the vehicle down and guided it toward a makeshift rest-stop. Turning off the ignition, he turned and faced Barbara. "Dearest, I know you've been through a lot and I don't want to seem insensitive, but I thought... well, you know..."

"That we had to face what our relationship will be. Isn't that it?" Barbara said as her crystal blue eyes gazed into Mauro Guzzo's. "You know, Mauro. while I was in the hospital I was afforded the opportunity to think over and contemplate a good many things. And one of them was you and me and where are we going? I have to confess that I have not been exactly aboveboard with some things and..."

"It is all right, Barbara. Look, I can't pretend I understand everything you've been through, what with your injury, and the doctors are still not sure about how extensive some of the nerve damage may have been, and—"

"Mauro, please, be quiet and listen to me. What I have to say has to be said," Barbara said as she placed a hand to Guzzo's mouth. "You are right, we cannot continue with this beating around the bush. Please, let me say this. I know you haven't said anything about this, but I know that you've been hurt. You've been hurt about what may have transpired between myself and Marcello Mastrani." Barbara paused, looking down at her lap, her hands twisting around one another. "I have to confess that I slept with Mastrani, and on more than one occasion. Part of it was to secure my ambition to drive for Maserati, and part of it was to fulfill a carnal desire. I know that now, I was foolish. I have for too long acted like every day must be lived to the absolute fullest immediately. It's taken me so many years and, well, I am not sure, but I no longer want to continue going down that road."

"Barbara, would you marry me?" asked Mauro Guzzo with a near pleading look in his eyes. After what he had just heard emanate from Barbara Danilo's lips, he directed the burning question he had had to ask.

"After what I have just told you, you still would want to marry me? I... I..." Barbara seemed staggered. "Mauro, oh, Mauro." She leaned forward toward Guzzo, cupping his face with her hands. "Yes. Yes, I will marry you. Yes."

Mauro Guzzo started up the Alfa's engine, put the car into gear and slowly accelerated back onto the A-12. Few words were exchanged between the couple for the remainder of their journey back to Rome.

Barbara must have dozed off somewhere around Pisa and when she awakened from her slumber she found the passing road sign indicating the next exit was for Livorno. She thought she might have imagined she may had been dreaming when Mauro had proposed to her. No, it had been no dream, and she was happier than she ever thought was possible. Mauro Guzzo was a good man, and he was a thoughtful man. And, he was also a consummate and practiced lover. Barbara Danilo now felt more than ever before that she was ready to enter a union with one man for the rest of her life.

* * *

In the early afternoon hours of Tuesday, Inspector Aldo Moretti met once again with Luigi Cardoso and Ernesto Monti. The weather in Rome was starting to reflect the approaching autumn, the winds now possessing more chill as they blew through the city. The atmosphere in Moretti's office was unsettled as well.

"All right, gentlemen, what do we have?" asked Moretti, who sat with his suit jacket off, exposing his Aldo Fieri suspenders. He hated the bloody things, but Francesca had once suggested them to lend a more dignified presence to himself.

Luigi Cardoso cleared his throat and began. "Well, Inspector, there may be a connection between the Carter and Dubnik murders. In addition, another body was discovered just the other night… in Genoa."

"Genoa!" interrupted Moretti.

"*Si*, Inspector. His throat had also been cut. This man has been identified as one Gianni Ravelli, but that's only an alias. His real name was Heinz Dornhoefer. He hails, or rather hailed from Liechtenstein," Cardoso reported as he periodically checked his notebook or would glance at Monti for affirmation.

"How do we know all this?" questioned Moretti with an arched right eyebrow. He stretched out one of those wretched suspenders. He suddenly lost control of the right one and it snapped back against his chest with a loud thwack sound. It lent a comical touch to the grim discussion the men were a party to. "Well, now do you see why I hate these bloody things, gentlemen? They're more suited for clowns in the circus," Moretti said with a laugh.

Luigi Cardoso allowed himself a small, contained laugh. Monti sat stone-faced. He didn't see anything remotely funny under the circumstances.

"We know this, Inspector, courtesy of my old friend, Stefano Lucca. When he heard, presumably through the grapevine, of the murders, he contacted me and filled me in on a few things. Such as he, Lucca, had been employed by Signora Rossi and Signorina Danilo. Apparently, they had been tailed by Ravelli on the order of Marco Dubnik."

"I see. Tell me, have you spoken with the Rossi woman or with Miss Danilo?'

Luigi shook his head. "No, not yet. We have reason to believe that Rosetta Rossi and her family have just returned to Rome. We're checking on Barbara Danilo and her whereabouts."

"*Bene, bene*. Please notify me as soon as you have word. I would like to inform Signora Rossi personally. I don't want her to hear of it through the press, or the grapevine. All right, what else do we have? Who do you think is linked to these apparently connected murders?"

Cardoso glanced over at Monti who now had a questioning look on his face, as if were doubtful as to whether he should speak up. Cardoso took the initiative. "Well, Inspector, it's Stefano Lucca's theory that these murders may well be traced back to Don Fabrizio Valpone."

"The Genoa overlord?" asked a startled Aldo Moretti.

"Yes, sir. You see, there is the Ravelli killing and his connection to Dubnik, whose body was found here in Rome. And since these killings involved what you could call extra-territorial, there would be no need for Valpone to obtain sanctions from the local crime boss here in Rome, Don Roberto Nofi."

"And what do you think, Luigi?"

"I agree with Lucca's hypothesis, sir."

Moretti looked over at Ernesto Monti who nodded his agreement to what Cardoso had just said. "All right, we seem to be making progress. But stay on it. I think I'll pay a visit to Rosetta Rossi's home this evening. Cardoso, let me know as soon as you have word the she's definitely back in Rome."

* * *

After they had finally settled in and been able to collect themselves, Bob and Rosetta Rossi, along with son Marco, enjoyed a light repast of cold cuts and cheese accompanied by, of course, some wine. Soon after, Marco excused himself and went off to join some of his friends for a night on the town. Ariana had already left to spend some time with her girlfriends.

"Rosetta, I've been thinking," mused Bob as he moved along one of the bookcases as if he were intending to select a volume from the collection.

"Yes?" asked Rosetta guardedly. She tried to relax herself in one of the room's settees.

"Yes, why don't we bequeath a gift to Cardinal Maggione. You know, I think there may be a way in which we can direct some of the recovered gold's value toward the Vatican. We could say that undoubtedly some of the Vatican's lost loot was most likely a part of the gold cache you and the girls uncovered off Vento Beach. What do you think?" Bob had now turned and was facing his wife.

"That might me a good idea, Bob. How much do you think we should give to the Cardinale?"

"Oh, I don't know, but Lt Edmonds thought the rough figure might be anywhere in the neighborhood of one to two million dollars. Say about $100,000? Also, that should cause Maggione to call off his dogs against you and Barbara, and your gym."

"I think you might have something there, my sweet," Rosetta agreed. Despite her being weary from the dives into the gulf and then their travel to Rome, she had been anticipating an evening of unbridled passion with her husband. The next thirty minutes would shatter that thought.

* * *

"I'm so sorry to disturb you, signora, and to you signore, but I felt the matter to be… to be… well, sufficiently urgent that I should speak to you directly," began a discomfited and slightly uneasy Aldo Moretti. The venerable chief inspector was now seated in the Rossi's spacious living room.

Rosetta sat next to Bob and at the inspector's words, she had reached for and clasped her husband's hand. She had the distinct impression she was now going to hear something very ominous. "It's quite all right, Inspector. You haven't disturbed us, although we have had a long and trying past few days," said Rosetta, her blood pressure rising.

"Yes, well, I do realize that you've just returned to Rome," continued Moretti, having only just been informed by Cardoso of the Rossi's arrival. "Well, I will come straight to the point," said Aldo Moretti, his eyes now dead level with Rosetta's. "You see, we discovered the body of your friend, Ann Carter, just a couple of days ago, and she—" Moretti did not have the chance to finish.

"*Nooo, nooo, it can't be!*" cried out a completely distraught Rosetta Rossi. Tears immediately welled up in her eyes and the air was literally sucked out of the room. She leaned heavily into Bob's own stunned body. Her chest began convulsively heaving and Rosetta thought that she might well pass out right then and there.

"I am so sorry, signora, but I felt you had to know. I would also like you to know that we at the Carabinieri are doing all we can to bring to justice the individuals who have perpetrated this... this monstrous and evil crime."

"How... how did she die?" The words barely quaked their way out of Rosetta's mouth. "I have to know." Her body was now heaving uncontrollably.

It was almost too painful for Moretti to watch, but he had his job to do. "Well, it was most, most unpleasant, signora," replied an anguished Moretti. He really did not want to have to tell this heartbroken woman the grisly details.

"Inspector, I have to know," implored Rosetta who by now was drying her eyes with Bob's assistance.

"The young woman's throat was cut. I am so sorry," intoned a now distraught himself Aldo Moretti. "Should anything new develop, I will notify you immediately. Again, my sincere and deepest condolences. I will see myself out." Moretti rose and briefly shook Bob Rossi's hand before he turned and left the apartment.

* * *

"You have your instructions, Puglio. You know what to do," commanded Don Fabrizio Valpone to his erstwhile and somewhat trusted lieutenant, Cesare Puglio. Valpone was seated behind his massive oaken desk at his palatial home. The surrounding night enveloped it in a forbidding gloom.

"Si, si, Don Valpone. I am to contact both Bob and Rosetta Rossi, but separately. I am to tell the signore that I am a trusted friend and associate of Stefano Lucca. He is to meet with Lucca at an apartment on Via Madonna. The number is 133. The appointment is to be for 7:30 in the evening on the 13th. It is most urgent and is in connection with the find off Vento Beach. And then, I am to do the same in regard to the signora."

"Excellent," hissed Valpone. "But remember, when you make the calls the two Rossi's must be in different locations. That is paramount if my plan is to work. Therefore, when we know earlier on the 13th you will be notified as to when to make your calls. If this works out as I have planned, the two Rossi's will be dealt with at the same time. Conveniently and quietly." Fabrizio Valpone sat back in a now contented frame of mind. He may not have gotten the gold yet, but he would have his revenge on these usurpers. And his nephew would be avenged.

* * *

"Do you believe this, Gonevento? Such rubbish!" stammered Cardinale Ernesto Maggione, as he stood in his office dressed in his nightgown replete with a ridiculous looking stocking cap. Gonevento could not remember even the last time he had observed the cardinal to be standing.

To Pasco Gonevento, the man had never looked less demeaning. Perhaps it was fitting to the novice priest. It would help him in his own news he had prepared that night for Maggione. "I don't know what you mean,

Cardinale," stammered back Gonevento, feeling a little less certain of himself than he had only a minute ago.

"This letter from the Rossi's bequeathing to the Church on my behalf the sum of $100,000 to be used for whatever good deeds we feel it can be used for here in Rome. It is from the gold cache they discovered from some wreck that was sunk during the war. You know what I think?" questioned Maggione, not pausing for a reply from Gonevento. "This is a payoff, a bribe so I will call off the dogs from the signora and her muscle-headed friends. That is what this is, a payoff!" thundered Maggione as he literally heaved the letter in Gonevento's direction.

The young priest hastily scrabbled to secure a grip on the offending missive. Gonevento quickly scanned the letter and turned his attention back to his fuming superior. "Does this mean that you will not accept their gift? Or will you accept it and then suspend further surveillance of the Rossi's?"

Ernesto Maggione stood silently, drumming his sausage-shaped, arthritic fingers on his desktop. "Regretfully, I am afraid that I must capitulate and accede to their offer. It gives me great distress. I do not like it. To be bought off like this. But, and I am reluctant to have to admit to this, mind you, what good would it do to continue this pursuit? Let these blasted women grunt and groan their way and develop their bodies. Why should we care?" conceded a now crestfallen and defeated Maggione.

Pasco Gonevento breathed a silent sigh of relief. At last it was over. He looked down at the forlorn Maggione and for a brief instant he felt a twinge of compassion for the man. But only for a moment. He would now deliver his own news. The news, that he, Pasco Gonevento, was going to leave the priesthood. He had had enough of the likes of Ernesto Maggione and others of his ilk within the domain of the Catholic Church.

* * *

Armed with the information he needed, courtesy of Don Valpone's contact, Cesare Puglio contacted Bob Rossi at his office and he thought was able to convince him that he, Puglio, was genuine, and then that Rossi should meet with him and Stefano Lucca at 133 Via Madonna at 7:30 that evening. Puglio waited for about an hour, as he had been instructed, before he placed his call to Rosetta Rossi. He knew she was in her own office. Once again, Puglio felt reasonably certain he had made a convincing argument to the woman. As it was past 5:00 PM, Puglio also felt confident the two Rossi's would not have sufficient time to coordinate a counteraction. Nevertheless, Don Valpone had assigned tails to each of the couple just to ensure nothing unforeseen would arise.

Incredibly, neither Bob or Rosetta Rossi had bothered to try and contact Stefano Lucca for some kind of verification. They had just taken Cesare Puglio at his word. In any event, even if they had tried to check with Lucca they would have been unable to, as the unfortunate man was figuratively tied up with two of his associates concerning some trivial art theft.

* * *

Bob Rossi finished up his paperwork just before 6:30. He then called Rosetta at her office and the two agreed to meet with Lucca and his associate at 7:30 at Via Madonna. Both Bob and Rosetta thought it to be rather strange to be meeting Lucca at this location.

Rossi bid a goodnight to his secretary, Carla Mangini, a comely shaped brunette, and left the building. Via Madonna was about four miles away from his office and, based on the circumstances, it couldn't hurt to arrive a little bit early. He had not neglected packing his US Army issued Colt .45 caliber sidearm.

Street traffic around Via Madonna was heavy. Apparently, a bad traffic accident had occurred on Via Cavour in the shadows of the ancient ruins, and the Colosseum, hadn't helped matters. Bob Rossi was able to secure a parking spot on a cross-street and then sat and waited. He glanced at his Benrus watch and saw that it was 7:15. Well, he decided, he would get out and walk around the corner to 133 Via Madonna. He had taken the time earlier to jot down some of the instructions given to him by Cesare Puglio. He was to go up to the first floor, and then he was to knock on the door of room 13. Nothing seemed strange or out of place to Rossi. For some unknown reason, he had let his guard down, but still…

After knocking, the door of #13 opened and Bob Rossi was met by a large and imposing brute of a man who merely nodded at him. The behemoth motioned to Rossi to enter and then swung his arm if in welcoming. Bob entered, knowing for certain now that something was desperately wrong. He then noticed another unpleasant looking older man seated behind a metal desk.

"Ah, Signore Rossi, please, do come in. It is a pleasure to finally meet you. Please, please, do come in. Let me introduce myself. I am Don Fabrizio Valpone and this is my associate, Paolo." Valpone gestured with his open right hand for Rossi to seat himself on the one folding chair set before the desk.

Realizing the gravity of his error, Bob Rossi stood mutely dumbfounded. Paolo Cardelli nudged him with one of his beefy hands. Rossi nearly stumbled as he made his way to the chair. Finally, Bob Rossi was able to find his voice, as Cardelli reached from behind and deftly removed his pistol. "What's this about? What's going on?" he stammered.

Valpone held up his right hand. "Please, signore, why don't we wait for the arrival of your lovely and charming wife. There is no need for me to go over the same things twice. Do you not agree?" Valpone said affably. "Eh, Paolo, why don't you go and leave the door open. I think we could use some air in here. It is rather stuffy and somewhat oppressive. And this may enable us to tell of the arrival of the signora."

Bob Rossi was now kicking himself for having been so stupid. Big and tough military man, and he had been completely duped by the mafia crime boss. Nervous sweat began to congeal around his wrists and ankles. He also realized he had no way of being able to warn Rosetta as to what awaited her. She would be walking right into a trap.

"I really wish things had not come to this. You know, Signore Rossi, I am a businessman and... well," Valpone again gestured with a wave of his meaty right hand. He appeared or, at least tried to appear, as if he were nothing more than an associate of the bank of Italy or of Olivetti.

* * *

262

The traffic was unusually heavy for this time of night as Rosetta tried to make her way from her AMGOT office on Via Coritalde to Via Madonna. As she waited behind a line of cars, Rosetta contemplated what could possibly happen at this meeting or as to why it was necessary. It now started to seem more and more odd. Perhaps she and Bob were walking into a trap. In any event, she was glad she was carrying her Beretta 9 mm semi-automatic pistol Bob had given her earlier in the year. She wasn't sure she would be able to bring herself to use it. Bob had given her a couple of simple and rudimentary lessons as to its handling: how to load it, how to aim and fire it. "Remember," he had told her, "squeeze the trigger, do not pull it." A shallow sense of not fear, but trepidation began to consume her body.

Some impatient motorists were now leaning on their horns, as if that would suddenly improve the situation. Rosetta merely shook her head, but her qualms and uncertainty kept building. Finally, she was able to break free from the logjam and started out again. At 6:45 PM, she crossed the Ponte Sisto bridge and drove onto Lunge dei Vallati, along the river. The October night was pleasant, but winter would arrive soon enough.

Rosetta drove by the Teatro di Marcello, long famed for its lovely and pastoral summer concerts, and then her route paralleled the ancient ruins of Rome, the times of Caesar Augustus and Trajan and Nero. At last, just after 7:00 PM, Rosetta Rossi made it to 133 Via Madonna. She slowed her car, looking for a parking space. She could have placed it anywhere, as Roman drivers had long been known to park anywhere they could and in any manner. It was not unusual to see a vehicle camped upon a sidewalk. But Rosetta would not do this. At last, she found a suitable space.

The fear and suspense kept building within Rosetta as she walked closer and closer to 133 Via Madonna. Once she arrived at the address, she paused and gently pushed open the front door, trying to be as soundless as possible. Thankfully, nary a sound was emitted as Rosetta stepped inside the building. She paused and thought she could hear voices from somewhere up the stairs. Rosetta decided to remove her flats from her feet. She placed them in her handbag and then took hold of the Beretta. She checked to make sure it was in working order and that the safety was off. Silently but steadily, Rosetta made her way up the stairwell.

"Well, I think it would be wise if you were secured, signore. It is not that I distrust you, Signore Rossi, but better to be safe than sorry," oozed Valpone, almost as if he truly believed in his own self-deprecation. "Paolo, if you would please tie up our guest."

Valpone's henchman was just gathering up the one-half inch diameter rope when suddenly all of the men were startled.

"Don't move! Do *not* move! Not one millimeter," commanded the stern voice of Rosetta Rossi as she stepped lightly through the open doorway. Her Beretta was pointed roughly half-way between Valpone and Cardelli. Rosetta held the firearm in a relaxed grip, not too tightly, and not too loosely. It was just the way Bob had taught her in their brief training sessions.

"Ahhh, Signora Rossi! How nice of you to make an appearance. You know, we were all just having a nice conversation, just between us men. It is rather nice when a feminine element can be added to the equation. We have been anxiously awaiting your arrival. Permit me to introduce my associate—" Valpone was suddenly cut off.

"Be quiet! I don't care to know who your associate is, Don Valpone. What have you done to my husband?" boomed Rosetta, her hazel brown eyes beaming their way like lasers into Valpone's.

"Why nothing, signora. As I was saying, we were—"

"Cut the bullshit, Don Valpone. You there… I would be very careful," Rosetta said as she pointed her Beretta in Cardelli's direction. "I should warn you, all, I haven't had extensive practice in the use of firearms and I may have an itchy trigger finger. You… drop that rope. Now!"

Bob Rossi looked up at his wife as if he didn't know her. He could not have been prouder. She was in command of the situation, and he would be dependent on her to save his life. He offered a faint, half-hearted smile.

"Such language, and from what I have always thought was such a dignified and mature woman," scoffed Valpone. "Now, do you not think you are behaving a little bit foolish? Really, Rosetta, if I may be permitted to call you that, why not be reasonable and just drop your gun. Do you really think you can overcome myself and Signore Cardelli?"

"Drop my weapon? And then you would kill my husband and then me," She noticed Cardelli reaching inside his coat pocket, as if for his own gun. "I am warning you, sir. Do not try my patience," Rosetta growled.

But Valpone's associate did not seem to pay heed to the woman's command, and he kept reaching for his own Beretta.

A shot rang out as Rosetta did not hesitate when she fired at Paolo Cardelli. Her bullet found its way to his upper left shoulder just a couple of inches above his heart. The man slumped backward onto his back.

Fabrizio Valpone saw this as his chance. He reached for Bob Rossi's Colt .45 on the table. He grabbed it and fired wildly in Rosetta's direction. The bullet sailed wide, barely missing her left ear. Bob thought he might well pass out.

At the sight of Valpone reaching for the gun, Rosetta went down onto her right knee. Whereupon she fired again into Paolo Cardelli's squirming body. This time, her Beretta round went under the killer's chin and then penetrated its way to the base of his brain. Cardelli went instantly dead.

By this time, Don Valpone had grabbed Bob by his coat collar and brought him up to his feet, the Colt now pointed at Bob's right temple. "My compliments, Signora Rossi. I was told you are a resourceful and determined woman. Your husband should be proud."

Rosetta now stood up carefully, her Beretta pointed squarely at Valpone. He knew she would not dare risk firing, not with his own weapon pointed at her husband's head.

"Now, Signora Rossi, we are going to perform a little dance. You will now move slowly to your left, while your husband and myself will move slowly to our left. We will then walk through the doorway and down the stairwell, and then out of the building. You are not to move. I do not want to see you stick your head out of the doorway. I do not want to see one strand of your lovely blonde hair. Do you understand?" asked Fabrizio Valpone, his black dead-set eyes smoldering at Rosetta. He tightened his grip around the Colt's stock, his index finger poised on the trigger.

Rosetta stood and mutely nodded. She knew she had to comply. She now hoped that Bob might be able to somehow trip up Valpone as they made their way down the stairs. Bob gave her look that indicated he understood what she was secretly thinking.

Valpone nodded and then proceeded to steer Bob Rossi out of the room. He and Bob watched as Rosetta kept her weapon trained and aimed at the Don's head. Bob Rossi was desperately trying to slow things down as Valpone held onto his collar with his left hand while he dug the .45 into Bob's ribs.

"Oh, come on, Signora Rossi, do not try and delay the inevitable," said Valpone. Just as the words had come out of his mouth, he felt himself being grabbed and pushed down the stairs. Bob Rossi had managed to get hold of Valpone's jacket and had been able to twist the man's body around until Valpone found himself hurtling down the stairs and crashing into the wall alongside the landing. Rossi, himself, had toppled over and crashed down the stairs, coming to a painful stop just feet from the gangster chieftain.

By this time, Fabrizio Valpone had decided to make his own getaway, sans Bob Rossi. He flew down the remaining stairs and rushed out through the front door and out into the street.

At the sounds of the crashes and bangs out on the stairwell, Rosetta ran to the doorway and looked down. Don Valpone was running out of the building and to the street, but not before he took a shot at Rosetta's head. It missed. Rosetta took in her husband, lying prostrate on the landing and moaning. She literally flew down them to Bob.

"Are you all right, dearest?" asked a fearful Rosetta as she began cradling Bob's bruised head within her bosom.

"I think… I may have broken my arm. My right one feels kind of funny. By the way, whoever taught you to shoot like that?" Bob asked as he closed his eyes in abject weariness and blessed relief.

"I guess I picked up a few things from when you taught me," mused a thankful and relieved Rosetta.

Less than two hours later at the Ospedale Memorial, Chief Inspector Aldo Moretti arrived to take a statement from Rosetta and Bob Rossi about what had transpired at 133 Via Madonna. "I'm glad to hear your husband is going to be all right, signora. I must say, you are the most incredible woman I have ever come across in all my years as a policeman. Your husband is a very lucky man. A lucky man, indeed."

"Thank you, Inspector, and I think he knows that."

"Oh, by the way, I thought you might like to know that just a short time ago some of my men discovered a crash scene on Via Muratori. Yes, you see, there is a construction site there and there was a truck parked along the street. On this truck was a beam that protruded outward from the tailgate. Anyway, your antagonist, Don Fabrizio Valpone, apparently did not see this obstruction as he was driving at a high rate of speed in his vehicle and..." Moretti let his words linger.

"Is he dead?" asked Rosetta hopefully.

"Yes, he is quite dead. It seems as if his head was taken clean off just above his neck. I don't think you and your husband and your friends will have to worry about him any longer."

* * *

Mauro Guzzo reported in one of his November columns in Corriere della Sera that the MS Moschilo salvage effort had yielded the equivalent of more than two million dollars. In his article, Guzzo had reported that approximately $500,000 would be distributed to the Bank of Italy and of that, nearly half would be directed to charitable work for destitute people in and around Rome. The remainder would be dispersed to the Vatican and to several banks in Italy, and even to one bank in Croatia.

The veteran journalist was about to enter new waters on his personal front. Barbara Danilo had agreed to his proposal of marriage. They would wed in a quiet ceremony in the spring of 1949. Meanwhile, Barbara's right shoulder had begun to heal and the initial fear of possible nerve damage was unfounded. Through extensive physical rehabilitation, Barbara was beginning to feel as if she were almost to the point of being a hundred percent. She had been able to resume weight training and some other physical calisthenics, including swimming laps in the Metropole pool.

More importantly to Barbara, her libido, which had wavered for a time in the immediate aftermath of the knifing and the subsequent drug treatments, had returned. She and Mauro were now at a point of having extremely gratifying sex several times each week.

* * *

"I called Captain Anderson the other day, Mother, to see how he was doing. I hope you don't mind," Ariana said cautiously. She had debated as to whether she should broach the subject to her mother. She and Rosetta were sitting in front of a warm fire glowing from the fireplace hearth. It was a chilly November morning in Rome. The two women had just been sitting around, casually sipping espresso coffee. Ariana thought she made a better espresso than Rosetta, but she would never reveal that to her mother.

"No, no, why would I mind?" asked Rosetta. Although, she had chided herself for not having reached out to the young man after the memorial service for Ann Carter.

"We've agreed to meet next week at Alfano's. You know, just a little get together." Ariana tried to sound as if she were not going out on a date.

"That's fine, dear, but, and I am not trying to put a damper on your meeting with Phillip, just be careful. He's in a vulnerable position. He's suffered great loss and…" Rosetta suddenly seemed at a loss for words.

"I know, Mother. And I realize he's several years older than me. I just feel so badly for him. I mean, he's now lost two women that he loved, not to mention his little girl."

"I know, I know," lamented Rosetta. She had reached a point to where she was hoping to move onto something else. There had to be a brighter future ahead for not only Phillip Anderson, but for many others throughout Italy.

* * *

Throughout the remainder of 1948 and into 1949, Rosetta Rossi, Ariana, and some of the other girls from the gymnasium continued their rigorous and demanding workouts. Rosetta seemed particularly intent on increasing the amount of weight she could dead-lift, press, clean and jerk over her head. She increased the weights she used on one-armed curls, as well as on leg curls.

Muscle was added to muscle until one day it began to occur to Rosetta that perhaps she had reached a plateau. What good was it of heaving ever greater amounts of weights? She felt as if she had trapped herself within the girders of her own body. Not that she would allow herself to let herself go and become a flabby mass of flesh. No, Rosetta slowly came to the realization to back off, just a little. There was no need to continue pushing the envelope any further on her weight training.

Meanwhile, Ariana had continued making steady progress and improvement in her own athletic regimen and even she had recognized there was a ceiling as to how far she should push herself.

Much to Rosetta's surprise, even Bob had joined his wife and step-daughter at the gym, having decided he should join his family in a worthwhile pursuit. Before this, Bob had worked out solely at the army's facilities. After a while, the three Rossi's would, at times, playfully engage themselves in spirited competitions. Rossi's former army buddies would have ribbed him unmercifully for allowing himself to being reduced to competing with women... but they would have had no idea as to the character and determination of these two women.

* * *

In mid-July 1949, Rosetta and Ariana Rossi went on holiday, ensconced once again in the Hotel Brentano. The air was a shade degree cooler than could be found in the Eternal City. Bob was to join the women in a few days, when he could free himself from his graves registrations' duties.

The Rossi women were greeted by the familiar face of the lovely signorina, at last freed from her previously deceptive espionage duties. After they'd checked into their rooms in the late afternoon, the women donned matching black bathing suits and gone down to recline around the hotels elegant pool. The water appeared as a crystal blue. Both took to the inviting water to swim some laps, and then they sipped gin and tonics in their chaise-longue chairs. Tomorrow, they would descend to Vento Beach to sunbathe topless. Some swimming would also be done as, after all, Rosetta and Ariana had to maintain some sense of their athletic regimen.

269

Tuesday dawned slightly cloudy, with few birds in the air, but the forecast promised the skies would clear by mid-morning. After Rosetta made arrangements with the ever-reliable Pasco Borrelli for the following day, she and Ariana made their way to the beach. There was no need to be concerned over any further spying being done on them. Marco Dubnik, Gianni Ravelli, and even the Church had receded into the nether reaches.

Once they had settled onto the soft sands of Vento Beach, Rosetta and Ariana peeled off their tops and there they stood, their magnificent fulsome cleavages jutting out proudly upon their chests. Both slathered on copious amounts of the Coppertone sunscreen. Neither one was at all self-conscious of how they looked. Both were proud of their magnificent-looking athletic bodies.

Within the hour, two well-built young men appeared in front of the women. The curly-headed male on the right leered at the topless women, as if deciding which of them he wanted for himself. Ariana dispatched the two with a few choice curse words. Rosetta had not even bothered to open her eyes at the advances of the two young studs. Out of sight, out of mind.

Mother and daughter swam in the gentle swells off the beach. Ariana kept pace and at times, exceeded Rosetta as the two women swam approximate 100-yard laps of the overhand crawl, butterfly, and breaststrokes. At one point, Ariana had the temerity to challenge Rosetta in an underwater swim-off. She lost, but not too badly. Ariana, while proud of her own body and athletic prowess, could not help but admire and be in awe of her mother's unbelievable stamina and endurance. It was as if she had been expressly built to swim and dominate the sea.

"I miss Ann, Mother," lamented a now sullen Ariana. She had turned onto her stomach and looked over at Rosetta, who was still lying on her back.

"I do too, dear. I think of her every day," replied a crestfallen Rosetta.

"Do you think it was worth it? I mean, you know, everything you and Barbara and Bob have been through," continued Ariana.

"I would like to think so. I really would. You know, Ariana, some time ago Enzo Stefani had said something about gold and how it tended to corrupt things and often endangered anyone involved in its pursuit." Rosetta now turned her body over and glanced at her daughter.

"But some good was done. The gold you found was sent back to its rightful owners. I suppose we should be thankful for that.'

"I suppose we should, dear," Rosetta said as she found herself commiserating with her own tortured soul. Had it all been really worth it?

The following day was to be a somewhat momentous and notable one for the Rossi girls. They would go out on Pasco Borrelli's small craft to a site not far from where the Moschilo had been found. The pair would swim and free dive in the gently swelling ocean waves. For Rosetta, it would mark her attempt to swim for a period of eight hours before she returned to the boat. It was to be her way of bestowing a tribute to her good friend, Ann Carter.

Rosetta and Ariana entered the water by 8:00 AM. They swam off from Borrelli in their matching black suits. To the old man, they resembled sleek and sure killer whales. He envied them their athleticism and he envied their youth, especially the younger one, Ariana.

Hour after hour, Rosetta and Ariana swam and dove. At one point, Rosetta thought they may have pushed things by staying nearly thirty feet under for more than four minutes. As much as Ariana admired Rosetta, she herself took great pride in seeing her daughter in the water; how the young woman had turned her life around, from one of drifting away aimlessly and in bad company to one with a purpose and meaning. Ariana had developed her body and her mind to peak condition, and she could more than hold her own in the water with Rosetta.

Just before noon, Ariana returned to the boat while Rosetta remained in the slowly rising tide. She took some mineral water sustenance. Rosetta kept herself moving, but she noted a slight chill to the water.

Ariana climbed into Borrelli's boat. She had to admit she was bushed. She looked outward to see her mother swim off a slight distance, and then she jackknifed her body over. Rosetta's legs slipped into the water. Ariana looked at her dive watch and waited for Rosetta to resurface.

Rosetta Rossi swam down to the ocean floor and had to admit she felt almost as at home here as she did on dry land. She truly loved and relished the sea and her own ability to be at one with it. Some sea turtles swam by her languorously, not paying any attention to the human intruder to their world. Sea bass were also in evidence. They, too, paid no mind to the diver in their midst.

Ariana was still looking at her watch. "Oh, Mother, please come up. You don't always have to prove yourself. You're not competing with Barbara." Finally after nearly five minutes, Rosetta broke the surface. She waved to Ariana, who waved back.

It was nearing two o'clock when Ariana decided to rejoin her mother in the water. She would stay in until the projected 4:00 PM target time. Ariana swam out to Rosetta's position about two hundred yards away.

"You've chosen to rejoin me, Ariana?" Rosetta smiled as she lifted her black framed goggles from her hazel eyes.

"Yes, I have. I wanted to join you in your tribute to Ann," Ariana said.

"*Bene, bene.* Then, let us dive together." Rosetta re-affixed her goggles back into place. She and Ariana gripped their hands together as in a silent tribute and prayer to the woman they had lost. Taking deep breaths, Rosetta and Ariana Rossi dove into the waters of the Gulf of Genoa. Their powerfully developed legs kicked up straight and upright as they slowly receded into the water.

From her vantage point high above them, a young Englishwoman smiled down in deep and abiding admiration, and love.

ABOUT THE AUTHOR

Gary Benassi was employed for more than 30 years by the Defense Department as an analyst of private defense contractors. He has degrees from the University of Rhode Island and Michigan State University. The subject of World War II and, in particular the Italian campaign have long held his interest. Gary is also the author of *The Monsignor*. He resides in the Providence, RI area.